MARRIED TO THE MILITARY

Dear Mom and Dad,

Everyone says the first year of marriage is the most difficult, but why? It seems everything should be peaches once you tie the knot, at least for the first twelve months. I mean, what could possibly go wrong?

Love, Natalie

◦   ◦   ◦

Their reunion was the same as always. Natalie couldn't imagine why she had worried it might be otherwise.

Step one, kiss.

Step two, hug.

Step three, get into a fight.

Standard operating procedure. Situation normal.

Natalie bit her lip to keep from saying something else that might create a conflict with Nick. She was getting this military stuff down pat.

By Elizabeth Bevarly

The Wedding
The Honeymoon

Available from
HarperPaperbacks

THE
HONEYMOON

Elizabeth Bevarly

HarperPaperbacks
A Division of HarperCollinsPublishers

This is a work of fiction. The characters, incidents, and dialogues are products of the author's imagination and are not to be construed as real. Any resemblance to actual events or persons, living or dead, is entirely coincidental.

HarperPaperbacks *A Division of* HarperCollins*Publishers*
10 East 53rd Street, New York, N.Y. 10022

Cover photograph by Herman Estevez

First printing: February 1995

Printed in the United States of America

HarperPaperbacks, HarperMonogram, and colophon are trademarks of HarperCollins*Publishers*

❖ 10 9 8 7 6 5 4 3 2 1

Prologue

The fifteenth day of October had dawned unseasonably warm in Cleveland. The sun shone brightly over the white frame church that sat on the corner of Elm and Oak Streets, throwing it into shade beneath a canopy of autumn trees stained with gold and red and orange. The church bells pealed joyously for some time, then gradually deferred to the organ rifts of Pachelbel's Canon inside. White satin and rose petals veiled the aisle, and the altar was virtually obscured by greenery and lavender flowers that sprinkled the room with their sweet fragrance. Four bridesmaids in lilac organdy grinned shyly at the expectant groom, who stood handsome in his Coast Guard uniform, awaiting the arrival of the woman he would take to be his wife.

A bride couldn't have asked for a more perfect wedding day.

Natalie Mason, however, wanted to throw up.

As she stood in the church foyer awaiting her cue, she clutched the beaded bodice of her gown and leaned forward, shoving away the cascade of white netting and pale blond curls that fell over her face with the motion. "Oh, Daddy, I think I'm going to be sick," she whispered to the man who grasped her arm to keep her erect. "You've got to let me sit down for a minute."

Daniel Mason tugged at the too-tight collar of his rented tux and eyed his daughter anxiously. "You'll be fine, sweetheart. Just fine. You can't sit down because all those people in there are waiting for you to make your entrance."

"Ooh," she groaned.

"You don't want to disappoint your mother, do you?"

"Oooohh."

"And Nick?"

"Ooooooooohhh."

"What will he think if his bride walks down the aisle all hunched over like Quasimodo?"

"Daddy, please."

"Now, come on, Natalie, take a deep breath . . ."

He inhaled vigorously himself, showing her how it should be done, then gestured for her to do the same. Natalie forced herself to stand up straight and mimic the action, but all she was able to manage was a little gasp.

"There, that's my girl," her father said. He patted her on the back and did his best to rearrange her veil. "You know your mother and I hate to see you go," he continued jovially as he urged her toward the entry to the chapel. "You're the last of our six girls to leave the nest after all. Yessirree, it tears us up knowing our little baby is going out the door. But we know you're in good hands with Nick Brannon. We'll talk on the phone all the time after your mother and I get settled in Pensacola—moving van's coming next week, you know. Now, let's get on with this wedding."

The organist began a second rendition of "Here Comes the Bride," and somehow Natalie was able to place one foot in front of the other. At the entrance to the chapel, she saw Nick standing at the altar, and she smiled at how handsome he looked in his dark blue uniform. The deep color made his eyes seem even bluer. His black hair was freshly cut and swept back from his forehead, except for the one stray lock that always refused to be tamed. He looked every bit as scrumptious as he had the day she'd met him two years ago. The sight of him injected her with a little more fortitude, encouraging her to walk all the way down the aisle. Her father handed her off in much the same way a relay runner relinquishes a baton—hastily—and then the ceremony began.

After that, she didn't remember much of anything other than the cool, heavy feel of her new wedding band as Nick slipped it over the fourth finger of her left hand, and the warm brush of his lips against hers as the minister introduced them as Mr. and Mrs. Nicholas Brannon. Then they sped back up the aisle, and down the stairs to lie low in the fellowship hall until the guests had all departed for the reception.

Immediately, Natalie threw herself into Nick's arms and, laughing, kissed him hard on the lips. When she pulled away, one of the ribbons pinned to his uniform caught on one of the beads sewn to her dress, and she laughed harder.

"Looks like you're stuck with me for good, Nick

Brannon," she said as she continued to shower him with kisses.

He grinned as he tried to unfasten the snag. "In sickness and in health," he told her.

"For richer or for poorer."

"For better—" They sprang apart as he freed his ribbon and laughed some more. "—or for worse."

"'Til death do us part," she whispered as she kissed him again.

He wrapped his arms around her tightly. "It'll take a lot more than death to keep us apart."

She touched her fingers to the lips she had just kissed, holding Nick's gaze intently with her own. "Nothing *could* keep us apart, could it?" she asked, suddenly feeling anxious for no reason she could understand.

He shook his head. "Nothing."

"You promise?"

"I promise."

The door to the fellowship hall crashed open then, and the couple was swept away by high spirits and the rest of their wedding party. Amid the laughter and the tears, the hugging and kissing, the congratulations and well-wishing, Natalie and Nick were separated. When she looked up again, she saw him on the other side of the room with his brother, and somehow he suddenly seemed very far away.

But that was nonsense, she tried to reassure herself. He was right here with her as he always would be, as it seemed he always had been. After another week of visiting with their families in Cleveland, they'd be leaving for Puerto Rico, where Nick was stationed, to begin their lives together on what they had joked would be their extended honeymoon.

Nothing could be more perfect, she told herself. She would be living on a Caribbean island with the man of her dreams, who looked absolutely adorable in his uniform. What woman wouldn't envy her?

Nick caught her eye and smiled at her, and some of Natalie's apprehension dissolved. She was a newlywed now, she reminded herself. Things could only get better from here. Couldn't they?

1

Dear Mom and Dad,

I'm still getting my bearings in San Juan, having been here only a matter of days. Nick has to go back to work tomorrow, which means going out on the cutter for a week, and I don't know what I'm going to do to keep myself occupied while he's gone. So far, I've only met one of his friends from the cutter, a guy named Luis who truly defies description. To be honest, I'm not quite convinced I'm going to like it here. Puerto Rico is nothing at all like Ohio . . .

Love, Natalie

The heat was the first thing Natalie noticed about San Juan. When their plane had lifted off in Cleveland that morning, the temperature had been a crisp forty-two degrees. She had donned a pair of lightweight, beige wool trousers and a matching blazer over a coral-colored silk blouse she felt was thin enough to be comfortable in the tropical climate. She had never flown on an airplane before and wanted to look smart for the event. And although she had been somewhat dismayed when her husband had emerged from the hotel bathroom in his baggy khaki shorts and a threadbare green polo, thinking the combination somehow inappropriate for honeymoon travel, she had refrained from commenting. She wasn't about to start off their marital adventure with an argument.

However, as their plane descended toward Muñoz-Marin Airport and she felt the heat begin to creep inside, she began to wonder if maybe she had chosen her outfit wisely after all. When they taxied down the runway, the warm winds of San Juan replaced the air-conditioned coolness of the pressurized cabin, and by the time she and Nick collected their things and approached the terminal, she was beginning to feel limp.

Immediately, she paused to shrug out of her jacket, stuffing it through the handle of her carry-on before she hurried to catch up with her husband, who hadn't noticed her stopping. All around her, the airport was alive with people. Some hurried past her going one way, while others sauntered leisurely in the opposite direction. Signs advertising local casinos in English gave way to concession stands touting their goods in Spanish. Languages met and mingled and clashed everywhere she went, and people of every variety blurred into the crush.

Natalie had never been comfortable in large

crowds. The people pushing into her made her feel anxious, and the foreignness of so much of her surroundings did nothing to put her at ease. Sweat dampened her underarms and trickled down between her shoulder blades and breasts, and matted her hair over her eyes and against her nape. Her bags became heavier with every step she took, and Nick had pressed onward a good thirty feet ahead of her. She inhaled deeply, blew as much of her hair out of her eyes as she could, and tried to catch up.

When she finally reached him at the baggage claim carousel, her mood had sunk from impatient to angry. She tried fanning herself with the airline magazine, but all she managed to do was to stir up more hot air. There were so many people here, and the heat was remarkable for autumn. She looked out the windows near the exit to see that San Juan was dark, but the absence of the sun had done nothing to lower the temperature. Unless, of course, it was even worse than this during the day, she thought with a frown.

"It's hot here," she said unnecessarily as they awaited the arrival of their luggage.

"I tried to warn you," Nick replied. "I told you to wear shorts because it would be in the eighties, but you insisted on wearing all that stuff instead."

Natalie glanced down at the once-crisp outfit, now wrinkled and puckered from the disagreeable environment. "But I bought this especially to wear on the plane."

"Yeah, well, it's nice, and you look beautiful wearing it, but you would have been cooler in something else."

She wiped at the perspiration forming over her lip.

"Well, you could have warned me a little harder about this heat."

Nick, too, was obviously beginning to suffer from their long journey and the warm evening. "You should have come down to visit me before we got married, the way I wanted you to," he told her. "Then you could have seen for yourself how hot it gets down here."

"I couldn't come and visit you because I was trying to finish school on time," she reminded him. "And I was working, in case you've forgotten, trying to save some money to get us started since you seldom sent any home."

"I sent you money," he told her.

She emitted a dubious sound. "Oh, sure, a few hundred dollars over twelve months. The rest of it wound up in the cash register of a bar on some island like Antiqua or Barbecue."

Nick rolled his eyes. "That's Antigua or Barbuda."

"Whatever."

"And I did not spend all my money in bars. I seem to recall sending you flowers on more than one occasion."

"Yeah, and I still can't believe you wasted all that money on long-stemmed roses right after the two of us had that huge argument about how little money we were saving."

"A lot of women would have said thank you and enjoyed them."

"A lot of women weren't working two jobs to save a few bucks for the future."

He turned to face her, opening his mouth to say something more, but stopped. Instead, he dropped his hands to her shoulders and smiled that toe-curling smile that always made her heart race. "Look," he said quietly, his voice no longer antagonistic. "We just got married. We're on our honeymoon, for God's sake. I don't want to fight with you."

Natalie smiled, too, ashamed of herself for needling him so mercilessly. "I'm sorry. I'm just tired, I guess. And the heat's starting to get to me. I didn't mean to pick a fight."

"Neither did I. I'm sorry, too. Let's just get out of here, get home, and relax."

She smiled and said, "The roses were gorgeous, by the way."

He smiled back. "Thanks."

"No, thank you."

"You're welcome."

The baggage carousel beside them wheezed to life then, and she breathed a sigh of relief. "It shouldn't be long now."

Twenty-five minutes later, the carousel continued to move in a laconic circle, completely devoid of luggage. Natalie sat on the floor beside her carry-on, certain her new trousers would now sport a black stain on the seat she wasn't likely to get out no matter how hard she tried. At the moment, however, she didn't care. Nick had gone in search of something cool to drink some time ago and hadn't yet returned. Just when she was certain things could get no worse, the steady hum of the baggage carousel became a high-pitched squeal, a sound that sent a blinding pain slicing through her forehead.

She had expected her new home in a tropical paradise would be a dream, she recalled. What she hadn't counted on was it being such a nightmare.

A solitary suitcase came sliding down the ramp onto the carousel, but it wasn't one of theirs. Natalie ticked off the passage of another fifteen minutes on her watch before Nick returned with two sodas. His arrival was accompanied by the appearance of just a few more suitcases.

"I'll go call Luis now," he said when he saw how much progress had been made.

"Who's Luis?" Natalie asked.

"He's one of the guys from the cutter. Since he doesn't live too far from the airport, and since a cab to Condado Beach would cost us about half our take from the wedding checks, and since he's been dying to meet you anyway, he said he'd pick us up and give us a ride home. But I didn't want to call him until I knew our luggage was on the way."

She eyed him warily. "You knew it was going to take this long to get our bags, didn't you?"

He shrugged. "Sure. You forget I flew into this airport twice after flying home to visit you, not to mention my arrival down here the first time. It's always taken my luggage at least an hour to show up."

All the fight had left her by now, replaced by an utter exhaustion that kept her from feeling as resentful as she thought she probably should feel. "You know, you could have said something to prepare me. I would have kept a book out or something. *War and Peace* might have been long enough to get me through."

He grinned. "I thought maybe this time it would be different."

She shook her head. "Go call your friend."

Ninety minutes after their plane had landed, Nick and Natalie had collected all but one of their suitcases.

"Which one are we missing?" he asked wearily.

"The one with my shoes."

"So it's not one you really need, right?"

"No."

"We could just sneak off without it."

"That's true."

Just then the bag in question came careening through the opening at the top of the carousel and fell with a muffled *plop* onto the conveyor belt. The couple stared at it for some moments as if unable to believe their good fortune. Before it was about to disappear again, Nick sprinted over to retrieve it, and together, they piled their booty onto a baggage dolly and pushed it toward the exit.

Luis was waiting for them outside. Natalie identified him immediately. Tall and rangy with short, razor-straight black hair, he wore sunglasses despite the total absence of sunlight, a red, skintight muscle shirt, and black jeans that looked as though they had been painted on. He was leaning against a well-lacquered black pickup truck, and he smiled when he saw them, then hurried over to help relieve them of their burden.

"*Mira,* I was beginning to wonder what happened to you," he said to Nick as he shook his hand. To Natalie, he said, "You must be Natalie. Nice to meet you. I'm Luis. Nick and I work together on the cutter."

"It's nice to meet you, too," she returned with a smile.

"Welcome to Puerto Rico!" he added as he spread his arms open wide.

"Luis grew up here," Nick said. "In Mayaguez. He spent a lot of time in the States, but he's home now, right?"

Luis smiled. "You bet I am. And I'm staying here

now. There's no place like home. San Juan's a great city, Natalie. You'll like it here."

"Is it always this hot?" she asked.

He waved his hand at her as if she'd just made a hilarious joke. "Are you kidding? What we have now is beautiful weather. You should feel it in the summer."

"It gets hotter?"

"And more humid."

"Great."

"Don't worry," Luis told her. "In the summer, you just go to the beach and you feel better."

"I hope so."

"Trust me."

Together, the two men loaded the luggage into the back of the truck, while Natalie listened to the sounds of Puerto Rico. The wind ruffled the palm trees overhead, and all around her crickets chirped and whistled.

"Boy, the crickets here are loud," she said as Luis tossed the last of their bags into the truck.

"Those aren't crickets," he said with a grin. "They're frogs."

She gaped at him. "Frogs? But they don't sound like frogs."

"They're called *coquis*. You won't find them anywhere in the world, except for Puerto Rico."

"Really?"

He nodded. "They're about this big." He held up his thumb and index finger about an inch apart. "And they sing at night like that all the time. You'll hear them everywhere, even in the business district of Hato Rey or the tourist section of Condado Beach. They're all over the island."

"Wow."

"So you ready to see some of San Juan?"

Natalie nodded vigorously and scooted into the cab between Luis and Nick. Luis turned the key in the ignition, and the truck roared to life.

"*Ai,* I love that sound!" he cried as he threw the car into gear. "Natalie, pop that tape in, will you?"

She reacted as requested, and the truck was filled with raucous horns and percussion, accompanied by fleet fingers along the keys of a piano. The music leapt and slowed, quickened and halted, and danced around like nothing she had ever heard before. She couldn't help but smile.

"Salsa," Luis said, as if he had sensed her silent question. "The greatest music in the world."

As if to punctuate the statement, he leaned across her and turned up the volume, until the whole truck seemed to shimmy in time to the sounds romping from the stereo.

"We'll take the scenic route to the Condado," he said over the din as they pulled out onto the highway. "That way Natalie can see some of San Juan."

"Really, Luis," Nick said, leaning forward to look past his wife at his friend. "We're pretty tired from the flight. We'd just as soon get home right away."

Luis waved his hand again and said, "Don't worry about it. Just sit back and relax. I'll take care of everything. Natalie's never been here before right?"

"Right," she told him, her mood improving now that she had left the confines of the airport.

"So, since you and I will be getting underway again soon, Nick, she needs to get a feel for San Juan so she won't go crazy after you're gone. Right, Natalie?"

Luis's high spirits were infectious, and she had to admit she was excited and anxious to see some of the sights, even under cover of darkness. "Oh, come on,

Nick," she said to her husband. "It won't take that long."

"No problem," Luis said. "I'll still get you home in plenty of time."

"Okay, okay," Nick relented. "Take the long way."

As the truck sped down the highway toward town, Luis began to sing along to the music from the stereo, belting out the verse in Spanish at the top of his lungs. Hot wind rushed into the truck cab from the open windows, and outside, San Juan went by in a blur.

Lights. That's what Natalie noticed most of all. Lots and lots of lights. As they sped down a highway lined with palm trees and richly colored murals of Puerto Rican life, she was impressed by the size and scope of the city. High-rise hotels near the airport gave way to sweeping plains of grass and corrugated tin shanties, then suburban stucco homes, then the centuries-old walls of the colonial part of the city, then cement and glass skyscrapers of the business district. And then everything changed again.

Natalie was overcome by the starkness of the transitions, and the speed with which they seemed to come. Through it all, she smelled the ocean, tasted the salt on her lips, felt its stickiness on her skin. Even though she caught only glimpses of it on her ride through town, the ocean seemed to be everywhere.

When they stopped for a red light at a busy intersection, Luis ducked his head out the open window and shouted at a group of teenaged girls. "¡Mira, damas! ¡Buenas noches! ¡Y que hermosa noche está haciendo! ¿Qué pasó, eh? ¿Quiéren venir conmigo? I can be back in a half hour, what do you say?"

The girls lifted their heads and shouted back in Spanish, waving and smiling at Luis as if they were agreeable to whatever it was he had suggested. Natalie glanced over at Nick, who smiled back at her and shrugged.

"Welcome to Puerto Rico," he said, echoing Luis's words of a short time ago.

"It's the greatest place on earth," his friend replied as he stepped on the gas again, waving to the girls he left behind. "*¡Hasta la vista, mijitas!*"

Natalie shook her head as she watched the girls wave enthusiastically. "Well, it's certainly a lot different from Cleveland," she said, not quite under her breath.

"It's like nowhere else in the world," Luis assured her.

And as he carried them deeper into the city, under bright lights and massive palms, past open-air restaurants and bars where lively music split the night, through neighborhoods where brightly clad people sat out on their porches chatting and playing dominoes, Natalie had to agree that Luis was probably right about that.

2

Dear Mom and Dad,

    Merry Christmas! I think I'm finally starting to get used to San Juan, but I hardly ever get to see Nick. We try to spend as much time together as possible when he's home, but it still seems like he's gone all the time. Except for Luis, I haven't even had a chance to meet any of his friends from the Point Kendall. Well, granted, when we do have time together, we sort of like to be alone. Still, it would be nice to have someone to talk to when he's gone. There are two girls who live across the hall, but they keep pretty funny hours. They certainly seem nice enough, though . . .

    Natalie stood at the window and gazed down on Ashford Avenue, watching for anyone dressed in dark blue that might possibly be her husband. She hadn't seen Nick for nearly three weeks. In fact, since the two of them had come to San Juan, she hadn't seen much of him at all. Less than a week after their arrival, his cutter had left for its usual patrol, and he had been gone for a week. On his return, he'd been assigned to an in-port watch in which he'd had to spend the night on the cutter, which had kept him away from her for another twenty-four hours. Later that week, he'd had to do it again. And right after that, his cutter had gone on another weeklong patrol. Such had been the pattern of the nine weeks since her wedding day.

She had spoken to one of her sisters on the phone that afternoon and had learned that it was snowing in Cleveland, a good, hard, heavy snow just perfect for Christmas Eve. But here in San Juan, even in December, even at eleven o'clock at night, the city shuddered under a tropical heat like nothing she'd ever felt before. She sighed, wondering if she should try to call the base, wishing she didn't have to go across the street to use the hotel pay phone if she did. Even after nine weeks in Puerto Rico, they still had no telephone. Apparently, getting phone hookup in San Juan was one part perseverance, two parts luck, and three parts whether or not the service person felt like coming over.

Her first Christmas as Mrs. Nicholas Brannon wasn't turning out at all the way she had envisioned it. For one thing, she was alone. For another, they had no Christmas tree, because she hadn't been able to find anyone selling any. At home, her father had always found the biggest, fattest, most fragrant evergreen in Cleveland, and Natalie and her sisters had spent hours decorating it with hundreds of ornaments and lights. Christmas Eve at home meant Bing Crosby on the stereo, mulled wine on the stove, and ham and cornbread stuffing for dinner.

Christmas Eve in San Juan evidently meant raucous salsa blaring from car radios outside, the aroma of *pin-chot* from a streetside vendor, and rum and tonic over ice. Natalie swallowed the final sip of her drink thoughtfully. Gee, maybe she and Nick could even eat dinner at Pizza Hut tomorrow, she thought dryly. They were advertising a holiday all-u-can-eat buffet with all-u-can-drink sangria. Just perfect for the season.

She turned away from the window and crossed the living room to the kitchen to refill her drink, a motion she completed in less than five steps. The Condado Beach apartment Nick had rented for them, was, to say the least, tiny. It had come furnished and suppos-edly boasted a view of the ocean. In fact, Natalie had glimpsed the Atlantic once or twice from the kitchen window—a flash of blue between two hotels across the street. And if she went to the bedroom window and tilted her head just so, she thought she saw the ocean there, too. Mostly, though, what she saw when she looked out the window was a guy with a really hairy back taking a shower in the apartment building across the street on the other side.

All in all, she supposed their first home together wasn't *too* bad—if you were a fan of beige, liked looking into other people's apartments, and didn't mind having only two rooms with a closet-size kitchen to your name.

Something quick and brown scuttled across the floor near her foot, and she stamped down on it hard. And if you didn't mind sharing the place with a few hundred *cucarachas,* too, she added to herself, wrin-kling her nose in disgust. Oh well. At least she hadn't seen any of those big, icky, flying cockroaches in the apartment. Yet.

From outside in the hall, she heard the sound of the

elevator coming to a stop. She abandoned her drink and hurried to open the front door, certain she would find Nick standing there with his overstuffed sea bag hauled over one shoulder and that big, goofy, "Boy-did-I-miss-you" grin on his face. Instead she saw a man standing at the front door of the apartment across the hall. When he jumped and pivoted around, his expression seemed kind of panicky, and Natalie wondered why. Then the other door opened, and the man returned his attention to her neighbor, Amber. Or was it Geneva? Natalie had met both women briefly, but could never keep them straight. No, the blonde was definitely Amber, she remembered. Geneva had dark hair.

"I'm sorry," she said to the couple gazing back at her. "I thought you were Nick. Uh, my husband, I mean," she added for the man's benefit, though why she was bothering, she couldn't say.

Amber smiled. "Have you let that man of yours out of your sight again, honey? You know you shouldn't do that. Not down here. Anything can happen to him."

Her voice was low and throaty, completely different from the lightly pitched tenor Natalie remembered. And why was she wearing a riding habit complete with riding crop? Surely that was impractical, even here in Condado Beach, where pretty much everything went.

Natalie nodded. "Uh, yeah. Well, gotta go. Merry Christmas."

The man flushed and mumbled something unintelligible, then darted inside the other apartment. Amber waved her riding crop and offered a hasty "Season's Greetings" back, then closed the door behind him.

Natalie was still wondering about the exchange when the dull whir of the elevator alerted her again.

She waited with the front door open to see if the new arrival would be Nick, hoping their reunion would be as sweet as it always was. For a moment, she heard faint strains of "The William Tell Overture" escape from the apartment across the hall. But before she had time to wonder further, the elevator door opened, and there was Nick, exactly as she had pictured him. His dark hair fell damply across his forehead, his crumpled, dark blue work uniform hugged every solid muscle, his tan was a little darker, and his blue eyes shone brightly with delight. She didn't even give him a chance to come into the apartment and relinquish his burdens. She threw herself against him and hugged him with all her might.

"I missed you," she mumbled against his neck. "I missed you so much."

He laughed and strode forward into the apartment with Natalie still clinging to him, until he could drop his things and close the door behind them. Then he wrapped his arms around her, too, squeezing until she felt every last ounce of worry finally wrung out of her.

"I missed you, too," he told her. "I'm sorry we were so late getting back. We were only two days away from San Juan when that damned EPIC check came through. Cost us an extra week and a half. Then we didn't even find any drugs on board. I wanted to shoot every member of their crew just for keeping me away from you."

"But you're back now."

He hugged her again. "I'm back now."

"And we have a whole week before you have to leave again, right?"

"With my regular watch duty," he reminded her. "Just like usual."

"Okay, okay, but besides that, I have you all to myself, right?"

"Well . . ."

"Nick," she said slowly, her words laced with warning. "What is it?"

He exhaled a breath, removed his ball cap and ran a big hand through his hair. "We're on B-2 this week."

Natalie narrowed her eyes at him. "What does that mean?"

"Bravo status. It means I'm on two-hour recall."

"But it's Christmas. Why would they recall you?"

"Any number of reasons. So don't get mad and yell at me like you usually do when I have to leave again."

She pulled away from him, but didn't remove herself entirely. She curved her hands over his big biceps and turned him to face her fully. "I don't always get mad and yell at you when you have to leave."

Nick emitted an incredulous sound. "Oh, yes, you do."

"Oh, no, I don't."

"Yes, you do."

"No, I don't."

"You do, too."

"I do not."

"Do."

"Don't."

"Natalie—"

"Nick—"

Yes, their reunion was the same as always, Natalie thought. She couldn't imagine why she had worried it might be otherwise. Step one, kiss. Step two, hug. Step three, get into a fight. Standard operating procedure. Situation normal. She was getting this military stuff down pat.

She bit her lip to keep from saying something else

that might create a conflict, led Nick to the sofa, and sat them both down. "Look," she said, "it's Christmas Eve. I don't want us to fight."

He tossed his cap into a chair opposite them, draped his arm over the back of the sofa, and grinned devilishly. "Okay. What *do* you want to do?"

She walked her fingers up his shirt to his top button, then unfastened it. "First, I want you to take a shower with me."

"I can do that," he said agreeably. "Then what?"

She slipped the second button through its hole and tangled her fingers in the dark hair on his chest. "Then I want us to make wild jungle love until neither one of us can stand up."

He chuckled, then cupped his hand over her breast. "Yeah, that sounds good, too. Then what?"

"And then," she whispered, dropping her hand to his belt, tugging the webbed cotton free from the brass buckle. She tucked her hand inside his pants until her fingers pressed against him.

Nick groaned as he leaned forward and nibbled her earlobe. "And then?"

"Then," she began again, moaning when he traced her ear with his tongue, "I want to open my presents."

"You're already halfway through your first one, you know."

She smiled. "You start the shower. I'll get the champagne."

"Oh, Nick, they're beautiful. Where did you find them?"

Natalie held up the earrings, watching the way the light caught and danced in the colored beads. Also nestled amid the cotton in the box were three enameled bangle bracelets to match. Immediately, she slid them over her wrist.

"Martinique," he said. "We put in there for a couple of days a while back on our way to St. Lucia."

"And what was it again you were doing in St. Lucia?" she asked as she slipped on the earrings.

"Training the local coast guard on search and rescue procedure."

"That's right," she said with a thoughtful nod. "You get to travel to all the exotic places, and I get to stay here and squash roaches and scrub the toilet."

"Natalie, it's not as glamorous as it sounds. I work, you know. It's not like I get to lie on the beach and drink piña coladas all day. That's *your* job."

She colored. "Touché."

"Still laying out on the beach behind The Palm Bar?"

"Sometimes."

"Well, watch yourself. I hear that place draws a questionable clientele. It *is* a gay bar, after all."

She shrugged off his concern. "It's the only place on the beach where I can sunbathe without being pestered by guys hitting on me."

"Nevertheless—"

"Besides, I think I'm going to start looking for a job soon. I could probably find something, even if I don't speak Spanish. Condado Beach is such a tourist draw, English is probably spoken more often than Spanish anyway." She pushed her blond curls away from her ears, and fingered the earrings gently. "How do they look?"

Nick leaned forward and kissed her briefly on the mouth. "Beautiful. And so are the earrings."

THE HONEYMOON 25 –

"Now open your present," she said, handing him a brightly wrapped package the size and shape of a shoe box.

He weighed it carefully in one hand, shook it slightly, listened to it closely, and narrowed his eyes in puzzlement. Natalie smiled. He always did this with a present. It was one of the few areas where they differed. She normally tore right into her gifts, but Nick had to play with his first.

"Well, go on," she said.

He had broken the ribbon and freed the paper from one end when a voice called out from the street below.

"Nick! Nick Brannon! I know you're home! I can see the lights!"

They both scrambled up from the sofa and peered out the window. Below them, Ashford Avenue was still heavily populated with people, despite being three A.M. on Christmas morning. But on the corner opposite their apartment building stood a large man dressed in a blue work uniform identical to the one Nick had worn earlier. He was also wearing a nasty expression on his face.

"It's Booker," Nick said. "Dammit." Out the window he shouted down, "Come on up! I'll buzz you in!"

Natalie watched him cross to the front door and jam his thumb against the button that would open the security door downstairs. Not only did the Brannons have no telephone, but their intercom was broken as well, something their landlord had been assuring them for seven weeks he would fix right away. So anyone who wanted to get in touch with them had to shout their names from the corner across the street. Until that moment, no one had ever had to. And

Natalie was suddenly certain no good would come of it now.

Nick's expression was troubled when he turned around and crossed to the bedroom. She followed quickly behind him.

"Nick? What is it? What's wrong?"

"Something's up," he said. "I'm going to have to go out."

"But—"

"I'm sorry, Nat, that's just the way it is."

He was halfway dressed in his uniform when a quick rapping rattled the front door. Natalie suddenly remembered she was wearing only a short, rather revealing gown in deference to the hot night and her earlier plans for her husband. Reluctantly she pulled on a robe as she followed him out of the bedroom.

He yanked open the front door. "This better be good."

"I'm no happier about it than you are," Booker said as he stepped inside. He was brown-haired and brown-eyed, and one of the tallest men Natalie had ever seen. "I was *this close* to—" He halted abruptly when he noticed her, colored somewhat, then hastily concluded, "She was from Idaho, Nick. *Idaho*. Do you know how much that would have helped me out? Nobody from Idaho ever comes to the Caribbean. The western states are by far the toughest to get."

His statement piqued Natalie's interest, but Nick apparently chose to ignore it, because without comment, he headed for the bedroom to finish dressing. Over his shoulder, he asked, "What are we in for?"

"SAR," Booker told him. He looked at Natalie and then clarified, "Search and rescue. I'm Billy Booker, by the way. I work with Nick on the *Point Kendall*."

"Natalie," she said softly, still wondering what was going on. "Natalie Brannon."

Billy Booker smiled briefly, but the smile never reached his eyes. Obviously he was no happier about this episode than they were. His next words were directed at Nick. "Some idiot had too much to drink, hit another vessel, and sank his boat. There were about twenty people more on board than there should have been. No life preservers for them, either, naturally. We've got to go help pull them out. The forty-ones are already underway. I told Skipper I'd pick you up since you're on my way."

"You're going out?" Natalie asked in disbelief. "Tonight? But it's Christmas."

Billy shrugged, a helpless expression replacing the one of exasperation. "Tell that to the shithead out there who sank his yacht."

She was about to say that she'd be more than happy to if they'd take her with them. At least then she might be able to spend a little time with her husband.

Nick came out of the bedroom tucking his shirt into his pants. He snatched his ball cap from the chair onto which he'd tossed it earlier and shoved it onto his head. He was almost out the door when he remembered to turn around and say good-bye. With a brief kiss for Natalie and a hastily uttered "I'll be back as soon as I can," he followed Billy out, slamming the door behind him.

Only then did she recall that he hadn't even opened his Christmas present yet, the present that had taken her weeks to select. She ran to the window and saw the two men get into Billy's Jeep.

"Nick!" she called after her husband.

But the Jeep eased into the traffic flow of Ashford Avenue, and Natalie was left alone again.

3

Dear Mom and Dad,

Nick wants me to meet some friends of his, but we still never seem to have much time to get out. The Ingrams sound really nice, though. They actually live on a sailboat, can you imagine? That's so romantic! They're probably adorable little lovebirds who don't let a thing in the world come between them. I can't wait to invite them over for dinner. Nick says they're the way he wants us to be when we get to be their age. But that's about fifteen years away. I can only imagine . . .

Sybil Ingram squinted at the thin plastic wand she measured between her thumb and index finger and frowned. Blue. Dammit, the tip of the thing had turned blue *again*. She fell to her knees and searched frantically through the wastebasket until she located the crumpled instruction sheet that had come with the kit, smoothed it flat on the toilet seat, and double-checked her findings for the third time. Yup, blue meant positive, all right. And positive meant pregnant. She sat down hard on the deck, buried her head in her hands, clutched two big fists full of dark blond hair, and wondered what the hell she was supposed to tell Jack.

How had this happened? she wondered. Of course, she *knew* how it had happened, technically anyway. But when? She and Jack were always so careful, always so conscientious about using protection when they made love. For eighteen years they had been careful and conscientious. But somehow, somewhere, something had gone wrong.

Immediately, she remembered Christmas Eve. Jack had been underway the two and a half weeks before, and she had spent the time trying to organize the perfect holiday celebration. She'd decorated the boat from stem to stern with all the traditional holiday trappings, thumbing her nose at the eighty-five degree temperature. Her mother had sent her some clippings from the big holly bush back home in Minnesota, and Sybil had hung them throughout the main cabin. As she'd strung lights from the mast and along the rail, their neighbor Catch had tossed over some mistletoe he'd found only God knew where, and she had taken it below to fasten it over the bed. She'd even cooked on Christmas Eve—turkey and mashed potatoes and those little shallot things just the way Jack liked them. Yes, Sybil had planned the event down to the last detail, had shopped for weeks and worked for days to make sure the two of them would have everything necessary for a happy Christmas.

Everything except, she remembered now, spermacidal jelly.

She tugged viciously at her bangs as the memory formed. After a late, romantic dinner and affectionate exchanging of gifts, she and Jack had retired to the forward cabin to become reacquainted after a nineteen day separation. When she had ducked into the head on the way in order to insert her diaphragm, she had realized much to her dismay that she didn't have a spare tube of jelly, as she had thought. At the time she had shrugged it off and reached for the Vaseline instead, thinking that as long as she had the diaphragm in, the little gizmo would be effective.

Overindulgence in wine always had made her overly optimistic, she thought. Fat lot of good that realization did her now. She groaned as she thumped her forehead against the sink.

"Sybil! Where are you?"

She groaned. The only thing that could make this day worse than it already was would be for Jack to come home early. Sybil stood, dumped the contents of the test tube down the drain, and stowed the remnants of her test into a cabinet, stuffing a few towels on top for good measure.

Maybe the test was wrong, she told herself, just as she had told herself yesterday and the day before, when the tip of the little plastic wand had turned blue on those occasions as well. The instructions said you could refrigerate your urine until later in the day and do the test at your own convenience—that is, when your husband wasn't home—and still achieve the same results. But what if the people who invented the test were wrong? What if refrigerating your urine automatically made the test come out positive, even if you weren't pregnant? Maybe tomorrow, if she could just hold her first morning pee until after Jack left, then maybe the test would come out differently. Like negative. Like not pregnant.

"Sybil?"

Yeah, and maybe tomorrow Glenda the Good Witch would float in on her pink bubble, wave her wand and make Sybil Queen of the Emerald City, too.

She splashed cold water on her face, ran a quick comb through her short hair, and reached for the latch on the door. When she heard her husband call out her name a third time, she drew a shaky breath. What was she going to tell Jack? she wondered again. Oh, God, what was she going to tell Jack?

"You're awfully quiet tonight. What is it, baby?"

Sybil's fork tumbled from her fingers and clattered to a halt on the deck beneath the table. "Baby?" she replied quickly. "*Baby?* No, no, there's no—" She halted when she saw Jack's expression—bland, mildly inquisitive, and completely at ease. "I mean, uh—" She took a deep breath and released it slowly, picked up her fork, and began to push around what was left of her dinner on her plate. "What do you mean?"

"Nothing. I just wondered what's wrong. You've hardly said a word all afternoon."

She studied him closely, convinced he must know she was pregnant and was just prolonging this torturous tension to punish her for screwing things up. But his face—the face that had looked on her with nothing but affection and honesty since the day she'd first seen it—belied nothing of what he might be thinking.

When Sybil first met Jack nineteen years ago, he'd had a luxurious red beard several shades lighter than his auburn hair. The beard had obscured much of his face, but she knew he'd sported it in much the same way a lion wears its mane—with pride, arrogance, and the full knowledge that such an adornment turned female heads.

Unfortunately, he had been forced to shave it off when the Coast Guard introduced a ban on beards. For months after the announcement, Jack had talked about getting out of the Guard instead of submitting to such an outrageous edict. But by then he'd been well over halfway through to his retirement. The morning the rule went into effect, he had lifted a razor for the first time since she had known him. Ultimately, he had decided a few lousy years without his beard would be worth it if he could still retire at thirty-eight. Then, not only would he grow his beard back, but he'd also begin drawing a pension large enough to allow the two of them to enjoy a lifestyle for which they'd both waited years—sailing the seven seas without a care or responsibility in the world.

Sybil pushed away thoughts of the future and concentrated once again on her husband. She still wasn't quite used to Jack's clean-shaven face, even after having looked at him this way for years. In many ways, she had more difficulty now reading his moods and thoughts than she had when his features had been partially hidden. His face had been oddly more expressive with the beard. She missed those expressions, missed tangling her fingers in the soft curls, missed the scandalous feel of his beard on her skin when they made love. She was looking forward to his retirement, too, if not for precisely the same adventures he craved.

"Sybil?"

She suddenly realized he had been talking to her for several moments, and she had heard not a word of what he'd said. "I'm sorry, I wasn't listening."

"No kidding." He smiled as he reached across the table and covered her hand briefly with his. "Is everything okay? You seem to have something on your mind."

She nibbled her lip anxiously and prayed for divine intervention. She listened for the rumbling of thunder and crashing of waves as the sea parted, but when no lightning bolts split the sky, she sighed.

"Jack, are you, um . . . are you still planning on retiring in a year?"

Oh, sure, *now* his face became expressive, Sybil thought. He looked like she'd just asked him if he wanted to swallow hemlock for dessert.

"What are you, nuts?" he asked with a laugh. "Of course I'm still planning on it. Why? You planning on skipping out on me? Leaving me without a crew?"

"Well, not exactly." She thought for a moment. Just how did one tell one's husband that the future he'd been planning and counting on for nearly two decades and which was just within his reach was about to take a nosedive off a cliff? "It's just . . . Well, I've been thinking that maybe you should stay in the Guard for a little while longer."

"*What?*"

"Well, think about it," she said. "You're only thirty-seven. If you retire at thirty-eight, you'll just get fifty percent of your base pay for your pension. If you stayed in a few extra enlistments—"

"A *few* extra?"

"—until you were, say . . ." She calculated quickly. If they could just get it into high school, then the kid could get a part-time job and work its own way through college. "Say until you were fifty-four—"

"*Fifty-four?* Jesus, Sybil, I might be dead by then."

"Oh, you will not." She tried to smile. "At worst you'll just be mildly senile. You'll still have most of your motor functions. I'll wipe your chin for you when you drool."

He glared at her. "Let's get one thing straight right now. I am *not* retiring when I'm fifty-four. I'm applying for retirement two months before I turn thirty-eight. I went into the Guard on my eighteenth birthday, and I'll leave it twenty years later to the day."

"But—"

"Christ, what the hell's gotten into you?"

Now it was Jack's turn to scrutinize her, and Sybil didn't like it one bit. She fidgeted with a button on her shirt, smoothed a hand restlessly over her hair, and tried to avoid his gaze. Only when she could no longer tolerate the silence did she finally look at him again. He did not appear happy.

"I asked you a question," he said.

She feigned confusion. "Did you? I'm sorry, I can't remember what it was."

"I asked what's gotten into you."

"Nothing. I've just been thinking, that's all."

"About what?"

"About us. About our future. About your wanting to sail around the world a few dozen times."

"About *our* wanting to sail around the world," he corrected her. "What about it?"

She squirmed a little in her chair, reached for her beer, remembered that she was pregnant and shouldn't be drinking, and ran a thumb over the condensation streaming down the can. "I'm just not sure that's such a realistic goal for two adults to have, that's all."

"That's the goal we've had since we got married," he reminded her.

"I know, but we were kids when we got married. Hell, we were still teenagers. Things change sometimes."

"They don't change that much." He reached over and curled a finger beneath her chin, turning her head until she faced him fully. "Do they?"

Tell him now, Sybil ordered herself. *Just tell him and get it over with.* Her lips parted to form the necessary words, but no sound emerged. Jack's dream—his *dream* for God's sake—was to sail around the world before he was forty, unhampered by the restrictions of society and the responsibilities of most men. Who was she to destroy his dream? she asked herself. Who was she to tell him he wouldn't be able to follow his heart after all?

Although she and Jack were equally responsible for creating the spark that had generated the life growing inside her, she couldn't bring herself to share that news with him just yet. She wasn't even sure how *she* felt about it. Did she want to be pregnant? Did she want to have a child? Funny, but she hadn't given either question a thought. Since her discovery her only concern had been for Jack's reaction, not her own. How did *she* feel about this? Her own future was at stake, too. Why wasn't she concerned about that?

She knew her husband was waiting for an answer, so Sybil shook her head. "No, Jack," she finally said. "Things don't change that much. I'm sorry. I didn't mean to suggest that we should alter our plans. I don't know what got into me."

When he seemed to relax, she knew she had lied effectively. She'd never tried to deceive Jack before, and the realization that such a thing had come so easily to her did not sit well. Worse still was the fact that he found such undeniable comfort in the lie.

"Are you finished with your dinner?" she asked as she stood to carry her dishes to the tiny galley.

He nodded and relinquished his plate. "I'll miss your cooking when I'm gone next week. I always do. This next patrol is going to be a real bitch. Especially now that I have to pull Nick away from his wife. That kid has been completely ineffective since Natalie came down here."

Sybil was grateful for the change of subject. She tossed Jack a dish towel as she ran water into the sink. "Well, can you blame him? They've hardly spent three weeks together since they got married."

Jack rose from his seat and leaned lazily against the companionway as he waited for her to start rinsing. "Yeah, but come on. How much time do two people need to spend together anyway?"

She gaped at her husband in disbelief.

He relented. "Okay, okay. Lots of time. Especially when they're newlyweds. But Nick's got a job to do, and he better not forget that." With one long swallow, he finished his beer and opened the refrigerator for another before continuing. "Have you met her yet?"

"Natalie?"

He nodded.

"No, not yet. I was going to call and invite them over for dinner one night, but they don't have a phone yet. I figure when they're ready to be with other people, they'll look up Nick's friends." She smiled, remembering a time when she was a newlywed herself. "For now, though, they probably just want to be alone. They need an adjustment period."

"Yeah, it's tough enough for two people living together for the first time without all the weirdness this place and Nick's job bring with them."

"Give them a chance. Nick will be fine, you'll see. I just wish you guys didn't have to go out again so soon. Can't you talk Baxter into staying in San Juan for more than a week at a time?"

"One week in, one week out," he said. "That's the way Skipper wants to do it, and that's the way Skipper gets it done. Besides, it's not entirely up to him. Schedule comes from higher up."

"Still, you'd think he'd want to spend more time with Carmen."

"No you wouldn't."

Sybil glanced up, surprised. "What do you mean? I thought they were wildly in love."

Jack smiled cryptically. "*Carmen's* wildly in love. Skipper's just mildly in lust. I think she's beginning to grate on his nerves. She's not trying to hide the fact that she intends to become Mrs. Baxter Torrance and move back to Baltimore with him to become lady of the manor. Christ, I can just see the look on all those tight-lipped, parchment Torrance faces if Skipper brought home a poor, Puerto Rican blackjack dealer to introduce as his bride."

"His parents wouldn't like it?"

Jack emitted a single, humorless chuckle. "I met his folks when they came down to San Juan for Skipper's change of command ceremony. Even after talking to them for about five minutes, I could see that white sheets with hoods run rampant on both sides of the family."

"They're bigots, you mean."

"Bigots, blue bloods, and biased. All those things with a capital *B*, and that rhymes with *T*, and that stands for trouble."

"But Carmen's very sweet. And I don't care what you say, Baxter obviously cares a lot about her. Between the two of them, they could probably win the Torrances over eventually."

Jack looked doubtful. "Don't count on it. And don't lose any sleep over it. You and I have troubles of our own to worry about now."

The glass Sybil had just finished rinsing slipped from her fingers as she turned, dropping to the floor between them with a shatter. "Troubles?" she asked softly as she stooped to gather the largest of the pieces.

Jack grabbed a broom and nudged her away with it. When he had completed the cleanup, his eyes met hers, dark and compelling to their very depths. "Yeah, troubles," he said as he reached for her. "I'm going to be gone for seven days without my wife, and I want to make sure she misses me as much as I'm going to miss her."

His kiss was long and deep and intense, demanding a response she returned with equal fire. When he pressed her back against the sink, cool water seeped through her shorts, and she instinctively pushed her hips forward to remove herself from the chill. He moaned and rubbed himself insistently against her, raking a thumb up over her rib cage to stroke her breast. The sensation that shot through her was exquisite. She had heard that pregnancy made the breasts more sensitive, but she'd had no idea such a thing would happen so soon. Somehow, the knowledge of the changes already occurring in her body made her eager to discover more, and she covered his hand with her own, urging it lower.

In no time at all, they were half-naked and completely aroused. Jack tugged Sybil toward the forward cabin, releasing her as they passed the head. When she continued to follow him back to their cabin, he turned to gaze at her, clearly puzzled.

"What?" she asked breathlessly.

"Your diaphragm," he said with a confused smile.

Her own smile faltered. "Oh yeah. I forgot."

"How could you forget that? Do you want to be saddled with a kid for the rest of your life? God, Sybil, something like that would ruin everything."

She nodded quickly as she ducked into the head and closed the door softly behind her, taking a few moments to make the proper noises that would effectively advance the charade. All the while, she wondered what she was supposed to do about the baby. And all the while, she fought back the tears.

4

Dear Mom and Dad,

I met Nick's commanding officer briefly today. His name is Baxter, but none of the guys on the boat are allowed to call him that, so they call him "Skipper." I can call him Baxter, though. He sort of reminds me of a Kennedy, only with blond hair. Nick says he doesn't usually associate much with the enlisted men, although there was this one party last year where Baxter and his roommate, some lieutenant, had too much to drink and put on a hula show. I told Nick maybe that's why he doesn't usually associate much with the enlisted men, but Nick said he thinks it's more because of his upbringing. Anyway, he seems like a decent enough sort to me . . .

"Hit me."

Carmen Fuente glared at the man seated opposite her at the blackjack table, wishing with all her heart that she could take his instruction literally. He had been leering at her since he sat down, his smile too white against the backdrop of sunburned face and scalp. Typical *turista,* she thought. Overworked, overweight, overeager. When she leaned forward to turn over another card, he sat up straighter in his chair and tried to look down her blouse. Again.

Unconsciously, she flexed her left hand into a fist before thumbing a playing card from the top of the deck in her right. An ace of spades joined his nine of clubs. It figured. Her luck had been running bad all day—ever since her fight with Baxter that morning—and had only gotten worse as the evening wore on.

"Ten or twenty, sir," she remarked without much enthusiasm. "How would you like to play it?"

Of course, he would stay, she thought, trying to refocus her attention on the game at hand. Only an idiot would ask for a hit on twenty, even if one card was an ace. But instead of voicing his intent to hold, the man continued to ogle her until her face became hot with annoyance.

"What would you say if I wanted to play with you instead?" he asked in a loud voice, punctuating his question with a horsy guffaw and the stench of bourbon.

Carmen struggled to be stoical and silent. It was not as if this man was any different from a hundred others she met in a week. On the contrary, his comment was unusually subtle. But tonight, she was in no mood to handle a *pendejo,* subtle or otherwise. Tonight, she wanted to be someplace else, far away from the din and smoke and glare of the casino. Someplace where she did not have to wear a tight black miniskirt and low-cut ruffles and smile at people who treated her like dirt.

She wanted to be with Baxter, wanted to apologize for arguing—even though it had been his fault—wanted him to hold her and tell her everything would be all right and that she would never have to put up with creeps like this one again.

"Hey, sugar, how 'bout joining me for breakfast tomorrow morning?" the man asked when he had finished wheezing. "I could come by your place and pick you up." He paused for a heartbeat before adding, "Or I could just roll over and nudge you, what do you say?"

She remained silent and continued to stare at him until his smile gradually faded. Finally he glanced back down at his cards and muttered, "Oh, hell, hit me again."

Do not tempt me, she thought. "Are you sure that is what you wish to do?" she asked instead.

The man nodded. She tapped the deck of cards in her hand before pulling one up. The ace of diamonds joined the other two cards beside the man's pudgy hand.

"Hey, looky there, twenty-one," he said.

She shook her head in disbelief. "No kidding."

A tap on her shoulder alerted her to the arrival of another dealer, and she turned to find Edgar Rojas offering her a grin of support. There was an hour left before the end of her shift, so she knew Ramon had sent him because word of her bad luck had made the rounds until it had arrived in the manager's office. Ramon kept a close eye on all of his dealers and knew with some strange sixth sense precisely when one of them began to lose consistently. He never let it go on longer than he had to.

"*Gracias,* Edgar," she said. Before leaving the table, she performed the usual ritual—extending her hands toward the players to turn them first palm up and then palm down, illustrating that she had, to put it simply, nothing up her sleeve—as if anything would fit up the skintight spandex material of her blouse to begin with, she thought.

Leaving her table, however, did not alleviate her tension. Although all thoughts of the leering tourist evaporated, worries about Baxter immediately replaced them. The two of them had been arguing more and more lately, and Carmen just couldn't understand why.

After stopping by the manager's office to pick up her paycheck, she headed straight for the women's locker room to change. She stuffed her uniform into an oversized straw tote and pulled on a loose-fitting, hot-pink tank dress that fell well below the knee. She wove her waist-length black hair into a fat braid, washed her face, and reapplied her makeup, then exited the hotel through the employee entrance.

Ashford Avenue was alive with activity at ten P.M. on a Monday night. The traffic crept by amid the thump-thump-thump of salsa music and a sprinkling of American pop from car radios. From the bushes behind her, the *coquis* sang out a comforting serenade. People crowded the sidewalk, coloring the night with bright reds, blues, oranges, and greens. The palm trees lining the avenue stretched and opened toward the dark sky, rustling and whispering in the warm breeze. But the smells were what Carmen noticed most of all—a combination of exhaust fumes, ocean breezes, and *paella* and fried plantains from the outdoor grill across the street. It was a familiar smell, one she enjoyed virtually every night.

Although she still lived with her family in Santurce,

she had always come to Condado Beach to have a good time. Littered with hotels, casinos, bars, and restaurants, the Condado was a main draw for tourists and locals alike, offering any excuse to party. Tonight, however, Carmen did not feel much like celebrating anything. Normally, Baxter would have been waiting for her when she left work, but this time he was nowhere to be seen. She would be walking home this evening, she thought, dreading the twenty-something block trek through town. No way was she wasting five dollars on a taxi.

The aromas from the grill across the street made her stomach rumble, so she crossed to grab a bite to eat before going home. She waved at a couple she recognized, then took a seat at the bar. As she waited for her *arroz con pollo,* she glanced surreptitiously across at the hotel, knowing she was watching for Baxter, cursing herself for wishing him there.

And then he was there, almost as if she had indeed wished him, pacing nervously near the employee exit, obviously waiting for her. Wearing crisp jeans and a white polo shirt, with his short, blond, military haircut, pale blue eyes and sunburned nose, he looked more like a tourist than a resident of San Juan. Carmen shook her head and smiled.

After having lived here for more than a year, he still could not get a suntan. She supposed people did not come any whiter than the Torrances of Baltimore. She looked down at her hands, at the dark skin below the bright red nails, and her smile faded. Baxter's family would be no more willing to include her among their own than her family was willing to include him in theirs, all because of something as insignificant as skin tone.

She was at the corner, ready to cross the street, when he saw her. He signaled for her to stay put, and she returned to her seat at the grill, watching as he crossed to meet her instead. Neither spoke as he sat on the stool beside hers. He ordered a hamburger and a beer, then turned his attention to Carmen.

"I'm sorry about this morning," he told her.

"I am sorry, too."

"I shouldn't have said some of the things I said."

"I should not have said some of the things I said, either."

He sighed, covering her hand with his, twining their fingers together. "It's just . . . I don't know, Carmen. Sometimes you just make me so mad."

She nodded, tightening her fingers around his. "I know. Sometimes you make me so mad, too."

A plate of yellow rice and chicken and two beers appeared on the bar between them, and Baxter released her hand so that she could eat.

"Why do we fight so much lately?" he asked her after enjoying a long swallow of the icy brew.

She hesitated, knowing it would be unwise to bring up the topic they had argued about most recently, but still unwilling to let it drop entirely. "Well," she finally began, focusing her attention on the rice she pushed around on her plate, "today it was because you are too ashamed of me to introduce me to your parents."

When she turned to gauge Baxter's reaction, she saw a deep crimson stain creep into his neck and cheeks. "I'm not ashamed of you," he said quietly. But he didn't look at her when he spoke.

She glanced back down at the dinner she still had not tasted. She had already known he was not ashamed of her, of course, but for some reason she could not resist those moments when she knew she could get a rise out of him. "Then why did you say you will you not let me meet your parents when they come to Puerto Rico in June?"

He sighed and reached for his beer once again. "I didn't say I wouldn't *let* you meet them. I said they were going to be too busy to meet you. Hell, they're not even coming down here to see me. They're going on vacation—their cruise ship just happens to leave from here. But since they had to fly into San Juan anyway, they thought they'd spend the night here first for a quick visit." Before she could comment, he hurried on, "Even I won't see them for more than a couple of hours. They keep to themselves when they travel."

Carmen finally lifted a forkful of rice toward her mouth, but halted the action midway and placed the utensil back on her plate. "Baxter," she said patiently, "we have been dating for almost one year. Any other girl in Puerto Rico would be planning her wedding after all we have done together. But I have not even met your family."

He rubbed the back of his neck, clearly agitated with the route their conversation was taking. "Yeah, well that's kind of difficult when they live two thousand miles and an ocean away, isn't it?"

"It is not difficult when airplanes fly those miles every single day."

His hamburger arrived then, but he, too, seemed uninterested in his food, because he spun around on his stool until he faced her fully. "Don't start up with this again. We've been through it a million times already."

"And every time, you end it before we can settle anything."

"That's because there's nothing to settle."

"I think there is."

"Like what?"

"Like our future."

There, she had said it. Carmen had known Baxter for eleven months, and for more than half that time, she had known he was the man with whom she wanted to spend the rest of her life. Yet he had never offered a single indication that he had similar plans in mind for her. The two of them had fun together. They laughed a great deal. She loved him, and although he had never told her he loved her, she knew he must care for her to some degree, otherwise he would not be with her. But things could not go on this way forever. His duty in San Juan would be over in September. And she wanted to know where she stood long before he left.

He glanced down at his watch. "Well, it's almost ten-thirty right now. If we hurry, our future could include that salsa band you like. They're playing at the bar in the Caribe Hilton tonight. Show starts at midnight."

Carmen opened her mouth to say something more, but Baxter leaned over and kissed her softly on her parted lips. His action surprised her, and he took advantage of her silence to kiss her again, this time prolonging the caress until she could scarcely remember her own name. When he pulled away he was smiling, and she was helpless to do anything but smile back.

"Come on, finish your dinner," he said as he turned back to survey his own food. "Then let's go dancing." Seemingly as an afterthought, he added, "Don't worry about the future, Carmen. The future will take care of itself."

❖   ❖   ❖

It was well after three A.M. when Baxter pulled his car to a halt in front of the Santurce apartment building where the Fuentes lived. On the eighth floor, in a corner unit, a light shone brightly in a window. Carmen's mother was still awake awaiting her return, just as she was every evening when her daughter went out with Baxter.

It was funny, Carmen thought, how her mother had never worried about her when she was underage and dating local boys. But now that she was twenty-five and old enough to know right from wrong, and dating a man with better prospects than any of her other boyfriends had ever had, Rafaela Fuente was suddenly concerned for the welfare of her little girl.

"Your mom's up," Baxter said quietly.

"A very big surprise, no?" Carmen replied. "That was Papi's job when he was alive. Mami just took up where he left off."

"I'll come up with you and say hello."

"Are you sure you want to put yourself through that?"

He smiled, lifting his shoulders in a halfhearted shrug. "Never hurts to try."

She waited for him to circle the front of the car and open her door for her, then stepped out into the warm, balmy night. Winter in Puerto Rico was wonderful. No humidity, no sudden storms, no threats of hurricanes. Just mild, languid days and nights so perfect, they often bordered on cool. Tonight was such an evening. When the breeze kicked up, it glided softly over her bare shoulders and left a chilly kiss in its wake.

Here in Santurce, the breeze brought with it none of the sweet saltiness of the sea, and instead of whispering through the palms, high-rises hindered its journey. But far in the distance, she heard the joyful sound of salsa followed by the shriek of a woman's laughter, and she smiled. Santurce was home.

A couple necking in the doorway paused as Baxter and Carmen approached, greeted them absently, then went back to each other. The elevator was cramped and smelled faintly of urine and Lysol, but was efficient enough in taking them to their destination. Carmen withdrew her key as they neared the apartment, but before she had a chance to use it, the door swung open to reveal her mother in her nightgown and robe.

Rafaela Fuente was an unassuming woman with a slight build and delicate features, a long, auburn braid left loose at the end cascading over one shoulder. But her eyes ignited with a determined fire as she observed the couple standing at her front door, and she seemed anything but unassuming.

"*Hola,* Mami," Carmen greeted her mother quietly with a kiss as she passed through the door. Her younger brothers and sisters would be in bed by now, fast asleep. Except for Marita, who at nineteen was certain San Juan belonged to her alone. And Orlando, of course, the second oldest Fuente child, who was no doubt causing trouble somewhere else in the city.

"Hi, Mrs. Fuente," Baxter added as he followed Carmen inside. "How are you this evening?"

"I am fine," she replied automatically. "But it is not evening, it is morning," she added.

Carmen ignored the comment and instead lifted her nose to the fragrance of freshly brewed coffee. "Is there more coffee?" she asked her mother.

Rafaela nodded. "*Sí.*"

Carmen turned to Baxter. "Would you like a cup before you leave?"

He nodded, too. "That would be great. Your mom makes the best coffee in Puerto Rico."

Rafaela inclined her head forward, but was obviously unimpressed by the flattery.

"Oh, I almost forgot," Carmen said as she unzipped her purse. "I got paid today." She withdrew her paycheck, signed the back of it, and passed it to her mother. "And here." She withdrew a roll of one- and five-dollar bills that comprised her tips for the evening, counted out fifteen dollars for herself, then handed the rest to her mother.

Rafaela folded the money and check in half, placed them in the pocket of her robe, then kissed her daughter on the cheek. "You are a good girl, Carmen."

Carmen smiled at Baxter and went to the kitchen to pour them some coffee. The trio sat at the table in the tiny kitchen and chatted for nearly half an hour, until the sound of a key scraping in the front door alerted them to a new arrival. Carmen's younger brother, Orlando, appeared in the doorway, a huge grin splitting his face until he saw Baxter.

"*Buenas noches, Mamá, Carmen,*" he said, deliberately omitting Baxter from his greeting.

Carmen bristled. Not that she was surprised at her brother's behavior of course, just that he continued to indulge in it after so many months. She started to object, but Baxter's words cut her off.

"Hello, Orlando," he said.

Orlando did not reply, but went to kiss his mother on the cheek.

"*¿Queda café?*" he asked. "*El café huele delicioso.*"

"Orlando, I have asked you over and over to speak

English when Baxter is here," Carmen said. "Be polite for once in your life."

Orlando glared at his sister. "Why does Baxter not speak Spanish instead?"

"Because he does not know any Spanish."

"Well, he should learn. He is living in Puerto Rico now."

"Which of course is an American territory," Baxter pointed out amiably.

Orlando ignored him. Carmen shoved her chair away from the table and stood eye to eye with her brother, ready to do battle.

"Carmen, don't," Baxter said. "Don't fight with your brother. I'll go."

Reluctantly, she backed down, knowing his suggestion was probably for the best. "I will walk out with you."

"No, that's okay. It's late. You stay here."

Where you belong. The words were unspoken, but hung in the air between them nonetheless. He lifted his fingers to his lips to throw her a kiss before closing the door behind him.

What was it with people? Carmen wondered as she watched him leave. She and Baxter had never once let their backgrounds interfere with their feelings for each other. Why was it so difficult for others to do likewise? She looked at her brother, who stared back at her with accusation.

"You had better get used to him, Orlando," she said, deliberately speaking in English. "Because I am going to marry him, and he will be a part of this family."

"Says him or you?" her brother asked in Spanish. "Even if you're dumb enough to believe he'd consider it, how do you think his rich, high-class family back in America would feel about you?"

Instead of replying, she turned her gaze back to the front door through which Baxter had just departed. Soon enough, she would find out, she thought. Because whether he knew it or not, and whether he liked it or not, she would meet his parents when they came to San Juan in the summer. She only hoped his family was a little more open-minded than her own. Unfortunately, thinking back on the conversations she had shared with Baxter on the subject, Carmen was unable to reassure herself at all.

5

Dear Mom and Dad,

Tonight, Nick's taking me to our first Coast Guard party, so after almost four months of living here, I'm finally going to meet all his friends. I haven't even met Reuben yet, can you believe it? After all Nick's talk about his best buddy, there hasn't been a single opportunity to meet the guy. Well, that's about to change. I only hope I like him as much as Nick does. And I sure hope he likes me . . .

"Are you ready, Natalie?"
Natalie tried to cinch her belt into the fourth hole as she always had but wasn't quite able to manage it. She couldn't possibly have put on that much weight since her wedding, she insisted to herself. She hadn't had that many piña coladas to drink. Thinking back on

the number of days she'd lain soaking up the sun and ordering refreshment at the beach, however, she wondered if maybe it was time to get out and get a little more exercise. Even getting a job might help some.

"Nat? We're going to be late. Hurry up."

"I'm coming!"

With an exasperated sigh, she pitched the belt into her dresser drawer and slammed it shut. She'd be more comfortable without it anyway. Her baggy yellow T-shirt dress was fine as it was. After stepping into leather thongs, she slung her purse over her shoulder and headed out of the bedroom. Nick was standing beside the open front door, staring at his watch. An odd thrill of apprehension ran down her spine when, for just the briefest of moments, her husband reminded her of her father. Dan Mason had stood precisely that way by the front door whenever he'd been waiting for one of his daughters to get her tail in gear.

But then Nick looked up to meet her gaze. With that unruly lock of black hair falling over his blue eyes, those tight, faded Levi's, and the well-developed muscles straining against the sleeves of a white T-shirt that read, "Still on vacation—USCG Base San Juan," all thoughts of her father evaporated. Nick Brannon was nothing at all like her dad, she reassured herself. Nick was sexy and fun to be around.

"I'm sorry," she said as she scurried past him. "I couldn't decide what to wear. This party is my first chance to meet your friends, and I want to make a good impression."

He smiled at her. "There's no way you could make anything *but* a good impression."

She returned his smile, but was no more reassured

by his conviction than she had been earlier. She had yet to meet anyone her husband worked with besides Luis and Billy Booker, the latter of whom she had glimpsed for a scant five minutes under less than social circumstances. She was sure that by now Nick's friends must have concluded she was some kind of ogre he kept locked away because he was ashamed of her. Still, she reminded herself, in the more than four months of living in San Juan, she had spent only a little over five weeks with her husband.

As they waited for the elevator, the door to the apartment across the hall opened, and Geneva exited wearing little more than a smile. Her red bikini bra covered about as much of her as she was legally obligated to cover, and her black vinyl miniskirt was more mini than skirt.

"Hi, Natalie, Nick," she said when she saw them. She gave her head a thorough toss so that her long, black hair streamed down her back like a rush of oil.

"Hi, Geneva," Nick replied with an enthusiastic grin. "Great outfit."

Natalie narrowed her eyes at him. "Hello, Geneva," she said as politely as she could.

The elevator arrived, and the three climbed aboard. Geneva was wearing enough perfume to gag a skunk, and Natalie had never felt more claustrophobic in her life.

"Going out on the town finally?" Geneva asked on the ride down. "It's about time the two of you left the apartment." Her smile broadened as she added, "You act like you're a couple of newlyweds or something."

Natalie tucked her hand into the crook of Nick's elbow and pulled him close. "Nick's taking me to a party tonight. All the guys from his boat are going to be there, along with a lot of his friends from the base."

Geneva raised her eyebrows. "Coasties?" she asked. "All of them?"

Natalie nodded.

Geneva turned her attention to Nick. "Do they, uh, need any . . . you know. Entertainment?"

Natalie answered before Nick had the chance. "Their wives and girlfriends are going to be there, too," she snapped. She wanted to say more, but the elevator chirped to announce their arrival on the first floor.

"Well, keep me in mind, Nick," Geneva said as she preceded them out the door.

Natalie clung to her husband's arm and held him back until Geneva was out of sight. Only when she was confident that she was well and truly gone did she begin a slow progress forward. When she met Nick's gaze, she could see that he was puzzled.

"What is the matter with you tonight?" he asked her. "Do I have to remind you again that we're running late?"

"I think Geneva and Amber are prostitutes," she whispered, ignoring his question.

Nick gazed back at her in disbelief. "*What?*"

"Geneva and Amber," Natalie repeated. "They're prostitutes, I'm sure of it."

He drew an impatient breath and released it slowly. "You're nuts, Nat, you know that? I think you've been out in the sun too much. Maybe you ought to cut down on your beach time for a while."

"Nick, I'm serious. Did you see the way she was dressed?" At his lascivious smile, she rolled her eyes. "You're right—I am nuts. Of course you saw the way she was dressed. You were slobbering all over yourself."

"Natalie . . ."

"And what do you think she meant by 'entertainment'?"

"Her boyfriend is a drummer in a local band, that's what."

Natalie didn't buy so simple an explanation. "Amber's no different," she said. "You don't see them that often, because you're hardly ever home, but you wouldn't believe some of the getups I've seen them wear, most of them unbelievably skimpy."

"It's hot down here," her husband reminded her. "You've worn some pretty skimpy things yourself."

She smiled, because this time she knew his leering expression was for her. "Okay, then explain the men who come and go at their apartment at all hours of the day and night," she told him. "Explain the riding habit."

His expression faltered. "What riding habit?"

"The one Amber was wearing a while back when some strange guy came to her door."

"Maybe he was her riding instructor."

"Or maybe he was her John."

Nick's mouth dropped open in surprise, then he laughed. "My, my, my. What a mouth my wife has developed. Where are you picking up this language, Natalie?"

She colored. "Channel thirteen has been showing old *Starsky and Hutch* reruns late at night. But you're trying to change the subject. It's not just the riding habit, it's the kimono, too."

"Lots of women wear kimonos."

"Not made out of leather, they don't."

He shook his head and nudged her forward. "We're late," he said again.

"And what about the little French maid outfit? And once she looked like a member of the cast from *Swan Lake.* Nick? Are you listening to me?"

But her words were swallowed by the sounds of San Juan as he herded her out into the warm winter night.

The party was hosted by Billy Booker and his two roommates, a radioman from the base named Enrique García, and a seaman apprentice from one of the buoy tenders named Glen something. Nick had filled Natalie in on what he knew of the guest list during the cab ride over, but at the moment, she could barely remember a word of what he'd said. Something about watching out for the guys from the buoy tenders, because they were real animals, that Billy would probably show up with yet another woman none of the others had ever met before because he had some kind of quota to make, and that Natalie was sure to get along fine with Reuben.

She had heard a lot about Reuben Channing, ever since Nick had been posted in San Juan a year before their wedding. The two men had arrived on base the same day and, as a result, had become fast friends, despite being assigned to different duty stations. Reuben, she had been told, worked on the base, so he spent all of his professional time there and never had to get underway like those assigned to sea duty. And in spite of being ten years older than Nick, he was the same rank, E-5, because he had joined the Coast Guard at the age of twenty-five as opposed to Nick's eighteen. And where Nick's professional record was exemplary, Reuben's was less so. Nonetheless, Natalie knew her husband carried a great deal of affection for his friend, and she knew it meant a lot to him that she and Reuben get along well.

"There he is," Nick said as he took her elbow and began to steer her across the crowded room.

They pushed a path through the bodies writhing in time to loud reggae music that pulsed from four huge stereo speakers. Natalie waved at Luis when she saw him dancing with a young woman and couldn't help but wonder if he'd met her by yelling at her out the window of his truck. Somewhere along the way, someone pressed a tall, cool-looking drink into her hand, and she sipped it gratefully as she felt her temperature gradually starting to rise.

"There's Jack and Sybil Ingram," she heard Nick say as he paused to indicate a couple on the opposite side of the room who looked to be in their thirties. "Jack's the XPO of the *Point Kendall*."

"XPO?" Natalie asked. "What's that?"

"Executive Petty Officer. Second in command. He's a good guy. And Sybil's terrific. She's looking forward to meeting you. Sorry I haven't gotten around to introducing you two yet. You'll like her."

He started to tug Natalie away again, then noticed someone else. "Oh, wow, look. Even Skipper came to the party tonight." This time the man Nick indicated was one about Natalie's own age with pale blond hair and a sunburned nose. "And he brought Carmen, too. That's kind of a surprise. I thought he'd broken it off with her. Again."

She caught a brief glimpse of a dark-skinned, slender woman with a long black braid falling over one shoulder, then Nick was towing her along toward his friend again.

Reuben Channing was nothing at all like Natalie had expected him to be. Although she knew he was thirty-two, he seemed much older somehow. His pale brown hair was liberally threaded with silver and, along with his bushy mustache, was probably barely regulation in length. His burnished face was grooved by deep lines along his mouth and around dark brown eyes lit with laughter. What appeared to be a very old scar slashed clear across the bottom of his chin. He wasn't exactly what she would call handsome, she decided, but there was something about him that would make a woman look twice. Or maybe even three times.

"Reuben," Nick said, circling an arm around her waist to pull her close. "This is my wife, Natalie. Nat, this is my buddy, Reuben."

"I've heard a lot about you," they both said at once, then laughed.

"It's nice to meet you, Natalie," Reuben said warmly, taking her right hand in his. His voice sounded as rugged as the rest of him looked.

"It's nice to meet you, too."

Turning to Nick, he added, "She's every bit as beautiful as you said she was."

Nick beamed, tightening his hold on her waist, and suddenly, for some reason, Natalie felt uncomfortably like a trophy. She squirmed out of the embrace, shifting her purse to her other shoulder as if that were the reason she wanted to separate herself from her husband. But he didn't seem to notice.

"So what exactly do you do in the Coast Guard, Reuben?" she asked to make conversation.

"I'm a quartermaster. I'm assigned to RCC."

"RCC? What's that?"

"It stands for Rescue Coordination Center. I'm basically a watch stander."

"And what does that involve?"

"I handle calls that come in to the base, coordinate SARs and law enforcement activities, write situation reports, that kind of thing."

"Oh, I see," she said, not really understanding much of it at all.

"Reuben's got a great schedule," Nick said. "He stands watch twelve on and twelve off."

"What does that mean?" Natalie asked.

"It means I work from six A.M. to six P.M. two days in a row," Reuben told her. "Then I get two full days off."

"Wow, that's great." She turned to her husband. "Why can't you get into something like that, Nick? Then you wouldn't have to be gone all the time."

"Nat, I'm not gone all the time. Jeez, would you quit harping on that?"

"I do not harp."

"You do about that."

"I do not."

"You do, too."

"Do not."

"Natalie . . ."

"Nick . . ."

Reuben Channing cleared his throat discreetly and excused himself to get another drink.

"There, see what you just did?" Nick muttered after his friend's departure. "You've only known Reuben five minutes, and already you're chasing him off."

Natalie frowned. "What *I* did? I didn't chase any-body off, Nick Brannon. You started it by calling me a harpy."

"I did *not* call you a harpy."

"You said I was harping. You said I harp."

"But I didn't mean you were a harpy."

"Well, what else could it mean?"

"Well, not that."

"Then what *did* you mean?"

"I only meant—" He inhaled deeply and dispelled the breath with a frustrated groan. "Nothing, okay? I didn't mean anything. I'm sorry, all right? Do you forgive me?"

She eyed him narrowly. "You don't sound like you're sorry."

"*Natalie.*"

"Oh, all right. I forgive you."

He leaned forward and pressed his lips against hers, briefly, but long enough to let her know that he was indeed sorry for what he had said.

"I'm sorry, too," she finally said.

By the time Reuben returned, all was well with them again. But as the three of them chatted, the party grew in number and volume, and normal conversation became difficult. Finally, Natalie gave up and decided to join in the fray.

"Nick, let's dance," she said.

"Aw, Nat, you know I hate to dance. Why don't you dance with Reuben instead? I'll go talk to Booker. See where his date tonight is from. He's been looking for a woman from one of the southeastern states, but this time of year, pickings are light from that area. Weather's too nice at home, I guess."

Natalie sighed, pushing her vague curiosity about Billy Booker aside. Yes, she knew Nick hated to dance, but she had hoped he might make an exception tonight since he was so anxious for her to enjoy this party. Well, fine, she thought. If he didn't want to dance, he didn't have to.

"Reuben?" she asked her other companion. "You want to dance?"

He shrugged and set his drink on a nearby table. "Sure. Why not?"

She threw her husband a smug, self-satisfied expression. "It's nice to know *some* men aren't afraid to face the music."

Nick made a face back at her, but smiled as he turned to go. The next thing she knew, Reuben was the one holding her hand, leading her out to the middle of the crowd. He stopped when he could go no further, then turned to face her. The song was an American oldie, fast, insistent, fun. That tune segued into a lively salsa number, which was then followed by smooth, melodic reggae.

"One more," Natalie begged when Reuben voiced his intention to quit. "I haven't been dancing in so long, and I love it so much. Nick will never take me."

"Okay, one more," Reuben agreed. "But after that, I've got to rest. An old man's heart can't take much more of this."

She uttered a sound of disbelief. "Old. Right. You're not that much older than me."

He smiled. "How old are you?"

"Twenty-two."

He laughed. "Sugar, I've got shoes older than you."

Her back went up at his patronizing tone, and she wondered if maybe she wasn't going to get along with him so well after all. "Oh, you do not. Nick told me you're thirty-two. You've had to have bought shoes since you were ten years old."

When the music began again, it was a slow number, so Reuben draped his arms lightly over her shoulders and hooked his fingers behind her neck, keeping a

polite, good six inches of space between them. Despite
its harmlessness, the position felt uncomfortable to
Natalie, and she found herself hesitant to touch him
back. Finally, reluctantly, she settled her hands on his
waist, telling herself she shouldn't get mad at him just
because he insisted on treating her like a child.

"What else did Nick tell you about me?" he asked
her.

She tried to meet his gaze, but found it difficult for
some reason. So she focused on some point over his
shoulder instead. "Well, he said you're from
Washington state originally—"

"Seattle, to be precise."

"And that you've lived all over the place—"

"I've done quite a bit of traveling, that's true."

She tried again to study his face, but found uncomfortable the straightforward scrutiny she received
from him in return. So instead she went back to scanning the crowd for signs of Nick. "He also said you've
been married twice—"

"And divorced twice."

"That you were in the Merchant Marines before
you joined the Coast Guard—"

"More stability in the Guard. Besides, there isn't
that much work anymore for the U.S. Merchant
Marines. It's cheaper to hire hands from third world
countries."

"Let's see," she went on, staring at the ceiling as she
feigned deep thought. "Before the Merchant Marines,
you worked on the docks somewhere. Philadelphia, I
think he said—"

"And before that in New York. Before New York, I
worked in New Orleans. And before New Orleans, in
San Diego . . ."

Natalie nodded before continuing, "He also told me how popular your annual 'Ides of March' toga party is with everyone on base."

"Those guys love any excuse to put on a toga."

"And," she concluded with a grin, "he said you get into trouble a lot."

Reuben laughed at that. "He did, did he?"

She nodded.

"Well then, I guess he's been pretty thorough in his description of me."

Someone dancing behind Natalie bumped into her, shoving her up against Reuben. She gasped, but was finally able to meet his gaze. For just the briefest of moments, she stared at him, feeling the heat of his body penetrate the fabric of her dress, noting the thump of his heartbeat as it pounded in time beside hers. Then with a muffled "I'm sorry" she released him and sprang away, wending her way quickly back to the sidelines to look for Nick. She found him talking to Billy and quickly looped her arm through his.

"Did you have fun?" he asked.

She nodded and was about to ask him to get her something to drink when Reuben came up behind her carrying two pale yellow refreshments.

"Thought you might be thirsty," he said as he handed one to her.

"Thanks," she said as she took the drink from his hand.

He didn't seem to be at all bothered by what had just happened, and that realization calmed her somewhat. Surely she had only been imagining things, she told herself. Surely it hadn't been desire for her she'd seen in his eyes a moment ago. Surely it hadn't been desire for him she'd been feeling herself. For Pete's sake, she wasn't even sure she liked the man.

"Natalie, you remember Booker," Nick said, drawing her attention back.

"Hi, Billy," she said. "Nice to see you again."

"And under much better circumstances," the other man agreed. He indicated the slender, dark-haired woman beside him as he continued, "This is Donna. She's from Alabama."

"Birmin'ham," Donna confirmed as she slipped her hand into Billy's. "I'm jes' down here visitin'."

Billy grinned. "Don't you love that voice? There's just nothing like a southern drawl."

Donna colored, but smiled prettily. "You been makin' fun of the way I talk all night, Billy. I'm gonna have to keep quiet from here on out."

"I'm not making fun," he said. "I love the way you talk. It's sexy as hell."

"Billy!" Donna swatted him playfully.

"Come on, let's dance," he said as he guided her toward the dance floor.

"What is it with him and states?" Natalie asked as she watched the couple depart. "Is he interested in geography or something?"

Nick and Reuben laughed in unison.

"Only anatomical geography," Reuben said.

Nick nodded. "Yeah, ever since he realized how often he meets tourists down here, Booker's had this goal to sleep with a woman from each of the fifty states before he leaves the Caribbean."

Natalie gaped. "You have got to be kidding. Not only is that morally, ethically, and socially reprehensible, but doesn't he realize how dangerous it is?"

"Don't worry," Nick told her. "Billy always practices safe goal attaining."

She shook her head. "How long has he been down here?"

The two men exchanged glances.

"About six months?" Nick asked.

Reuben nodded.

Natalie didn't know why she was even bothering, but asked anyway. "And how's he doing so far?"

"Eighteen last I heard," Reuben said.

"No, nineteen," Nick corrected him. "You missed it. You were on St. Thomas a couple of weeks back when he met the woman from Maine."

Reuben whistled low. "No kidding? What a windfall."

Natalie shook her head at both of them. "I can't believe you guys. What he's doing is despicable, and you act like it's some sporting event."

"Hey, I've got twenty-five bucks in that says he's going to make it," Nick told her.

"Nick!"

"Only twenty-five?" Reuben asked. "I'm in for two hundred."

"Yeah, but you're not a married guy who has to worry about every nickel, are you?"

"Nick!" Natalie said again.

He smiled at her, letting her know he was only kidding. "Hey, why don't we all head over to Rico's for a beer? It's getting awfully crowded here."

"But I've hardly gotten to meet anyone you wanted me to meet," she said.

Nick searched the crowd. "Well, looks like Skipper and Carmen have taken off, and Jack and Sybil are talking to Chief Saunders and his wife. If it's all the same to you, Nat, I'd rather avoid Chief right now. Ever since we got back from that last underway, I'm not real high on his list of favorites."

"*You* got on Chief's bad side?" Reuben said. "What did you do?"

"I'd rather not talk about it."

"Great. If he's mad at you, Mr. Do-Everything-Right, where does that leave me? The guy's hated my guts ever since the Coast Guard Day Picnic last year."

Nick turned to Natalie again. "So you see, it might be best if we just got going. It's about time you saw Rico's anyway."

"What's Rico's?" she asked.

"It's a bar in Old San Juan where a lot of the Coasties hang out. It's kind of a dive, but we call it home."

Her gaze traveled from her husband to his friend and back again. "Okay," she said. "Rico's it is."

6

Dear Mom and Dad,

Good news! I finally found a job! Although I'm not exactly using my degree in child development, what I'm doing sort of goes along with children's behavioral studies. In a way. Kind of. You'd be proud of me, Daddy, because I'm sort of in public relations, like you were before you retired. How is your new place in Pensacola, by the way? Your postcards have been beautiful, but how about a letter now and then . . . ?

  Actually, to call Rico's a dive was to pay it a kind compliment, Natalie thought as she spun around on her stool between Nick and Reuben an hour later. Only two dusty windows broke the monotony of dark-paneled walls, and through those windows she could see nothing of picturesque Old San Juan outside—

just a nondescript side street and the brick wall of an equally nondescript building across the way. An old Bob Seger tune blared from the jukebox, punctuated by the click of billiard balls and pool cues. The moment she had stepped over the threshold, she'd felt as if she had left San Juan and returned to the industrial Cleveland neighborhood where she'd grown up. Still, there was something oddly likeable and cozy about the place.

The party at Billy's seemed to have simply changed locations shortly after their departure, because Rico's gradually filled with familiar faces Natalie had seen only a short time ago. Jack and Sybil Ingram sat on Nick's left, and Baxter and Carmen seemed to be wrapped up in a less-than-intimate chat at the other end of the bar. When Carmen started to raise her voice about something, Baxter tugged her up from her seat and led her to the dance floor in what Natalie supposed was an effort to quell the argument before it got out of hand. She hoped she and Nick never wound up at each others' throats that way.

When Nick and Reuben got up to throw some darts, Sybil Ingram moved to occupy one of the vacated seats beside Natalie. With her short blond hair, slender build, and dark tan, she reminded Natalie of a surfer. Had Nick not already told her the other woman's age, Natalie would have thought her to be only a couple of years older than she.

"Nick tells us you just graduated from college last summer," Sybil said during a lull in the music. "What's your degree in?"

"Child development," Natalie replied.

For some reason, Sybil's expression faltered, but

she recovered quickly. "Really? How interesting. Are you planning to pursue a career in teaching?"

"I'd like to. I'm hoping to get my master's in education when we get back to the States. But I'm not sure how easy it will be to establish a career with the Coast Guard moving Nick around every couple of years."

"Oh, there are ways to get around that," Sybil told her. "I know a few people in the Guard who've managed to keep the same billet for a long time before being transferred out. So you like kids, huh?"

The change of subject should have seemed abrupt, Natalie thought, but Sybil made it feel as if they'd been talking about children all along. "I love kids," Natalie told her. "I'm the youngest of six girls, so I never had any younger siblings to watch out for. I have a lot of nieces and nephews to baby-sit for, though. I can't wait until Nick and I can have a few of our own."

"Really?" Sybil said again, her expression bland despite the obvious interest she seemed to take in Natalie's answer. "Why would you be thinking about that already? The two of you just got married. You're so young. You have your whole lives ahead of you. You should enjoy it while you can."

Natalie shrugged. "Why can't we enjoy it with our kids, too?"

Her question seemed to stump Sybil, who didn't reply right away. Finally, she said, "Well, of course you can . . . I just meant . . . Um . . ."

"Besides," Natalie continued, "the longer you wait to have children, the greater the physical risks become. The female body is best equipped to handle a pregnancy in its early twenties."

"Is that so?"

"Oh, sure," Natalie continued, warming to the subject and feeling the effects of the God-only-knew-how-many planter's punches she had consumed so far that evening. "Once you hit thirty, you have all kinds of things to worry about. And after thirty-five, well . . ." She waved her hand through the air. "You might as well just forget about it."

Sybil's smile fell, and she reached for her ginger ale. "Why should you forget about it after thirty-five?"

"Well, because any number of things could happen. Chromosomal abnormalities could affect the child. And hypertension, diabetes, anemia, and autoimmune diseases could affect the mother. Not to mention the fact that miscarriages happen more frequently as women age. Plus, of course, there's the increased possibility of multiple births."

"Multiple births? You mean like twins?"

"Or triplets."

"*Triplets?*" Sybil gasped.

Natalie nodded.

Sybil inhaled a shaky breath. "You seem to know an awful lot about it."

"I've done a lot of reading," Natalie said as she lifted her drink to her lips. "Like I said, I'm looking forward to the time when Nick and I can start a family."

Sybil ran a shaky hand through her hair before leaning forward to rest her elbows on her knees. "Oh, man, I've got to get to a doctor," she said under her breath.

"What?" Natalie asked, leaning forward to bring her face even with Sybil's. "I'm sorry, I didn't hear you. The music's so loud."

"Nothing," Sybil mumbled through the fingers covering her face. "Never mind."

"So," Natalie went on, "have you and Jack ever thought about having kids?"

Before Sybil had a chance to respond, Jack hooted out his answer with a loud guffaw. "Not bloody likely!" he shouted. "Sybil and I are in no way the parental types, are we, Syb?"

Sybil shook her head miserably, still resting her forehead in her hands. "No," she agreed with a helpless sigh, "we most certainly are not." Well, at least that much was the truth, she thought. Nice to know she was still capable of an occasional bout with veracity, considering how often she'd lied to Jack lately.

"Nope, we have no plans to add on to the Ingram clan in the future," Jack continued as he signaled Rico to bring him another beer. "Ain't no room on the boat or in our lives for the pitter-patter of little feet. Although I might consent to getting a dog one day. A small one that doesn't make any noise and can pretty much take care of itself. Maybe. Someday. Sybil's always wanted one."

Sybil couldn't prevent the near-hysterical giggle that escaped her lips at Jack's comment.

"You okay, Syb?" he asked.

"Fine," she assured him with another giggle. "Just fine, Jack. I'm just a little surprised to hear your comments about getting a dog someday. Maybe. Someday."

He shrugged, clearly unconcerned. "Well, if it would make you happy."

Sybil suddenly felt tears stinging her eyes and abruptly excused herself to flee to the women's room. Latching the door behind her, she twisted the knob on the faucet marked *C* until it would turn no further, and waited for the water rushing from the spigot to change from brown to clear. Then, filling her palms with the icy water, she splashed her face over and over again, until the threat of tears subsided.

Dammit, she hated to cry. Crying was a sign of weakness, a frail emotional response that indicated a complete lack of self-control. But ever since discovering she was pregnant, she seemed capable of doing little else. She had never felt so helpless in her life. No matter how hard she tried to will it away, there was a baby growing inside her. With each passing day, its heartbeat grew stronger. With each passing week, some phenomenal new change in its development occurred. And no matter how hard she tried, there was nothing—nothing—she could do to stop it.

Well, actually, she thought as she reached for a paper towel to dry her face and grimaced at the scratchy feel of the harsh paper against her skin, there was one thing she could do. She could have the pregnancy terminated. Jack would never even have to know it had happened. But she would know, she reminded herself. And she would never forget. And frankly, she wasn't sure she'd ever be able to live with the memory.

Certainly Sybil faulted no woman for opting out of a pregnancy. And now that she had experienced for herself the trauma that accompanied the realization of impending motherhood, she thought she could sympathize even more with why a woman would want out. But she knew she couldn't do it herself. Whatever happened between her and Jack now was out of her hands. She had no idea what the future held.

By the time she found her way back to the bar, Nick and Reuben had rejoined Natalie. Her blond curls bounced merrily as she turned her head from one man to the other. Sybil couldn't help but marvel at the younger woman. Natalie Brannon was so incredibly naive. A kid away from home for the first time in her life, who'd managed to get herself thrown onto an exotic island surrounded by the kind of people her parents would certainly shelter her from if they only knew. She would learn, Sybil thought with a wistful smile. Before she left San Juan, Natalie would surely know what life was all about.

"Rico," Sybil said as she took her place beside Jack once more, "give me another ginger ale, will you?"

Rico Gomez was a harried-looking man with lively blue eyes and a perfect circle of scalp exposed at the crown of his dark head. At the moment he was also breathless and sweaty from rushing from one end of the bar to the other all evening.

"What was that, Sybil?" he asked as he swiped the grimy sleeve of his yellow *guayabera* shirt across his forehead. "Rum and ginger ale?"

"No, just a ginger ale."

"You sure ain't been drinking much lately," he remarked as he plucked a bottle out of a cooler of ice and twisted off the cap for her. "Anything wrong?"

She shook her head and quickly changed the subject. "Why are you working all alone on a Saturday night? Where's Ted? Where's Buck?"

"Bastards," he said, spitting on the floor at the mention of his two bartenders. "They took off for Tortola yesterday afternoon. Eloped. Never said a word to nobody. Hell, I don't even know if they're coming back."

"I guess you never know what people in love are capable of doing."

"Yeah, well they took four cases of Heineken with

'em, too," Rico muttered. "Now, I don't mind buying the two of 'em a wedding present and all that, but the least they coulda done was let me pick it out. And they left me shorthanded to boot. Where am I gonna find a bartender who can start work Monday?"

"Uh . . . I could probably do that," a third party offered.

Sybil and Rico looked over at the source of the soft, feminine voice that had answered the question. And if the expression on Nick Brannon's face was any indication, he was as surprised as they were to discover it was his wife.

"Got any bartending experience?" Rico asked.

Natalie shook her head. "No. But I've got a college degree."

Rico shrugged. "Hey, that's good enough for me. Can you start at ten Monday morning?"

"Sure."

"I'll see you then."

Carmen stared silently into a glass of cabernet she had barely touched and listened absently to what appeared to be an argument ensuing at the other end of the bar between that newlywed couple Baxter had pointed out to her earlier at the party. Baxter sat beside her, freely sipping his third beer of the night, slapping his hand against his thigh in time to the howling of Mick Jagger that blared from the jukebox speakers.

All was right with his world, she thought. As long as his girlfriend did not create waves, Baxter Torrance never had a care to trouble him. He had never had to share a small apartment with eight other people, had never awakened in the morning to hear his mother crying in the next room because she did not have the means to care for her children. He had never come home from school to discover the only thing to eat for dinner was *frijoles negros* and rice *again*. Where he came from, people ate black beans in expensive restaurants because it was a trendy dish.

No, Baxter would never have to worry about supporting himself or his family. He would never have to be concerned that some unforeseen force would disrupt his way of life and shatter everything he took for granted now. His future was completely mapped out for him until the day he died, and there were no treacherous mountains or valleys in the cartography. Carmen could not imagine what that kind of security must feel like.

"You look beautiful tonight, Carmen."

She glanced up from her wine and smiled, but the compliment did little to ease the tension she had felt escalating between them all evening. "Thank you," she said as she leaned forward to kiss him on the cheek.

"No, I mean it," he told her more insistently. "I don't think I tell you that often enough. I'm not sure I've ever met a woman more beautiful than you."

She smiled again and blushed at the praise for some reason. In her line of work, she never lacked for men telling her how attractive she was, and normally, she ignored such comments automatically. But to hear the words coming from Baxter, entirely unsolicited and completely out of the blue, was oddly disconcerting. Or perhaps it was precisely because he was speaking to her in the same way as the men who sat at her blackjack table ogling her that she now became uncomfortable. Lately, she had not been certain of her feelings in any way.

"Thank you," she said again. "It is sweet of you to say so."

When he said nothing more, but continued to gaze at her as if she were some fascinating specimen of life, Carmen began to feel even more detached. "Tell me something," she said suddenly.

"Anything."

She hesitated for a moment. "That first time you saw me, that night at the bar, why did you ask me to dance? I was with four other girls, none of us with dates, but when you walked over to our group, I was the one you asked to dance."

"You were the best looking of the bunch," he said with a careless shrug and a long swallow of his beer. "There was no contest."

She felt her hackles rise at the quickness of his reply. "So that is what it all came down to that night? You liked the way I look?"

Baxter nodded. "Sure."

"Then why is what I look like exactly the reason you do not want to introduce me to your family?"

He swiveled around on his stool and slammed his beer down on the bar with such force that she feared he would shatter the bottle. "Oh, Carmen, don't start this again. What you look like has nothing to do with—"

"I cannot help it. This is very important to me. It is all I think about lately."

"But there's no reason to—"

"There is every reason," she insisted. "I love you. I want to be your wife. But you refuse to talk about any future we might have beyond tomorrow evening."

When he did not reply—when he did not even look at her to acknowledge what she had said—Carmen knew she was losing him. She sighed sadly, lowering her eyes to the fingers twisting fretfully in her lap. "I am a good person, Baxter," she said quietly. "I would make a good wife for you. If you will let me meet your parents, they will see how much I love you. They will see how good we are together. What I look like . . . it does not matter."

He emitted a single, humorless chuckle. "Sure they will. In exactly the same way *your* family has seen how good we are together, and in exactly the same way that what *I* look like doesn't matter to *your* family, right?"

"I do not deny that my mother and Orlando are very unfair to you. But at least we are trying with them. You . . . you have been very unfair to me. I do not deserve to be just a . . . a sexual convenience for you while you are living in Puerto Rico."

A long moment stretched taut between them. She did not—could not—look up to see how he was reacting, but could detect no sign of motion from him.

Finally, he shifted on his seat a bit and replied as quietly as she had spoken, "Well, being a sexual convenience was good enough for you the night we met, wasn't it? And how the hell am I supposed to know how many other strangers you've jumped into the sack with the first night you met them? How do I know how many times it's happened since you met me? Who says it's your looks that prevent me from introducing you to my parents? Maybe it's your morals."

Carmen closed her eyes tight to halt the tears she knew would come. Tears of frustration, tears of anger. When she finally did glance up, Baxter had lifted his beer to his lips again to down what little was left. She stood, waited for him to finish drinking, waited for him to replace the bottle on the bar, waited for him to turn and look at her again. And then she slapped him as hard as she could.

"*Cabrón*," she said evenly, surprised at how calmly she delivered the insult. "Your morals are no better than mine. They are worse, because I would never say something to you that you did not deserve. And as *loco* as it sounds, I am willing to forget what you just said, because I do not think you truly meant it."

When he still refused to meet her gaze, she gripped his chin firmly in her hand and jerked his head around until he was staring at her eye to eye. "But I will tell you one thing, Baxter Torrance," she added. "Until you can talk openly about any future we might have, until you can be honest with me—and with yourself—I do not think I want to see you again."

And with that she spun around and disappeared into the throng of dancers crowding the stained hardwood floor of Rico's. She did not miss a step as she made her way through the writhing, sweaty bodies, and she did not look back once.

7

Dear Mom and Dad,

What was it like for you guys before you had all us girls? I mean, it could be years before Nick and I know each other as well as we should before we become parents. Seems like having children would only make that process take longer. So how did you two manage it when Mom got pregnant the first time? You were about the same age as me and Nick when it happened, weren't you? Was it scary? Were you happy? I was just kind of wondering is all . . .

      Natalie watched Sybil Ingram slice a cantaloupe in half, wondering why the woman looked as if she had been crying. Maybe she had allergies, she thought. Although Nick had allergies, too, and they'd never bothered him in Puerto Rico. Sybil sniffled as she scraped the orange gook out of the center of the fruit, then rubbed her nose vigorously with the hand holding the knife. Natalie held her breath for a moment, certain that the other woman was going to cut off her nose if she wasn't careful.

"What's wrong?" Sybil asked when she turned around and caught Natalie studying her.

"Nothing," Natalie replied quickly. Maybe too quickly, because Sybil eyed her warily. "I was just admiring your boat," she added.

Sybil smiled. "Thanks. We've put a lot of work into her over the years. She's finally pretty much at the point where we want her. When we bought her, she was bare bones and on her last legs. Her decks were a mess, her underbelly was covered with all kinds of muck, her shower was busted, her refrigeration unit was shot, and her cabins looked like someone had sent the cavalry through them."

Well, all that had certainly changed, Natalie noted, taking in once again the teak paneling and plum-colored cushions. Printed curtains were pushed back from the long, narrow windows, and the brass fixtures gleamed in the sunlight streaming through. The boat rocked gently against the pier, its hull creaking slightly with every subtle dip and rise it made. Through the open companionway leading to the cockpit, she heard Nick's laughter mingle with the deep-throated chuckles of Jack Ingram and the Ingrams' neighbor, who had been introduced simply as Catch. She wished when the time came for her to invite people over for dinner, they would be coming to a place as nice and as welcoming as the Ingrams', instead of to a tiny cracker box full of bugs.

"Jack says your boat is forty-two feet long?" Natalie

asked as she rose from the settee, comparing the size of the boat to the size of her own apartment only to find the boat much more accommodating. She crossed the cabin in a half-dozen strides to join Sybil in the galley.

"Forty-two to the inch," Sybil said.

"Seems bigger."

The other woman laughed. "Obviously you don't have to live on her. To me, she seems a lot smaller."

"How old is it?"

Sybil thought for a moment before she went back to slicing cantaloupe. "She's coming up on thirty-five years, I guess. Though we've only had her for about twelve."

"*Errukine,*" Natalie said, voicing the name she'd read on the back of the boat as Jack and Catch had helped maneuver her aboard. "That's a nice name. What does it mean?"

Sybil chuckled. "It's actually pronounced, 'Eh-roo-kee-neh,'" she said. "Jack chose the name. His grandmother was Basque. Her name was Errukine. It means 'merciful.'"

"You guys named your boat after his grandmother?"

Sybil nodded. "Jack always said since he wasn't planning to have any kids—" She halted abruptly as the knife slicing into the cantaloupe skidded danger-ously close to her hand, but she recovered quickly. "Since he wasn't going to have any kids, he would name his boat after the relative who meant the most to him."

Natalie hoisted herself onto the only available counter space in the galley, feeling oddly at home here with Sybil. "Nick and I have already told all our relatives that we're not naming our kids after anybody

when we have them. There are too many people to
choose from. Someone's feelings might get hurt, and
family politics can get pretty ugly. We don't want to
create any bad blood."

Sybil smiled, but didn't look up. "That's probably a
wise idea. So you two are going to start a family right
away, huh?"

Natalie sipped her beer thoughtfully before replying. "Actually, we probably will wait a little while. It's
like you said at Rico's that night a couple of weeks
ago. We do want to have some fun together alone
first. I guess there are a lot of things you can't do once
you have kids to consider."

Sybil dumped the sliced cantaloupe into a bowl
with an assortment of other fruit and reached for a
papaya. "Jack and I are going to sail around the world
after he retires."

"Wow," Natalie replied, impressed. "That sounds
great. How long before he retires?"

"Less than a year. His enlistment is up next
January."

"Is that why you guys don't want to have any kids?"

Sybil jerked up her head to fix Natalie with a
pointed gaze. "I didn't say we don't *want* kids. I said
Jack wasn't *planning* to have any."

"Oh," Natalie replied in a small voice. "I'm sorry, I
thought—"

"It doesn't matter what you thought."

Sybil squeezed her eyes shut to wipe out the image
of Natalie Brannon looking horrified, then lifted a
hand to her forehead and rubbed vigorously at a
headache that had sprung up from nowhere. What on
earth was the matter with her? She had no cause to be
tearing a piece off of Natalie. The kid was just making

conversation, and she was too young and inexperi-enced to realize how loaded a question like the one she just asked could be.

"Look, I'm sorry, Natalie," she said quietly. "I didn't mean to bite your head off like that. The fact is that you're half right. Jack doesn't plan on having kids because he doesn't want any."

"But you do?" she asked, her own voice low.

Sybil dispelled a breath of air that sent her long bangs flying, then tossed the knife onto the counter. "Right now I'm not sure what I want."

Natalie placed a hand on her shoulder. "Well, it's not like you have to decide right away. You're young. You still have time."

Sybil laughed, but there wasn't an ounce of humor in the sound. "That's not what you said at Rico's."

Natalie looked puzzled. "What do you mean?"

"Boy, how many of those planter's punches did you have that night? Don't you remember telling me about all the terrible things that happen to pregnant women over thirty-five?"

Natalie colored. "Uh, gee . . . now that you mention it, I guess I do. But I didn't mean to imply that—I mean, uh . . . Well, statistically speaking anyway, more women are putting off having kids until they're in their thirties, and very few experience any kind of problem with their pregnancies. That night at Rico's, I guess I was just being a, uh . . . "

"A know-it-all?" Sybil supplied.

"Actually, 'an obnoxious geek' was the phrase I was looking for," Natalie told her with a smile. "Fact is, you're still plenty young enough to have a family. Heck, my mom was forty when she had me. You don't have to decide right away. You and Jack have lots of time."

Sybil took a deep breath, released it slowly before turning her attention back to the bowl of fruit salad and muttered, "That's what you think, kid."

"What do you mean?"

She glanced up at the open companionway, but could hear the men above in deep conversation about something. Still, she kept her voice low when she met Natalie's gaze and said, "I'm almost nine weeks pregnant, and Jack doesn't know a thing about it."

Natalie's eyes widened. "You're pregnant? But that's wonder—"

She bit her lip in an obvious effort to keep from saying more. If Sybil hadn't been feeling so lousy, she would probably have laughed at Natalie's awkward expression.

"Oh, no," Natalie continued, "and I said all those terrible things about pregnancy after thirty-five. That's what upset you that night, wasn't it? I'm sorry, Sybil."

Sybil lifted a hand to halt the apology. "Believe me, the things you said at Rico's don't worry me nearly as much as other more immediate, and infinitely more probable, things do."

"And you haven't told Jack yet?"

Sybil shook her head. "No. And you can't say a word about it to anyone. Even Nick. God, especially Nick."

"But—"

"I mean it, Natalie," she said emphatically. "No one can know about this."

"But Jack's going to find out eventually. I mean, if you're nine weeks along . . . "

"*Almost* nine weeks," Sybil repeated. "There's still time, if I decide to . . . you know."

"To end it?" Natalie asked, her voice scarcely audible now.

Sybil curled a hand instinctively over her womb. Even though she knew she didn't have it in her to have an abortion she had the unsettling feeling that Jack might ask her to do just that.

"You can't tell him," Sybil repeated. "Not yet."

"Okay, I won't. I promise."

Sybil released a breath she hadn't been aware of holding and wondered why she had confided her dilemma to a virtual stranger. She barely knew the kid standing here looking at her like she was some kind of lunatic. And hell, Natalie *was* little more than a kid. Sybil had almost fifteen years of life experience on her, and even at twenty-two, Natalie Brannon seemed a bit less worldly than most women her age. She recalled Nick saying that his wife had lived with her parents until the time of their wedding. So she supposed Natalie had never really had the opportunity to be on her own. Sybil couldn't even remember if she had ever been that innocent herself.

"I apologize for burdening you like this," she told her. "You've probably never kept anything from Nick before, have you?"

The question reminded Natalie instantly of the party she and her husband had attended two weeks before, bringing up memories of the way she had felt for that single moment in Reuben Channing's arms. "Oh, maybe one or two things," she replied without meeting Sybil's gaze.

"It's just for a while," Sybil promised. "I'll tell Jack soon." Her fingers splayed open again over her lower abdomen, where Natalie could detect nothing to even hint at the other woman's condition. "When I have to."

"Do you need anything?" Natalie asked.

"No, thanks," Sybil told her. "I haven't had any morning sickness or anything. I feel fine. I just get tired sometimes is all. If it weren't for the damned pregnancy tests, I could almost convince myself I wasn't pregnant."

"Why don't you want Jack to know? I mean, would he really be that unhappy about it? Maybe he'll surprise you. Maybe he'll be ecstatic about the whole thing."

"No way. Before we even started getting serious, Jack made it clear that he didn't want any children, ever. Hell, he doesn't even really want a dog. His dream, his lifelong dream, has been to retire before he's forty and sail around the world, putting in at whatever port seemed interesting. He simply doesn't want to live by other people's rules."

"He joined the Coast Guard," Natalie pointed out. "That means he's willing to live by other people's rules if he has to. Maybe—"

But Sybil cut her off with a wave of her hand. "Oh, Jack will tolerate that way of life for now, while it's necessary, but only because it's a means to an end. Trust me on this, Natalie. He *won't* be happy about the baby."

"Are you so sure about that?"

"Very sure."

Natalie was about to object again, but Jack shouted through the companionway, "How's everything coming down there?"

Sybil threw her a cautioning look as she shouted back, "Fine. Dinner will be ready soon."

Nick stumbled down through the companionway with Jack and Catch on his heels. The Ingrams' neighbor had intrigued Natalie from the moment she'd lain eyes on him. With his sun-bleached hair, golden eyes, and brown skin lined permanently from what was obviously far too much time in the sun, there was no way to discern his age. Catch might be eighteen or fifty-eight, or anything in between. He seemed disinclined to overt conversation, but was, nonetheless, pleasant enough.

His home—berthed in the slip next to the Ingrams'—was absolutely gorgeous, a long, sleek sailboat even larger and older than *Errukine*. Catch's boat, named *Saracen,* had a wooden hull, and its mast and decks were a dark, polished mahogany, covered by a dark green canvas bimini top. The main cabin was huge, and potted plants dotted the outside all the way around. Even without Sybil's telling her the boat would bring a fortune at auction, Natalie had been able to see it was something special. She wondered how someone who seemed to be unemployed had come to enjoy such a lifestyle.

All three men laughed as they tossed out their empty beer cans and reached into a nearby cooler for refills. When Jack came forward to plant a kiss on the back of Sybil's neck, Natalie jumped down from the counter to sit between Nick and Catch on the settee in the main cabin.

"Jack's been telling me about his retirement plans," Nick said as he stretched his arm across the back of the settee and tangled his fingers in Natalie's ponytail. "He wants to start in Miami, point *Errukine* east and sail until he hits Mexico. Then he wants to turn around and do it all again."

"But not by myself," Jack clarified. "Naturally I'll be taking along my spouse. Couldn't get by without my crew."

"But you guys don't have an automatic pilot," Catch pointed out. "Will two people be enough to take this boat around the world?"

Natalie considered the question pretty ominous in light of the situation. Behind Jack, she saw Sybil's body stiffen.

"Two will be perfect," Jack said. "We're planning to have an automatic pilot installed before we go. Been saving up for it for a while now. *Errukine* is just the right size for a long voyage with two people. Any more than that, and you blow the entire balance." He smiled as he added, "Not to mention a beautiful relationship. Right, Sybil?"

Natalie wanted to cry when she saw Sybil's expression and had to force herself to keep seated and not cross the room to take the other woman in her arms.

"Right, Jack," Sybil said softly as she turned away. "And we wouldn't want to do that, would we?"

8

Dear Mom and Dad,

*I know you were worried about my coming
down here because you think I'm so shy, and that
I wouldn't go out of my way to meet people when
I left Cleveland, but you'd be so proud of me! I'm
making all kinds of new friends in San Juan. The
people are all so interesting, too! With some of
the most fascinating jobs, you can't imagine . . .*

*P.S. And no, of course I'm not pregnant. Whatever
gave you that idea?*

Natalie leaned back on her aching arms,
dug her toes into the warm sand behind the Hotel La
Concha, and sighed deeply with satisfaction. It was
one of her few days off since going to work at Rico's
three weeks ago. She'd had no idea that tending bar

could be so physically exhausting. Since Nick was underway this week, she intended to spend all her time today doing exactly nothing. Tilting her face back toward the bright blue bowl of the sky, she pushed the straps of her bathing suit off her shoulders, closed her eyes, and listened to the sounds of Condado Beach: to the radios blaring salsa all around her, to the sea gulls squawking for handouts, to the soft lap of the ocean licking the shore, to the—

"Party time! Puerto Rican party time! Rum and Coke! Piña colada! Ice cold Budweiser!"

She opened one eye to see the drink vendor picking his way through the throngs of sunning bodies. His pink-and-orange flowered trunks hung low on his hips, the baggy legs long enough to skim his knees. A gold cross dangling from twine winked at his midsection, and dollar bills were threaded through his fingers.

"*Hola,* Natalie," he greeted her when he arrived.

"*Hola,* Esteban."

"The usual?"

She nodded. "With an extra piece of pineapple, okay? I need my vitamin C."

He smiled. "You got it. Party time!" he shouted again as he made his way back to his cooler. "Puerto Rican party time! Rum and Coke! Piña colada! Ice cold Budweiser!"

As his voice faded away, another soon replaced it. The sunglasses vendor, dressed in his usual army fatigues and tank top, a Cincinnati Reds baseball cap perched on the back of his head, meandered along the shore advertising his own wares.

"Sunglasses! I got sunglasses! Calvin Klein! Gloria Vanderbilt! Liz Claiborne!"

Yet another man approached from the opposite

direction, wearing a homemade straw hat and a billowing yellow-and-red sarong wrapped double around his ample waist. His torso was bare, as dark and flawless as a Caribbean sky at midnight. Behind, he dragged a long mesh bag filled with green coconuts.

As if harmonizing, he chimed in with the sunglasses vendor, singing out, "Coco, coco! Coco, coco! I got coconuts! Fresh cut coconuts! Coco, coco!"

Natalie lifted her hand to the coconut vendor and he waved back, taking his time as he approached her.

"You want coconut today, Natalie?" he asked, grinning brightly.

"They're not dry like they were last week are they, Samuel?"

He shook his head vehemently. "No, no, no. I got a new supplier. These are fresh from Venezuela. Mouthwatering." He smacked his lips for effect and she laughed. "The most succulent coconuts you will ever taste."

She smiled. "Oh, okay. Hack me one up."

He withdrew a machete from the back of his sarong, searched through the bag until he found a coconut he deemed suitable for her consumption, then proceeded to hack it to bits. With swift, deft motions Natalie was certain would result in the loss of a limb should she attempt them herself, Samuel cut away the husk of the coconut and presented it to Natalie with all the flourish of a five-star restaurant wine captain.

"One dollar, please," he said.

She paid him and said, "Looks delicious. I'll miss stuff like this when Nick and I have to go home."

"But I thought this was your home," Samuel said as he tucked the dollar bill into a tailored, very expensive-looking eel-skin wallet, which he also returned to the folds of his sarong. "I've been seeing you on this beach for months."

She furrowed her brow. "Well, since you put it that way, I guess San Juan is my home . . . in a way . . . for now. I just meant . . . Oh, never mind. If you ever decide to move to the States, Samuel, let me know which one, okay?"

"Nope. Been to the States. Don't like it up there. This beach is just fine for me." He grinned again as he added, "Nice clientele."

He rose, then turned to thread his way through the sunbathers once again. "Coco, coco! Coco, coco!" he called out as he went.

"Sunglasses! I got sunglasses!"

"Party time! Puerto Rican party time!"

"Coco, coco! Coco, coco!"

"Gloria Vanderbilt, Liz Claiborne!"

"Rum and Coke, piña colada, ice cold Budweiser!"

Natalie laughed at the clash of the voices, then lay back on her towel. Puerto Rico was her home, she realized for the first time since moving there—hers and Nick's. Their very first home together. And all in all, she decided with a sigh as she rolled over onto her stomach, it wasn't such a bad place to begin a life together.

"It is Natalie, yes?"

Natalie opened her eyes some time later, shading them from the sun as she squinted at the person staring down at her. All she saw was a dark silhouette of a woman whose body was far better equipped to wear the tiny bikini it had on than hers was for her own one-piece that had lately begun to strain at the seams. She sat up straight and squinted harder.

"Oh!" she exclaimed when she finally recognized the woman. "You're Carmen, aren't you? Baxter's girl-friend?"

Carmen emitted a derisive sound. "I am not Baxter's girlfriend right now. May I join you?"

Natalie gestured toward the empty sand to her right, where Carmen was already spreading a brightly colored beach towel. "Sure," she said unnecessarily.

She waited while Carman took her time in getting situated, winding her long hair up onto her head, and using some mysterious technique to keep it there despite the absence of a barrette or clip. She slathered on suntan oil—SPF number two, Natalie noted enviously—then leaned back on her elbows, closed her eyes, and tilted her face toward the sun. Natalie shook her head. What she wouldn't give to look like Carmen Fuente.

"Men are such pigs, don't you think?" Carmen said.

Natalie's eyebrows shot up in surprise. "Pigs?"

Carmen nodded without opening her eyes. "I am beginning to think Puerto Rico should be renamed *Puerco* Rico, because the men who live here are just pigs."

"*Puerco* is Spanish for pig?"

Carmen turned to smile at her. "*Sí. Habla Español?*"

Natalie shook her head. "Not really. I've picked up a few phrases down here—'*¿Dónde está el baño?*' '*¿Dónde está mi esposo?*' '*Lo siento, no hablo español*'—that sort of thing. But nothing really important."

"Oh, I disagree. I think it is important to know where the bathroom and your husband are, not to mention that people understand you do not speak the language. No offense, but we Puerto Ricans usually assume you *Americanos* do not know Spanish anyway."

"We're that bad, huh?"

Carmen nodded. "Usually."

As if cued by their conversation, an obese woman straining against a bikini to rival Carmen's stood up on the quilt she and her family had spread nearby. She wore neon green sun block on her nose and lips, a huge straw hat with what appeared to be a dead bird affixed to the top, and little else. She waved her flabby, sunburned arms over her head, and in a voice redolent of northern New Jersey and shrill enough to raise goose bumps on Natalie's arms, she screeched, "Oh, Peedro! Peedro! Harry, what *is* that Porto Rican boy's name who brings us the drinks? Isn't it Peedro?"

"*I* thought his name was Peedro," Harry replied from his prone position without looking up. He, too, wore the neon green sun block on his nose, but had completely neglected the rest of himself, and his ample body shone bright red in the mid-morning sun. His swim trunks were skimpy briefs patterned like the Union Jack, and the flesh below his knobby knees waved in the breeze like a banner. "Maybe it's Julio," he told his wife. "Try that, Marge. I bet it's Julio. Or maybe Jesús. That's a pretty common name with these people, isn't it?"

"No, I'm sure it's Peedro. Peedro!" she shouted again, waving her arms more furiously. "Hey, Peeeeedro! Bring us a coupla more Cuba libras! Pronto!" She settled her hands on her hips—at least, Natalie thought they were her hips—and shook her head hopelessly. "He's ignoring me, Harry. I swear, the people in this place are just morons. Lazy Porto Ricans. You can't get them to do anything. I *told* you we should have gone to Yosemite."

"*I* wish they had gone to Yosemite," Carmen said quietly beside Natalie.

Although Marge certainly didn't deserve any help, Natalie didn't want to be here all day cringing each time the woman shouted out every Spanish-sounding name she could remember. "The guy who sells drinks is named Estéban," she called out.

Marge ignored her and turned to Harry instead. "Well, where did I get Peedro?" she asked her husband.

"How should I know?" he asked. "I thought his name was Peedro, too."

Carmen shook her head. "They think every man in Puerto Rico is named *Peedro*. And every woman is named María."

"Okay, so there are some real jerks who come down from the States to visit," Natalie conceded. "You can't blame us all for that. And not every Puerto Rican I've met has been the nicest person on the planet, either."

"I agree that there is a strong anti-American sentiment among some on the island. But not everyone feels that way. It is the same here as it is anywhere— there are good and bad people. And unfortunately, people always dwell on the bad."

Natalie nodded. She supposed that was true all over, too. "At least they're just visiting," she said of Harry and Marge. "They'll go home soon."

"And be replaced by two more who are just like them or worse."

"So then it's not just the men on the island who are *puercos*," Natalie said with a smile.

Carmen shaded her eyes from the sun and smiled

back. "No, I suppose not. But they are the biggest ones. May I ask you a personal question?"

"Sure."

"What is it like to be married?"

Natalie laughed. "To be honest, I'm not sure. I don't much feel like I'm married."

Carmen looked puzzled. "Why not?"

Natalie picked up a handful of sand and idly let it sift through her fingers. She considered the ring on her left hand as she said, "Oh, I don't know. Maybe it's because Nick and I have only been married a few months and it hasn't sunk in yet. Maybe it's because living in a place like this just makes me feel like we're still on our honeymoon. Or maybe it's just because he's gone all the time, and when he's home, all we do is—" She halted abruptly, unable to stop the blush that heated her cheeks.

"You spend all of your time in bed," Carmen guessed with a chuckle.

"Yeah," Natalie admitted. "You'd think being able to have sex as often as we want without having to worry about logistics and getting caught would make me feel married, but in a lot of ways, that just makes me feel more single. I mean, everyone's always told me that after you get married, sex drops off dramatically. But, boy, not with Nick and me. We're at it like rabbits, day and—" She broke off again when she realized how frankly she was speaking.

Carmen's chuckle became full-fledged laughter. "That is nothing to be embarrassed about, especially considering how long the men are out to sea. It is the same with Baxter and me." After a brief pause, she added more quietly, "At least, that is how it *was* with Baxter and me."

Natalie didn't want to pry, so she turned the conversation back to the original topic. "See? That's my point exactly. You and Baxter aren't married, but you act like Nick and I do, so what's the difference?"

"There is much difference," Carmen said quietly.

"You mean because we live together and stuff."

"No, I mean because it is more to be a wife than to be a girlfriend."

This time it was Natalie's turn to laugh. "Yeah, I get to pick up after Nick and wash his underwear and iron his uniforms. I never did that as his girlfriend. His mother did all that."

"You also have the respect a wife commands. And the knowledge that he will love you for the rest of his life, because he took a vow to do so."

"That's true," Natalie agreed. "But when Nick and I first got engaged, I thought being married was going to be a lot different."

"In what way?"

"I don't know. I thought we'd wake up in the morning and share the paper in bed over coffee and toast. Then I'd kiss Nick good-bye and send him off to work, then go to work myself, and teach first grade at some outrageously expensive private school. At night, I thought we'd sit down to a dinner representing each of the four basic food groups, then talk about how our days went, bitch about work, worry about our financial situation, complain about the kids, that kind of thing."

Carmen smiled. "But it is not like that."

Natalie laughed. "No, not really. Instead, what happens is that the alarm goes off at five-thirty, and I'm always too tired to get up with Nick, so he grabs a cup of coffee on his way to the base. Then I go pour drinks at Rico's all day, and by the time we get home, both of us are way too exhausted to fix anything. More likely, we wind up at Pizza Hut or this little Italian place down the street. And if Rico needs me to work a night shift, forget it. Then I don't get to see Nick at all."

"You could quit your job," Carmen suggested. "And spend your time making a home for your husband."

"No, I can't. Not that there's anything wrong with being a homemaker, but I just wouldn't be happy doing that. And in spite of Nick's complaining about how I work too much, he knows as well as I do that we need the money. Worrying about our financial situation is the one part of my imagined marriage that has come true. Condado Beach may be one of the nicest places to live in San Juan, but it sure isn't one of the cheapest. Besides, I really do like working at Rico's. And it helps to pass the time when Nick's underway and I'm stuck here alone."

"I wish Baxter would complain that I work too much," Carmen said. "It does not seem to bother him at all that we see so little of each other. And for the past three weeks, we have seen nothing at all of each other. But every time I complained about not spending time with him, he was never concerned."

"Maybe he was afraid to let you know how much it bothered him."

Carmen looked at her thoughtfully. "What do you mean?"

"Maybe he thought that if he overreacted, it would let you know how much he cares about you, and maybe he didn't want to let on until he was sure of your feelings for him."

"There is no way Baxter could misunderstand my feelings for him. He knows that I love him. Even when I fight with him, he knows how much I care."

"Then maybe he's afraid for other reasons."

"His parents," Carmen said. "His parents are coming to Puerto Rico this summer, and even though I have told him I would like to meet them when they are here, he will not let me."

"Why not?"

"I think it is because his parents would not like it that I am Puerto Rican any more than my family likes it that he is not."

"They're like Marge and Harry over there, huh?"

Carmen shook her head. "Marge and Harry could never produce a child like Baxter."

"Okay, so Baxter doesn't want to introduce you to his parents because you're Puerto Rican," Natalie said. "But is it his parents or himself he's more worried about?"

"No, no, no, you are wrong," Carmen was quick to contradict her. "My being Puerto Rican does not bother *Baxter*. It bothers his *parents*."

"Are you so sure about that?"

Carmen opened her mouth to say "Of course," but the words never quite emerged. Could there possibly be any truth in what Natalie was suggesting? That Baxter was as ashamed of being involved with a Puerto Rican girl as his parents would be if they knew? She had been assuming it was his wish to protect her from their bigotry that prevented him from arranging a meeting. And she had been convinced that she could overcome—and maybe even alter—his parents' narrow-mindedness.

But what if the prejudice was on Baxter's part? She had been so sure his reluctance to make a commitment to her was because he feared the repercussions from his family, and not because he did not love her.

But what if during all this time that she had been sure he was in love with her, she was in fact little more than a pastime until he left the island?

"What if you are right?" she finally asked Natalie. "What if it is true that Baxter is ashamed of me?"

"Whoa, I didn't say he was. I'm just saying it's something else to consider. At any rate, people can unlearn what they've been taught, especially if they're given the right examples to follow. Maybe you and Baxter can change Mr. and Mrs. Torrance's way of thinking."

Carmen was silent for a moment, lost in thought. "So you believe that people can change?" she finally asked.

"Sure they can," Natalie replied as she leaned back down on her towel. "You just have to have a little perseverance."

9

Dear Mom and Dad,

There are times when I wish I could be a fly on the cutter when Nick gets underway. I'd love to know what goes on when those guys go out on their patrols. I imagine it's a lot of that macho stuff. They probably all sit around in their underwear, smoking cigars and talking about sports, and pee off the side of the boat. Then they retreat to the beach and ogle the tourists in their little string bikinis. Men. They just have no concept of civilized behavior . . .

Nick Brannon sat on the bridge of the *Point Kendall,* sipping a cup of very strong, very bad coffee and staring out the window at the sky. The quarter moon dodged wispy white clouds, and stars winked like tiny bits of crystal strewn about black velvet. The deck vibrated ever so slightly from the hum of the cutter's engines far beneath him, a sound so familiar by now, he scarcely noticed it. It was three o'clock in the morning, they were cruising through Pillsbury Sound between St. Thomas and St. John, and all was right with the world.

"There's a lot to be said for Jack's retirement plans," he told Booker, who was seated at the helm. "There's nothing, *nothing* I can think of, that's quite like a night at sea."

"Hey, you don't have to tell me about it, "Booker areed. "I love this part of the job."

To escape the aroma of diesel and bring himself closer to the night that beckoned, Nick exited the bridge and leaned against the rail outside. Mingling with the smell of fuel now was an almost intoxicating scent of the sea, and mixed with the thrum of the engines was the sound of the wind whipping across the cutter. It tangled itself with a smack in the flag before rattling the anchor line, then nudged a lock of Nick's hair into his eyes. He didn't bother to push it back.

Even if he stayed in the Coast Guard for the rest of his life, he thought, he would never have another billet like this one. He was lucky to have been assigned to the *Point Kendall* right around the time he and Natalie had become engaged. His duty on the cutter had provided the two of them with a honeymoon they sure couldn't have managed otherwise.

"Nick?"

He turned to find Baxter pulling himself up the ladder nearby. "Skipper," he said straightening.

"What are you doing up here?" Baxter asked. "You don't have to report for duty for another hour yet."

Nick shrugged. "I caught some z's this afternoon while we were underway. Besides, Pillsbury Sound is my favorite passage. I didn't want to miss it."

Baxter nodded. "It's beautiful all right. Nice night for it, too."

The two men stood in silence for a while, enjoying the ride. Finally, Baxter seemed to grow restless and asked, "So how's married life treating you?"

"I like it just fine," Nick told him. "I don't get to see as much of Natalie as I'd like, but it's better than it was while we were engaged. I didn't get to see her at all then."

Baxter laughed derisively. "Actually, there's a lot to be said for that, too."

Nick knew he was talking about his own relationship with Carmen, but didn't press the issue. He didn't know his commanding officer that well, and although he considered the skipper to be a good guy, he was certain Baxter wasn't the sort to confide in his men. Life on a Coast Guard cutter was more casual than in other branches of military service—and even elsewhere in the Guard—but there was still a definite, albeit fine, line between officers and enlisted. And Nick was no more inclined to cross it than Baxter was.

"Yeah, women," Baxter went on, and suddenly it occurred to Nick that he might have been wrong about that line-crossing business after all. "Let me ask you something, Nick."

"Yeah, Skipper?"

"Does Natalie ever do things that make you want to wrap her in a tarp and dump her out at sea?"

Nick laughed. "Yeah, sometimes. A lot of times, actually."

"Like what?"

Nick sighed. Where to begin? "Well, most recently, she's taken this job at Rico's tending bar."

"Yeah, I've seen her working there and wondered how you felt about that. She doesn't seem to me quite the bartender type."

Nick nodded. "Join the club."

"So you're not too crazy about her working there?"

Nick turned his back to the view and leaned one elbow on the rail. "Hell no, I'm not crazy about it. I don't want her working around a bunch of drunks."

Baxter smiled. "Even if those drunks are all guys like us?"

"Oh yeah, like that's supposed to reassure me? And I don't like the late hours she has to keep sometimes. She's made it even more impossible for us to spend time together."

"So tell her to give up the job."

Nick knew Baxter was the product of a privileged upbringing, but even rich people couldn't be that stupid, could they? He shook his head. "Uh-uh. No can do."

"Why not?"

"Natalie's a grown woman. I can't tell her what she is and isn't allowed to do. Besides, I know she gets bored when I'm underway. I don't mind her working. Hell, we could use the money. I just wish she would have found something in the Condado closer to home and with better hours, that's all."

Baxter seemed to take a moment to digest this information, then asked further, "So what else has she ever done?"

His willingness—even eagerness—to pursue the topic surprised Nick. "What do you mean?"

The pale light streaming from the moon and stars gave Baxter's blond hair a ghostly whiteness. He eyed the sky thoughtfully as he asked, "What's the worst thing Natalie's ever done? Was there ever anything that made you want to end it for good?"

Nick thought for a long time before he answered. "Well, once, not long after she and I started dating, she went out with her old boyfriend behind my back a couple of times. I don't think she would have told me about it, either, if I hadn't heard about it from someone else. That made me pretty mad."

"It was a pretty lousy thing to do."

Nick shrugged. "It wasn't as bad as it sounds. The two of them had some unfinished business. By the time I found out about it, they were through for good."

"So you didn't break up with her for doing it?"

"Nah."

"Why not?"

Nick shrugged again. "I don't know. Just . . . " He paused for a moment, searching for the right way to put what he had to say. "As soon as I met Natalie, I knew there was something about her that I'd never seen in anybody else. Something that I was never going to find in anybody else again."

"What was that?"

"That's what's weird. I don't know. Just . . . something. I love her. You know?"

Baxter nodded, but said nothing.

Nick stared down into his coffee cup as he ventured, "So, uh, so how's Carmen doing?"

For a moment, Baxter didn't answer, and Nick was afraid he'd pried where he shouldn't have. But when he looked up to find his skipper staring off into space, he realized it was because the other man's mind was on something else.

He wasn't going to ask again, but the question must have finally registered, because Baxter turned quickly and replied, "Carmen? She's fine, I guess. Pissed off and not speaking to me, as usual, but otherwise okay. I was going to introduce her to Natalie at Booker's party last month, and then later at Rico's, but both times we had to leave early."

Meaning both times they'd gotten into a fight, Nick thought. He didn't think there was a person in Rico's that night who hadn't seen Carmen haul off and land one squarely on the skipper's jaw. "That's okay," he said. "I'm sure we'll run into you guys again."

"Oh, I'm not so sure about that," Baxter said softly. "I haven't seen her since that night."

"She'll come around."

"She's mad at me because I won't introduce her to my mother and father when they visit Puerto Rico this summer," Baxter continued as if Nick hadn't spoken. "What she doesn't realize is that I'm saving her a lot of grief. My parents aren't the easiest people to get along with. Especially—"

"Especially?"

Baxter seemed to remember who he was talking to then, because he pushed himself away from the rail and said, "Well, especially when they're traveling. They keep up a pretty hectic pace."

Nick nodded. "Yeah, I know what you mean. My folks are like that, too."

"No, they're not," Baxter said with a decisive shake of his head as he turned away and reached for the handle of the bridge door. Not quite under his breath, he added, "They can't be. Nobody's folks are like my folks."

He lifted a hand in farewell as he went inside, leaving Nick alone with the night and the stars and more than a little confusion.

It was raining in Frederiksted. Baxter sipped his imported Dutch beer and stared at the murky turquoise waters off St. Croix. Beside his table on the covered balcony of Dino's Bar, the spray of leaves from a huge palm spread open, rustling beneath the raindrops, dancing in the breeze. From somewhere downstairs he detected the sound of a reggae band warming up, and overhead a seagull screamed. The wind gusted, tossing a cool spray of rain over his bare arms and face, and he shivered.

Even when it was raining, this place was gorgeous, he thought. There was nothing he would like more than to spend the rest of his life here in the Caribbean, away from the restraints of everyday society, away from the dictates of his family, away from all the bullshit that made life difficult in general. But unfortunately for him, he was destined for greater things. It was something of which his father had always reminded him while he was growing up.

As a twenty-three-year-old lieutenant junior grade, Baxter was just a year and a half out of the academy and already commanding his own vessel. From the decks of the *Point Kendall* he would only go up, in vessel size and ultimately, in rank. He'd probably have to go ashore at some point in his career, maybe finagle an assignment at HQ in Washington, D.C. or something, but for the long-term, he had his sights set high. Eventually he wanted the command of a three-seventy-eight.

Of course, if he wanted to please his parents—something he was desperate to do but was certain was next to impossible—he'd ultimately have to become the Commandant of the United States Coast Guard. They hadn't wanted him to join the Guard in the first place and had assumed he would major in business at Harvard and follow in his father's banking footsteps. But ever since he'd learned to sail as a boy, Baxter had felt the lure of the sea. Enrolling in the academy was the only thing he'd ever done in his life that completely disregarded his parents' instructions. But dammit, he'd wanted *something* for himself.

And there was nothing to stand in his way now, he thought. He could have everything he'd ever wanted in life, anything his heart could desire. Except for one thing: Carmen Fuente.

He set his beer down on the table and cradled his chin in his hand. Why did his thoughts always circle back to Carmen? And why couldn't he just split with her once and for all and forget about her? She was no more to him than any other girl had ever been, and in many ways was a lot less. He'd met her in a Condado Beach bar shortly after his arrival in San Juan. They'd danced and shared a few drinks, then they'd gotten a hotel room. That was supposed to have been the end of it, he reminded himself. But more than a year had passed since then, and he still couldn't quite let her go.

He hadn't even told his parents about her. Christ, he could only imagine how well that news would go over. His father would understand the whole episode with a wink and a nudge, until Baxter explained that he really cared for her. That's where his old man would draw the line. And his mother . . . she would recoil at even the thought of her son sharing a bed with someone like Carmen Fuente.

"Looks like the rain is letting up."

He glanced up at Jack Ingram, who had returned from the bar with two more beers. Baxter swallowed the last of his first and reached for the second. "Never seems to last long down here," he said.

Jack took the seat he had vacated earlier. "Nothing lasts long down here," he said. "Rain, beer, time . . ."

"Oh, now I have to disagree with you there. I think time lasts forever down here."

Jack thought for a moment before nodding his head in agreement. "Yeah, maybe you're right at that."

"How long have you and Sybil been married?" Baxter asked suddenly.

"Eighteen years. Why?"

"Can I ask you a question?"

"Sure, Skipper."

"Something personal?"

Jack nodded again. "Okay."

"Has there ever been a time when you and Sybil had . . . you know. Problems?"

"What kind of problems?"

"Marital problems. Problems bad enough to make the two of you split up."

"Never," Jack replied immediately.

"Never? Not even once?"

Jack smiled and shook his head resolutely. "Not even once. Sybil and I have a relationship that is completely unlike anyone else's I've ever met. We've just never had a disagreement about anything, ever."

"Not even over something like . . . like . . . money?

Or . . . or household chores? Or your hours on the cutter? Most of the wives and girlfriends hate that," he pointed out.

"Nope. Number one, we make enough money to get by, and we both have very modest needs. Number two, Sybil takes care of the inside of *Errukine,* and I take care of the outside. And number three, frankly, I think she likes having the time alone when I'm gone as much as I like being underway. We're just one of those rare couples who gets along without a hitch."

Baxter frowned. Jack wasn't helping at all.

"We both share the same philosophy about life," Jack continued. "We have the same beliefs, the same feelings, the same dreams. There's never been anything between us to raise even the slightest problem. And there never will be."

Baxter seized on the other man's final statement. "But what if there was?" he asked.

Jack halted the movement of his beer bottle just shy of his mouth. "What do you mean?"

"What if you found out something about Sybil you didn't know, or what if she did something that made you want to leave her?"

"That will never happen," Jack said with infinite confidence before placing the beer to his lips to enjoy a hefty swallow.

"But what if it did?" Baxter insisted.

"It won't."

"Are you saying the two of you could work through it if something did go wrong?"

Jack eyed his commanding officer squarely. "No, I'm saying it won't happen. Sybil wouldn't do that to me. And I wouldn't do that to Sybil. What's up? You and Carmen still having problems?"

Baxter expelled a long, impatient breath before replying. "You don't sound too surprised to hear it."

"Yeah, well it's no secret the two of you haven't had the steadiest of relationships, is it?"

"No, I suppose not."

Jack tipped his beer back for another long, thirsty swallow. "Well, then," he said when he'd completed the motion.

"Well, then," Baxter echoed.

"You want to talk about it?"

"Not particularly." Then, counter to his assurance, Baxter said, "What's weird is that there's really nothing about Carmen I don't like. No one particular thing that I can stay mad at her about."

"So what's the problem?"

"So I can't identify anything so special about her that I *do* like, either."

"Meaning?"

"Meaning I can't figure out why I want to be with her. She is in no way different from other women I've met."

"She's beautiful," Jack pointed out.

"So are a million other women on the island."

"She's smart."

"So are a million other women on the island," Baxter repeated.

"She laughs a lot. She's fun to be around."

"So are—"

"—a million other women on the island," Jack chorused in conclusion. After a moment, he added quietly, "But unlike a million other women on the island, she's the one you're in love with."

"But why?" Baxter demanded as he rose from his chair and paced to the side of the balcony that overlooked the beach below. As soon as he reached his destination, he turned abruptly and paced back to the table. "That's what I want to know. Why?"

"Who knows why?" Jack asked. "Hell, who cares why? Just let it happen. It's unbelievably good once you find the right person. Trust me."

Jack Ingram surveyed his commanding officer with a smile. Jesus, he couldn't believe he was serving under such a kid. The Coast Guard sure was getting younger, he thought. No way did it have anything to do with his getting older. Academy or not, Baxter Torrance had a lot of growing up to do.

"You know, Skipper, it's been my experience that a lot of people create their own problems from nothing. Don't sweat the small stuff. That'll kill you faster than anything else in life will. I guaran-damn-tee it."

Baxter sighed, raked his hand through his hair, and slumped into his seat once again. For a long time, he said nothing, only stared blindly out to where the grayish-blues of sea and sky became smudged together. "Jack?" he said finally.

"Yeah?"

"Do you think women worry about us as much as we worry about them?"

Jack laughed knowingly before replying, "No way, Skipper. No way."

10

Dear Mom and Dad,

We went sailing with the Ingrams this week. Their neighbor, this guy named Catch, and Baxter and Carmen went, too. It was wonderful. Now Nick's all fired up to buy a sailboat. I've tried to tell him I think there's more to sailing than attaching a piece of fabric to a boat, but he's sure he knows what's best. He sort of reminds me of Dad that summer on Lake Erie. How long did you have to wear that cast anyway, Dad . . . ?

"Nick, could we do something different today?"

Natalie studied her husband as he folded over another page of the *San Juan Star* and read some more. The huge, block headlines on the front screamed out at her like a bad tabloid, something about a local politician caught in a compromising position with a flamenco dancer named Jorge. "Family and friends shocked!" the smaller print read. The accompanying photograph was a grainy snapshot that took up three-quarters of the page and featured two men in very brief swimsuits who might have been anyone.

"Like what?" Nick asked.

She shrugged as she rose to get more coffee for them. "I don't know, but I'm starting to get kind of tired of going to the beach every time we have a day off together."

"But I love the beach. And I hardly ever get to spend time there."

"I know," she repeated as she refilled their mugs. "But after four months of it, it's starting to get a little boring."

"Boy, if our friends in Cleveland could hear you now. Do you know how many of them would give their teeth to be living the way we do? With the ocean right across the street and nothing but warm temperatures every single day? This place is paradise, Natalie. Better take advantage of it while you can."

In the street below, a car alarm sounded loudly out of nowhere, and she jumped, spilling a good portion of the coffee on herself and the floor. That sound was followed by yet another loud stereo blaring salsa, and then the hollering of two men who seemed to be in a quickly escalating argument. She wasn't sure she would ever get used to the noise that went with city living; or the smell of exhaust that seemed to permeate everything in the apartment; or the black grit that covered every flat surface every morning when she arose, despite her best efforts to keep the apartment clean.

When she replaced the coffee carafe on its burner, a large roach scuttled out from behind the machine. She squealed, jumped away, and grappled for the flyswatter, but by the time she slapped at the insect, it had disappeared into a crevice between the kitchen counter and stove.

She hooked the flyswatter back onto its usual resting place, blew an errant strand of hair out of her eyes, and wiped away the sweat that rose on her forehead even at seven A.M. Paradise, huh? she thought. Maybe for someone who spent eighty-five percent of his time on the deck of a boat, with the warm tropical breeze whiffling through his hair, beneath a sunny sky, out in the middle of the vast blue Caribbean, on his way to yet another gorgeous St. Somewhere, this place was paradise. But there were times when Natalie thought San Juan was beginning to lose some of its charm.

"Roach?" Nick asked when he noticed her flurry of action. Absently, he flipped over another page of the *Star.*

"Yes, they're getting nervier everyday. Usually they only come out at night. But that's not a problem anymore. Since the sun goes down around six o'clock, I always make sure I'm drunk by then, and the little buggers don't bother me so much. It's when they jump out at me during the day, when I'm sober, that sets me on edge." She studied the small crack between the counter and stove where her most recent tormenter had disappeared. "I'm pretty sure that one was Raúl. He's their leader."

Nick finally dropped the paper into his lap and turned to stare at her. "Raúl?" he asked. "You're actually naming the cockroaches now?"

Natalie nodded. "Sure. There's Raúl, his wife

Consuela, their kids—who I'd name, but there are hundreds of them—a really big one named Bubba . . ."

"Bubba?"

"Yeah, he migrated here from Mississippi on a freighter."

"He told you that himself, did he?"

"Well, not in so many words, no. It's his accent that gives him away."

This time it was Nick who nodded, slowly and with great deliberation. "I see."

She returned to her seat and sipped her coffee. "Well, I have to have something to do to pass the time when you're gone."

"So you party with all your little six-legged friends."

She nodded again. "And then, when they're not looking, I kill them."

"I see," he repeated. "You know, I think you're right. You do need to do something a little different today. What say I make you an appointment with the base shrink?"

"Very funny."

He relented then, folding the newspaper closed and setting it on the table. "Actually, Jack did mention yesterday that he and Sybil were taking the boat out today. And he invited us to come along."

She stared at him incredulously. "And you didn't jump at the chance?"

"Well, I thought you'd want to go to the beach."

"No, you knew *you'd* want to go to the beach. I can do that any time."

"Well, I can't. I'd like to go to the beach today."

"Oh, you go to the beach a lot, and you know it. And you get to go to all the nicest ones in the Caribbean. On Uncle Sam's tab, too."

"Yeah, well, I'm also out on a boat a lot. Maybe I don't want to go out with Jack and Sybil on theirs today."

"Well, I never get to go out on a boat. Oh, come on. I've never been sailing before. Can't we go? Is it too late to accept?"

He crossed his arms over his chest and pouted. "Probably not," he muttered. "I could go across the street and give them a call."

"Please?" Natalie asked further.

He pushed himself away from the table with a scrape and stood. "Oh, all right," he said.

She could see that he was none too happy about having to do something that would require bodily motion today, and was pleased that he would make the sacrifice for her.

"Thanks, Nick," she said with a smile, rising to throw herself against him for a kiss. "It will be fun, you'll see. Jack and Sybil know better than anyone how to have a good time."

"Glad you two could make it after all," Jack said as Nick and Natalie climbed aboard *Errukine* an hour later. "Skipper and Carmen and Catch are all aboard, too. It should make for an interesting cruise."

"A booze cruise," Catch added as he popped the tab on a beer. "The best kind."

Natalie didn't think there was another area in the world where people drank more alcohol than they did in the Caribbean. At barely nine in the morning, nearly everyone on board had already started. When Catch held up one for her, she shook her head. "I think I'll wait a little while," she told him.

"Okay. Nick? How about you?"

He shrugged. "Sure. Toss me a cold one."

Sybil, who stood in the companionway between the cockpit and main cabin, smiled at Natalie and asked, "How about some o.j. instead?"

Natalie nodded gratefully.

"I know it's heresy among this crowd," Sybil said as she ducked below. "But some people actually enjoy a little something nutritious for breakfast."

Her comment was met by hoots and accusations that she had no sense of adventure whatsoever.

"Maybe not," she replied. "But I'm going to feel a hell of a lot better tomorrow than you guys will."

"Don't let Sybil fool you," Jack told them. "She can outdrink any man alive. And has, on more than one occasion."

"Well, not today," she assured her husband. "Someone's got to see clear enough to steer this bucket out to sea and back into her slip. You know, the Coast Guard really frowns on drinking and operating a boat."

Everyone made faces at the warning, but didn't comment further.

"So I'll be the designated driver," she added.

"And I'll be the designated navigator," Natalie offered.

"You know how to navigate?" Sybil asked.

"Not a whit. But that shouldn't make me any less qualified than these guys will be in a few hours."

"Enough talk!" Jack called as he reached for one of the lines securing *Errukine* to the dock. "Avast ye, mateys, and shiver me timbers! Let's get this cruise under way!"

"Cap'n Jack is a scurvy dog!" Baxter cried as he

tended to a second line. "I say we mutiny and take this ship to the Spanish Main!"

"Aye!" Nick joined in. "And we'll keep the rum rations for ourselves! Yeoman Catch?"

Catch snapped up and saluted. "Aye, matey."

"Slap Black Jack in irons. We'll keelhaul him later."

"May I finish my beer first, sir?" Catch asked.

"Oh, aye. Of course."

Carmen joined Natalie and Sybil near the companionway. "Is this the way they act when they are together on the cutter?" she asked.

Sybil shook her head. "I imagine so. Give a man a boat, even a military vessel, and he can't help but regress back to the time when he was floating leaves down a rain-filled gutter. Some genetic thing, I guess."

The other women nodded as they watched the men go about getting the sailboat underway with lots of "arghs," the occasional "avast ye," and numerous references to Davy Jones's locker. Finally Jack guided *Errukine* easily out of her slip and slowly through the waters of the marina. The moment Natalie felt the breeze tangling in her hair, she moved from the cockpit forward to the bow. It seemed to take a long time to clear the marina, and even after they did, instead of hoisting the sails, as she had thought they would do, they continued along under motor power until they were well out into the harbor.

From her perch at the bow, with her feet dangling over each side of the boat, Natalie had a panoramic view of San Juan she had never enjoyed before. The small craft of Club Nautico gradually gave way to larger commercial vessels docked on both sides of the harbor—vast, rusting metal freighters she was frankly amazed could possibly float.

Nick joined her shortly and pointed out some of the more pertinent sights along the way—the Bacardi distillery to her left, and near it a triangular-shaped building he said he thought was a library. After that, and on the other side, they passed the gorgeous high-rise art deco splendor of the Banco Populare, and nearby the Coast Guard base itself. They waved at Luis, who stood watch on the cutter. Beyond that, and further out to sea, was a long stretch of peninsula dotted with palm trees, and directly across from it the looming specter of El Morro, a four-hundred-year-old Spanish fort that looked as if it had not changed at all since its last battle.

Only when they had cleared the debris of the harbor completely did Jack cut the engine, and he and Sybil moved to raise the sails, with Catch and Baxter assisting. Amid the shouted instructions and warnings, the rattle and clink of the sail lines as they hit the mast, and the wind rushing about her ears, Natalie watched in fascination as the white sheet unfolded and caught the breeze. Immediately, the motion of the boat changed, rocking to the side a bit as the stiff, canvas fabric grew fatter.

"We have achieved sail," Sybil said with a smile as a cheer went up around her. "Give old Neptune a nip, will you, Catch?"

Catch reached for a fresh beer from the cooler, moved to the bow of the boat near Natalie, twisted the top off the bottle, and poured the contents into the ocean. "Enjoy it, old man," he said with a smile.

"Why did you do that?" Natalie asked him.

"For good luck. And to keep Neptune appeased. He gets a little miffed if we mortals are up here having a good time while he's down there with nothing.

You should always toast the gods of the sea before you get underway and give them a little of what you're having yourself. It's good PR."

Natalie smiled. "Sounds like a fair deal."

"Can't hurt," Sybil said. "We need all the luck we can get."

The morning flew by. Jack steered *Errukine* straight out to sea without hesitation, and it wasn't long before San Juan was completely out of sight. Gradually the waters changed color from green to a deep, dark midnight blue, and the water that sprayed up on Natalie from time to time as the boat dipped over a swell was icy cold. The wind blasted her hair about her face, and a fine film of salt covered her sunglasses. She found herself removing them frequently to clean them, then finally succumbed and removed them completely.

She also discovered the hard way that it was probably best if she didn't go below unless she had to. Looking out the cabin window at the shifting horizon made her stomach lurch, but as long as she remained on deck, she felt fine. Therefore, when Sybil asked for help in putting together lunch in the galley, Natalie—though she felt bad for doing so—had to decline. But Sybil said she understood, assuring Natalie she wasn't the only one who suffered from seasickness. Jack, too, it seemed, refused to go below when they were under sail.

As afternoon became evening, the beer supply began to dwindle substantially. And as the beer disappeared, the men grew proportionately more mellow. And just as the sun descended into the sea, they began to sing sea chanteys.

"Oh, no," Sybil said from her seat at the tiller. "Not again."

"Do they do this often?" Natalie asked.

"Only when they are very, very, very drunk," Carmen replied. "It has not happened for a long time."

"Oh, no," Sybil said again when the men began a particularly raucous number. "This one is the worst."

"There's a girl named Bea," the men sang out, "who waits for me, whenever I'm sailing the deep blue sea. She sits on the stair, braiding her hair without a stitch to cover her bare. I told her before not to wait by the door, 'cause many a man can see her. But instead of obeying, she only starts baying and asks for another beer."

"What's so bad about that?" Natalie asked when the men seemed to be finished.

"That's the clean verse," Sybil said with a smile. "The second one is awful."

"Last time I went out," the men continued, their voices growing louder with every line, "I left her some stout, to keep her away from trouble. But she gave it away to a lad from the bay, who promised her more of it double. I shouldn't be sad she treated me bad, I guess I'm just being fussy. 'Tis true she was good, always gave when she could, but I'll sorely miss the—"

"Don't say it or you'll all go overboard!" Sybil yelled.

The men paused for a moment to trade glances, then concluded as if on cue, "Hussy!"

Sybil released a breath and laughed along with them. "Thanks," she said. "I appreciate it."

Natalie puzzled over the song for a moment before asking "Were they going to say something else besides 'hussy'?"

The men laughed harder, and Sybil turned to look at her incredulously. "How old did you say you are?"

"Twenty-two."

Sybil nodded but said nothing more, and instead asked Carmen to go below and switch on the running lights as the men launched into another tune. It was full dark by the time they made it back to Club Nautico, and Natalie was glad Sybil had remained sober. None of the men was in any shape to do much of anything, and she knew she'd have her own work cut out for her just walking Nick back to the apartment.

As if she'd read Natalie's thoughts, Sybil turned to her after securing the last of the lines and said, "You guys might as well stay on the boat for a while. Looks like the power's out in the Condado again anyway."

Natalie looked toward the high-rise hotels of her neighborhood, clearly visible from the cockpit of the boat. Most were dark, and the hazy glow that normally arced over the Condado was gone.

"Besides, there's still some beer," Jack said. "And since Catch was so nice to bring it along, I don't think we should hurt his feelings by leaving any."

The men murmured their agreement.

"I think I'll make some coffee," Sybil said.

"I will help you," Carmen offered.

"Me, too," Natalie agreed.

The three women went below just as the men started to sing another song, this one about a girl from Dorset and her filthy corset.

"Where do they pick that stuff up?" Natalie asked.

"Who knows?" Sybil said.

"They are men," Carmen remarked, as if that explained it all.

When the coffee was ready, the three made their way back up to the cockpit, and took their seats next to their mates. Catch sat by himself above the tiller, but seemed not to notice that he was the only one alone. Instead, Natalie noted, he only watched the others with a faint smile, sipping his coffee and keeping a low profile.

"This is a great boat, Jack," Nick said as he draped an arm over Natalie's shoulder.

"The best," Jack agreed.

"Nat, I think we should buy a boat just like Jack and Sybil's and spend the rest of our lives sailing."

"But we don't know how to sail," she pointed out.

"No problem. I've got it all figured out. All you have to do is get the sail thingy stuck to the top of the mast and tie it down over there somewhere." He pointed in the general vicinity of the middle of the boat. "The wind does the rest."

Sybil chuckled at him. "Oh, yeah. You're ready to tackle the high seas, all right."

"See?" Nick said as he pulled his wife closer. "I told you so." To Jack, he added, "We'll just follow you guys around the world next year."

Jack winked, then made a circle with his thumb and index finger, lifting the other three in a sign of okay. "I just hope you can keep up with us."

"Can we do it, Nat?" Nick asked as he laid his head on her shoulder and stared at her balefully. "Can we buy a boat and sail around the world with Jack and Sybil?"

She looked down at him and smiled at the glazed look in his eyes. He wouldn't remember any of this in the morning. "Sure we can, Nick," she told him. "We'll clear out the bank account Monday morning. Three hundred and twenty-eight dollars ought to buy us a real nice boat."

He smiled back at her as his eyes fluttered closed. "Thanks, Nat. You're the best. I love you."

She ruffled his hair and looked over at Sybil, who grinned back and opened her mouth to comment. But Jack prevented whatever she had planned to say when he dropped his own arm over her shoulder and pulled her close for a kiss.

"Nick," he said, "I beg to differ. With all due respect to your wife—and she is a very lovely one—I'd have to put Sybil here in the number one position."

Sybil laughed. "Oh, get out of here. You're so drunk, you don't even know what you're saying."

"I do, too," he told her. "And I know you're the best."

"Nope," Nick objected amiably. "Natalie is."

"Sybil is."

"Natalie."

"Sybil."

"I'll fight you for it."

"Okay. Best two out of three falls."

"Okay."

But both men remained seated firmly in place.

"Tomorrow," Jack said after a moment, tilting his head back to study the moon.

"Tomorrow," Nick agreed.

"You see?" Carmen said, taking Baxter's hand in her own. "Just because people get married does not mean they stop loving each other. Look at these people. They are all more in love now than they have ever been."

"They're also a lot drunker now than they've ever been," Baxter pointed out.

"Not all of them."

But Baxter ignored the comment, and instead

turned to the one man who had been noticeably silent during the conversation. "Catch, you're a single man. You got any regrets?"

Catch shrugged. "Sure. But none that have anything to do with being single."

Baxter turned to Carmen. "See?"

"I bet he is also very lonely."

"Catch," Baxter called out again. "You lonely?"

"Not usually," the other man replied.

"But sometimes you are?" Carmen asked.

"Sometimes. But I think everyone is lonely sometimes, whether they're single or not."

No one responded to that statement. Instead they all remained silent and enjoyed the quiet evening. Sometime after midnight, Catch excused himself and climbed over to his own boat, and after that, the party began to break up. Sybil helped Natalie fold Nick into a taxi, then both women helped Carmen get Baxter stretched out in the backseat of his car so that she could drive him home.

The power was still off in the Condado when Nick and Natalie arrived home, and they had to maneuver their way up the stairs to the fifth floor in complete darkness. When she had gotten them both into bed, she snuggled up close to him and kissed the back of his neck, then leaned over and watched him as he slept.

"Nicky?" she asked after a moment. "Are you awake?"

"Mm-hm."

"Do you really think I'm the best?"

He nodded. "Absolutely. The very best."

"Thanks for today."

"You're welcome."

"I had a good time."

"Me, too. Natalie?"

"Hmm?"

"I love you."

She smiled as she settled in beside him. "I love you, too, Nick," she replied on a soft sigh. "I love you, too."

11

Dear Mom and Dad,

  *You remember the Ingrams I told you about?
You remember a while back how I said they were
probably little lovebirds who were totally devoted
to each other? Remember that? Well, there's been
a slight problem . . .*

  Sybil lay on her back staring at the blackness between herself and the ceiling and listened to
Jack breathe with the mellow regularity that comes
with deep sleep. She had finally been to see a doctor
that afternoon. And when he had told her what she
already knew—that she was approximately eleven
weeks along in her pregnancy—she had promptly
burst into tears.

  Funny, she thought now. She hadn't realized that
such a big part of her had been holding out for the

chance that she must have made some kind of mistake with all those pregnancy tests. She supposed she would rather have discovered the reason for her absence of periods was some heinous disease that would require all kinds of horrible treatment. At least in a situation like that, Jack would have stayed by her side. But now she had no reason to keep the knowledge of the baby from Jack.

None except for the fact that the announcement would completely alter the lifestyle the two of them had come to know and love, not to mention the future they had been planning for nearly twenty years. None except for the fact that on learning of her condition, her husband would probably never speak to her again.

She looked over at him. He lay on his stomach with one arm thrown over his pillow, scrunching it into a tight ball beneath his head. His dark auburn hair was swept back from his forehead, revealing a hairline that had ventured back farther with every passing year. She smiled sadly when she recalled how much it bothered Jack that he was losing his hair. It had made the forced removal of his beard an even greater burden to bear. Strange, the things that upset men, she thought.

"Jack," she whispered, poking him gently in the ribs.

He stirred slightly, uttered a muffled sound, turned his face away from her and went back to sleep.

"Jack," she said again, a little more loudly this time. She rose on her elbow until she was leaning over him, and lightly traced the curves of his ear with her finger. "Oh, Jaaaaaack," she sang out when still he did not respond.

"Mmmmpf," he replied without moving.

"I need to tell you something," she began softly, her

voice lowering as she continued. "It's very, very important."

"Mmmmpf?"

Quietly, so quietly she could barely hear the statement herself, she told him, "I'm going to have a baby."

"Rrrrph?"

Sybil nodded and brushed his hair away from his ear with a slow, soothing gesture. "Yes, really," she said, her voice still hovering just under a whisper. "I'm eleven weeks along."

"Skax."

She started at the sound he made, recognizing it as a distinctly negative reaction to her news. "Hey, it caught me by surprise, too, you know. It's not like I planned it."

"Yuud."

"I did not, either. But everything will be okay. You'll see. We'll manage somehow. I know we will."

"Nnnng."

This time she ignored his objections. "Dr. Juncos recommended a book for me to read, and I picked it up after I left his office. It's amazing what's already happening down there. I'm surprised I can't hear little power drills and hammers at work." Instinctively, the hand she had left lingering at his nape moved down to curve over her belly, over the soft rise that only she seemed able to detect. "At eleven weeks, the baby already has all its organs. It has fingers and toes, and eyes and ears. It's almost like a real baby. Everything's there—it just needs to get bigger and more refined. Can you believe it? After only eleven weeks, all this stuff has already formed. I even got to hear its heart beating today, Jack. Its heart—"

She broke off when she felt something warm and

damp on her cheeks and only then realized she had
started to cry. Rolling onto her back, she draped her
arm over her eyes, and bit her lip to prevent the silent
weeping that shook her body from becoming great,
wracking sobs. She lay that way for a long time. At
least she thought it was a long time. Nights had been
strange since she'd become pregnant. She awoke frequently, often from bizarre, incredibly vivid dreams.
On such occasions she would then fade in and out of
sleep, never quite sure when she was truly awake until
Jack stumbled out of bed in the morning.

So it came as little surprise to her that she was wide
awake when the alarm buzzed at six as it always did,
and her husband turned toward her to kiss her good
morning. What did surprise her, though, was when,
instead of kissing her as he normally did, he said, "I
had this weird dream last night that you told me you
were pregnant."

Wow, Sybil thought. Right off the bat and just like
that. No "Good morning," no "I love you," no warning
whatsoever, and absolutely no chance to prepare.
"Really?" she said. "I wonder what could have caused
you to dream about something like that."

Jack's face was rigid. "I have no idea. Do you?"

She tried to smile, but was pretty certain the gri-
mace she managed fell well short of one. "Well, you
know, actually it is kind of funny, you dreaming that I
told you I'm pregnant."

"Is it?"

"Uh-huh."

"Why's that?"

"Because I . . . I sort of . . . am . . . pregnant."

He didn't react at all. He didn't move, he didn't
speak, he didn't blink. He just looked at her as if she

were the vilest form of life he had ever had the displeasure to encounter. Finally, he said, "So what are you going to do about it?"

"What am *I* . . . Jack, this sort of affects us both."

"You're the one carrying it."

"Yes, but it's your child, too."

"So I do have some say in this thing?"

"Of course."

"Then I vote you get rid of it."

A great fist seized her insides and squeezed hard. Her stomach burned, and her heart pounded harder. "Just like that?" she asked, the words feeling raw in her throat. "Don't you even want to think about what that would mean?"

"It would mean things could go on just the way they have been," he said. "Nothing would have to change."

Sybil shook her head. "No matter what we do about this, everything is going to change. We can't just pretend it never happened."

"I can."

"Well, I can't."

She scooted to the foot of the bed, then stood to face him fully. "I'm almost three months along. It may be too late to have a . . . a . . ."

"An abortion," he said, enunciating the term as if it were one foreign to her. "Abortion, I think, is the word you're looking for, Syb."

"Actually, I think that's the word you're looking for," she countered. "I'm fully prepared to have this baby."

"Then you'll do it alone."

A sudden, almost debilitating weakness came over her then, and she slumped forward like a ragdoll. "Oh, honey, don't be like this. Think about what you're saying. I know this is a shock for you, but this baby . . . it's a part of us, both of us. It's a human being that's here because we created it together. And even though I'm not the most religious person in the world, I feel like there must be a reason this has happened."

He glared at her. "Great, in addition to saddling me with a child, now you're going to turn into the pope on me, too."

She flexed her fingers vigorously to keep herself from wrapping them around his throat. "Look, let's start over, all right? This isn't exactly the way I had planned to tell you about the baby."

He set his jaw viciously, a nerve twitching in his left cheek. "No, you were no doubt going to wait until it was too late to get rid of the damned thing. Hell, you just said yourself it may already be too late. So much for my having a say in this, too, right?"

"That's not true." She sighed heavily and flattened her palm against her forehead. "Look, why don't you go ahead and shower, and I'll fix us some coffee. Then you can call Baxter and tell him you're going to be a little late this morning, and we'll take some time to talk about this."

"Like hell I'm going to go in late this morning. There's nothing to talk about. We've had a plan for almost twenty years, and I for one intend to stick to it. We agreed long before we were married that we would remain a blissfully child-free couple. If you insist on having this kid . . ." He sighed fitfully and ran a big hand over his face as if to wipe away any expression that might give him away. "Then like I said— you're on your own."

She shook her head. "Honey, you don't mean that—"

"The hell I don't. I'm not the one who needs to think about this. You are. And, hey, I'm a generous guy. Take the whole day to do it. Tomorrow, I'll even go with you to the doctor's when you have the—" His voice broke off without completing the statement.

"Abortion?" she bit out. "Is that the word you're stumbling over?"

"Abortion," he repeated. "Exercise your right to choose, Sybil. It's either that kid or me."

"I can't believe how cavalier you're being about this."

"And I can't believe how seriously you're taking it. Abortion is no big deal, you know. Thousands of women have them every day."

"Thousands of women have no other alternative," she countered. "They're poor, sick, scared, or unmarried. And I'll bet no matter what their reasons, very few of them would say what they're doing is no big deal. Don't ask me to choose between you and this baby, Jack. Because you might not like the choice I make."

He rose from the bed and reached for his clothes. Only when he had finished dressing did he finally look at her. But his expression was cold and distant, and his eyes never completely met hers. He looked away again as he said, "Don't bother with coffee. I'll shower and shave on the cutter. And when I get home, this all better be settled."

Sybil watched as he gathered his things, then stood aside to let him push his way past her and through the passageway to the main cabin.

"Don't worry," she called out after him. "This will be settled long before you get home."

Normally, after Jack had finished a day at work, he drove home to see his wife with the anticipation of a newlywed. Even after eighteen years of marriage, not a day passed that he did not marvel at his magnificent good fortune in finding such a perfect mate. Sybil was everything to him—wife, best friend, lover, teacher . . .

 . . . and now the mother of his child.

He pushed the thought away. He didn't like to think of her as such. And not because of some Freudian hooey about madonnas, whores, and mothers, either. A baby simply didn't fit into their game plan in any way. They had no room for a child in their lives, literally or figuratively. *Errukine* was finally the boat Jack had always dreamed she could be. She was perfectly equipped for what he and Sybil had planned, just commodious enough for the two of them to sail away together forever. The *two* of them, he repeated emphatically to himself as he turned his car into the parking lot of Club Nautico. No more.

And, he conceded, recalling uncomfortably his threat of earlier in the day, no less.

He shifted the car into park, but didn't unfasten his seat belt. Instead he stared out at the marina, at the forest of silver aluminum masts that bobbed and leaned in the breeze. Every one of those masts was attached to a boat, and every one of those boats housed someone's dream. Jack was certain people didn't buy boats just because they were exotic possessions to own. People bought boats because they had to. Because something in their psyches commanded it, some mystic lure, some continuous calling. A boat didn't become a possession just because someone happened to own one. A boat became an extension of what that person was himself. And if boating was a way of that life, then sailing was the pinnacle of that life. Just the sun and the wind and the water—the very essence of creation.

It wasn't selfishness that generated Jack's desire to sail around the world. It was a mystical pull as old as time. And there was nothing—absolutely nothing—he could do to change it.

Errukine bumped softly against the pier as he approached her, her white hull gleaming in the late afternoon sun, her sail lines lapping against her mast with an irregular *ping, ping, ping . . . ping-ping.* Somewhere in the harbor, a whistling buoy caught the wind and threw its deep tone back toward land. Above him, a seagull cried out in a lonesome call. Usually, he felt the day's tensions begin to unwind from his body when he reached this point. But today they only doubled.

Catch lifted a hand in greeting as Jack passed by and invited him over for a beer. But he shook his head. For a moment, he envied the other man his single status, his freedom to do as he pleased without considering anyone else. Then he remembered the last eighteen years with Sybil, and he couldn't help but smile. No matter what happened now, he knew he had been right in attaching his life to hers. Even if that union wound up being less permanent than he had originally planned, it had been nice while it lasted.

"Sybil?" he called out as he climbed into the cockpit. A tiny explosion erupted somewhere in his midsection when there was no reply. "Syb?" he called out a little more loudly as he made his way down the companionway. "I'm home. Where are you?"

The curtains had been drawn in the main cabin, and the table was set with the china Sybil's mother had given them for a wedding present. They hadn't used it since about their fifth anniversary, and he had begun to think she'd sent it back to her folks for permanent storage. She'd also fished out the silver candlesticks his grandmother had given them, and two slender tapers flickered softly in the dim cabin. Fresh cut flowers filled the small room with a sweet aroma, and slow-moving reggae music wafted from the stereo.

"This was how I had originally planned to tell you about the baby," Sybil said as she came through the passageway on the opposite side of the cabin. She wore a filmy peach nightie and little else, and Jack wasn't sure he'd ever seen her looking more beautiful.

But he shook his head at her and said, "It won't work, Syb. I'm not going to change my mind about this."

"Maybe not," she conceded. "But at least you're going to talk about it."

He removed his ball cap and buried his fingers in his damp hair. When he realized his hand was shaking, he shoved it into the pocket of his uniform trousers. "There's nothing to talk about."

She laughed, but sounded none too happy. "Oh yeah. There's plenty to talk about. Sit."

Reluctantly, he did as she requested, but deliberately chose a spot on the settee as far from the romantic arrangement on the table as he possibly could. Sybil duly noted the gesture, shaking her head as she went to the refrigerator to open a ginger ale for herself and a beer for Jack. Once she had filled two glasses, she realized there was little she could do to stall any longer, and she joined him on the settee.

She handed him his glass, then lifted her own in a toast. "To change," she said halfheartedly.

He didn't echo the sentiment, which didn't surprise her. Instead, he stared morosely into his beer and remained silent.

"All right, then," she tried again. "To life."

His head snapped up at that, and she saw that his eyes were red-rimmed and damp. "How could you do this to me, Sybil?" he demanded. "How could you do it to *us*?"

She lowered her glass and frowned at him. "Hey, I wasn't working alone here. We're both responsible for this child. Don't you dare try to turn me into the bad guy."

"You're the one who won't even consider an abortion."

"And you're the one who won't even consider what having an abortion would involve."

"It would give us our life back. Don't you see that?"

"And it would take it from our baby."

"Oh, come on, it's not a baby at this point," he objected. "It's just some little wad of flesh. Hell, you're not even showing yet."

"It *is* a baby, dammit. And it's a part of us both."

"And it's going to change everything. Don't you understand?" Restless, Jack rose from his seat and paced to the other side of the cabin. "Don't you like what we have now? And in less than a year, when I'm out of the Guard, we'll have everything we've always wanted. Everything we've busted our asses for two decades to get."

His anguish was almost palpable, and Sybil couldn't bear the realization that she was the one responsible for causing it. Unable to tolerate his intense gaze, her own fell to the glass she still clutched in her hands. "I love things the way they are. You know that. And I know full well how close we are to realizing the dream we've had since we got married. God, I remember how hard we've worked. And I understand that we're just now at a point where we can sit back and enjoy it. But things change, Jack. And sometimes there's nothing we can do about it."

"In less than a year—*in a matter of months*—I'll be out of the Guard for good. We'll have nothing but complete and total freedom to go wherever we want, whenever we want to. Freedom, Sybil. That's what we've been reaching for ever since we got married. And we're so close to grabbing it. So damned close."

She felt hot tears spilling over her cheeks, but was helpless to do anything that would stop them. She'd never felt more miserable in her life, and she had no idea what to do. "I know that. Don't you think I can feel it, can taste it, too?"

"But you're willing to just throw it all away?"

Unable to tolerate the conflux of emotions tearing her up inside, Sybil gripped the drink in her hand and hurled it against the opposite wall with all her might. It shattered with what seemed an almost deafening crash, leaving a stain behind. "Dammit, I have agonized over this decision for two months!" she shouted. "*Two goddamned months!*" She looked up then, fixing Jack with a steady gaze. "You just found out about it this morning. Hell, I thought about ending it, too, when I first found out I was pregnant. But then I thought about what that would mean. I began to understand that this is a whole lot bigger than just you and me. Don't you dare judge me until you've lived with the knowledge of this baby as long as I have."

Jack had jumped when she threw the glass, but he'd

recovered admirably. Now he glared at her as if she were a recalcitrant child in the throes of a major tantrum. "You didn't answer my question," he said mildly. "Are you willing to throw away everything we've worked so hard to achieve? Are you willing to throw away our dream?"

She stared at him for a long time, wondering how the man she had married so long ago could have turned into a stranger overnight. "Yes, I am," she said softly. "I have to."

A long moment passed before he spoke again, and when he did, his voice was low, his expression thoughtful. "You know, it's not just the fact that we'll be losing our dream that we should consider. If this kid is born, it will be with us for the rest of our lives."

She inhaled a shallow breath, feeling hopeful for the first time since she had realized she was pregnant. At least he was finally speaking in terms of "us" now. "Strange as it may seem, that thought did occur to me," she said quietly.

"We'll never be rid of it. It will be there every waking moment of the day."

"I know."

"We'll be responsible for its health, its education, its values."

"Yes."

"It will cost us a small fortune to get it into adulthood."

"I know."

He lifted a hand to rub his cheek. It was a nervous gesture that had been common to him when he'd had a beard, but she hadn't seen him do it in years. She wondered if he even realized he was doing it now.

"I don't want a child, Sybil," he said evenly.

The tiny ray of hope that had begun to penetrate the darkness in her heart flickered out when she noted the certainty that punctuated his statement. "Well, that's too bad. Because you're going to have one."

"No," he said softly, "you are. I'm leaving."

She shook her head in disbelief. "You can't. You wouldn't."

Jack looked at her for a long time without speaking, then went into the forward cabin and closed the door behind him. She sat in stunned silence, listening as he opened and closed drawers, certain he was only bluffing, that he was just waiting for her to run in and tell him she'd do anything if only he'd stay. But she remained firmly seated where she was and waited to see what would happen.

When he emerged, he had changed from his uniform into jeans and a V-neck T-shirt and was clutching a sea bag that bulged with his belongings. He propped it against the companionway stairs and returned to the forward cabin, exiting this time with a stack of manuals and a portable stereo.

"I didn't think you'd mind," he said, indicating the tape player. "You'll have the good one here. You can keep the TV, too, even though you don't watch it much. There's one on the cutter. Sorry, but I'm going to keep the car. Since you do all your sail-mending work here at the marina anyway, you won't need it. We can talk about what we're going to do with *Errukine* later."

"What about doctor's appointments?" she asked. "I'll need the car for those."

He looked past her for a moment, tried to meet her gaze once more, but glanced away again. "Maybe

Catch can give you a lift. He owes you for all those dinners anyway."

"You're really going to do it?" she asked, rising. "You're actually going to leave me?"

He pushed past her and occupied himself with inspecting the knot on his sea bag. "I'll be staying on the cutter for a while, until I can find an apartment in town. If you need me for anything—"

She emitted a single, humorless chuckle. "And what would I possibly need you for?"

He straightened, but kept his back to her. "In case anything goes wrong, or—"

"If something happens to the baby, you mean. If I lose the baby, by whatever means, then you'll be glad to come back, is that right?"

He didn't answer, but finally turned to face her.

"Well, forget it," she told him. "Baby or no, once you walk off this boat, that's the end of it for us. I told you before that this baby was going to change things between us, regardless of what we did about it. And if you leave me now because of it, I won't take you back later. No matter what happens."

In response to her threat, Jack hefted his sea bag over one shoulder and balanced his books and stereo in the other. He studied her for a long time, and she was certain he wanted to tell her something. So she waited for some sign, some clue that there was still a chance to put things right between them. But he turned away, shoved his things up through the companionway, then climbed up and out behind them.

The last Sybil saw of him was when he bent to pick up his things. His face was in profile, the setting sun lighting bright fires in his hair. He was long overdue for a haircut, she thought inanely after he had disappeared from view. Baxter was sure to come down on him hard for letting it get so long.

As he disappeared from view, she recalled how much she hated for Jack to get into trouble. He never did handle it well.

12

Dear Mom and Dad,

Sorry, just a quick postcard this week. Nothing much going on, really. Weather's been great, wish you were here and all that. Really, like I said, nothing's going on. Nothing. Not one thing. Nada. Zip. Zilch. I mean absolutely nothing . . .

"It's awfully nice of you to do this, Reuben, but it really isn't necessary."

Natalie stood in the lobby of her apartment building and looked at the man framed by white sunlight streaming in through the security door behind him. Nick wanted her to get along with his best friend, wanted her to be as close to his buddy as he was himself. And on the occasions when she and Nick encountered him together, she got along with Reuben just fine, despite the fact that she was none too sure

she liked him. It was only when she was alone with
him on those occasions when he visited her at Rico's
that Natalie felt uncomfortable. And thanks to Nick's
requests that Reuben check up on her now and then
when he was underway, alone with Reuben Channing
was where she was finding herself more and more
often.

"Of course it's necessary," he told her as he opened
the door behind him and ushered her through it.
"Nick's been concerned that you're getting stuck at
home, alone and bored, way too often. He asked me
to spend time with you when I could, and I promised
him I would."

A wave of damp heat swept over her when she
stepped through the door and into the sunny morning. That was something she supposed she would
never forget about Puerto Rico. The way the heat surrounded her, the way it filled her nose and mouth and
lungs. There were times when she thought she could
actually taste it.

"But you already waste half your afternoons giving
me rides home from work," she objected. "It's not
necessary to waste your mornings with me, too."

He frowned at her. "It's not a waste. I don't mind.
Hell, I never do much of anything on my days off anyway. Lay on the beach. Drink at Rico's. That's about it."

Natalie was going to protest again, but his look
silenced her. She had decided some time ago that the
best course to take where he was concerned was to
simply avoid him whenever she could. In spite of her
decision, however, she seemed to see more of him
than she did of her own husband. And now, because
of Nick's concern for her welfare, she would be
spending an entire day with him.

"But—" she began.

"No buts," he said, holding up a hand to silence her. "Now be honest. It's been almost six months since you came to San Juan. How much of Puerto Rico have you actually seen since you moved down here? Not including that time you got on the wrong bus and wound up at Luquillo Beach," he added when she was about to offer up exactly that location.

After a moment's thought she spent trying to convince herself that she and Nick must have done more since moving down here than she now recalled, she said, "We went sailing with the Ingrams last month. Before the two of them split up."

Reuben nodded. "Okay, that's a good start. What else?"

"And we've been to Plaza las Américas lots of times."

He gazed at her mildly. "The shopping mall."

"It's a big mall," she pointed out. "There are lots of stores there that we don't have in Cleveland." Of course, there were lots of stores they *did* have in Cleveland, too, she recalled.

"Yeah, but it's a mall, Natalie. What other tropical hot spots has Nick taken you to see?"

The sun glinted off the white stucco of the Condado Beach Hotel across the street, and she shielded her eyes from the reflection. "We've borrowed the Ingrams' car a few times and driven over to Fort Buchanan," she said. "To buy groceries."

"I see."

"Hey, that commissary is really something. Have you ever been there?"

Reuben shook his head.

"They have one whole aisle devoted to nothing but soup."

"Imagine that."

"It's a really big aisle, too."

"I don't doubt it for a moment."

"Virtually thousands of cans to choose . . ." Her voice trailed off. "My mother was amazed when I told her about it."

Why did Reuben so thoroughly rub her the wrong way? Natalie wondered. He was a perfectly nice, perfectly polite, perfectly harmless man who had never once come on to her in even the slightest way.

And why on earth would it even occur to her that he *might* come on to her? What a silly thing to think. Even if he did come on to her—and she was quite positive he would not, as he was her husband's best friend after all—she would just remind him she was a happily married woman, remind him, too, that her husband was his best friend, and set him straight once and for all.

As she followed him reluctantly down the tile stairs that led to the street below, she couldn't help noticing the way his snug jeans hugged his trim hips, and couldn't overlook the solid muscles bunching beneath the sleeves of his tight, faded purple polo shirt. Natalie wondered where all these bizarre, errant thoughts today were coming from and tried to recall where else Nick had taken her.

"How about El Morro?" Reuben asked suddenly.

His interruption into her train of thought was a welcome one. "The big castle?" she asked.

"They call it a castle, but actually, it's an old fort," he told her. "Have you seen it yet?"

This time it was Natalie who shook her head. "Not really. Only from a distance when we went out on the Ingrams' boat."

"It's the perfect place to begin. We can explore there, then walk into Old San Juan and see something other than the four ugly walls of Rico's." He smiled as he seemed to think of something else. "Today's Thursday isn't it?"

She nodded.

"The cruise ships are in today. You know what that means, don't you?"

"No, what?"

His smile grew wider. "Whenever the cruise ships are in, all the jewelry stores in Old San Juan give away free piña coladas to lure in the tourists. You can go from one shop to another and get pretty loaded without spending a dime."

She laughed. "Sounds like a nice way to pass the afternoon."

"Oh, it is," he told her with a chuckle. He held out a hand. "Come on. Nick wants me to show you a good time. And showing a lady a good time is one thing I do exceptionally well. We'll have fun today. You'll see."

An awkward moment passed while Natalie stared at the hand he extended toward her. For some reason, she didn't want to take it, didn't want to touch him in any way. But she didn't want to be rude, either. Slowly, reluctantly, she lifted her fingers toward his. And before she had a chance to pull away, Reuben wove them with his own. As they made their way toward his car parked at the curb, she felt her heart pounding. All she could think about was how warm and rough his palm was, and how utterly exhilarating it felt to have it so close to her own.

*   *   *

El Morro's yellow-gray walls were stained and pocked by the passage of four hundred years, rising up against the crisp blue sky like battered conquistadors. Natalie stood at the center of them, studying the guidebook intently. Beneath her, a labyrinth of cool, dark dungeons wound through the rocky promontory on which the Castillo de San Felipe del Morro sat, while this level was studded with barracks and ramps. She closed her eyes for a moment and tried to imagine what life here must have been like all those years ago, tried to recreate in her mind the smells of military food, the shouts and songs of the soldiers, and the colorful uniforms of the early Spaniards.

But her eyes snapped back open quickly. Because all she could think about instead was the fact that she wished she were here with her husband instead of her husband's best friend.

Almost instinctively, she made her way toward the sound of the ocean, and before long she found herself standing in one of the fort's tiny, stone ramparts. On one side of her, the dark blue Atlantic swept out to meet the sky, while on her other side, the high-rise hotels and skyscrapers of San Juan jutted like metal fingers toward the clouds. The salty scent of the sea assailed her, and she inhaled deeply of the fresh, clean fragrance. Below her, the ocean lapped against the base of the old fort as it had for centuries, no more successful at felling the structure than El Morro's countless other assailants had been. She closed her eyes once more, wondering what it must have been like for the soldiers who stood watch here as Sir Francis Drake's ships approached, scurrying to prepare themselves for battle.

She felt more than heard Reuben approach her

from behind and opened her eyes again as she stiffened. He paused just beyond the doorway of the stone rampart, too tall to stand inside comfortably. "Nice view from up here," he said.

She nodded. "What's that over there?" She pointed toward a nearby section of town perched at the edge of the ocean where pastel-hued buildings huddled together like scattered beads.

He followed the line of her finger. "That's La Perla."

"It's lovely. What is it?"

He made a sound that was at once derisive and full of humor. "La Perla is a ghetto. The quality of life there is probably worse than anywhere else on the island. It's an unbelievably dangerous place for someone like you. You're right, though. From up here it looks great."

"What does 'La Perla' mean?"

"Pearl. Ironic, isn't it? That a place like that was named after one of the most beautiful things in nature?"

"It probably wasn't always a ghetto," she said softly.

"No, probably not."

"Besides, sometimes looks can be deceiving. Things can seem to be something they're not."

"That's true."

Natalie turned to face Reuben then and suddenly felt even more confined in the small space. The stone walls surrounding her had been cool at first, a welcome relief from the heat of the sun. But with him standing so close, that coolness evaporated like steam, to be replaced by a heat that had nothing in common with the sunny afternoon.

She waited for him to move aside, but he leaned

forward to rest his forearms above the opening of the rampart and stared at her. His gaze was speculative, his expression somehow grim. Just as she was about to ask him to move so that she could exit the rampart that was fast making her feel claustrophobic, he pushed himself away, turned around, and began to make his way toward the interior of the fort. Natalie released a breath she had been unaware of holding, then followed slowly behind him, surprised to discover that she was trembling.

They left El Morro and crossed the green, grassy slope that separated the old fort from the Museum of Art and History. Reuben invested the three dollars required of a vendor to buy a kite, then laughed as Natalie tangled herself in the string trying to get the thin paper contraption aloft. Afterward, they explored block after block of cobblestone streets that wove through Old San Juan and joined together the pastel-colored buildings like the threads of an elaborate tapestry.

They ate lunch outdoors, at a restaurant called La Mallorquiña. As she enjoyed her *asopao* and *gazpacho*, Natalie fell in love with the restaurant's Old-World Spanish courtyard, with its delicate arches and antique clocks. Later, she marveled at the quiet beauty of the Cathedral of San Juan, photographed Reuben as he stood beside the statue of Christopher Columbus at Plaza Colón, and bought wind chimes and a papier-mâché mask at Puerto Rican Arts and Crafts.

And at some point in the afternoon—whether it was when Reuben and an elderly Puerto Rican man tried to teach her the finer aspects of the game of dominoes, or when he introduced her to the splendid spectacle of nature housed inside The Butterfly People, she wasn't sure—Natalie decided that maybe her husband's best friend wasn't such a bad guy after all.

They ended their outing with a late dinner at an Ashford Avenue restaurant situated at the edge of Condado Lagoon. The dry heat of the day surrendered to the cool breezes of the night, breezes that rustled and danced with the lush foliage that decorated the restaurant patio. All around her, the songs of what sounded like hundreds of *coquis* whistled like air running through the finest of flutes. Out on the lagoon, two day-sailers bedecked with multicolored lights skimmed lazily over the black waters, while white stars winked in the ebony, moonless sky overhead.

Natalie filled her mouth with another sip from her planter's punch, her straw sucking air as she emptied the glass. She wanted another one, but knew two was her limit. Or had she had three? After all those piña coladas at the jewelry stores in Old San Juan, she couldn't quite remember now.

Reuben had already signaled the waiter for another round before she could stop him. Oh, well, she reasoned. Her apartment was only a few blocks away. It wasn't as if she had to get in a car and drive somewhere. And there were always taxis at the hotels and casinos that lined Ashford Avenue. Reuben wouldn't have any problem catching a ride home.

She glanced up from her empty glass to find him staring at her and she smiled. "What?" she asked. "What are you looking at?"

He shook his head, smiling back at her. "You. You're drunk."

She giggled. "So are you."

"I'm not drunk," he assured her with a decisive shake of his head. "It takes a lot more than a couple of fruit juices to do me in."

"Oh? And just what would it take to bring the mighty Reuben Channing to his knees?"

His smile broadened then, changing from a simple expression of delight to something Natalie could only liken to dangerous. She was intrigued.

"You don't want to know, Natalie," he said quietly. "Trust me on that."

She was going to say more, add a comment that was flip and teasing, but something in his voice stopped her from doing so. And when the waiter placed a fresh drink before her, she leaned forward and popped the straw into her mouth, sipping the rum-laced concoction with much gusto.

"Well, I'm not drunk, either," she said after she'd swallowed. "I'm just full and satisfied from having such a good time today."

"Did you have fun?"

She didn't answer right away. Instead she looked out over the water, tilted an ear to the frenetic drums of *bomba* music rising from somewhere far off in the distance down the lagoon, and closed her eyes against the cool breeze that nudged her hair down over her eyes.

"Before Nick and I got married," she said quietly, "we joked about how we were going to Puerto Rico for our honeymoon, and that it would be the longest honeymoon in history. But since we arrived here, it hasn't felt like a honeymoon at all." She looked back at

Reuben as she added, "Until today. Today was what a honeymoon should be like. And my husband wasn't even here to share it with me."

Reuben said nothing, but continued to gaze at her. The breeze tugged at his hair, too, lifting the short, pale brown strands before releasing them. Suddenly, for some odd reason, Natalie wanted to reach over and touch his moustache.

Instead she shrugged off the sensation and looked back out at the water again. "I miss him a lot when he's gone," she said. "He's out there doing things and seeing things that I'm not a part of. I'm not sure I like that. I always kind of thought that when you married someone, you automatically became the focus of his life, and he became the focus of yours. But that's not how it works at all, is it?"

Reuben sighed before he replied, "I'm probably not the guy to be asking on that score. Both of my marriages ended pretty badly."

"Marriage just isn't what I thought it would be," she said, turning back to look at him once more. "Although maybe things will change. They say the first year is the toughest. I guess it's even tougher when the couple involved spends the majority of their time apart."

"There are those who would argue that separation only makes the relationship stronger."

"Yeah, well, I'm not one of them. Nothing good can come of it when you don't see enough of the person you love."

"I suppose not."

The drums of the *bomba* grew louder then and she smiled. "Let's find out where the music is coming from and go dancing."

He watched her thoughtfully for some moments. "Okay," he finally said. He lifted his hand to the waiter, who promptly brought their bill, then reached into his wallet for his credit card.

"Oh, no, let me treat you," she said, staying his hand by placing her own over it. "You paid for my lunch and my kite—"

"Which about now is probably hanging from a tree in El Yunque," he said with a smile.

She smiled back. "Maybe next time we go out, we can go to El Yunque and find it. I've never been to a rain forest before."

He glanced down at the hand covering his own, then back at Natalie. "Next time?" he asked.

She felt the heat of a blush staining her cheeks and snatched her hand back. "With Nick, I meant," she said quickly. "Maybe I can get him to take me there soon."

"If he won't, I will."

She inhaled a shaky breath, but couldn't quite meet his gaze. "Thanks. I'll remember that."

"Please do."

She fumbled in her purse until she found her wallet, took out her own credit card, and went to place it on the check. By the time she managed to complete the action, though, the waiter had already left with Reuben's card instead.

"Next time," he said when her gaze met his. "You can treat me next time."

Natalie swallowed hard, but found herself nodding in agreement. "I probably should be getting home," she said when the waiter returned.

Reuben didn't look up from signing his name on the receipt as he asked, "Don't you want to go dancing?"

"I thought I did, but I guess it is getting kind of late. It's been a full day. I'm pretty tired."

"Okay," he said, ending his signature with a wide loop on the g. "I'll drive you."

She shook her head. "Oh, no. You and I have had way too much to drink. Neither one of us should try to operate any heavy machinery. I'll walk. You take a cab home."

"It's okay, I only live in Isla Verde. It's not that far—a straight shot out Ashford—"

"Reuben," she said, exasperated, "you have to promise me you won't drive. I'll worry about whether or not you got home safely."

"I'll call you when I get there."

"We still don't have a phone."

"Still? How long has it been now?"

She stared at him from beneath long bangs, then blew her hair out of her eyes with an errant puff of air. "Don't try to change the subject. Promise me you won't drive home."

"Natalie—"

"Promise me."

"Jesus, you sound like my wife."

"Which one?"

Reuben relented with a chuckle. "All right, neither. They were both mean, nasty, horrible women. You're a pretty nice kid. Nick's a lucky guy."

His compliment made her feel warm and wary at the same time. Nevertheless, she replied quietly, "Thanks."

"You're welcome. And if it's such a big deal to you, then I promise to take a cab to Isla Verde. But not before I walk you home. The streets of the Condado can be treacherous. Especially at night."

Natalie laughed. "Yeah, you've got to watch out for those grandmothers from Pittsburgh—come between them and their casinos, and they can be lethal. And those honeymooners—" She shuddered for effect. "They're absolute monsters. Not to mention all those dangerous transvestites."

"And the pickpockets, hookers, hustlers, and drug dealers," he added. "Some guy was macheted to death on your block not too long before you moved down here."

She shrugged, unimpressed. "It was a crime of passion. I heard all about it from my neighbors, Amber and Geneva."

"Speaking of hookers," Reuben said.

Natalie lifted her brows. "Nick thinks they're just nice working girls. He says they probably work as housekeepers at one of the local hotels."

Reuben uttered a rude sound of disbelief. "Oh, I don't doubt they're responsible for the sheets being changed in some of the area's finest, but not because they're good at hospital corners, that's for sure. It figures Nick would think that. He's almost as naive as you are."

"I'm not naive. I know they're prostitutes."

"And it doesn't bother you, their living across the hall that way?"

"Hey, to each his own. Or her own. Besides, Amber promised to loan me this gorgeous sequined bikini she has. Nick would love it."

Reuben grimaced as he pushed his chair away from the table. "Please, spare me the gory details. Come on."

As usual, the Condado was alive with people. When they passed an open-air bar, Natalie heard the regular

Thursday-evening steel drum band pounding out a lively rendition of "The Girl from Ipanema." One of the tourist police was nodding his head as a frantic elderly woman screeched about her stolen purse. And Gus, a seventy-five-year-old cross-dresser who had told her he'd once had a very steamy summer affair with J. Edgar Hoover, was out walking his shihtzu, his tangerine fingernails coordinating beautifully with his tiger-print separates.

As Natalie and Reuben neared her apartment building, Amber and Geneva approached from the opposite direction and nodded a quick greeting, hoisting a rather inebriated sailor between them.

Natalie sighed. She was a long, long way from Cleveland. And she didn't miss it at all.

Across the street, in front of the convention center that connected two hotels, they discovered a band complete with extensive percussion and horns performing. The men wore red satin shirts darkened in front by the stain of perspiration, and their tight white pants were bound at the waist with bright blue sashes. The music was infectious, joyful, and impossible to resist. Soon enough, Natalie and Reuben were swaying in time with the crowd who had gathered to watch and enjoy.

Unable to stand still a moment longer, she took his hands in hers and tugged him close, swiveling her hips in rapid rhythm to mimic the beat of the conga drum. The aroma of fried plantains wafted around her from somewhere, and a single, warm raindrop fell onto her cheek. She laughed at the sensation, and over the sound of the horns heard someone shout, "*Mira!* Hernando!" And the next thing she knew, Reuben was kissing her.

At first she was too stunned to do anything but stand still and let him do it. And then, to her horror, she realized she was kissing him back. Immediately, she jerked her head away from his, but he dipped his head forward and took her mouth again, more insistently. This time when Natalie pulled away, she also pushed Reuben backward, then spun around, and ran blindly toward the street.

"Natalie!" he shouted as he ran after her. He caught her wrist and jerked her up off the curb just as a *público* sped past her. "What the hell is the matter with you? You could have been killed!"

The only inkling of danger registering in her brain was the one presented by the man who held her wrist so tightly. She yanked her hand free and turned again, but Reuben gripped her shoulders firmly and spun her around to face him.

"Are you all right?" he asked breathlessly.

For a long time, she could only stare at him, could only shake her head in silence.

"Natalie? Are you all right?" he repeated.

"Why did you do that? Why did you . . . kiss me?" she finally asked him, her voice breaking on the last two words.

"Why did you kiss me back?"

She shook her head again. "I didn't."

"You did, too."

"You surprised me."

He chuckled low, but the good humor never registered in his eyes. "You surprised me, too. A lot."

He lifted his hand to cup her jaw, stroking his thumb softly over her cheek. Natalie tilted her head away from the caress, moving backward until she was free of him.

"I have to go," she said.

This time she checked the street before she stepped out onto the pavement, but when she did, her departure was no less hurried than it had been before. She ran with all her might until she reached the security door of her apartment, wrestled with her keys until locating the right one, then slammed the door behind her once she was inside. She made her way to the elevator on shaky legs, pressing her forehead against the cool metal doors as she awaited its arrival.

Once on the fifth floor, she vaguely registered the strains of an old Shirley Temple ditty called "The Codfish Ball" coming from the apartment across from her own, but the recognition of Amber and Geneva's adventures did nothing to lighten her spirits tonight.

Only when Natalie was safely tucked in bed a half hour later did she allow herself to think about how her day with Reuben had ended.

And only then did she let herself cry.

13

Dear Mom and Dad,

I never thought I'd see the day when I got tired of going to the beach, but after so many months of it, I have to admit that it leaves a lot to be desired sometimes. You never know who you're going to run into, and it seems like there's almost always someone there who wants to hassle you about something. I hope Nick doesn't have this kind of trouble when he's underway. Of course, he always talks about how much he loves to go to the beach . . .

"*Oh, Nick, Luis*, get a load of that one."
Nick shook his head knowingly at Luis then turned to look in the direction Billy Booker indicated, even though he already knew what he would find—a beautiful young woman with big, naked hooters, leaning

back in the sand to soak up as much of the hot Guadeloupe sun as she could.

"She's got a decent set, too, Booker," he said as he returned his attention to applying sunscreen.

"Yeah, she seems pretty nice," Luis said with an agreeable nod.

"Nice?" Booker asked. "Decent? What are you guys, blind? My third grade teacher Miss Martin was nice and decent. That one over there . . . oh, baby, she is one hot mama. I wonder where she's from?"

"She's probably from Europe," Nick told him. "She wouldn't do a thing for your quota."

Booker smiled. "Yeah, but imagine what she'd do for the rest of me."

Nick shook his head. "You're incorrigible, you know that?"

His friend nodded. "That's what they tell me."

Nick lay down on his back and shut his eyes. "Uh-huh. One wild dude, that's you all right." Something hovered over him, blocking the sun, and he opened his eyes once again to find Booker glaring at him. "What now?" he asked.

"You're actually going to just lie there and do nothing?" the other man asked incredulously.

"I thought that was kind of the point to days off. Am I wrong, Luis? Is there something else we do on our days off?"

Luis shook his head and lay back on his towel, as well. "No, I think you got it down just fine. You leave the cutter as fast as you can, before somebody remembers something you're supposed to do, and you get yourself to a beach and a beer ASAP."

"Right," Nick continued. "Then you perform an activity called *relaxing* for the rest of the day. I know that kind of thing eludes a guy who's always on the make, like Booker here, but some of us kind of enjoy it."

"Yeah, those of you who are nauseatingly married," Booker said, clearly disgusted by the idea.

"Marriage has nothing to do with it," Nick said defensively.

Booker snorted. "Hey, all I know is before that wife of yours came down here to live, you were always up for a little further investigation. But since Natalie's arrival on the scene, you're afraid to even look."

"I'm not afraid to look."

"Then look at those three girls over there." Booker lifted a hand in the opposite direction, pointing back over his shoulder. "They've been checking us out since we sat down."

"He's right about that," Luis said. "The little red-head, she's especially attractive."

Reluctantly, Nick turned on his side and looked past Booker, where he saw three women a short distance away gazing back at them. They were smiling bashfully in spite of the fact that they had shamelessly shed the top halves of their bikinis. The blonde lifted her hand in a shy wave, then lowered her head to her chest flirtatiously before looking up again. Telling himself he didn't want to appear rude, Nick lifted a hand in return before rolling onto his back once again. He squeezed his eyes shut and tried to think of Natalie, but all he saw instead was the deeply bronzed, quite naked, torso of the woman to whom he'd just waved.

"This place is unbelievable," he heard Booker murmur low beside him. "Here we are, surrounded not only by sunshine, palm trees, and the Caribbean, but by beautiful women, too. Women who, I might also point out, are half-naked. And it's legal. Not only legal, but customary! Encouraged even! And we're here, you guys, because—and this is the best part—because this is our *job!*"

As much as he wished he could dismiss his friend's enthusiasm, Nick supposed that even after all this time, he was no less awed by his situation than Booker was. Every time the *Point Kendall* got underway, he found himself on some exotic island where the people, language, and customs were completely foreign to his own. Each place vied with the others for which was most beautiful, and everywhere he turned, he was struck by the magnificence of nature's elemental beauty.

And sometimes, he thought further, when they found themselves in places like Guadeloupe, where topless bathing was a convention, he discovered an even more elemental kind of beauty to be found in nature.

He snuck another peek at the three girls still staring back at him and his companions a scant thirty feet to his left. Nick couldn't deny his friend's assertion that he had been a more than willing participant in occasional flirtations before he'd been married. Even during the time he was engaged, he and some of the other guys had been known to actively pursue the tourists. But things had never gone too far, he was quick to remind himself. A brief kiss here and there, and okay once some pretty serious groping that almost got out of hand, but he'd been truly drunk that night. And nothing had happened. Nothing serious, anyway.

But since he'd become a married man, Nick had

left all those frivolous pursuits behind. He had scarcely even noticed other women since Natalie had joined him in the Caribbean, and he certainly had no intention of groping—or even kissing—anyone other than his wife anymore. Still, he thought, no one ever said he couldn't look, right?

"Okay, Booker, they're beautiful," Nick said. "Why don't you go over for a little chat?"

Booker shook his head. "Why don't *we* go over for a little chat?"

"Whoa, no. I'm not going over there."

"Oh, come on, why not? There's three of them and three of us. It's destiny."

"Destiny my ass. I'm a married man, you jerk."

"Yeah," Luis agreed. "His destiny is already sitting in the Laz-E-Boy with the remote control. Leave him alone."

Booker persisted. "Oh, what's marriage got to do with anything?"

"Well, let me explain this to you, Booker," Nick said. "Generally when someone gets married, they sort of have an obligation to be faithful to the person they married. It's all part of the package. That vows thing you hear so much about."

"Jesus, Nick, I'm not telling you to take one of them back to her hotel, I'm just asking you guys to go talk to the other two while I cozy up to the brunette."

"Why can't you cozy up to all three of them?"

Booker's expression became decidedly libidinous. "Well, as much as I might enjoy that, there are certain rules one must follow in playing this game of love."

"And you, no doubt, are an expert."

His friend nodded sagely. "You know it. And one of those rules—perhaps the most important—is one-man, one-woman. At least to start things off. All I'm asking you and Luis to do is make friendly with the blonde and the redhead while I lure the brunette to her downfall."

"Well," Luis said with a smile as he sat up on his towel and ran his hands through his hair to slick it back. "I'll do what I can. I don't think I'll have a problem with both the redhead and the blonde."

"No, no, no," Booker said. "There's a system at work here. Three of us, three of them. Hell, Natalie wouldn't find fault with Nick's being polite to the tourists."

This time it was Nick who erupted with a rude noise. "Oh, yeah. I can see Natalie's reaction to the news that I was sitting next to a topless woman exchanging touring tips. No way, Booker."

"Come on, Nick . . ."

"You're forgetting something anyway."

"What's that?"

Nick lifted his left hand, letting the bright afternoon sunlight shimmer off the wedding band circling his fourth finger. "I'm branded," he said with a smile.

Booker covered Nick's hand quickly with his own and shoved it back down into the sand. "Will you put that thing away?" he hissed. "Do you want every woman here to see it?"

Nick chuckled as he closed his eyes to the glare of the sun again. "If I go over there with you, they're going to see it."

"Not if you take it off, they won't."

His eyes snapped open again. "Don't even think about it. Natalie would kill me if I took this ring off."

"He's right," Luis said. "It's bad luck to take off your wedding ring once you put it on."

"There you two go again, worrying about the little woman. I swear, Nick, if I spent half the time you do wondering what other people think of me—"

"It's not other people I worry about. It's my wife."

"Man, you are getting so pussy-whipped."

Nick's back went up at the charge. "I am not."

"You are, too. Natalie's three hundred miles and an ocean away from here, and you're scared to death of her."

"I am *not* scared to death of her. I love her."

"If you love her, then you shouldn't be worried about what she'll think."

"Booker, you have no idea what you're talking about."

"Oh, yes, I do. What I know is that this time last year, you were a lot of fun to be around. You laughed a lot, joked a lot, and didn't mind stirring up a little trouble. But now that you're a married man, you're humorless, uptight, and no fun at all."

Nick turned to Luis for confirmation. "Is that true?" he asked.

Luis shrugged. "Well, you haven't been the party animal you used to be. But that's understandable. Married men usually do lose their sense of fun after they tie the knot. Even us Puerto Ricans. It's only natural. Don't worry about it."

Nick remained silent for a moment, his friends' words soaking in, despite his best efforts to repel them. When another thought struck him, he fixed on it. "Even if I take my ring off," he said, "which is not to say that I have any intention of doing so—" He twisted the band up over his knuckle and added, "Look, I have a tan line there. I really am branded."

Booker thought for a moment, then glanced down

at the high school ring he wore on his right hand. "Here," he said, tugging it off. "See if this fits your left hand."

"Don't do it," Luis cautioned him. "It's bad luck. And it isn't right. You'll be sorry."

Nick looked at the wedding ring that was halfway off his finger already and spun it in a continuous circle above his knuckle.

"Well, don't be all day about it," Booker told him. "They're going to figure out what you're up to."

"I shouldn't do this," Nick said.

"Oh, will you calm down? You act like you're already in bed with the girl. All you're going to do is talk to her. Natalie will never know about it."

No, but I will, Nick thought, removing his wedding band completely. He tucked it into the topsider that was holding one corner of his beach towel in place, then stuffed his T-shirt in on top of it to make sure it didn't fall out. Hastily, he took the high school ring Booker held out to him and slipped it over the white mark the absence of his wedding band had left behind. The class ring was heavier and looser and didn't fit very well, but it would do the job.

"Perfect," Booker said with a smile. "Now let's go party."

He hadn't done anything wrong, Nick tried to reassure himself the following evening as he stood outside the bridge of the *Point Kendall*. It was after midnight, the sea was calm, the night sky was black and flawless, they were headed home . . . and he felt like hell. All he could do was replay in his mind what had happened on Guadeloupe the day before, and as much as he tried to change what happened, the ending always came out the same.

He, Booker, and Luis had spent the better part of the afternoon in the company of Toni, Jeannette, and Marie, who worked as typists for a group of lawyers in Rheims, France, when they weren't vacationing in Guadeloupe. He had loved the way the three women had spoken, had enjoyed hearing about France and their travels all over Europe. Toni, the blonde, had been particularly avid in her conversation, and when Booker and Marie and Luis and Jeannette had taken off for strolls down the beach in opposite directions, she had invited Nick to join her for dinner later.

So there he'd been, sitting on a tropical beach with a gorgeous Frenchwoman whose bare breasts were two of the most incredible examples of anatomical perfection he'd ever seen, and she was inviting him to dinner. What was he supposed to do? he asked himself now. Say no? He hadn't wanted to be an Ugly American. And he had very much enjoyed her company—more than Booker's and Luis's that was for sure. Dinner was dinner, he'd told himself then. It didn't have to turn into anything more.

And it hadn't. He had met her at her hotel in Petit Havre and they had walked the short distance to a nearby cafe that served Creole cuisine. They'd talked some more, laughed, and had taken a stroll along the beach afterward. There Toni had kissed him—on the cheek and only one time, he reminded himself—and had invited him back to her room. But he'd politely declined, had told her goodnight, and had been back on the boat by eleven. He'd done nothing wrong, he assured himself again.

Well, except for losing his wedding band somewhere along the line, he amended as acid churned in his stomach. He supposed that was something.

God, how could he have been so stupid? he asked himself now. How could he have let Booker talk him into such a crazy stunt? Natalie was going to kill him. And frankly, he couldn't blame her one bit.

He turned and entered the bridge, only to find Booker at the helm when he got there. Nick couldn't help but glare at him, and the other man frowned.

"You still haven't found it?" he asked.

"No, I still haven't found it," Nick mimicked. "By now it's probably in the pocket of some old geezer from Des Moines who's making his way down the beach with his Sears metal detector."

"You should have checked your stuff before we left the beach."

Nick's glare intensified. "You wouldn't let me, remember? You were afraid Toni and Marie and Jeannette would catch sight of it."

"Yeah, well, it probably wasn't such a good idea for you to take it off in the first place."

Nick's hands doubled into fists at his sides. "Boy, you are some piece of work, you know that?"

"Hey, nobody held a gun to your head, you know. All you had to do was say no."

As much as he wished he could blame Booker for what had happened, Nick knew he had only himself to kick in the ass. "You're right," he said. "It's my own fault. But you might have had the decency to—" His voice broke off, and he ran an unsteady hand over his face. "Look, never mind. What's done is done. But I have no idea what I'm going to tell Natalie."

Booker thought for a moment before suggesting, "Why don't you just stop in one of the jewelry stores in Old San Juan before you go home and pick up another one? They can't be that expensive."

"What are you, nuts? Natalie and I looked all over Cleveland for the right rings before we finally decided to design some ourselves. There are no other rings like ours anywhere. I'm going to have to order a new one from the jeweler at home. And it's going to cost us a few hundred bucks we really can't afford."

"Nick, I'm sorry," Booker said quietly. "I shouldn't have egged you on like that."

Nick lifted one shoulder in a halfhearted shrug. "Forget about it. It's not your fault, it's mine. I knew better. I guess I'm just still not used to being married. Still not used to being responsible."

Booker clapped a hand over his shoulder and pushed him toward the door. "Your watch is almost over," he said. "Get some sleep. We'll be home soon. Maybe things will work out better than you thought. Hell, why worry about it? Natalie probably won't even notice your ring is missing."

Nick inserted his key into the front door lock as carefully as he could, hoping against hope that he'd be able to enter the apartment without Natalie hearing him. That might just buy him a little extra time, he thought as he silently turned the key, maybe gain him a good ten or twenty seconds more to come up with a reasonable excuse for why he wasn't wearing his ring.

Despite his efforts to remain undetected, he was surprised when his wife didn't immediately greet him as she normally did when he came home. She had to be in either the living room or bedroom, both locations no more than a few feet from the front door. No matter what time he got back from an underway, she was always home, awake and anxious, waiting for him. Slowly, he pushed the front door forward and poked his head through the small opening. Today, however, there was no sign of her in the apartment.

"Natalie?" he called out. "Honey? I'm home."

He grimaced at the way he had worded his announcement, feeling like Ward Cleaver returning from a hard day at work doing whatever it was Ward Cleaver had done for a living. If he wasn't careful, Nick thought, soon he'd be wearing cardigan sweaters with patches on the sleeves, smoking a pipe while he read the paper in an overstuffed chair, and saying things like, "Now, dear, you know how much I love having your tuna casserole every Wednesday night."

"Natalie?" he called out again. "Where are you?"

But there was no reply to his question. Feeling more relieved than curious about her whereabouts, Nick entered the apartment and pushed the door closed behind him, thanking whatever providential force it was that had supplied him with a few extra moments to gather his wits. He had actually already come up with a pretty good excuse to give Natalie for why he wasn't wearing his wedding band. He figured he could tell her that he'd had to remove it to do some manual labor on deck, but hadn't secured the ring as well as he should have. Then, when an errant wave had come up out of nowhere to tip the cutter, the ring had fallen over the side. It seemed a likely enough story to him. It could have happened. Probably. Hey, hurricane season was approaching.

He went to the bedroom and dumped his sea bag into the corner, skimmed off his topsiders with first one foot, then the other, shrugged out of his uniform shirt, and collapsed onto the bed. It was only a little past three in the afternoon, but he was beat. Constructing an effective lie, he thought vaguely as he drifted off, took a lot out of a man.

He wasn't sure how long he'd lain in bed dozing when he heard Natalie's key in the front door. The sound awakened him at once, however, and he leapt up in bed, rubbing furiously at his eyes. He padded barefoot out of the bedroom to find her crossing the living room, carrying four plastic bags of groceries from the local Pueblo. She hadn't heard him moving around, though, he realized, and didn't know he was home.

"Natalie—"

Immediately, she spun around, dropping two of the bags onto the floor. A few stray oranges emerged from one and rolled under the couch, but neither much noticed. Nick wasn't sure what she was thinking about then, but what caught his attention most was the look of utter panic in her eyes.

"Nat? What is it? What's wrong?"

She shook her head vehemently, then bent to scoop up the contents of the bags that had spilled. "Nothing," she said quickly, sounding skittish. "You just scared me is all. I wasn't expecting you until tomorrow."

"But today's Saturday. I always get home on Saturday."

"It is?" She stretched an arm under the sofa for one of the runaway oranges. Still she did not look at him. "I thought it was Friday. I guess I've been a day behind all week." She laughed, a stilted, anxious sound. "You know, sometimes I'm not even sure what week it is. What month even."

He eyed her suspiciously. "Is everything okay?"

"Of course. What would make you think it wasn't?"

"Well, for one thing, you haven't even said hello to me. You haven't kissed me."

She stowed the last of the groceries into one bag and stood, making her way not toward Nick, but hastily to the kitchen. "I need to get this meat and stuff in the fridge. It's a half-hour walk from the Pueblo, and it must be over ninety degrees today."

He remained silent as she put the groceries away, noting that she didn't seem at all upset by his lack of communication, indulging in her own form of it as she was. Her movements were quick and awkward, as if she were unfamiliar with the surroundings of her own home, and he wondered what it was that made her behave in such a strange manner.

"You want to tell me what's going on?" he asked when he could no longer tolerate her silence.

"Nothing," she said quickly. When she finally looked at him, she was smiling, but there was something about her expression that didn't seem quite right. "There's nothing going on, there's nothing wrong. You just surprised me. I wasn't expecting you today."

"Then you want to come over here and welcome me home the way you usually do? Where's my kiss? Where's my hug?" He grinned. "Where's my grope?"

She laughed then, and the tension that seemed to have burned up the air between them suddenly vanished. Natalie pressed herself against him, circling her arms around his waist for a fierce hug. Then, framing his face with her hands, she rose up on tiptoe to kiss him tenderly on the lips. Immediately, Nick turned what she had begun as a chaste welcome into a heated

manipulation of her mouth with his own. She allowed
him to pull her closer, to cup his hands over her der-
rière, to taste her deeply with his tongue. But when
he moved his hands up over her waist and brought
them around to settle them over her breasts, when he
began to work feverishly at the buttons of her blouse,
she hastily pulled away.

"Don't," she said, taking a giant step away from
him. Her breathing was shallow and ragged.

Nick's expression would have been the same if she
had just called him the vilest name she could remember. When Natalie realized what she had just done—
recoiled from her own husband—she felt shocked.
But the thought of throwing herself back into his arms
was suddenly repugnant somehow, and she was helpless to do anything but stand still and wonder about
her reaction.

"What the hell's the matter with you?" he
demanded.

She shook her head. "Nothing."

"Don't give me that. I've been gone for a week, and
you suddenly don't want to touch me? What's the matter, Natalie?"

"Nothing," she said again. "I just . . . It's just . . ."
She ran a shaky hand through her bangs. "God, Nick,
why do we always have to jump into bed the minute
you get home? Why can't we at least talk first?"

"Talk?" he repeated. "Are you serious? About
what?"

"Well, I don't know. Your trip. My week. Whatever.
I just . . . It's not normal having sex all the time when
we hardly ever talk to each other."

"Natalie, we talk plenty."

She opened her mouth to object, but Nick continued on relentlessly, "And when two married people go this long without seeing each other, it's only natural that they're going to want to . . . you know . . . get close . . . as soon as possible when they're reunited. Especially when they're going to be separated again."

"I know," she said softly, losing some of her conviction. "But we have a whole week together before you have to leave again. We have lots of time to make love."

He took a step toward her, his intention clear. "And we have lots of time to talk, too. Later."

For each step he took toward her, Natalie retreated an equal distance. "But I don't want to right now."

Nick stopped. "Why not?"

She sighed, exasperated. "I don't know. It's hot. I'm tired. I just don't feel like it, all right? Jeez, Nick, sometimes I feel like the only reason you married me was so you'd be able to get it any time you wanted. Can't you think about anything else?"

"Not when I've been gone from my wife for a week, I can't."

"Well, you're just going to have to wait, because I'm not in the mood."

"Why not?"

"What do you mean, 'Why not?' A person can't be turned on all the time, you know."

"You always have been before."

"Well, I'm not now."

They stood in the center of the living room for a long time glaring at each other, neither saying a word. Finally, Nick rubbed his hand over his face, shoving his hair out of his eyes in a clearly frustrated gesture.

"I don't get you," he said. "Everything was fine

when I left home a week ago. What happened this week that's got you all worked up like this?"

Natalie's heart thumped wildly behind her rib cage as her memory of Reuben's kiss flared up like a bazooka blast in her brain. "Nothing," she said quietly. "It was nothing."

"What was nothing?"

But she only shook her head mutely.

"Natalie . . ."

Almost instinctively, she clasped her hands together behind her back, her right fingers anxiously twisting the ring on her left hand. It was a nervous habit she had just picked up over the last couple of days, this fiddling with her wedding band. For some reason, spinning the ring on her fourth finger offered her a vague reassurance that everything would be all right. Her gaze dropped to her husband's left hand, as if seeing the ring that matched her own would reinforce her conviction.

"Nick, where's your wedding band?"

His eyes widened in panic at her question, and he tucked his left hand into his pocket as if doing so would make her forget what she had just asked him.

So much for Booker's assurance that Natalie wouldn't even notice the ring was missing. "I, uh . . . I don't know how to tell you this, Nat," he began slowly, "but while we were on this last underway, I kind of had an accident—"

"An accident?" she interrupted. "Were you hurt? Is everything all right?"

"Yeah, everything's fine. It wasn't that kind of accident." This time it was Nick who moved hastily toward the kitchen. "Is there any beer?" he asked as he reached for the refrigerator door, knowing the question was an obvious and lame attempt at stalling even as he uttered it.

Natalie ignored the query, replying instead with one of her own. "If everything's fine, then where's your wedding band?"

"Well, like I said," he began again as he twisted the cap off a beer and returned to the living room, "I had this little accident, and I . . . I'm sorry, but I lost my ring."

"You *lost* it?"

He closed his eyes at the sound of her voice, so full of disbelief and accusation. "Yeah. I'm real sorry, but I did."

He crossed to the sofa and sat down, stretching his arm across the length of the back, a gesture that normally caused Natalie to join him there. This time, however, she remained standing.

"How on earth did you lose it? Why did you take it off to begin with?"

"It was an accident," he repeated.

"So you've said."

Nick suddenly had no desire to tell her some story he'd made up. Mainly because he was certain she'd know in a heartbeat that he was lying. Suddenly feeling more married than he had since his wedding day, he decided to tell his wife the truth. Married people were supposed to be honest with each other, right? And if he had recently turned down a no-strings-attached roll in the sack with a gorgeous French blonde in a tropical paradise, he was most definitely married. Besides, he wouldn't have to tell Natalie *everything*, would he?

With a restless sigh, he said, "I took it off because Booker asked me to."

She narrowed her eyes. "Why would Booker ask you to do something like that?"

"Because he was trying to meet some girls, and he thought being with a married guy would only hinder his chances."

"Why would being with a married guy hinder *his* chances?"

Nick shrugged fitfully. "I don't know. Booker's got a warped philosophy. You know how he is."

"Yes, I do. But that doesn't give me any insight into why you would go along with him. Especially since *he* was the one who wanted to meet these girls. It *was* him who wanted to meet them, wasn't it, Nick?"

"Of course it was. Him and Luis, anyway. How can you ask me something like that?"

"Maybe because you're the one sitting here without your wedding ring. Aside from all the disturbing symbolic implications of this, do you know how much it's going to cost to get it replaced? And how long it's going to take to get it after we order it?" She expelled a ragged breath of air and looked like she was going to cry. "God, I can't believe you lost your ring because you wanted to look like you were single to some girls."

"Natalie, it wasn't like that."

"Of course it was like that. You just told me it was."

"It was Booker and Luis who wanted to meet them, not me."

"If that were true, you would have left your ring on."

He opened his mouth to object, but something prevented him from doing so.

"See? You're not even bothering to deny it," she said.

Natalie shook her head in silent disbelief. But as

much as she tried to focus on her husband's errant behavior, she was instead remembering her own. It wasn't the same, she tried to tell herself. Reuben had kissed *her*. *He* had been the aggressor, the one who created the situation, not her. And she wasn't the one who had been behaving like an unmarried person, Nick was. She'd done nothing wrong. So why did she feel so miserable inside? Why did everything suddenly feel so hopeless?

"How would you like it if I took my wedding ring off when I worked at Rico's so I could get better tips?" she asked, forcing her thoughts back to Nick's misbehavior. "That would work, you know. Guys would be more inclined to flirt with me if I were single, and if I flirted back, they'd leave better tips. Rico told me so."

Nick sat up straighter on the sofa. "You wouldn't do that."

"Wouldn't I?"

"No, you wouldn't."

He watched helplessly as Natalie studied the ring on her own left hand. Except for being much smaller, it was identical to his in every way, a tangle of ivy vines entwined in silver and gold. She twisted it a few times, then, with some difficulty, pulled it up over her knuckle much as he had done that afternoon on the beach. Then she plucked it off her finger completely.

"Natalie, don't—"

"Feels funny," she told him, inspecting the untanned band of flesh that remained behind. "Feels like I still have it on."

"You should still have it on."

"So should you."

Nick inhaled an impatient breath and released it

slowly. "Look, I said I was sorry. What more do you want me to do?"

"I want you to be honest with me."

"I have been. How many guys do you think would honestly tell their wives they took off their wedding rings to talk to some girls on the beach?"

"On the beach?" she repeated. "You didn't tell me they were on the beach. You were in Guadeloupe this time, weren't you?"

"Yes."

"Those are topless beaches there, aren't they?"

"Yes, but—"

"Oh, Nick," she said miserably, shaking her head.

"It wasn't like that, Natalie, I swear it wasn't."

But she only stared at him in silence, uncertain what made her hurt more—envisioning her husband with a trio of beautiful naked women, or picturing herself kissing Reuben Channing after what had been the most wonderful day she'd spent in San Juan. She wasn't sure why she did what she did after that, but instead of saying anything more to her husband, she turned and went into the bedroom. Nick followed her, only to find her tucking her wedding ring into her jewelry box.

"What are you doing?" he asked.

"If you don't have to wear yours, then I don't have to wear mine."

"Natalie—"

"See how you like it, Nick."

As he watched his wife close the jewelry box lid without a second thought, Nick decided he didn't like it at all.

14

Dear Mom and Dad,

I know everyone says the first year of marriage is the most difficult, but why is that? It seems like everything would be peaches once you tie the knot, at least for the first twelve months. I mean, what could possibly go wrong . . . ?

"You're not wearing your wedding band."

Reuben punctuated his comment by enclosing Natalie's wrist with his fingers as she placed an open bottle of beer before him on the bar. Two weeks had passed since the night he had kissed her, but neither of them had mentioned the incident in any way. It was as if they had reached some mutual, unspoken agreement to forget it had ever happened, and for Natalie at least, that was just fine.

But now when she glanced down at the white line

of flesh circling the ring finger of her left hand, so stark against the deep tan it had taken her months to cultivate, her stomach churned furiously. She met his gaze levelly as she pulled her wrist free from his grasp. "No, I'm not," she replied.

"When did you take it off?"

She shrugged, hoping the gesture looked careless. "A couple of weeks ago."

He tipped back his beer and eyed her speculatively. "A couple of weeks ago, huh? Interesting. Any particular reason you chose to take it off?"

"Not because of anything you did. Of that you can be certain."

A tense moment passed while neither spoke, and Natalie wished with all her heart that Reuben wouldn't pursue the subject.

But naturally, he did. "Well, since you're the one who brought up that wonderful day and night we shared—"

"We did *not* spend a night together."

"Maybe not. But we could have."

"Oh, no we couldn't."

He ignored her comment and instead said, "If memory serves, I wasn't the only willing party that night."

Natalie felt the heat rising in her cheeks. "Then your memory must be getting pretty faulty in your old age," she said without looking at him. "You caught me off guard that night, that's all. And it won't happen again."

"What would you have done if I hadn't caught you off guard? What if I had given you fair warning? Would you have still kissed me back?"

"Of course not," she was quick to reply. Before he

could pursue the subject further, she added, "Excuse me a minute. I have to get some more bourbon from the stockroom. Keep an eye on the bar for me."

Reuben glanced around at the empty room. "Why? There's no one here."

"Just do it, all right?"

She ducked under the bar and hurried down the hall that led to the stockroom, pressing her cold hands against her hot face to steady her nerves as she went. Before she could close the door behind her to be blissfully alone, however, Reuben was in the room with her, cupping one of his hands gently over her shoulder to turn her around to face him, then curling the fingers of his other hand under her chin.

Somehow, his presence there didn't surprise her. But when he tipped her head back to look her in the eye, she lowered her lids and refused to meet his gaze. And when he leaned forward to kiss her, she pulled her head away.

"Somebody has to keep an eye on the bar," she told him.

"Somebody has to keep an eye on you," he countered.

His remark rankled her. "No one has to keep an eye on me. I can take care of myself."

He smiled. "Sure you can, Natalie. That's why you're running around married to one man and kissing another."

"I only kissed you once."

His smile broadened. "Well, at least now you're admitting you participated. Why don't you take one step more and admit that you wanted it to go even further that night?"

She tried to shake her head, but only managed to complete the action halfway and found herself staring at the wall. Reuben must have taken her silence and her gesture to mean she was agreeing with him, because he lowered his head to hers and pressed his lips softly against her cheek. When he did so, she crossed her arms over her chest and looked down at the floor, an action that must have exposed the side of her neck, because he kissed her there, too. Then he turned her head and tipped it backward and descended on her again.

Reuben's kiss this time was different from the first, Natalie thought vaguely as he explored her mouth with his own. There was none of the demand, none of the desperation, that had been present that night two weeks ago. A warm sputter of delight rippled through her midsection, circling her heart and numbing her brain. This time Reuben kissed her as if he were trying to persuade her of something, and at the moment, she wasn't altogether certain she wanted to resist.

For that reason, she tried to tell herself it was a good thing Nick showed up when he did. She started at the sound of his voice calling out her name in the empty bar, then pushed Reuben away with such force that he stumbled backward.

"Here," she said quickly, picking up a case of bourbon and thrusting it into his arms, "make yourself useful." Then she sauntered to the stockroom door and called out, "We're back here, Nick! Reuben's helping me restock the bar."

"Impressive," Reuben said quietly as he followed her back out toward the main room of Rico's. "You're getting real good at juggling two men, Natalie. Is this something that goes on a lot with you?"

"Be quiet," she snapped over her shoulder. "And don't ever do something like that to me again."

He feigned innocence. "Something like what?"

"Don't try to catch me off guard like that anymore."

"Did I do that *again?* Well, my goodness." He moved closer behind her as he added, "You know what they say, Natalie. 'Fool me once, shame on you. Fool me twice, shame on me.'"

"It won't happen again," she vowed under her breath when she entered the main room to find Nick leaning over the bar to grab her soda gun and pour himself a Coke.

"Seems I've heard that before," Reuben told her.

She opened her mouth to say more, but Nick looked up at them and smiled. He still wore his blue work uniform, but had discarded his ball cap to lay it on a nearby stool. Lifting the cold soda to his lips, he downed half of it before he spoke.

"Taking good care of my girl, Reuben?" he asked by way of a greeting.

Involuntarily, Natalie clamped her jaw shut. She wasn't sure what bothered her the most at the moment—the fact that Reuben had just professed that she needed watching over, the fact that her own husband had asked someone else to keep an eye on her, or the fact that Nick didn't think her qualified of managing the task on her own.

"Yeah, God knows I couldn't get along by myself, that's for sure," she muttered as she ducked under the bar.

"What?" Nick asked.

Natalie studied the two men staring back at her, suddenly furious at both of them. "Nothing," she said as she reached for the case of bourbon Reuben had placed on the bar for her. "I didn't say anything."

"Well, if you'll both excuse me a minute," Nick said,

rising from his stool, "I have to pee. Top that Coke off for me, will you, Nat?"

She glared at her husband as he strode carelessly down the hallway toward the men's room, then uttered an angry, guttural noise, snatched his glass from the bar with enough force to send the remaining contents sloshing over the edge and jammed it under the soda gun. When she slammed it back down on the bar with a fury, she saw Reuben grinning at her.

"So how come you're not wearing your wedding band?" he asked again as he sat back down. "You never did tell me that."

"It's getting too small for me," she lied.

Reuben's smile broadened, which did nothing to reassure her. "Getting a little uncomfortable, is it? Starting to feel a bit smothering?"

"Well, I've put on a little weight since moving down here," she told him, reluctant to realize the truth in that. "And the heat makes my fingers swell. The same thing has happened to Nick."

"Yeah, I just noticed he seemed to have taken his ring off, too."

Neither of them said anything more, but Reuben tipped his beer back to drain the last few swallows. Natalie could feel him watching her, even when she turned her back on him to feign rapt attention in organizing the day's bar tabs. She wished Nick would hurry back in spite of the animosity she was still feeling toward him.

"So I guess you won't be needing a ride home tonight," Reuben said finally.

"Yes, she will," Nick told them when he returned. "I have to get back to the cutter. Skipper was supposed to stand watch tonight, but something's come up and I agreed to switch nights with him. I just came to get a bite to eat and say hi to Natalie, tell her what's going on. Then I have to go back."

She frowned at him. "But I thought we were going to go out tonight. You promised to take me to see that new Mel Gibson movie."

He shrugged. "Sorry, Nat. Duty calls. Maybe you and Reuben could go."

"Sounds good to me," Reuben said. "I've been wanting to see that movie myself."

"But—" Natalie started to object.

"There, see?" Nick interrupted. "No problem. Reuben will take you. Can you place an order for a burger and fries for me? I've only got about half an hour before I need to be back."

Natalie felt betrayed. All she could do was stare at her husband and wonder how on earth Nick could so easily deliver her into the hands of Reuben Channing. Automatically, she filled out the order for his dinner and took it back to the kitchen. When she returned, Nick and Reuben were chatting like old chums.

Once his order arrived, Nick wolfed down his dinner and tossed back another Coke, glanced at his watch, and kissed Natalie quickly goodbye. "I'll see you tomorrow afternoon," he said as he swept back his hair and shoved his ball cap onto his head. Then, gripping Reuben briefly on the shoulder, he added, "Thanks again for keeping an eye on her. Enjoy the movie, you two." Smiling, he wagged a finger at them. "But don't stay out too late, you hear?"

And with that final warning, he turned and exited Rico's, whistling under his breath a song Natalie recognized as the one they had danced to at their wedding reception.

She turned to Reuben. "You don't have to take me to the movie tonight. And you don't have to take me home."

He met her gaze. "Why not? I'm looking forward to it."

"Thanks, but I think I'll walk home."

His expression indicated he was skeptical. "It's a five mile walk," he told her.

"Through some of the most beautiful parts of San Juan. I've done it before. Besides, I could use the exercise. Maybe walking will help me get my wedding ring back on."

"Come on, Natalie. It's a hot day. The streets are crowded with tourists. You'll be miserable by the time you make it to your apartment. Let me give you a ride. Even if we don't go to the movie, we can stop for a bite to eat, then I'll take you home. Nick would never forgive me if I left you to wander the streets of San Juan alone."

She wanted to hit him for that. Unfortunately, she knew he was right. Nick would be mad if he found out she had turned down a ride from Reuben in favor of walking home alone. And he'd want to know why she'd do such a thing. Why she would insult his friend and inconvenience herself over something as silly as a ride home.

"All right," she finally said. "Buck should be here for his shift in half an hour. But if you can't hang around that long waiting for me, I'll understand. Believe me."

Reuben smiled and lifted his bottle, then emptied it before pushing it back toward her. "Sounds like just enough time to enjoy another beer."

❖   ❖   ❖

"This one's on me," Natalie said some time later when the waiter at La Zargonzola brought their bill. "You paid the last time we had dinner together, and I promised to cover it this time."

"Don't worry about it," Reuben told her. "Let me get it."

"No," she insisted, pushing his hand away when he reached for the bill. "It's my treat this time."

He sat back in his chair and studied her. "Okay, fine. I'll get it next time."

"No. We're even. From now on—"

"From now on?" he asked.

"Nothing," Natalie concluded, uncertain what she had meant to say in the first place. Something about there not being a next time with him. As she searched in her purse for her wallet, she also tried to reassure herself that their conversation did not sound like that of a couple who had dated frequently and intended to keep doing so.

Their dinner tonight had felt like a date, though, she admitted reluctantly as the waiter disappeared with her credit card. She couldn't imagine why she had once again let him talk her into eating out before taking her home. And because most Puerto Ricans dined late—around nine or ten P.M.—she and Reuben had been virtually alone in the restaurant at six. There had been few other people for the strolling guitarists to entertain, so the two men had returned often to the couple's table to serenade them. The Mediterranean decor of the establishment had been exotic, the Spanish cuisine delicious, and as much as Natalie wished Reuben would behave like a boor, he had been nothing but charming and sweet, in spite of their earlier antagonism.

And attractive. Dammit, she wished the man wasn't so attractive.

She had no idea what it was about him that made him so appealing. He wasn't especially handsome in a conventional way, and she didn't agree with him about much of anything. He was considerably older than she, almost the product of a different generation, yet they always found something interesting to talk about. She supposed if she were forced to admit the truth, she would have to confess that she had enjoyed more lively conversation with Reuben than she ever had with Nick. Reuben spoke to her differently than her husband did. She couldn't quite put her finger on it, but there was something . . . well, *different* . . . about him.

"Let's go visit Nick tonight," she said suddenly, as surprised by her suggestion as Reuben seemed to be.

"What? Why? He's standing watch."

"But it's okay to go by and say hello, isn't it?" she asked. "I mean, his workday is over. He's probably just sitting around reading or watching TV, right?"

"Unless something's come up," Reuben said. "Unless there's been a SAR or there's a mechanical problem on the cutter or something."

"Oh, how often does stuff like that happen?"

"Well, not often, but—"

"So it's okay to visit him, right?"

"Well, sure, but—"

"He won't get into any trouble or anything if we're there, will he?"

"No, but—"

"Then let's stop by," she concluded with a smile. "If he's busy or in the middle of something, we don't have to stay. But it would be fun to surprise him, don't you think?"

Reuben clearly did not think it would be fun, Natalie thought as she contemplated his frown. But the more she thought about it, the more she liked the idea.

"We're in the neighborhood," she added. "The base is practically on our way home."

"The base is *not* on our way home."

"But it's not that far from where we are now."

"All right," he finally relented. "We'll go and visit Nick for a little while. But don't be surprised if he's too busy to do much more than say hello and chase us off. There's a lot you have to keep track of on a cutter."

"Okay, okay. Sheesh."

When they exited the restaurant, Natalie was again overcome by the feeling of having stepped back in time. Dwellings painted in pastel pink, blue, yellow, and green, and trimmed in white lined the cobblestone streets in exactly the same fashion that they had hundreds of years before. Bright red geraniums and lush potted ferns dotted many of the houses' windows and doorways. A striped cat lounged in a window, making Natalie miss her own cats at home fiercely. She paused to scratch the animal under its chin. Clearly as mellow as everyone else on the island seemed to be, the cat purred its contentment and closed its eyes.

"I love it here," she said as she stroked the animal one last time. She turned to Reuben with a smile. "When Nick told me we'd be living in Puerto Rico after we got married, all I thought about was how great it would be to lie on the beach all day. But there's so much more to this place, isn't there?"

Reuben smiled back, and she knew at once he felt the same way she did about their surroundings. "It's definitely different from anywhere else I've ever lived."

As they walked slowly to his car, she continued, "My parents weren't too crazy about the idea of my coming here, even with Nick. They thought there was a strong anti-American sentiment and that the language barrier would be a problem. They didn't think I'd like it here."

"But you do?"

"Oh, yes. It's been fascinating. I mean, it's beautiful and all that—that goes without saying. But it seems like every day I experience something I never have before or meet someone unlike anyone else I've ever known. And always in the most unlikely places."

"Yeah, I know what you mean. The woman who runs the market up the street from me was married to some high-ranking official in Batista's regime in Cuba. Her husband was killed during the coup, and she barely made it out alive with her two kids."

Natalie nodded. "One of the cabbies I met used to be a boxer back in the forties, all over Central and South America, but he quit because his manager got involved with gangsters. He was so interesting to talk to."

The drive to the base was a short one, and their conversation became more animated along the way. By the time they reached the pier where the *Point Kendall* was docked, Natalie was chuckling merrily over a story Reuben was recounting about his difficulty buying groceries at the local Pueblo because he couldn't speak Spanish. Her giggles grew to laughter as he concluded the story, and when she stumbled over an uneven board on the dock, she leaned heavily on his arm to steady herself as she laughed some more.

"Oh, Reuben," she said between chuckles. "You're just going to have to learn to speak the language. That's all there is to it."

"Yeah, or else stay out of the Pueblo."

He draped his arm over her shoulder when she leaned against him, holding her up until her laughter subsided. When the two of them arrived at the cutter and looked up, they found Nick standing on deck, glaring back down at them. He gripped a rope in his fist, and if Natalie hadn't known better, she would have sworn he looked as if he were ready to fashion a noose out of it.

Her forward motion came to a stop almost as immediately as her laughter did when she saw the expression on his face. Reuben bumped into her from behind at her abrupt halt, and she straightened and pulled herself away from him. When he glanced up to see what had caused her to stop, he promptly dropped his arm back to his side.

"Hi, Nick," Natalie greeted him with a smile. She crossed the gangplank onto the boat and leaned up to kiss him on the cheek. "We were in the neighborhood and thought we'd stop by to say hello."

Reuben followed behind her, but kept his distance once he was aboard. "We decided to skip the movie," he said. "Natalie insists on seeing it with you. So we just went out and grabbed a bite to eat instead."

"Where did you eat?" Nick asked.

"This place in Old San Juan," Natalie told him. "Reuben suggested it. La Zargonzola."

Nick nodded. "Nice place. Very romantic atmosphere from what I recall. You guys seem to eat out together a lot before heading home."

"Yeah, well groceries are so expensive, sometimes

it's cheaper to eat out," she replied. "This place *was* very nice. The food was great. What's the matter? You seem kind of angry. Is everything all right? Did we come at a bad time?"

Nick went back to coiling the line he held. "You know, I could hear you guys coming from a mile away. You might want to try keeping your voices down next time."

Natalie smiled again, pivoting around to her dinner companion. "I know, but I couldn't help it. It was so funny. Reuben was just telling me about this time when he—"

"You guys want a cup of coffee or something?" Nick interrupted her. "I just made a fresh pot."

"Coffee would be great," Reuben said. "Natalie? Would you like some?"

"Sure," she replied, turning back to look at Nick, still puzzling over his behavior.

"I'll get it for you," Reuben offered. "Light on the cream and one heaping spoonful of sugar, right?"

She smiled over her shoulder at him. "Right."

Reuben disappeared down the companionway, and Natalie was left alone with her husband. She watched as he focused on the heavy rope he spun at his feet, an activity that seemed to demand an inordinate amount of his concentration, because he didn't look at or speak to her once.

"Nick?" she asked. "What's wrong?"

"Nothing's wrong," he told her. "I'm just busy is all."

"Are you mad because we showed up without calling first?"

He dropped the rope in his hands and finally spun around to face her. "No, I'm mad because you two showed up here hanging all over each other, and I'm worried about what other people might think."

Her mouth dropped open in surprise, and she felt her face flush with heat. "Hanging all over . . . What *other* people might think?" She expelled an exasperated sigh. "We weren't hanging all over each other. I was just laughing so hard, I was about to lose my balance, and Reuben was holding me up. He was keeping me from falling flat on my face."

"Well, the two of you looked mighty cozy if you ask me."

"I didn't ask you," she retorted. "And I don't know who you think you are insinuating something like that. In case you've forgotten, *you're* the one who took his wedding band off and lost it just because he wanted to look single for a bunch of bathing beauties."

"And *you're* the one who took her wedding ring off to get even with me." He paused for a moment, hands on his hips in challenge, before adding, "Or maybe you didn't take it off for that. Maybe you took it off for another reason. Like maybe you wanted to look single, too."

"*What?*" This time it was Natalie who dropped her hands to her hips. "What is the matter with you? Have you been out in the sun too long today?"

"No, I'm just saying maybe you've been dying for an excuse all along to ditch your ring and forget you're a married woman."

She shook her head in amazement, wondering at the source of his ideas, scared to death to realize they had a certain amount of foundation. "Yeah, well it wouldn't be that hard to forget I'm married, seeing as how my husband is never around anyway."

"That's not my fault and you know it. It's my job. I told you before we got married how it would be down here."

"And I told you I could handle it. And I can. What I can't handle is a suspicious husband. Especially one who's suspicious without reason."

"Are you telling me there's nothing going on between you and Reuben?"

"Oh, for Pete's—" She crossed her arms over her breasts, trying to keep her voice calm when she replied, "God, Nick, ever since we came down here, you've been badgering me about making friends with him." She mimicked his voice as she continued, "'Be nice to Reuben, Natalie. Don't be such a harpy around Reuben, Natalie, you'll scare him off. I want you to make friends with Reuben, Natalie.' Well, I made friends with Reuben, Nick, just like you said. And now you're telling me you're mad because of it?"

"No, I'm not mad because of that." He lowered his voice some as he added, "I'm mad because you two were all over each other, that's why I'm mad."

"We were not . . . all . . . over . . . each . . . other," she said again, enunciating the words slowly and clearly as if she were speaking to a child. "He saved me from falling."

"You two seemed awfully chummy to me."

She expelled an exasperated breath. "That's because we *are* chummy. Because *you* wanted us to be chummy."

"He even knows how you take your coffee."

"So does my mother. It's because we eat dinner together a lot."

"And that's another thing I'm starting to wonder about. The two of you eating dinner together all the time."

"Because you always ask him to pick me up after work when you can't meet me. Dinner is a logical thing for Reuben and me to do after work when you're not around, because I don't like to cook for just myself. And why should I eat alone when I don't have to, especially when I can eat with my husband's best friend who he wants me to get along with so badly anyway? And what's the matter with you suddenly? A couple of hours ago, you were foisting me off on Reuben, telling us to go to a movie together. How can you be so mad at me because I'm doing everything you've asked me to do?"

"That's not my point."

"So what is your point? Just what is it you want me to do, Nick? Stop seeing him? Fine. I don't care. I don't like him that much anyway. You're the one who keeps telling him to check up on me. You're the one who keeps asking him to give me rides home from work. You're the reason he and I spend so much time together in the first place."

"All right!" Nick finally relented with a shout. "All right. Jesus. You're right. I'm sorry. I didn't mean to sound so suspicious." He inhaled a deep breath and released it slowly. "I guess I overreacted. I know you two would never do anything like that. You're my wife, after all. And he's my best friend. I should be ashamed of myself for even thinking about it."

"Yes, you should," Natalie told him quietly.

"I'm sorry. Just . . . seeing you two together like that, I guess it hit me that Reuben sees more of you these days than I do. Realizing that makes me a little angry. It's nobody's fault. It's this damned job. It gets to me sometimes, you know?"

She nodded. "I know. It gets to me sometimes, too."

He smiled at her, then took her hand in his and lifted it to his lips. "Getting coffee doesn't take that long. It's nice of Reuben to stay away so we have a chance to work this out."

She laughed a little nervously. "Yeah, he's a hell of a guy all right."

"The best friend a guy could ask for."

Natalie didn't comment on that. Instead she just tilted her head toward the companionway and said, "We better go get our coffee before it gets cold."

It was after dark when Reuben took her home. The power was out in Condado Beach again, and her apartment building loomed dark above them. The hotels across the street were well lit as usual, though, thanks to the generators that hummed like huge, angry beasts somewhere on the beach. The hotel spotlights cast harsh white light into an otherwise black sky, and Natalie squinted as she looked across the tiny confines of the car at Reuben.

"I hate it when this happens," she said.

"Does it happen often?"

"A couple of times a month. It's not so bad inside the apartment, because the hotel lights make it pretty easy to see. You can even read if you sit by the living room windows. But getting up to the apartment is a real pain. You have to use the stairs, and of course, the stairwell is pitch black. And the boys are always out prowling around in the dark. That's something else you have to worry about."

Reuben frowned. "The boys? What boys? Do you have a gang living in your building or something?"

She nodded. "Yeah, a bunch of big ugly guys. Hector, Joey, Denzel, Chico. They call themselves 'Las Cucarachas.'"

"The Cockroaches?" he asked. "That's a pretty stupid name for a gang."

"Fits these guys to a tee. Trust me."

"Well, I'll walk up with you then. I don't want you to have to tangle with a bunch of lowlife scum. Especially in the dark."

Natalie bit her lip. It probably wasn't a good idea to have him accompany her any farther than his car. Despite the numerous assurances to the contrary that she had just delivered so passionately to her husband, she didn't trust Reuben not to try something. But she vividly recalled a time when she had been climbing the steps in the dark and had put her hand down on the stair rail to find it already occupied by one of the building's larger six-legged inhabitants. That coupled with the crunching sound the big bugs made when she stepped on them decided her once and for all.

"Will you walk up first?" she asked.

"Sure."

"Okay."

She stopped short of asking him to carry her piggy-back. She supposed that was going a bit too far. They made it to the fifth floor with relatively little trauma, then Natalie had to fumble for the appropriate key in the blackness that consumed the foyer. Inevitably, there was music coming from the apartment across the way. She marveled at her neighbors' ingenuity at using battery-powered accessories in their line of work.

"What's that music?" Reuben asked.

"It's Geneva and Amber," she told him. "I imagine something like a blackout would be good for business."

"What's that they're playing though? Sounds like . . . 'La Marseilles'?"

"The French Revolution," Natalie said absently as her fingers closed over her front door key. "Louis the Sixteenth, Marat, that sort of thing. I think they wear purple and spend a lot of time in the bathtub with that one. I found my key. Come on in."

Inside the apartment, the rumble of the generators sounded as loudly as it had on the street below. Natalie crossed to crank the windows shut, despite her certainty that such a gesture wouldn't alleviate the noise much. It also cut out a good deal of the white light that had scattered across the room in stripes, but there was still enough present for them to see what they were doing. She went to the bedroom and tossed her purse on the bed, then opened the windows in there to stir some of the air around. On that side of the apartment, the generators weren't quite so loud. When she came out she bumped into Reuben, right near the bedroom door.

"I, uh, I thought maybe you were waiting for me to follow you," he said quietly.

Her heart thumped hard against her rib cage at the sound of his voice in the darkness. "Into the bedroom?" she asked.

She felt more than saw him shrug. "I wasn't sure."

"Well, let me assure you now that I don't want you anywhere near my bedroom, okay?" Unfortunately, she didn't sound nearly as adamant about that as she wanted to.

"Okay," he said.

He lifted a hand to her face, cupping her jaw before skimming his hand back to thread his fingers through her hair. In the pale light of the apartment, only half his face was illuminated, the other thrown well into darkness. The hum of the generators outside became

a dull buzzing in her ears, a sound that still did nothing to silence the pounding of her heart. When he
lifted his other hand to her face, she closed her eyes
and swallowed hard.

"Reuben, don't," she said softly. But she didn't pull
away.

"Why not?"

"Because I don't want you to."

"Are you sure?"

"Yes, I'm sure. It isn't right."

"Why isn't it right?"

"Because . . ."

When she let her voice trail off without giving him
an explanation, he curved his fingers over the back of
her neck. "No surprises," he told her. "I'm going to go
slow, and you can stop me whenever you want. I won't
catch you off guard this time, Natalie. Whatever happens now won't be happening because you didn't
expect it."

Her eyes had adjusted to the darkness by now, and
she could make out the shadowed side of his face
more clearly. He was watching her closely, waiting for
some sign, some clue about how she wanted him to
proceed. But all she could do was shake her head in
silence, and lift her hand to cover his. Whether she
was trying to push him away or bring him closer,
though, even Natalie wasn't certain. She felt as if she
were suspended in time, as if there was a vacuum
around her, and all she could do was stand there.

When she made no further move one way or the
other, Reuben leaned toward her, slowly. Instead of
moving away, she stood still where she was and
watched him. She didn't close her eyes when he
pressed his mouth against hers, nor did she kiss him

back. But as his lips brushed gently over hers, her heart began to race, her cheeks began to heat, and something deep inside her burst into flames.

"You taste good," he said when he pulled away. "You feel good."

And then he leaned in again. This time his body followed his mouth, his thighs and abdomen pressing insistently against hers. He dropped a hand to her hip to pull her closer still, and this time when his lips met hers, Natalie did close her eyes.

She wasn't sure how long Reuben kissed her— maybe seconds, maybe hours. But when he finally pulled away, her breathing was as rough and uneven as his was, and when she ran her tongue across her lips, she detected a lingering taste of him there.

"Just a little while ago," she finally said, "I was fighting with my husband, trying to reassure him that there was nothing going on between you and me."

"And nothing is going on between us," Reuben told her. "Not really. Not yet anyway."

"Nick said he should be ashamed of himself for even suspecting there was. That I was his wife, and you were his best friend. He said he knew he could trust us."

Reuben said nothing in response, but drew his fingers along her jaw and lightly over her lower lip.

"We shouldn't be doing this," she said.

"No, we probably shouldn't."

"Why are you doing it?"

"Why are you?"

She wished she had an answer for that. Wished she could come up with some reason for her behavior. "I don't know," she said finally, honestly. "But for some reason, I have a feeling you know more about what you're doing than I do." When he didn't contradict her, she added, "You'd better go."

"Natalie, I—"

"Please, Reuben. Go home."

He stepped away, even though she could tell he was reluctant to do so. The heels of his shoes scraped across the tile floor as he moved toward the front door. Once there, he paused for a moment, and she thought he was going to say something more. But he only opened the door and walked through it, closing it with a soft *click* behind him.

When he was gone, Natalie collapsed onto the sofa and covered her face with shaking hands. But this time she didn't cry. This time she only lay there and wondered about what kind of a wife she had become.

15

Dear Mom and Dad,

I've been reading in the newspaper lately about a political group down here called the Macheteros. Nick says that literally translated, it means 'Machete wielders' and that what they want is to make Puerto Rico an independent republic. I think that's great and all, but they do weird stuff, sometimes violent, to try and get their point across. Why is it, do you think, that some people just go out of their way to not get along with other people . . . ?

Baxter stood outside the door of his parents' Condado Beach hotel room for a long time before knocking. He hadn't seen his mother or father in more than a year and a half, not since they'd come down to San Juan for his change of command. Even at that, he had seen them for no more than a couple of hours. They had stayed only long enough for the formalities of the ceremony and had skipped the reception afterward. His father had been anxious to leave for the other side of the island and inspect all seventy-two holes of golf the Hyatt Resorts in Dorado had to offer. It was, after all, they told him, the main reason they had come to Puerto Rico.

Baxter hadn't known Carmen then. If he had, he might have introduced her to his parents. It would have been easy, because he wouldn't have known her very well. She would have just been a woman he had recently started dating, someone with whom he had a good time when he had nothing more pressing to do. His father would have slapped him on the back with a knowing wink and an envious smile, and his mother would have been stiffly polite. Afterward, they would have left without giving the woman with their son a second thought, and everything would have been fine. Tonight, he had no idea what would happen.

He recalled again his conversation with Carmen, the one they had had shortly after making up a few weeks ago. He had assured her that his family would feel about her exactly as hers did about him. Except that his, he had warned her, wouldn't be quite as polite about their prejudice as the Fuentes were about theirs. But that, she had told him, was precisely the point. At least she and Baxter had confronted her family. Now she wanted the same opportunity with his. She had told him if the two of them tried hard enough, they would make all the world see how wrong it was to disapprove of the feelings they shared for each another. And although he had finally conceded to her request to meet his parents, Baxter was certain Carmen couldn't be more wrong about that.

Before he could chicken out, he rapped loudly on the door to his parents' suite three times.

"Just a moment," his mother called out from the other side, her voice sounding muffled and distant. In fact, several moments went by before Elaine Torrance opened the door. When she finally did, it was to brush her lips quickly over Baxter's cheek before turning away to rush to a mirror on the other side of the room.

"Excuse me for a moment, won't you, Baxter, darling? I'm having a terrible time trying to get this earring in. They're supposed to be diamonds, but who knows for sure? Your father bought them for me at a store in town this afternoon. I told him we should wait to buy anything until our ship docks somewhere more reputable, but your father insisted."

"Actually, Mother, San Juan has some pretty nice jewelry stores. You really can get some great deals here. And there's no sales tax."

"Well, of course the jeweler assured us we were getting a more than fair price, but you know how these people are. You just can't trust them. I warned your father that when we get back to the States and have the earrings appraised, we're going to find ourselves with two very expensive pieces of glass." She waved her hand toward the other side of the room. "He's in the bathroom shaving, by the way. He'll be out shortly."

As if on cue, the bathroom door opened then, and Davis Torrance emerged. "Is that Baxter?" he asked.

"Well, who else would it be, dear?" Elaine said, rolling her eyes.

Davis was wrapped in one of the hotel's royal blue

bathrobes, his hair as white as the steam that blus-
tered out behind him, his tan deeper than ever now
that he was fully retired. "Come shake your old man's
hand," he said as he approached his son.

Baxter extended his hand toward his father, who
took it, shook it once, and released it. "Good to see
you," he said. "Hope the Coast Guard is treating you
well."

"Great, Dad," he replied. "Just great."

He looked down at the hand his father had so
quickly released. What Baxter really wanted to do was
hug his father, just throw his arms around him, and
squeeze with all his might before turning to his
mother and grabbing her in the same way. There had
been a time in his life when such a gesture wouldn't
have been at all out of the ordinary. A time when his
parents had made it a habit every day to tell their son
how much they loved him, how vitally important he
was in their lives, how they didn't know what they
would do without him. The time before he had joined
the Coast Guard.

Baxter was his parents' only offspring, born as a surprise late in their lives after the couple had given up
in dejection the hope of ever trying to conceive a
child. As a result, he had been the bright, shining
promise of the Torrance household while he was
growing up. He had lacked for nothing in his child-
hood and teen years, and had been nearly smothered
by all the affection the two elder Torrances had shown
him.

And he had always, always, done whatever they
asked of him. He'd attended the same schools his
father had attended, even though all of his friends had
gone elsewhere. He had taken the riding lessons his

mother insisted on for seven summers, despite the fact that he was terrified of horses. He had even asked Lucinda Monroe to the senior prom, because his mother and Mrs. Monroe had been such good friends, and poor Lucinda couldn't get a date to save her life and had always had a fierce crush on Baxter.

He had been a good son. He had done everything they'd asked him to do. Until the summer of his eighteenth year, when instead of packing his bags and heading off to Harvard as his mother and father had wanted, he had enrolled in the U.S. Coast Guard Academy.

Ironically, it was because his parents had also insisted he take sailing lessons that he had become so interested in the sea to begin with. The moment he'd been cut loose on that wide, blue expanse of ocean, Baxter had come to love it passionately. And he had decided early on to make a career of it. When he was eight years old, he had wanted to be a pirate. But he had thought better of that by the time he was twelve. Pirates—at least, the pirates he'd known about back then—simply didn't have the state-of-the-art equipment he demanded on a vessel.

So he had joined the Coast Guard instead. His parents had considered the work common, and completely inappropriate for a Torrance. For eighteen years, it had been understood that Baxter would go to college, earn his MBA, and go to work at the bank with Davis. It had simply been understood. He had always been such a good boy, his parents had reminded him, and had always done what he was supposed to do. Where this sudden rebellion had come from, they had no idea, but there was no way on earth that they would ever condone it.

His father had threatened to disown him when Baxter had refused to change his mind about the academy, and his mother had cried for days. They hadn't invited him home for the holidays that first year he was gone, or for the summer that followed it. Instead, they had told him it would be better if he stayed in Connecticut. The second year, they had come up to Groton on Christmas Eve, had taken him out to dinner, and then spent the night at a hotel. But they had left early Christmas morning because they were expected at the Monroes for Christmas dinner.

By the time he graduated, they had allowed him into the house again. They even smiled when they saw him and spoke to him as if nothing in the world were wrong. But they scarcely touched him. They never told him they loved him. And they never did anything to even suggest he was an important part of their existence.

Baxter had done what *he* wanted to do only once in his life, and it had cost him the affection of his parents. He didn't even want to consider what they would take away from him if he went counter to their wishes a second time.

"We are *so* looking forward to this cruise tomorrow," Elaine said when she finally had her earring in place. "Your father has been counting the days, haven't you, Davis?"

"Since the day we made the reservations," his father replied. "It's one of those something-for-everyone cruises. There will even be a golf pro on board for those of us who want the advice of a professional." He swung an imaginary club as he added, "I can't imagine what I'm doing wrong with my stroke."

"And I get to learn origami," Elaine said, clapping her

hands in delight. "Taught by an honest-to-goodness Japanese person. Won't that be exciting?"

Baxter nodded. "Sounds like you two are in for a thrilling week. Uh, listen," he added suddenly, wondering what might be the best way to spring the news about Carmen even as he changed the subject. "I just wanted to stop by and make sure you two were settling in all right, but you're obviously okay, so I was wondering if I could meet you at the restaurant in about an hour. I . . . there's someone I need to pick up."

"Pick up?" his mother asked. "Who?"

"Her name is Carmen. She's . . . she's a friend of mine. She's going to be joining us for dinner tonight. If that's okay."

"A date," Davis told Elaine in an aside. "Our son is bringing a date with him this evening."

"That's fine, dear," Elaine said. "Just remember that your father and I will have to get back to the hotel early. We board the ship at eight tomorrow morning, and who knows whether or not we'll be able to find a taxi that early."

"Mother, I could give you a lift to the ship. It's no problem."

"Oh, no, Baxter, that's not necessary. We'll take a cab."

"But—"

"She's right, son," Davis said. "There's absolutely no reason for you to have to get up that early on a Saturday."

None except that he might want to spend a little more time with his parents, he thought. "Okay, if you're sure," he said.

"Of course we're sure," Elaine told him. "Now go

get your little friend, and we'll meet you at the restaurant in an hour."

Carmen stared into the cracked, faded mirror over her vanity and applied her eyeliner carefully. She was being very careful about everything she did this evening, determined to make the best impression possible on Baxter's parents. She had chosen a sleeveless white cotton dress from her closet, a modest little number that fell just below her knees and was cut high above her breasts. Her long hair was wound into a tight bun at the nape of her neck, held in place with a silver clip Baxter had given her for Christmas.

Mr. and Mrs. Torrance would see that Carmen Fuente was a nice girl who was perfect for their son, she thought. Once they met her, they would see how much she loved him, how beautifully the two of them went together, and they would offer their every blessing for their son's future happiness. She pulled a tube of lipstick from the caddy that housed dozens of shades of red and wound it up to inspect the hue.

"That one is no good," Marita said.

Carmen glanced into the mirror again, studying the reflection of her teenaged sister, who was sprawled on her bed, flipping idly through the latest issue of Puerto Rico's most popular teen magazine. "What is wrong with this color?" she asked, holding it next to her brightly painted fingernails to compare them.

"It is too red," Marita said without looking up again. "Those *Americanos* you are trying to impress tonight will not like it."

"Oh, and what makes you so certain of that?" Carmen asked before applying the color amply to her mouth. She rubbed her lips together and blotted them on a tissue, liking the effect just fine. "Baxter loves this color on me."

Marita rolled her eyes in the way teenaged girls do when they must deal with someone who is less experienced than they are themselves. "You still do not get it, do you, sister? Baxter loves it, because Baxter is a little boy who is away from home for the first time and trying to do all the things that his parents do not approve of."

Carmen frowned at her sister's reflection. "You have been talking to Orlando again."

"So?"

"So, Orlando is bitter and spiteful like his *machetero* friends because he thinks Baxter stands for everything that is wrong with the United States. Baxter is a 'have' and we are 'have-nots.'"

Marita turned over onto her back and jackknifed up on the bed, meeting her sister's gaze intently in the mirror. "Are you denying that such a thing is true?"

Carmen shrugged. "Of course not. But it is not Baxter's fault that he is rich and we are poor."

"Orlando thinks you are turning your back on your heritage."

"Orlando does not know what it means to fall in love with someone."

"And you do?"

This time Carmen spun around on her stool and stared at Marita eye to eye. "Yes. I do."

Her sister looked doubtful. "What makes Baxter so different from other boys you have dated? Besides the fact that he is not Puerto Rican."

"For one thing, he has a good job. A job with a future."

"And his job is what made you fall in love with him? Then maybe Orlando is right. Maybe you just want a ticket out of Santurce."

"That is not true at all. And that is not what made me fall in love with Baxter," Carmen countered. "He also treats me better than any other boy I have ever dated."

"Because he has more money," Marita said. "He can afford to treat you better."

"No, because he has more respect for me," Carmen replied. She rose and gathered the things she would need for the night ahead, stowing them in an over-sized straw bag. "The boys down here, they do not know how to treat a girl. They drive around in their cars, shouting out the windows, telling us we have a great ass or a nice set of chi-chis. And they think we should be flattered. They think behavior like that is a compliment."

"It is a compliment."

Carmen paused in her search and took her sister's shoulders in her hands, forcing her to meet her gaze. "No, Marita, it is not a compliment. And do not ever think that it is, because that is the first step toward losing yourself."

Marita narrowed her eyes. "Well, what about all the *turistas* at the casinos? They treat you the same way, and they are not from down here."

"That is true," Carmen conceded, releasing her sister to tuck the last of her cosmetics into her purse. "And I am not defending them. I am defending Baxter. He is much different than the *pendejos* who sit at my table and give me a hard time."

"Are you so sure about that?"

Carmen nodded her head once, hard. "Yes. I am sure."

"Well, you better hope so," Marita told her. "Because if his family is anything like Orlando thinks they are, you are going to need all the help from him you can get."

The Torrances were already seated and enjoying cocktails by the time Carmen and Baxter joined them. Her first impression of them was how blond and pale they appeared with the candlelight flickering across their faces. Baxter's father looked as she guessed Baxter would look in forty or fifty years, with his conservatively cut white hair and his golf clothes that combined two colors she would never think of matching together herself. Baxter's mother, on the other hand, was perfectly coordinated, her flat aqua pumps *exactly* the same color as her short-sleeved silk top and matching pants. All in all, the Torrances seemed harmless enough, she thought, feeling the tension that had knotted her stomach beginning to ease some.

Their table at the restaurant in Old San Juan overlooked the harbor, and the blood-red sun was hanging low over the water. In the distance, a two-masted tourist schooner skimmed at full sail along the water, its billowing sheets changing from pink to yellow to orange in the pale illumination of the setting sun. Carmen had recommended the restaurant to Baxter precisely because of such sights, and because the establishment was well known among tourists and locals alike for producing delicious—and authentic— Puerto Rican fare. A salsa band played downstairs and added to the tropical ambience, the mellow strains of one of her favorite songs lifting into the evening air and easing her tension a little bit. She sighed in relief. The night was not off to such a bad start.

Baxter's parents looked up as he and Carmen approached. Davis Torrance rose to shake his son's hand and nod in greeting to Carmen, and Elaine Torrance briefly kissed the air beside her son's face as he leaned toward her.

"Mother, Dad," he said as he circled his arm around Carmen's waist, "I want you to meet Carmen Fuente. Carmen, these are my parents, Davis and Elaine Torrance."

"It is very nice to meet you, Mr. Torrance," Carmen said with a smile as she extended her hand toward Davis.

He seemed surprised by the gesture, but only momentarily so, then took her hand for a light squeeze.

"And you, Mrs. Torrance," she said further, nodding toward Elaine. When Baxter's mother did not immediately respond, she wondered if she had made some grievous social error. She had not *thought* she was supposed to curtsy, but something about the other woman's demeanor almost demanded it.

"Hello," Elaine finally replied, skimming her gaze from the top of Carmen's head to the silver sandals on her feet, then back up again. A platinum-blond eyebrow that hadn't been arched before was now. "It's nice to meet you, too . . . Carmen. Baxter, dear," she added quickly, turning her attention to her son, "you might have chosen a restaurant that offered a little more culinary variety. You know how your father's ulcer acts up when he eats this ethnic food."

Carmen opened her mouth to apologize for her oversight, but Baxter cut her off.

"Since you and Dad are only going to be in San Juan for one night, we wanted to make sure you experienced the city in the best way possible. Old San Juan is the most picturesque part of town, and we thought you might enjoy sampling some Puerto Rican dishes. I'm sorry. I should have remembered Dad's stomach."

"It's all right, son," Davis Torrance said. "The food will be fine. It's this music they're playing that's upsetting my stomach. We've heard it constantly since we arrived on the island. It's perfectly awful."

Carmen wanted to offer a defense of the music she had grown up with and dearly loved, but once more, Baxter's interruption halted her.

"It's called 'salsa,'" he said, his voice strained. "It's very popular down here."

"Yes, well you'd think they would play something else for the tourists," his father grumbled. "Something a little more familiar. A little more palatable."

Baxter threw Carmen a halfhearted smile as he pulled her chair away from the table and waited for her to sit down. "Well, you know, Dad," he said as he rounded the table to take his own seat, "there are those who would argue that the reason people visit foreign places to begin with is to experience something a little different from what they get at home everyday."

"Don't get smart with your father, young man," Elaine said sharply. "You know exactly what he meant. Places like this thrive on tourism. The least they can do is try to accommodate their paying guests."

Carmen started to speak again, but again Baxter cut her off.

"I'm sorry. I didn't mean to be smart. All I meant was—" He sighed fitfully and picked up his menu.

"Never mind. Have you two decided what you want for dinner?"

When the waiter returned for their orders, both elder Torrances ordered steaks, while Baxter opted for the grilled swordfish. Carmen chose a conch salad to start, *piononos*—a dish consisting of plantains and chicken—for her main course, a local vegetable called *yautias* on the side, and flan for dessert. Then, after snapping the menu closed, she spoke at length with the waiter in Spanish, just to remind Baxter how perfectly capable of speech she was. And, she had to admit, maybe by speaking her native language so enthusiastically, she wanted to make Mr. and Mrs. Torrance just the slightest bit nervous.

After the waiter left, Elaine rubbed at a water spot on her knife with her napkin, Davis sipped leisurely on his scotch and water, Baxter stared out toward the Atlantic, looking as if he wished he were on the *Point Kendall,* miles out at sea, and Carmen grew more and more uncomfortable. Maybe Baxter had been right, she thought. Maybe meeting his parents now had not been such a good idea after all.

"So, Carmen, what does your father do?"

She looked up to find Davis staring at her intently. For some reason, the expression on his face reminded her of so many of the men who sat at her table when she dealt blackjack, and she had to fight to keep herself from squirming.

"My father died four years ago," she said. "But he worked in a rum distillery when he was alive."

Elaine's lips curled back over her teeth in something Carmen supposed was meant to be a smile, but the gesture fell well short of the mark. "How interesting," she said.

Carmen's back went up at her tone of voice. "Actually, it is very interesting," she replied. "If you and Mr. Torrance have a free day before you go back to Maryland, I can take you to the Bacardi distillery. They have tours everyday. It is fascinating what goes into the making of rum."

"I'm sure it is," Elaine said. "And your mother? What does she do now that your father is gone? It must be very difficult for her."

"Carmen's mother works for one of the larger hotels in Condado Beach," Baxter said. "Isn't that right, Carmen?"

"Yes, my mother works as a—"

"Rafaela's assigned to one of the most important departments there, isn't she?" Baxter interrupted her before Carmen could elaborate. He threw her a warning look, silently urging her to end the discussion there.

Carmen ignored him. "My mother is in housekeeping," she said. "She is a hotel maid. And I help her by working as a blackjack dealer in one of the other hotels."

"I see," Elaine said. "It must be difficult making ends meet with . . . how many children does your mother have?"

"Eight," Carmen said.

"*Eight,*" Elaine repeated, her eyes wide with surprise. "Imagine bringing *eight* children into the world when you couldn't possibly afford them. She and your father must have been very devout Catholics."

Carmen's jaw clenched, and she allowed a slew of insults to pass through her head fiercely in Spanish before replying politely in English, "They were, Mrs. Torrance. And my mother still is. So am I. Will that be a problem?"

Elaine clearly did not understand what Carmen was talking about. "Why on earth would it be a problem?"

"Because your son will be marrying into the Catholic church. Some people who are not Catholic have a problem with that."

She felt Baxter's foot nudge her own hard beneath the table, and only then did she realize what she had said. She snatched her foot away from his and frowned at him. Maybe she *was* being a bit forward. After all, he had not proposed to her yet. But something in Elaine Torrance's face had just been asking for it, she thought. Baxter's mother needed for someone to take her by the shoulders and shake her hard. And maybe, she decided further with a little smile, Carmen Fuente was just the person to do it.

"Our children will be raised Catholic, too, of course," she threw in for good measure.

Baxter rubbed his temple and shook his head at her. "Carmen, you know better than to do this."

"Baxter," Elaine began quietly. Carmen thought her voice surprisingly level in light of the situation. "You didn't tell us you had asked this . . . had asked Carmen . . . to marry you."

He sighed wearily. "I haven't asked her to marry me."

"Then why is she talking as if you did?" Davis asked. "Don't you remember the little chat we had about this before you went overseas, son? You never, ever, promise a woman what you can't deliver."

"Davis, please," Elaine said.

"Mr. and Mrs. Torrance," Carmen said, "Baxter and I love each other. And we have been dating for more than a year. It is only natural that we should get married. Is that not right, Baxter?"

He shook his head. "Don't ask me a question like that, Carmen. I never once said anything to you about getting married. You're the only one who's ever brought up the subject."

"Well, that's a relief," Elaine said after a hefty sip of water from her glass. As an afterthought, she asked, "It *is* safe to drink the water here, isn't it, Baxter?"

Baxter emitted an impatient sound and ran his hand through his hair. "Of course it's safe, Mother. This isn't the Third World."

"Well, you could have fooled me. These people—"

"Puerto Rico is the wealthiest island in the Caribbean, Mrs. Torrance," Carmen interrupted. "Many, many American and European companies have offices here. San Juan is a metropolitan city in every sense of the word. It has many facilities to rival those found in the United States."

Elaine's gaze traveled from Carmen to Baxter and back again. For a long time, she didn't speak, only continued to stare at the young woman who had so recently stated her intention to join the Torrance family. "My," she said after a moment, "you do speak English well. Did you pick that up from your . . . clients at the casino?"

"No, I learned it in school. Catholic school," she added. "You would be surprised how many Puerto Ricans speak English perfectly."

"I dare say I would."

Carmen ignored Elaine Torrance after that, focusing her attention entirely on Baxter. "And I am surprised how many Americans say one thing and mean another," she said softly. "In Puerto Rico, when you love someone, really love someone, you spend the rest of your lives together. You respect each other. You support each other. But you *Americanos* must have a different idea of what love means."

"Carmen," Baxter began.

"But you know what is really funny?" she went on, still looking only at Baxter. "I think finally, after all this time, I understand now what you mean when you say you care for me. And it does not have anything to do with love at all, does it?" She stood, threw her napkin onto her empty plate, then fished in her wallet until she located a twenty-dollar bill. "This should cover the cost of my dinner," she said, her gaze never leaving his. "Anything else you might have to offer is much too expensive for me. Good-bye, Baxter."

"Carmen, wait."

But she ignored his plea, weaving her way through the tables and ignoring the startled looks of the other diners as she hurtled past. Baxter caught up with her just as she hit the street outside, grabbing her arm to spin her around to face him. She said nothing, waiting for him to explain, to say he was sorry, or to do whatever it was he felt it necessary to do. This time, however, she would not be swayed by his pretty apologies. This time, he would have to do a lot more than say he was sorry if he wanted her forgiveness.

For a long time he looked at her, then released her arm with a sigh. Finally, he shook his head and said, "Why did you have to wear so much makeup tonight?"

Her heart plummeted. She wanted to scream at him, wanted to shake him, wanted to bash his head against the wall until he came to his senses.

"That is all you have to say?" she asked, nearly choking on the words. "After all that, you are only concerned about my makeup? You have never minded before how I looked. You have always liked it."

"Yeah, well I've never been introducing you to my parents before, have I?"

She shook her head at him hopelessly, her heart sinking to the pit of her stomach. "So Orlando was right about you after all."

"What are you talking about? What's Orlando got to do with anything?"

She eyed him thoughtfully for a moment before saying, "Tell me something, Baxter."

"What?"

"Why have you never learned to speak Spanish?"

"Why . . . Carmen, what are you going on about? You're not making any sense. What's this got to do with my parents?"

She ignored his questions and pursued her own instead. "You have been living in Puerto Rico for a long time and will not be going home for many months. You have told me the Coast Guard offers free Spanish classes on the base, yet you have never signed up for them. Why not?"

"Why should I?"

"Because you are living in Puerto Rico, and in Puerto Rico, we speak Spanish, that is why."

"So?"

"So if I were a Puerto Rican moving to the United States, you would expect me to learn English, right?"

"Of course, but—"

"Yet you are not willing to learn Spanish just because you are living in Puerto Rico. Does that make sense to you?"

His lips flattened into a tight line. "Yes. It does. And I still don't understand what this has to do with anything."

"It tells me much about the way you were raised,"

she said. "About the way you are and the way you will always be."

"Look, I warned you about my parents," he reminded her. "You can't say I didn't."

"Yes, you warned me about your parents. What you did not warn me about, Baxter, is that you are just like them."

She turned away and headed down the street, a big part of her still half expecting that he would object to what she had just said and come running after her. But of course he did not. When she finally looked back, he was entering the restaurant again, no doubt going back to sit obediently between his parents and without uttering another word about her.

And not so deep down inside, Carmen had to concede that that was probably exactly where Baxter Torrance belonged.

16

Dear Mom and Dad,

    Enclosed is a postcard of El Morro, a Spanish fort of great historical significance here in San Juan. I drew a little arrow beside the rampart where Nick made an indecent proposal. It was a great day. Really. Probably the very best day I've spent in Puerto Rico since coming down here. I don't guess I'll ever forget it . . .

      "Nick?"
"Hmm?"
"Could we go to El Morro today?"
Nick dropped the newspaper into his lap and looked at his wife, who sat opposite him at the table, pouring herself a second cup of coffee. A half-eaten supermarket danish roll sat on a plate between them, and a glorious, uneventful Sunday lay ahead. At least,

he'd thought it was going to be uneventful. Evidently, his wife had other ideas.

"That came out of nowhere," he said. "Why would you want to go to El Morro? I thought you went with Reuben a while back."

"But I haven't been with you."

"What's the difference?"

She looked at him for a moment before replying, and when she did it was to ask a question of her own. "Have you ever been?"

"No."

"Well, wouldn't you like to see it?"

He went back to scanning a story about a barge collision in the harbor to which the forty-one footers had responded earlier in the week. "No, not really."

Natalie was clearly disappointed by his reply. "Why not?"

"I don't know. I'm not much for tourism, I guess. Give me a good beach and a cold beer, and I'm happy."

"But there's so much more to Puerto Rico, to San Juan. Do you realize how much history there is here? Ponce de León is buried in the Cathedral of San Juan. Did you know that?"

Nick turned a page and read some more. "Nope."

Natalie tried again. "It's a nice day. After we go to El Morro, we could fly kites in that big field beside it. That might be fun."

"We don't have any kites."

"You can buy them there."

"I'm not much good with kites."

She sighed. "Well then, maybe we could go shopping in Old San Juan."

"Why? We can't afford to buy anything."

"You don't have to have money to shop. It's fun to just look around. Some of those little stores have great stuff in them."

He reached for his coffee and took a sip. "Sounds like you've already seen them all."

"Not all of them," she said quietly. "And there are some cute restaurants in Old San Juan that aren't that expensive. We could have lunch out. That might be fun for a change."

Nick shook his head. "The local food doesn't agree with me. I think it's the peppers."

"Please?"

He dropped the newspaper into his lap and stared at her. Where Natalie's sudden urge to get up and go had come from, he couldn't for the life of him figure out. When they'd first come to Puerto Rico, she'd been perfectly content to lie on the beach and relax, just as he liked to do. Now, lately, all she wanted to do was play the tourist. He would have thought she'd gotten that out of her system by now, after all the adventures she had described having with Reuben. Still, he supposed he hadn't much taken her anyplace himself since her arrival.

It was just that he wanted to be *home* with Natalie, the way two married people should be. He spent so much time away from her, so much time visiting other places, that it was nice to come back to San Juan and spend what little time they had together alone. At home. Where no one else could disturb them. Considering the barely tenuous peace they had managed to maintain since the lost ring fiasco, being home alone with her seemed even more imperative to him now.

"All right," he finally relented, unable to tolerate

her forlorn expression. "We can go sightseeing today."

Her smile was dazzling, and Nick thought maybe it would be worth it to sacrifice a day alone with her if she would look at him like that more often. It had been too long since she had smiled at him with such obvious delight.

"You have to be the guide, though," he told her. "Despite having lived here for a while, I'm like one of those New Yorkers who's never visited the Statue of Liberty or the Empire State Building. I'm just not into the tourist thing."

"No problem," she assured him, leaning over to place a quick kiss on his mouth. "I have the itinerary all worked out."

It wasn't the same, Natalie decided as she watched Nick wolf down a bologna sandwich at home some time later. She had taken special care to make certain the day she spent with her husband mirrored the one she had spent with Reuben in every way, from luring him into one of the ramparts of El Morro to rounding off the day with a romantic dinner by the lagoon that night. But at the old fort, he had spent much of his time asking her if she had seen all she wanted to see. The kite vendor apparently didn't work on Sundays, and many of the shops in Old San Juan had been closed. Those that had been open had repelled her husband because they were too small, too expensive, too hot, or too crowded. They had eaten lunch at McDonald's. And when she had proposed they dine at a little bistro near Condado Lagoon because there was so little fare to choose from at the apartment, he had suggested they go home anyway, since they had already eaten out once that day.

She sighed for perhaps the hundredth time since they had set off on their journey that morning, and gazed down into her bowl of chicken noodle soup. It hadn't been the same as it had with Reuben. It hadn't been the same at all.

"Oh, jeez, I almost forgot," Nick said suddenly, jumping up from his seat and racing over to the TV set. "*Murder, She Wrote* is coming on. I've had to miss it the last couple of weeks."

As the opening credits showed quaint little shots of Cabot Cove, Maine, Nick moved his soup and sandwich to the coffee table and settled in for the evening. After *Murder, She Wrote*, he would want to watch the movie, Natalie thought, regardless of what it was—unless it was one of those Danielle Steele things, in which case he'd probably watch something on cable. Nick Brannon was nothing if not dedicated to his Sunday night television. It was the one time he took to relax in such a way, and she didn't have the heart to deny him after he'd spent the day indulging her.

Ever since coming to San Juan, she reminded herself, she had been growing tired of exotic surroundings and odd work schedules, had been pining for a married life with her husband that was normal, predictable, and comfortable. She had wanted nothing more than for the two of them to just be happy together, enjoying the most mundane of activities, like real married people did. And now, as she watched Nick swallow the last of his sandwich and rise to go to the kitchen for another beer, as she listened to the familiar theme music of her husband's favorite show blare out from the TV, as she leaned back in her chair and stared hopelessly at the ceiling, she was overcome by the certainty that she was, at that moment, experiencing exactly the kind of lifestyle she had so desperately thought she wanted for her marriage.

Unfortunately, having gotten what she wanted, Natalie felt more depressed than ever. Because what she had been so certain she wanted wasn't anything at all like what she'd had that day with Reuben. It wasn't romantic, it wasn't full of laughter, it wasn't much fun.

Reluctantly, she moved her own dinner to the table beside Nick's and sat down on the sofa to join him. Later, she thought, as she snuggled up close and leaned her head on her husband's shoulder. Surely the two of them could make up for the day's shortcomings later.

But later, when she sidled up to him in bed, tangled her fingers in his hair, and kissed his earlobe in that way that normally sent him over the edge, Nick took Natalie's hand in his, kissed it softly, and set it back on her hip.

"I'm sorry, Nat," he told her, "but I'm pretty tired. All that walking today, I guess. And those two beers with dinner made me sleepy."

"But—"

"Not tonight, okay? I have to get up earlier than usual tomorrow."

She lay her head back on her pillow and stared at the ceiling, feeling the heat close in on her as quickly as the darkness seemed to do. It was okay, she told herself. They didn't have to make love all the time. Hadn't she herself pointed that out to her husband not long ago? It was just that tonight she had wanted to be certain that things between them were still okay. It seemed almost significant somehow that Nick would turn away from her tonight, and she didn't like the feeling of hopelessness his unwillingness brought with it.

To reassure herself, she cuddled close behind him and fitted herself to him spoon fashion, draping one arm over his midsection and covering his foot with hers.

"Nat?" he said softly.

"Hmm?"

"Could you, uh . . . would you mind moving over to your side of the bed? It's awfully hot tonight."

Without comment or hesitation, she pushed herself away from him, scooting as far to her side of the bed as she could without sending herself over the edge of the queen-size mattress. He was right, she thought. It was pretty hot tonight. In spite of that, however, she reached for the sheet at the foot of the bed, and pulled it up to her chin. The two of them had slept in the buff since marrying, both because they were newlyweds, she supposed, and because the nighttime temperatures of San Juan were uncomfortable. Somehow, though, after tonight, she thought she'd probably start sleeping in a T-shirt or something. The mosquitoes had become fierce in the summer months, and there was no reason to submit herself to torture like that if she didn't have to.

Closing her eyes restlessly, Natalie tried to empty her brain and settle in to sleep. Unfortunately, sleep was long in coming that night. The thought of another day—and another man—were more than enough to keep her awake.

17

Dear Mom and Dad,

Remember back in junior high when you told me not to worry when things looked bad, because they were always better than they could be? I'm not sure that was such a good thing to tell a kid at such an impressionable age. I took it to mean that no matter how bad things get, they can always get worse. It's really stayed with me over the years . . .

Jack inventoried the contents of the apartment he had inhabited for nearly a month now and threw his sea bag on the bed with an idle toss. One damned room. That's all he was able to afford. The outside of the apartment house in Old San Juan was nice enough—mint green stucco with white trim, red geraniums in every window facing the street, white wrought-iron security gate. What he hadn't realized was that the furnished apartments available in his price range didn't have geraniums in the windows. Mainly because the affordable dwellings didn't have windows, either. What they did have was a single room measuring about ten by fifteen feet, an alcove with a gas stove and college dorm-size refrigerator, and a shower stall. A bed with an orange chenille bedspread took up half the room. What little space remained was occupied by a metal bookcase full of paperback romance novels and a table with four plastic chairs.

"Welcome home," he muttered to no one in particular.

He tried to comfort himself with the reminder that the apartment was essentially no smaller than the innards of *Errukine*, and he'd survived just fine on her for years. Still, *Errukine* had offered him a few portholes to allow in the sun, and a wide open deck to retreat to whenever the close quarters of the boat began to feel confining. He'd also had the fresh ocean breeze coming down through the hatch in the forward cabin, the continuous, lulling lap of the ocean against the hull, the laughter of neighbors as they passed on the pier outside, and the comforting cries of the seagulls.

And Sybil, of course. He'd had Sybil then, too.

He pushed that last thought away and turned his attention to unpacking his things and getting settled after another week underway. That accomplished in less than fifteen minutes, he then decided to go to the grocery and stock up on supplies. When he opened his front door to exit, however, and found Sybil standing there with her fist poised ready to knock, he recognized quickly that he was going to be a bit delayed.

It had been more than three months since he had left her alone on *Errukine*. And her belly had swollen a lot. She was quite obviously pregnant now and had gained a little weight in her face and breasts, too. She seemed kind of round all over, and he grudgingly had to admit that she wore her pregnancy well.

"What are you doing here?" he asked her.

She dropped her fist to her side and met his gaze levelly. "I came to talk to you."

"How did you find me?"

"Baxter told me where you were."

He frowned. "Well, I was just going out."

"You'll stay long enough to hear what I have to say."

"Which is?"

Sybil inhaled a deep breath and pushed her way past her husband, making herself comfortable on the edge of his bed. But instead of launching into the speech she had spent weeks perfecting, she only looked around and muttered, "Hey, Jack, nice digs."

He frowned. "It's all I could afford, under the circumstances."

"You could come back to the boat, you know."

"Why would I want to do that?"

She tried to bite back the sarcasm she wanted to hurl at him, but wasn't entirely successful. "Well, gee, for one thing you'd be more comfortable there. For another, it's where you belong."

Jack closed the door softly, then crossed the tiny room to sit at the table opposite. "Not anymore. Too much has changed. It's different now."

Sybil's hands doubled into fists she pressed fiercely into the soft mattress beneath her. She had known coming to see Jack wasn't going to be easy. But she had thought he might at least help some.

"You've had three months to play the injured little boy," she said quietly. "Now I think it's time you came home and started acting your age. Behaving like a child is pretty odd for someone who seems to hate them so much."

"I don't hate children."

"You could have fooled me."

"I don't hate them," he insisted. "I just don't want any of my own."

She rose from the bed and joined him at the table, folding her arms over the flat surface and meeting his gaze levelly. "Well, like I said before, that's too bad. Because you're going to have one anyway. And you're as responsible for it as I am."

"Look, I'll pay whatever I'm required by law for child support. But that's all you're going to get out of me."

She sighed restlessly. This wasn't at all how she had planned for things to go. But Jack had started this. She might as well finish it. "You're damned right you'll pay child support," she told him. "I've already talked to a lawyer about it."

"You *what*? That's nuts. The baby's not even born yet."

"Yeah, but considering your job—the fact that you move around so often and spend a good bit of your time on foreign soil—I figured it might be a good idea to have someone keeping an eye on you from the get-go."

He glared at her. "You've got some nerve."

She gaped back. "*I've* got some nerve? Just who in the hell do you think you are saying that to me?"

Suddenly impatient, she stood and began to pace the minuscule room with much agitation. Jack scooted his chair away when she approached him, as if he were fearful of having her touch him in any way. Her movements became even jerkier at the realization.

"I didn't come over here to fight with you," she said as she swallowed back the tears she felt threatening. "I came over here to make you see reason, to make you understand."

"I understand just fine," he told her. "I understand that you've made your decision and I've made mine and that there's nothing more to be said between us."

"There's plenty more to be said," she countered.

But for the life of her, she had no idea where to begin. So she continued to pace in silence, growing more and more frustrated by the minute. Finally, she turned around and demanded, "Do you realize how much I always worried about you every time you got underway? There are so many things that could happen to you. You guys could board a boat looking for drugs and get shot by some crazy lunatic. There could be some mechanical failure on the cutter and some horrible accident could result. You could fall overboard at night and get eaten by sharks. You could hit foul weather and wind up capsized. You could get drunk in some bar and end up knifed in a brawl." Running a hand viciously through her hair, she added, "Hell, I even worried that you'd meet some sweet young thing on a topless beach and decide she had a lot more to offer you than I did."

She sniffled, swiped at her nose, and briefly covered her face with her hands. "Every time you went out," she continued after a moment, "I wondered if it was the last time I was ever going to see you. And now my worst fears have been realized. Not because of any terrible thing I've ever imagined, but because of something as harmless as a child. Our child. This separation doesn't have to be permanent, Jack. I'm willing to forget everything we've said to each other and start all over again. The decision is yours."

She stopped pacing and turned to look at him, and nearly sobbed out loud at the hopeless expression on his face. She'd lost him. She knew it then with all her heart. There was nothing she could say or do that would make him change his mind. One thing about Jack, she recalled belatedly, was that he was stubborn as hell. When he made up his mind that the world was going to work in a certain fashion, nobody could change his way of thinking.

"Don't do this," she pleaded. "Come home with me—now, to stay. We can work through it, I know we can. But not if we're apart."

"It's too late, Syb," he said quietly. "This isn't some little disagreement we can sit down and talk out over dinner. This is a life-altering situation, and there's no way we're going to find a middle ground for it. I can't live with things the way you want them. I just can't. And there's nothing we can do to compromise."

"What about *Errukine?*" she asked him miserably, knowing it was a last-ditch effort. "I won't move off her. And I'll fight you for custody."

He sounded exhausted when he said, "Keep the damned boat. I'll get another one somewhere and start all over again. Maybe I'll even find someone to help me whip her into shape. Someone who knows the value of a good thing."

Sybil didn't even try to hide her tears after that. She stood, approached him slowly, and lifted her hand toward his cheek. All she wanted to do was touch him—she had almost forgotten what that was like. But when he pulled back before she could make contact, she dropped her hand to her side and turned away.

"Dammit, Jack," she said softly. "You always have known exactly what to do to drive me crazy, haven't you?" When he said nothing in reply, she told him, "This was your last chance. I'll send the rest of your things to you here, and I don't want you coming near the boat again. Should you come to your senses about this, I guess it's all right for you to call me. But I can't promise I'll be willing to talk to you. And I can't promise I'll ever forgive you."

When she crossed to the front door and reached for the knob, he said, "I'm not looking for your forgiveness."

She twisted the knob and pulled the door open. Without looking back, she said, "Maybe not now. But you will be. Someday. And by then it just might be too late."

She left before he could comment further, closing the door quietly behind her. Slowly, she made her way down the dark steps of the apartment building, then squinted her eyes against the stark sunlight that greeted her outside. Her pace remained sluggish as she made her way through the streets of Old San Juan, and she noticed nothing of her picturesque surroundings.

She cried out when a sharp pain sliced through the lower part of her abdomen. It wasn't the first time she had felt such a pain, but this one was far worse than the others she had experienced. When the cramp grew more unbearable, she pitched forward and doubled over into a ball on the concrete sidewalk. As she cradled her belly in her hands, she began to cry freely. And when an elderly Puerto Rican woman hastened toward her to see what was wrong with cries of "*¿Mira, qué pasó? ¿Mijita? ¿Qué pasó?*" all Sybil could do was repeat over and over and over, "My baby, my baby, my baby . . ."

Jack had noticed the little market up the street when he'd first looked at his apartment, and now he found its front door wide open when he approached. He knew before entering that what he would find inside would be typical of a neighborhood establishment. The interior would be close and comfortable, aged and run-down, but spotlessly clean. The few aisles would be narrow and crowded with as much stock as they could hold, the items blending nicely despite an apparent absence of organization. Bottles of Pepsi would appear on a shelf beside cans of Goya guava juice, and the Häagen-Däzs key lime and cream ice cream—the flavor that he loved but had never been able to find in the States—would be in a freezer right next to the frozen calf brains.

A young Puerto Rican woman looked up from behind the counter and smiled as he entered.

"*Buenos días,*" she said. "Can I help you?"

"Hi," he replied. "No, I just need to pick up a few things."

"Okay. Let me know if you can't find something."

"I will."

Beside the cash register was a high bar stool, and sleeping curled up on the stool was a black cat with white paws. It was fat and well fed, obviously more than content to make the market its home. As Jack passed further toward the aisles, he noticed a makeshift cradle on the floor beside the counter, and sleeping inside as soundly as the cat was a baby. It lay on its stomach with one chubby, little fist curled near its face, its head covered with thick, black hair.

"How old is the baby?" he asked before he even realized he had formed the question in his head.

The young woman looked up at Jack before glancing down at the sleeping infant. "She is six months old today."

"Six months?" he repeated incredulously. "But she's so small."

The woman laughed. "*Ai*, you think she is small now, you should have seen her when she was born. Violeta weighs three times as much now as she did then."

As if summoned by the mention of her name, the baby stirred, uttering soft little sounds and pushing her fist against her eyes. She raised herself up on fat, unsteady arms, then turned her head to the left, as if trying to look over her shoulder. The young woman bent to lift her out of the cradle, burying her face in the baby's neck before kissing her soundly on the cheek. When the baby laughed out loud, Jack smiled.

"She laughed," he said, knowing he must sound stupid in light of the baby's obviously amused state.

"Violeta is a very happy baby."

The woman turned the child in her arms so that Violeta was facing Jack fully. Immediately, the baby fixed him with a gaze so intent, he had to fight off a squirm. Her eyes were a strange mixture of blue and green and gray, with incredibly long, dark lashes. She stared at him without blinking for some time, and for a moment, he got the odd sensation that Violeta knew what he had asked Sybil to do to their child so many months ago, knew that he was in no way happy about the arrival of another baby—his own baby—into the world. Then she smiled at him, a wide, genuinely delighted smile, and he felt relief wash over him.

"*Mira,* she likes you," the woman said with a chuckle. "You must have children of your own."

"No," Jack replied quickly. "No, I don't have kids."

She nodded as if in understanding, but he was certain she didn't understand at all. "It takes a long time sometimes," she told him. "My husband Arturo and I, we waited a long time for Violeta. We lost our first baby before it was born. It was a very difficult time for us."

Jack didn't ponder the intimacy of the woman's revelation. He had learned long ago that the people of Puerto Rico were generally gregarious and inclined to conversation, even of a personal nature. "You lost it?" he asked. "How?"

"I do not know the English word for it," she told him. "But I was pregnant for only eleven weeks when it happened. It was very sudden. And it was a very long time before I got over it. I do not think people realize how much you love a baby as soon as you know it is there."

Oblivious to the tragic subject of the conversation, Violeta let out a piercing squeal and then laughed. She moved her arms vigorously up and down, then extended them toward Jack.

The young woman laughed, too. "She likes you very much. Would you like to hold her?"

"No!" Jack replied quickly. "I mean, thanks, but, I've never been around kids much, and I wouldn't know how to hold her."

"It is easy. I will show you."

"No!"

She smiled at him again, probably mistaking his adamant refusal as simple fear that he would harm the baby in some way. "Okay. I understand. My Arturo was scared to hold her at first, too. Fathers, I think, have many more worries with their children than mothers do. It is only natural."

Jack bobbled his head up and down quickly. "Uh, I really do have to get going."

"But don't you need to buy some things?"

"I, uh, I just remembered an appointment. I've got to run. I'll just come back tomorrow."

"Ah, you are living in the neighborhood?"

He backed slowly toward the door, his eyes never leaving those of the baby. "Yeah, I just moved in up the street about a month ago."

"Well, welcome to the neighborhood. Violeta and I will look forward to your visits."

"Great," Jack said as he stumbled back through the door. "See you."

He squinted at the sunlight outside and turned back toward his apartment. But the idea of returning there held no appeal, and he turned again, in the opposite direction. That way led back to the base, but there was little reason for him to go there now that his workday was ended. Turning forty-five degrees to his left pointed him in the direction of Club Nautico, where *Errukine* was berthed, and he wondered why he had pivoted that way.

So Jack turned once again and found himself staring out at San Juan Harbor, the blue waters sparkling as if someone had scattered diamonds on their surface. That was where he belonged, he told himself. Out on the ocean. But even as the thought formed, he couldn't make it stay. The call of the high seas didn't seem to be as loud as it had been before, back when he had been planning to rise to the challenge with Sybil. Faced with doing so alone now, the prospect held little of the allure it once had.

He stood for a long time on the sidewalk outside the market, trying to decide in which direction to go. Finally, he chose the one that would take him to Rico's. At least there he would be among friends and compadres, he thought. At least there he could get a good, stiff drink.

And right now, for some reason, that seemed to hold as much appeal as anything.

Unfortunately, he had forgotten about Natalie Brannon working there. She glared at him when he entered as if he were a walking, talking piece of the devil's work. When he sat down at the end of the bar that was farthest away from her, she took her time in approaching him. She was talking to that friend of Nick's, the one from RCC—Reuben something, Jack thought the guy's name was—and she made sure she finished her conversation before she came down to take Jack's order.

"I'll have a draft," he told her.

She nodded but said nothing more, placing the beer on the bar before him with a resolute thump. Some of the frothy head sloshed over the side, but she didn't bother to wipe up the spill. Instead, she only glared at him some more.

"Nick says you've got an apartment now," she said finally.

Jack nodded. "In Old San Juan. Skipper threw me off the cutter. Got tired of my wet panty hose hanging in the head all the time." He ventured a smile, but Natalie was clearly not in a joking mood.

"Have you told Sybil?" she asked him.

"She knows where I am. Baxter told her."

"So someone else had to let her know where you were. What if she'd needed to get in touch with you?"

"She's been in touch with me."

"Then you know about the bad spells she's had with the baby this past month."

Jack abruptly pulled the mug away from his lips, and a dribble of beer trickled down his chin. He swiped it away with his hand and took a swallow, then placed the mug back on the bar, hoping his hand wasn't shaking as badly as he felt it was. "What bad spells?"

Natalie frowned at him. "You don't know? She's had some pains on a couple of occasions. She won't admit it, but I think she's been scared there's something wrong with the baby."

"Has she been to the doctor about it?"

"No, she hasn't mentioned it to him. She's read that cramps are normal in pregnancy, but I can tell she's scared anyway."

Jack consumed another hefty swallow of his beer. "So?" he finally forced himself to say afterward.

"So?" she repeated. "*So?* Is that all you can say?"

"Look, Natalie, what's going on between me and Sybil is none of your business."

"Sybil is my friend," she countered. "That makes it my business."

"Well, what Sybil does now is none of *my* business, then."

"She's still your wife."

"She sure doesn't act like it."

Natalie crossed her arms over her chest and studied him carefully. "Did you know she found out the sex of the baby when the doctor did amniocentesis?"

Jack told himself he didn't want to know anything more about Sybil or her baby. Nevertheless, the fingers wrapped around his mug closed over it more fiercely, because he knew if he didn't hold tight, Natalie would see his hand trembling. Still, he said nothing, convinced that he didn't care.

"It's a girl," she went on. "And all the tests came back okay. She's a perfectly healthy little girl."

A great gust of air left Jack's lungs in a long *whoosh*. A girl. A daughter. He recalled Violeta, the way the baby had laughed and smiled and reached out to him. For a moment, he couldn't reply, and when he did, his voice was quiet and not a little unsteady. "That's good. Sybil should be pleased about that."

"I'd think you would be, too."

He lifted his shoulders in what might have been a shrug. "Doesn't make any difference to me."

Natalie shook her head. "Yeah, I should have figured."

She said nothing further, and Jack was relieved that she decided to let it go. He wished he could put it all out of his mind as easily. He wished the last three months of his life had never happened at all.

He closed his eyes to dispel any lingering thoughts of Sybil. But what he found himself seeing instead was infinitely more disturbing: a baby girl with his auburn hair and Sybil's blue eyes. And try as he might to make the image change, it only grew clearer instead. The infant studied him intently, laughed and smiled, then held out her arms to her father.

Jack jumped up from his stool so abruptly, it fell with a clatter onto the floor behind him. Without picking it up, and without paying for his beer, he stalked out of the bar, completely forgetting the drink he had thought he needed.

18

Dear Mom and Dad,

No, everything with me and Nick is going great. I can't imagine what I could have said to give you the impression that there was something wrong. Really, things have never been better between us . . .

Natalie awoke with a start and stared into the darkness surrounding her, trying to still her ragged breathing, licking the sweat from above her lip. She lifted a trembling hand to her forehead as she tried to remember what she had been dreaming about to cause such a reaction. But when she did manage to recall—all too vividly—she closed her eyes again, squeezing them tight to banish the images replaying in her mind. It had been a dream like none she'd ever dreamed before, a dream she wasn't likely to forget anytime soon. In it, she had been with a man, hot and naked and tangled up in sheets, doing things she had scarcely even considered doing with any man before. Unfortunately, the man in question hadn't been her husband. The man had been her husband's best friend.

She rolled over quickly and surveyed the slumbering form beside her. "Nick," she said, poking him as she did so to rouse him more quickly. "Nick, wake up."

He groaned and grumbled, but turned onto his back. In the dim light that filtered through the blinds from the casino spots outside, she saw his eyelids flutter open. He sighed deeply before closing them again.

"Don't go back to sleep," she said, scooting closer to him, flattening her hand against his jaw to turn his face toward hers.

"What?" he mumbled, opening his eyes again. "What is it? What's wrong?"

"I had a bad dream."

In the darkness, she wasn't sure if he was sympathetic to her concern or not. "About what?" he asked as he rubbed his eyes sleepily.

She shook her head. "It doesn't matter. Just hold me for a little while. Please?"

He sighed again, opened his arms to her, and Natalie snuggled close. She lay her head against his chest, listening to the steady *thump-thump-thump* of his heart, and tried to match her still unsteady breathing to his more leisurely respiration. Slowly, gradually, the pounding of her own heart lessened, and she was able to put a little distance between herself and her dream.

"Is that better?" Nick asked quietly. He stroked her

head, bunching her hair in his fist before dropping his
hand lower to caress her back.

She nodded. "Mm-hm."

"Do you want to talk about it?"

"No."

"Are you sure?"

"Yes. Just hold me."

"Okay."

He settled his arms around her, cupping his hands
at the small of her back, and Natalie felt a little better.
For a long time she simply lay quietly, recalling other
occasions when he had held her this way, and trying to
forget she had ever met Reuben Channing. She
wanted to tell Nick she loved him, wanted to hear him
say the words back to her. But for some reason she
remained silent instead, wondering why she would be
dreaming about one man when she was certain she
loved another.

It didn't make sense, she thought. Nothing about
Reuben made sense. Nick was her husband, the man
with whom she had fallen irrevocably in love, the man
with whom she had chosen to spend the rest of her
life. She had made a promise to love him always. But
more than that, she had made plans. Plans for a future
with him—for a home, for children, for old age.

Since nearly the day she had met him, she had
spent hours at a time visualizing what her life with
Nick Brannon would be like. She had known backward and forward how the two of them would be
together. How they would spend their days, where
they would vacation, when they would start a family,
where they would move when they retired. Secretly,
she had even named their children. And although she
knew she shouldn't expect things to be falling per-

fectly into place scarcely nine months after marrying, already Natalie's plans were beginning to unravel.

Unwillingly, she thought again of Reuben. He was a man ten years her senior, with whom she shared little in common, and who sometimes infuriated her. He had been married and divorced twice, had never stayed in one place for very long, and until the Coast Guard had never held a job for much longer. With him, she could imagine no future, no children, and certainly no retirement. She wasn't even sure she *wanted* to imagine such things with him. Reuben Channing represented at best a temporary distraction potentially unlike anything else she'd ever known, but with no guarantee of security, happiness, or fulfillment. And at worst, he could wreck her marriage.

Natalie curled her fingers over Nick's heart and listened to him breathe. Maybe it wasn't in truth Reuben himself that pulled at her so fiercely, she thought. Perhaps it was simply what Reuben represented. Something completely at odds with what she had found with her husband—what she had thought she wanted from life. Reuben lived in a way she had never considered for herself before—a way that was unpredictable, unmapped, uncertain. A way that was different. Something she had never thought she wanted. Until now.

"Nick, don't say anything, just listen to me," she said quietly. "There's something I have to tell you, but I don't want you to take it the wrong way, so just think about it before you respond."

She felt his arms relax around her. When he said nothing in reply, she continued, "This dream I just had, I think it was a warning of some kind. I'm worried about things. About us. Something's happening to us—or at least to me—and I'm not sure what it is. I mean, look at us. We haven't even been married a year and we fight like two old warriors. We hardly ever just talk anymore. We're not even wearing our wedding bands."

When still he said nothing, she added, "I just think we should stop for a minute and reevaluate our relationship, talk about what we want, what we need, what we expect from each other. There's something wrong in a marriage when a woman has a dream like I just had. A dream about . . . about . . . about a man who isn't her husband."

She halted, waiting to see what Nick's reaction would be. When he remained silent, she held her breath, chewed her lip, and decided to be more specific. "A dream about her husband's best friend," she added quickly.

Still, Nick did not react to her revelation. She wondered if he was angry beyond speech or doing as she'd requested and thinking about what she'd told him. For a long moment she didn't move, just continued to press her face against his chest to listen to the steady rhythm of his pulse. Finally, when she could tolerate his silence no longer, she tipped her head back to look at him. His head was listing to the side on his pillow, and his eyes were closed. She realized then that he had fallen asleep some time ago and had not heard a word of what she'd said.

For some reason, Natalie felt the bizarre urge to laugh. But instead, she only lay motionless in her husband's arms, oblivious to the warm tears that dampened her face and his chest.

❖   ❖   ❖

"Natalie! Natalie, are you home?"

Natalie started at the sound of her name rising on a shout from Ashford Avenue below. Before she even arrived at the window she knew who she would find down there summoning her, but she still gazed warily at Reuben when she saw him. He was standing on the opposite street corner, hands settled impatiently on his hips, looking worried about something.

Her dream of the night before was still fresh in her mind, and she hadn't yet recovered a feeling of rightness or normalcy since she had awakened from it. Nick hadn't seemed to notice her withdrawal that morning as he'd made himself ready for work, but she supposed that wasn't surprising. She seldom rose to join him in the morning. Why should today have been any different?

"I need to talk to you!" Reuben called out. "Can I come up?"

Her instincts told her to refuse him, but Natalie found herself nodding instead and gesturing toward her front door. When she saw him bolt across the street, she made her way slowly across the living room, punched her thumb reluctantly against the button to unlock the security door downstairs, and sat on the edge of the sofa to await his arrival. She didn't have to wait long. At his quick knock, she rose and opened the front door, taking a step backward to keep from touching him as he strode past her. The front door latch seemed to click ominously in the otherwise silent room as she closed the door behind him.

"What did you need to tell me?" she asked without preamble.

He spun around to face her. "I went to Rico's, but they told me you were off today. I—"

He halted as quickly as he had begun and simply

stared at her. She could see that he definitely had
something on his mind, and she wasn't sure she
wanted to know any more about it. Nevertheless, she
ventured, "Reuben? What is it?"

He drew himself up more fully, met her gaze evenly,
and tried again. "I just . . . I can't . . ." He ran a hand
through his hair and muttered, "Dammit, this is ridicu-
lous. I feel like I'm in seventh grade." He paused, then
tried again. "Look, Natalie, the fact is . . . what I need
to talk to you about . . . what I need to tell you is that . . .
I can't stop thinking about you. About us. I've been
having these unbelievable dreams about us, and I . . ."
"I just can't stop thinking about you," he said again.

A month had passed since the night he had kissed
her that third time, the time when he had not caught
her off guard, and she had allowed him to complete
the action. But just as before, neither had spoken of
the kiss afterward. Natalie had almost begun to think
she had imagined the whole episode. Almost.

Yet she hadn't quite been able to keep her thoughts
of Reuben at bay, either. She had been thinking about
that night, too, lately, about that kiss, and about what
might have happened if she had let him stay with her
that night as he had wanted.

"You should leave," she said, reaching for the door-
knob again. "And we should both forget you came
over today."

He took a step toward her. "No, wait. Just hear me
out. There's something here, Natalie, something
between us. I don't know what it is or why it's happening. Nick's my best friend—I can't forget that—and
you're his wife. But God help me, I can't stop thinking
about making love to you. I can't stop thinking about
what it would be like with us. Together."

What it would be like with them together, she repeated to herself. Hadn't she also been spending a lot of time lately wondering about that? Yet somehow, she couldn't help but believe that the two of them had been thinking about entirely different possibilities. Was Reuben thinking about how they would be together in a lifelong experience that included every facet of existence? Or simply what kind of sparks they would generate during a sexual encounter that might or might not ever be repeated?

"And I've seen the way you look at me," he continued when she didn't reply. "I've felt the way you respond to me. You're every bit as curious as I am about the two of us. You've been wondering, too."

"Yeah, I have," she told him, the words drawn from her almost unwillingly. "But wondering and doing are two totally different things. I'm married to Nick, not you. I *love* Nick, not you. You can't expect me to just forget that for a little while so we can go exploring this . . . this *curiosity* we have. Because curiosity is all it is. There's nothing more to it than that."

He sighed, clearly agitated. "Are you so sure about that? Because I'm not."

"And what's that supposed to mean?"

He inhaled another deep breath, released it slowly, and stared at her intently. "I'm not just saying this off the top of my head—I've given it a lot of thought. I was attracted to you the minute I met you at Booker's party. But you're Nick's wife, so I just shrugged off the feeling and tried to let it go. But it wouldn't go. And as time has passed, it's turned into something else. There's more to what I feel for you than an idle attaction. Natalie, I . . . I think I might be falling in love with you."

She chuckled nervously. "Oh, Reuben, get real. That's—"

"No, I mean it. I know it sounds crazy. Hell, you're my best friend's *wife*. And you're just a kid, for Christ's sake. But I . . . I *feel* things for you that I've never felt before. And I can't just forget about it."

"Well, you're going to have to forget about it. Because I don't have feelings for you—not important, 'til-death-do-us-part feelings anyway. Besides, Nick and I are getting along better than ever. I'd be nuts if I did anything to jeopardize what I have with him."

Reuben eyed her thoughtfully. "You sure haven't been acting like a woman who's getting along with her husband better than ever."

"I beg your pardon?"

He approached her slowly, leaning in close as he said, "You don't even wear your wedding band anymore."

"I told you that's because—"

"And not too long ago, you were standing right here in your dark apartment, kissing another man as if you meant to devour him alive."

Her heart rate picked up speed at the gravelly tone of his voice. "I think you have that backward," she said quietly. "I think it was you who was trying to devour me."

"Okay, so we were intent on consuming each other. That still doesn't seem to me the behavior of a happily married woman."

Natalie had nowhere to focus her gaze except on Reuben, who was watching her now as if he had every intention of ravishing her on the spot. Her pulse quickened even more. "I am, too, happily married," she insisted. But she sounded unconvincing, even to herself.

"Natalie . . ."

She covered her ears with her hands with the hope of silencing him. "This isn't happening," she said as she hastened to the only other room in the apartment—the bedroom—in an effort to escape. "This can't possibly be happening."

When Reuben followed her, she pivoted around, intending to push past him to retreat to the living room again. But he caught her by the wrist and pulled her back toward himself, preventing her from fleeing.

"Don't," he said softly. "Don't be like that."

"Like what?"

He lifted his hand to her face, cupping her jaw in his rough palm. When she tried to pull away, he tangled his fingers in the hair at her nape and cradled her head firmly in his hands. "Don't try to deny your feelings," he told her.

She uttered a sigh that was a combination of confusion and frustration. "Don't deny them?" she said as a fierce longing shook her. "How can I deny them when I don't even know what my feelings are anymore?"

He dipped his head to hers and kissed her, brushing his lips gently over hers in a whisper of a caress. Natalie let him do it simply because she was too tired to turn him away. Something did stir inside her at his touch, but whether she was aroused by his nearness or simply reacting to something inside herself, she wasn't quite sure. Nevertheless she only stood still as he continued to ply her mouth with his, knowing what she was doing was wrong, but somehow helpless to keep it from happening.

She could only imagine how their embrace must have looked to Nick when he rounded the bedroom door and found her there with Reuben. She only knew that one minute, she was nearly lost in her confusing emotions, and the next, her husband was yanking her back with a less-than-gentle tug on her shoulder.

"What the hell is going on here?" Nick shouted as he glared at her. "What the hell are you doing?"

"Nick," she said breathlessly, wiping her hand over her mouth as if the gesture would remove any incriminating remnants of the kiss. "It's not what you think."

"Oh, yes, it is," Reuben countered. "It's exactly what you think."

She gaped at him, startled by his statement, then realized she shouldn't be shocked to discover that she would be getting anything but help from him. "No, it isn't," she said.

Nick stared at his wife, shaking his head in disbelief. "I don't think you want to know what I'm thinking right now," he told her. To Reuben, he simply said, "You . . . you're supposed to be my best friend. I know I asked you to keep an eye on her, but this . . ."

Reuben held up a hand as if trying to ward off a blow. "Nick, I—"

"And *you*," he continued, ignoring the other man to turn to his wife again. "You . . . you . . ." He laughed, a sound that was anything but joyful. "Just how long have you been screwing my best friend?"

"It's not what you think," she repeated miserably. "It's not what it looks like. We haven't—"

"It looks to me exactly like what I think it is."

Natalie opened her mouth to explain, realized she had no idea how to go about doing that, and closed it again. She turned to Reuben. "You should go," she told him.

"I'm not going anywhere until we get this settled," he said.

"This is between me and Nick."

"Oh, no, it's not," Nick said. "I'd say this involves the three of us."

"No, it doesn't," Natalie insisted. "This has nothing to do with Reuben."

"I come home for lunch to find you and my best friend about to tumble into bed together, and you say it doesn't involve him?"

"No, it doesn't. Because we weren't about to tumble into bed together."

"Oh, yes, we were," Reuben said. "Nick, there's something you should know about me and your wife."

"Hey, I think I've got it figured out just fine, Reuben. I don't need you to paint a picture, all right?"

"Stop it," Natalie said. "Both of you. Neither one of you has a clue about what's going on here." Her horror at being caught in a compromising position was fast turning into anger. She doubled her hands into fists and studied both men. "You guys are so damned blind. You can't think of anything but yourselves. This really has nothing to do with either one of you. It has to do with me. *Me.*"

As both men simply stared at her in silence, she felt more exhausted than she ever had in her life. "Reuben, you go home. Nick and I need to talk."

"I told you, I'm not going—"

"Go home," she repeated firmly.

He looked as if he were going to object again, but he said nothing more. Natalie and Nick watched in silence as he went to the front door.

"It isn't settled between us, Natalie," Reuben said as he left. "Not by a long shot."

And with that, he was gone, and she was left alone with her husband. Left to explain something she didn't understand herself. She lifted a hand to cover her eyes, unable to bear Nick's expression of absolute betrayal.

"First off," she began, "let me correct Reuben. Anything that might have been going on between him and me is definitely settled."

Nick crossed the room and slumped down onto the sofa. "So you admit you've been having an affair with him."

She moved to join him, but when she did, he stood and took his seat in the chair opposite her, clearly wanting to put distance between them. She shook her head morosely, then stared at the ceiling. "No, we haven't been having an affair. But I . . . I do think about him sometimes. And I wonder about what it would be like with him."

"So you decided to find out this afternoon, right?"

"That wasn't what was happening when you found us."

"Oh? And just what was happening when I found you? You sure as hell weren't playing Parcheesi."

"Reuben was telling me—" She supposed it probably wouldn't be a good idea to tell her husband that his best friend had told her that he was falling in love with her. Nevertheless, this probably wasn't a good time to lie to Nick, either. "He said he thought he was in love with me, and he was just trying to convince me of that."

"My best friend was telling my wife he's in love with her."

"Yes."

"And you were probably eating it up, weren't you?"

"No, Nick, I—"

"You wouldn't have gone to bed with him just now if I hadn't shown up?"

She thought for a moment before responding. "I don't think so."

"You don't *think* so? You're not sure?"

She shook her head again. "I don't know what would have happened, Nick. I've been so confused lately."

"Confused? That's a strange word for it."

She began to feel angry again, though she could no longer identify who the target of that anger was. Maybe Reuben. And maybe Nick, too. But mostly, she decided, she was angry at herself. "Yeah, well, confusion is exactly what it is."

He studied her for a long time without commenting. Finally, he asked, "Is this the first time something like this has happened?"

"No."

"You've . . . kissed him before?"

She hesitated a moment before replying, "He's kissed me. It's happened a couple of times. That day we spent together sightseeing was the first."

"This has been going on that long?"

"Well, not constantly, and not the way you think, but . . . it all started back in May."

"What happened?"

"I'm not sure. We were having a good time that day, but nothing seemed out of the ordinary. At dinner, I talked about how much I missed you when you were gone, about how we had joked that Puerto Rico was supposed to have been our extended honeymoon. I told Reuben that the day I'd just spent with him was what a honeymoon should feel like. Except of course for the glaring fact that my husband wasn't with me. Then he walked me back to the apartment and suddenly . . ." She shrugged. "Suddenly everything changed."

Nick thought about that for a moment. Natalie fancied she could almost see his brain cells churning as they digested the information she had just offered him. She was about to say more, but he looked at her intently and asked, "That day when you wanted to go to El Morro and shopping and everything with me?"

"Yes?"

"I've always had the feeling there was more to that than just your wanting to spend a day away from the apartment. That was a test of some kind for me, wasn't it?"

She nodded. "In a way, yeah. I guess it was."

"So, how'd I do?"

She smiled sadly. "Not too well. Then again, I don't suppose I made much of a passing grade, either."

When he didn't comment, she added, "All I've ever wanted was for us to do things together and be happy as a couple. But you're gone so much of the time that when you are home, we always seem to overcompensate for being apart so long. We wind up spending most of our time in bed or arguing about being separated. I wanted us to be happy together. I wanted things to be more romantic. Instead, it all just feels so routine. Even our lovemaking has become predictable. I mean, here we are living in these incredibly romantic surroundings, Nick, but there's no romance in our lives at all."

A moment passed, and Natalie wondered if Nick had heard or understood anything she had said. Finally, he asked, "So you fantasize about having sex with Reuben?"

"Sometimes," she said softly.

"Did you ever do that with me?"

She nodded. "Before we were married."

"But you haven't lately?"

"No, not lately."

"Why not?"

"I wish I could tell you that, but the truth is, I don't know."

"Tell me again that you haven't slept with him."

"I haven't slept with him. I swear it."

"Then what's the matter? What's gone wrong?"

"I don't know," she repeated. "Things between you and me . . . they're just not what they should be, not what they're supposed to be."

"I thought everything was fine."

She looked at him squarely as she asked, "Are you happy, Nick? I mean completely happy?"

"I was until this afternoon."

"Well, I'm not. Not completely."

"But why not?"

Tears filled Natalie's eyes when she realized she didn't have an answer for that question, either. How could she tell him what she wanted when she couldn't identify that herself? How could she explain her sadness when she didn't know the source of it? How was she supposed to describe the emptiness she felt inside when she didn't know what it was that had been taken from her?

"I don't know why I'm unhappy," she finally said. "I just know there's something wrong. It isn't a question of wanting Reuben over you. It's about missing something inside of me. Things with us . . . they just aren't what they used to be, aren't what I thought they'd be. I'm not sure what I want anymore. Nothing is making any sense. I—" She choked back a sob before concluding, "I think you and I should be apart for a while. Until I figure all this out."

He leapt up from his chair and in three quick strides he stood over her, glaring. "Until *you* figure it all out?" he demanded. "What about *me*? What about *my* feelings? You're not the only one who has a say in this marriage, Natalie. This isn't just about you. There's two of us now. Don't be so goddamned selfish."

"Selfish?" she cried, rising to her feet, as well. "Here I am all torn up inside over this, and you're calling me selfish?"

"You're damned right I am. You forgot awfully fast that we're married now and that there are two of us who are going to be affected by this. Of course things are going to change after you get married. They're supposed to. Quit whining about being unhappy. You can't use that as an excuse to go running off. If something's wrong, we should be facing it together. But if you're so willing to just write me off and dwell on yourself, then maybe you're right. Maybe we do need to be apart."

He moved quickly after that, packing a few meager belongings in the bag he took along when underway. "You know, when Jack walked out on Sybil, I was so pissed off at him. I couldn't imagine anything that would make a man want to be away from his wife. But now I think I understand. You women just get so wrapped up in yourselves, you never stop to think about what you're doing to us guys."

"That's not it at all, Nick, I—"

"You want romance, Natalie? Well, romance isn't something you can keep up forever. Not in the way you mean anyway. It changes, too, just like everything else does when you get married. And it means something different to everyone. Romance is what you make it. *I*, at least, thought we had plenty of it. But you and I obviously have different ideas about romance. So, you're right. We probably shouldn't be together."

Faced with the reality of what she had suggested and what was about to happen, Natalie felt the first tremors of panic. "Nick, that's not true! Look, don't go. You're right. We should stay here and talk this out. We're married now. We have to face this kind of stuff together."

"No way, Nat. You're too caught up in your own feelings and too quick to forget about mine." He picked up his bag and reached for the front door. Turning slightly to look at her askance, he added, "And dammit, I won't lie in bed at night and wonder if you're lying next to me, thinking about Reuben."

"But I won't be thinking about Reuben anymore."

His expression told her he didn't believe her.

"It's true! I told you this wasn't about Reuben, it's about me."

"Yeah, and now it's about me, too," he said as he tugged the door open and stepped into the hall. "Now I'm unhappy. Now I'm confused. Now I'm the one who's not so sure about things."

"Nick, don't—"

Deliberately, he punched the button to rouse the elevator. And desperately, Natalie tried again.

"Don't go," she repeated. "I made a mistake."

"Yeah, you did," Nick agreed as the elevator doors opened before him. "And I'm beginning to think I made a mistake, too. A whopper. The minute I asked you to marry me."

She watched helplessly as the metal doors folded before him and left her alone, then she covered her face with her hands. What had she done? Natalie wondered wildly. Oh, God, what had she done?

19

Dear Mom and Dad,

Another quick question about pregnancy: have they ever figured out what it is that makes women sick? Is it hormones or something? Or is it just because of the way other people react to you . . . ?

　　　Sybil lay on the settee in the main cabin with her arm thrown over her eyes and cried with all her might. She had never felt so devastated, so alone, so empty in all her life. Dropping her hand to her belly, she cried some more. Catch knelt on the floor beside her, holding her other hand and patting it slowly.

"You're okay, Sybil," he said softly. "The baby's okay. Dr. Juncos said so, right?"

She nodded, but her fingers gripped his hand hard.

"He said according to the latest ultrasound, the baby is fat and healthy and everything is fine."

"And you've been feeling her moving around a lot, right?"

Sybil nodded again. "She's been dancing around as if Tito Puente himself were playing 'Lady of Spain.'"

"Then you shouldn't be worrying about the baby."

"I'm not worrying about the baby."

"What then? For the past month, you've been moping around like every day is your last one on earth. You've got to stop feeling so anxious. It's not good for you or the baby."

"I'm not anxious. Not anymore. Not about the baby anyway."

"The pain then? Are you still worrying about what happened after you visited Jack a while back? The doctor explained what caused that, right?"

She nodded, but continued to stare off into space. "He said it was probably bowel related," she recited. "That the hormones of pregnancy do funny things to the digestive system. He told me to drink more water, eat whole grain products, and consume at least five servings of fruits and vegetables everyday. If that doesn't help, he said I should try a natural fiber supplement." The fingers over her womb curled into a fist. "I'm lying there on the ground, scared senseless that I'm about to lose my baby, and it turns out I'm just having a bad spell with gas."

He chuckled. "Hey, it happens to the best of us." He reached out and covered the hand over her abdomen with his own. "Look, everything is going perfectly according to plan. You're fine, the baby's fine. So why are you still so upset?"

Sybil sat up on the settee, folded her elbows onto

her knees, and dropped her head into her hands. She began to cry more freely. "Because I can't forget about that day I went to see Jack. I can't forget about what happened when I felt that pain in my belly. When I was lying there on the sidewalk frightened out of my mind that something was happening to my baby, I realized something that terrified me even more."

"What's that?"

She didn't answer right away. She still didn't like to think about that afternoon. About Jack rejecting her again, about her fear that something was terribly wrong with the baby, about what she had realized about herself as a result. Finally, she lifted her head from her hands and studied Catch levelly.

"As I was lying there waiting for that woman to get help," she said softly, "all I could think about was the baby. About what I would do without her. About how empty my life would be if I lost her."

"So?"

She sniffled, palming her eyes to fend off the tears that came again so readily. "So what I *didn't* think about was Jack. Not for a moment. Not even once. After it was all over, after I talked to Dr. Juncos and he reassured me that the baby was okay, it occurred to me how absent Jack had been from my thoughts." She began to cry freely once again as she concluded, "And then I realized that could only be because this baby has come to mean more to me than he does. And nothing has ever meant more to me than Jack."

Catch said nothing, but moved up to sit beside her, dropping a hand around her shoulder. He held her while she cried, rubbed her arms reassuringly, and went to retrieve a box of Kleenex when the one she wadded up in her fist became little more than a crumpled piece of lint.

He held a fresh tissue to her nose and instructed her quietly, "Blow."

She obeyed without questioning in the way a toddler would its mother.

"Better?" he asked.

She nodded. He handed her the box of tissues, and returned to his seat beside her.

"Under the circumstances," he said, "I don't think it's strange that you would be putting the baby first and foremost in your mind, even before thoughts of your husband. Jack hasn't exactly been much of a husband to you, lately, anyway."

Sybil shook her head. "No, you don't understand. What Jack and I have—had—is unique. We always came first to each other, over everything. Our jobs, our families . . . even *Errukine* was a distant second to the obligations we had to each other. A baby shouldn't change that. Even if Jack is acting like an idiot right now, I should still be worrying about setting things right with him before worrying about the baby."

"That's nuts, Sybil, and you know it. When you're doubled up on the sidewalk in pain like that, of course you're going to be more concerned about your baby."

"But there should have been some thought about Jack, too," she insisted. "I should have wondered about the repercussions of this on him."

"No, you shouldn't. Stop being so hard on yourself. You haven't done anything wrong here. You're the wounded party, not Jack."

She shook her head vehemently. "No, Jack is the wounded party. I betrayed him by getting pregnant in the first place, and now it's as if I'm more than ready to turn my back on him in favor of the baby."

Catch jumped up and took her shoulders in his hands. "Listen to yourself. If Jack was saying these things to you, you'd defend yourself to the end. But it's okay for you to berate yourself, is that it?"

Sybil stared at the tissue she twisted in her hands, wanting to deny what he said. Nevertheless, she couldn't quite shake the notion that she was the one who had messed things up. If only she'd told Jack they couldn't make love that night. If only she'd explained the state of things with him, had asked him to hang on for a minute while she ran out for some spermacidal jelly. Of course, that late on Christmas Eve, there wouldn't have been any stores open, and they had gone more than two weeks without seeing each other. . . . But if she had just told him there was a chance she could get pregnant, and if they'd gone ahead and made love anyway, then he *would* be as responsible for the baby as she.

"Catch?" she asked quietly.

"Yes?"

"Have you ever been married?"

Sybil was surprised to realize how very little she knew about him. He had been berthed in the slip next to theirs when she and Jack had first come to Club Nautico, and the two men had quickly become friends. Somewhere along the line, Catch had become a regular guest at dinner when he was in port, and the three of them often went out together. Despite that, their conversations seldom covered personal subjects, and Sybil was hard-pressed now to figure out why.

"Why do you ask?" he wanted to know.

She shrugged. "I don't know."

He sighed, a thoughtful sound, and ran a ruddy hand through his hair. "No, I've never been married."

"Have you ever come close?"

"No."

"Why not? Never been in love?"

"Oh, I've been in love."

His voice was tight when he made the comment, and Sybil began to wish she had never started this conversation.

"I've just never thought about marriage," he finally concluded. "I don't think I'm the marrying type. You, uh . . . you having second thoughts about it?"

Instead of replying one way or the other, she said, "You know, I honestly thought Jack would be home by now. I thought he'd take off and be steamed at me for a few weeks, and I knew things wouldn't be easy once he got back, but I did think he would have come home by now. He's never done anything like this before."

"He's never had to face the prospect of fatherhood before, either."

"The baby isn't what's really bothering him, though," Sybil said.

"No?"

She shook her head. "It's not even the fact that we're not going to be able to sail around the world together now."

"Then what's the problem?"

"It's me. Jack thinks I betrayed him. Anything else, he could deal with. He could get over it. But that . . ." She sighed deeply, sadly. "I guess I was kidding myself when I thought he'd get over that. I don't guess he'll ever come back."

"He'll come back," Catch told her.

"How do you know?"

"Because he loves you."

Sybil tried to smile, lifted a hand to his face, then dropped it back to her lap. "Sometimes love isn't enough."

"At the risk of sounding like a romantic—something I assure you I most certainly am not—love, true love, is always enough, Sybil. Don't ever forget that."

She studied his face for a long time, noting the deep lines grooving his lips and eyes, eyes that told her he was absolutely convinced of what he had just told her. She wished she could believe him, wished she could feel as confident of Jack's return as Catch seemed to be. Instead, she only felt more defeated.

"Oh, Catch," she said quietly. "What am I going to do?"

"I'd say you've done just about all you can do. It's up to Jack now. He'll come around, Sybil, I know he will. He's just a stubborn man. It might take him some time, but he'll do the right thing. I'm sure of it."

She emitted a doubtful sound. "Well, that makes one of us."

"Come on, let's get off the boat for a while. Let me buy you some dinner. You name the restaurant. I'll treat."

She smiled up at him. "That's awfully sweet of you, but you don't have to."

He smiled back, reaching a hand out toward her. "I know. But I insist."

She rose a bit unsteadily, leaned on him for support, and sighed. "You're a good guy, Catch. I don't know why some woman hasn't snatched you up and carried you off into the sunset by now."

"Many have tried," he assured her.

"But none have held on long, is that it?"

He shook his head. "It gets complicated."

"That it does," she agreed.

When they climbed out of the cockpit and onto the dock, she linked her arm through his. Not far up the pier, they encountered a group of sport fishermen who had just returned from their day's adventure with a four-hundred pound marlin in tow. The once majestic fish, more than twice the size of Sybil, now dangled from a scale, its formerly rich blue flesh having faded to a dull gray in the bright, killing sunlight. The black eyes were flat and lifeless, and the mouth was slightly parted, as if it had died trying to reason with the people who had reeled it in. The four men responsible for the feat stood around the big fish cheering, downing beer and slapping each other on the back in congratulations.

Sybil stood for a long time staring at the scene, recalling a time when she and Jack had sailed *Errukine* from St. Thomas to San Juan. They had seen a marlin on that trip, had watched it leap from the ocean in an arc of sparkling water over and over again. She'd never seen a big fish behave in such a way before, nor had she witnessed such a sight since. She remembered asking Jack why the marlin would do something like that. Jack had shrugged and said probably because it was fun.

Catch nudged her from behind and they began their approach toward the marlin again. As she drew nearer and passed along the fish's underside, Sybil realized its belly was distended and bloated. No, not *its* belly, she noted. *Her* belly. The marlin was female, she thought. And the marlin was pregnant. She knew it with every ounce of certainty she possessed. A shudder wound through her at the realization.

"What are you going to do with her?" she asked one of the men as she passed the group.

He looked at her as if she had spoken to him in a foreign language he couldn't understand, yet all were clearly American.

"Do with it?" he replied. "What do you think we're going to do with it? Gut it clean through and stuff it. Then hang it up in our waiting room. We're OB-GYNs," he added parenthetically. "We just opened a practice in Chicago. This will fit right in with our decor. Here—" He reached into one of the many pockets of his fishing vest and extracted a rumpled business card. "If you're in the windy city when it comes time to drop that bundle you're carrying . . ."

Sybil nodded and automatically reached for the card he extended toward her, but felt the bile rising in her throat. Before she could reply, the meager contents of her stomach revolted, and the next thing she knew, she was on her knees at the edge of the pier, vomiting into the water. Even after her insides were empty, dry heaves continued to wrack her body in spasms. Catch was right behind her, rubbing her back and making soothing noises, but she scarcely noticed him. All she could see was the marlin's swollen belly, its dead eyes and pallid skin. And all she could do was heave some more.

It was a crime, she thought, how pregnant women were treated these days.

20

Dear Mom and Dad,

The casinos here are fabulous! The decorators for these places must have gone to the same school as the one who did Aunt Camille's parlor—you know, the one you always thought was so tacky? Ever since that first night at the Condado Plaza, though, Nick will only let me play the nickel slots. It's amazing how high some of these people bet. Talk about taking chances . . .

Baxter stood at the casino entrance and scanned the cavernous room for the blackjack tables. The walls around him were scarlet, the carpeting beneath his feet a mixture of red and gold and green. At the center of the ceiling was a huge crystal chandelier that must have been fifty feet in diameter. The place was packed with bodies in every shape, size, and

color he could imagine. All around him, the steady
hum of slot machines droned like giant insects, interrupted frequently by shrill bells of alarm whenever
someone hit a jackpot. Voices rang out in a variety of
languages, in no way muffled by the pervasive haze
and aroma of cigar and cigarette smoke.

All in all, a pretty gaudy place, he thought. Not the
kind of environment he'd choose to work in himself.
Then again, he supposed if Carmen had a choice, she
probably wouldn't be working here, either.

He'd never been inside the casino where she was
employed. He'd always waited for her outside the
hotel, or had met her at the grill across the street.
Why he'd never taken an interest in her job before, he
couldn't say. And he couldn't understand what he was
doing here now, when he hadn't seen or spoken to her
for almost two months.

"Buy a girl a drink, mister?"

He heard the voice murmur in his ear at the same
time he felt the hand of its owner cupping his fanny.
He turned to find himself gazing up at a very beautiful face, a face heavily decorated with cosmetics and
adorned above by a platinum blond wig. A face he was
fairly certain did not belong to a woman.

He smiled as he removed the hand—larger than his
own—from his behind. "Maybe some other time.
Right now I'm looking for someone."

His companion smiled at him. In a deep, rumbling
baritone, she replied, "So am I. Aren't we all?"

"Yeah, well, like I said, maybe some other time."

She sighed dramatically and touched a finger to her
hair. "Well, if you don't find who you're looking for,
my name's Trixie. Just ask anyone. They all know me
here. You'll remember, right? Trixie?"

"I'll remember," Baxter promised. Boy, would he remember.

He shook his head as he watched her leave, marveling at the sway of her hips beneath the purple-sequined dress. He had never been able to figure out how a woman could walk in spike heels, let alone a man who probably weighed more than one-eighty in his panties and garter belt. Oh, well. The Condado was nothing if not interesting.

He strolled through the room for some time before he finally found the area where all the blackjack tables were grouped together. There were about a dozen in all, and he didn't see Carmen standing behind any of them. But he knew her schedule backward and forward, and Thursday was definitely one of her nights to work. She must be on a break, he reasoned. Surely she'd be back soon.

He found an empty seat at one of the tables, opting for one displaying a five-dollar minimum bet sign as opposed to a twenty- or fifty-dollar minimum. Pulling two twenties from his wallet, he pushed them across the table to the dealer and exchanged them for chips, then sat back to wait for Carmen's return.

He had been up by one hundred dollars at one point, but was down to his last two five-dollar chips when she finally appeared on the other side of the room. He watched her closely as she moved toward the tables. She lifted a hand in greeting and smiled at some of the other dealers as she passed. At one point she laughed at something a man said to her in Spanish, and she responded in the same language with something Baxter didn't understand, but which he thought definitely sounded flirtatious.

She didn't seem to be too miserable without him,

he thought. Although, as she drew nearer, she did seem kind of preoccupied about something.

She passed him without even noticing him and went to relieve one of the dealers at a fifty-dollar table. Great, he thought, pulling his wallet out again and inspecting the contents. Eleven dollars and chips totaling ten. He wouldn't even be able to sit at her table unless he had fifty bucks, and that would only last him one hand. Then he recalled how most of the casinos in San Juan were nice enough to provide ready-cash machines just outside their doors. If a person had a major credit card, a person could borrow cash against his balance all for a small transaction fee, and that small matter of inflated interest. Then a person could play blackjack all night.

Baxter knew he couldn't afford what he was going to do. But having thought a lot about Carmen over the past seven weeks, he wondered if he could afford not to.

Without thinking more about it, he pushed himself up off his stool and left the casino, returning fifteen minutes later with two hundred and fifty dollars in his wallet. All six seats at Carmen's table were taken, so he hung back and waited a while until one of the men got up. As soon as one did, Baxter slid onto the unoccupied seat. And then finally, finally, Carmen looked up.

"Baxter," she said softly when she saw him. "What are you doing here?"

He flexed his fingers and cracked his knuckles, and when he trusted his hands to remain steady, slid two one hundred dollar bills across the table.

"I need chips, please," he told her.

"But—"

"Yeah, gimme a couple hundred more, too, sweet cheeks," the man seated to his left said.

Baxter bristled at the way the man spoke to Carmen, but said nothing. Instead he held her gaze with his, marveling at how beautiful she was, amazed to realize he had missed her even more than he had thought.

Carmen had been staring at Baxter intently, but blinked at the other man's comments and rushed to accommodate his request. Then she exchanged Baxter's cash for chips and made sure the other players had what they needed. When everyone was settled, she dealt a hand, her gaze frequently darting up to meet Baxter's. She fumbled over the cards, in no way graceful about her dealing. Considering the fact that she had been doing this for years, he could only assume that the reason for her jitters was because of his presence at her table. He thought it was a good sign.

"Well, hell, sweetheart, just skip right over me, why don't you?" the man seated on Baxter's other side said when Carmen neglected to turn up a card for him.

"I . . . I am sorry," she said quietly. "I was not paying attention."

"I'll say you weren't. Of all the stupid—"

"I am sorry," she repeated. "I will start over with a new deck. It will not happen again."

"Jesus, pal, it was an accident," Baxter said to the other man. "It could have happened to anyone. Leave her alone."

"You mind your own business, boy," the man replied, turning on his stool to glare at him. "This is between me and her."

"She said she was sorry. What more do you want?"

The man ignored him, turning on his seat again to watch the cards Carmen was shuffling. "Porto Ricans," he muttered, not even trying to hide the contempt in his voice. "Can't do anything right anyway. I don't know why anybody even hires them. This one ought to be home wiping her kids' noses, not trying to do some job that's obviously beyond her intelligence."

Baxter watched Carmen's cheeks turn red with anger and waited for her to fire off some retort. But she remained silent, looking down at the cards she continued to shuffle with what he thought was more vigor than necessary.

"What makes you think she's got kids at home?" he asked the man beside him, amazed that he was able to keep his voice level.

"They all do. They breed like rabbits."

Baxter turned to stare at the man more fully. "If you hate these people so much, why do you come down here?"

"Got no choice. I'm here on business."

"Baxter," Carmen interrupted. "Do not start trouble. They will throw you out."

The man was probably twice Baxter's age and certainly twice his size, with big, beefy hands. Getting hit by a hand like that would hurt plenty, Baxter thought. Nevertheless, he didn't back down, but continued to glare at the man.

"Listen to her, boy, and don't worry too much about my manners," his adversary said. "You mind your own, you hear? And you," he told Carmen when he turned on his stool again. "Try to deal this hand right for a change, will you?"

She nodded quickly and dealt out another hand, this time not looking at Baxter at all. The other players at the table were silent, each studying his hand intently. Baxter didn't bother to look at his.

"Carmen," he said, "I need to talk to you."

"Baxter, I—"

"Hit me," the man at the other end of the table said.

She hurried down to turn over another card, then moved to the next player. When she stood in front of Baxter again, her expression was worried, but all she said was, "Do you want another card?"

He glanced down to see what he had. A two and a seven. "Yeah, give me another card."

A four joined his other two cards. Great. On top of everything else, he couldn't get a decent hand to save his life. Carmen left him again then to make her rounds, and when she came back, he asked for another card. Oh, sure, *now* he got a king, he thought. "I'm out," he said under his breath.

"No, you are not."

He looked up to find Carmen smiling at him, but she said nothing more. She cleared away his cards along with those of the other players who had gone over, then dealt another to each of the two men who remained.

"Busted," one of them said when he went over.

"The dealer has eighteen," she said.

"And I've got twenty." Baxter's adversary chuckled in delight as Carmen set a stack of chips before him. Why did the jerks always seem to win? he wondered.

He was down two hundred dollars before there was a lull in the action again. "We need to talk," he told Carmen once more. "I have something I have to tell you. When do you get off work?"

"You know, that's something I've been wondering

myself, sweetheart," the other man said. "You've brought me some pretty good luck tonight. I'd like to make it up to you."

"She'll be busy," Baxter told him.

"Maybe she wants to decide that for herself."

"Maybe I'll decide it for her."

"Listen, sonny, you've been making trouble since you sat down, and I don't like it. Now what would a girl like her want with a scrawny little runt like you when she could have a real man?" He threw Carmen a lascivious look as he added, "A man who can afford to keep her."

The hairs on Baxter's neck prickled. "And what's that supposed to mean?"

"Just that a fine-looking woman like that is probably used to having a real man around, not some young pup like you who has no idea what he's doing. Isn't that right, sugar?" he asked Carmen. What he asked her next was unforgivable, a proposition so profoundly offensive that it made Baxter's stomach recoil. He could only imagine how it had made Carmen feel.

That was when he decided he'd had enough. He could no more have prevented what happened after that than he could prevent the sun from rising in the morning. He flew off his stool and landed a good, solid punch squarely on the other man's jaw, who, stunned for only a second, retaliated by lifting Baxter from the floor and throwing him over the blackjack table.

The next thing Baxter knew, the two of them were rolling on the carpet at Carmen's feet, and Carmen was crying out his name. When the man straddled him and began to punch his face with more gusto, he saw her loop her arms around his neck and pull back hard. The man didn't seem to notice, however, and instead planted a fist hard against Baxter's temple.

After that, things went a little fuzzy. The pain that shot through his head quickly became numb, and then he heard Carmen scream. The last thing he remembered before passing out completely was the arrival of two big goons in tuxedos who pulled the man off him. After that, just like in the movies, everything went black.

When Baxter opened his eyes again, he was lying on a couch in a room as gaudy and red as the casino, but infinitely smaller. Above him, a ceiling fan whirled around slowly, and to the right of that was Carmen's face. She cradled his head in her lap as she gazed back down at him. She looked worried and anxious, and she had a big red spot on her cheek. He wondered how that had happened.

"Are you all right?" she asked as she smoothed his hair away from his forehead. "How is your head?"

He didn't answer her question, but instead lifted his hand to her cheekbone. "What happened to you? Did that sonofabitch do that to you?"

Her hand joined his, cupping his fingers gently before she lifted them away from her face. "I do not think he meant to. I was trying to pull him off you myself when Cosmo and Stephen did it for me. When they did, the fist he was aiming at you flew back and hit me instead. He apologized."

"Awfully damned big of him."

She shrugged, as if this sort of thing happened to her every night. "He was drunk."

"Are you trying to excuse his behavior?"

She shook her head. "No. No more than I would try to excuse yours."

He nodded as he looked around at his surroundings again. "Where are we?"

"In Ramon's office. He is the casino manager. Cosmo and Stephen—they are two of the bouncers— brought you in here. They took Mr. Dolan to another room. Ramon has sent for a doctor. You have not been unconscious for long. Mr. Dolan does not look too bad. I do not think he is going to press charges against you."

"I'd like to see him try."

Neither one spoke for a moment after that. Baxter continued to brush his fingers lightly over her cheek, and Carmen brushed his hair back from his face.

"Do you have to put up with creeps like that all the time?" he finally asked.

She shrugged again, but he could see that the gesture was anything but unconcerned. "This man tonight, Mr. Dolan, he was worse than most. But no, it is not unusual for someone to speak to me that way. It will not be a problem anymore, though. Ramon has fired me."

Baxter jerked up. "What? Why?"

"I think it has been coming for a long time. He says I have not been paying attention to what I am doing at work. He thinks I lose too often. I am costing the casino money. And now tonight, my ex-boyfriend comes in and starts a fight . . ." She sighed. "It is not good for business."

"I'll talk to him," he said. "Maybe if I apologize—"

"No. It is not necessary. I do not think I wish to work here anymore anyway. I will find something else. Maybe in one of the shops in the Condado or Old San

Juan. The money will not be so good, but I will like it better, I am sure. My little brother Ramiro is sixteen now. He is old enough to go to work. He will make up the difference."

When she looked up at Baxter again, her eyes were dark and fathomless, and he had no idea what she was thinking about. He recalled then that she had referred to him as her ex-boyfriend a moment ago, and the label struck him oddly. Before he could dwell on it, however, she spoke again.

"What was it you wished to talk to me about?"

"What?"

"Earlier you said that you wished to talk to me. Now is a good time, no? The doctor will be here soon."

His mind raced as he thought about everything he wanted to say to her. But not here. Not like this. "Listen, I don't think I need a doctor. Could we just get out of here? Go someplace where we won't be disturbed?"

She looked at him doubtfully. "You do not think you need a doctor," she repeated. "You have not looked at yourself in a mirror."

"It can't be that bad."

She uttered a skeptical sound and threw her hands into the air. "At least go to the men's room and wash up. You will scare all the *turistas*. You have a big bump on your head, your eyes are black and blue, and there is blood on your mouth. It is not attractive."

He smiled. "I'd rather go back to my room and wash up."

"All the way to Old San Juan?"

"No. All the way to the third floor."

Carmen eyed him suspiciously. "What are you talking about?"

"I got us a room."

She frowned. "A room for *us?* Why?"

"So we can be alone."

"You are presuming much, Baxter. I am not even your girlfriend anymore. The last time we were together, you chose your parents over me. You insulted me. That is not something I will forgive easily."

"How did I insult you?"

Her gaze drifted away from his as she said, "You told me I wore too much makeup. You spoke to me as if I meant no more to you than a prostitute. And you did not stand up for me when your mother and father said things that were not so nice."

He knew he couldn't deny any of it. All he could do now was try to make it up to her. How he would do that, however, he didn't know. He still wasn't sure why he had come to the casino tonight. He had only known he missed her terribly and wanted to see her to be sure she was all right. And she had been doing all right, he recalled with a frown. Until he had stepped in and lost her job for her.

"You're right," he said. "I should have been there for you, and I wasn't. But you have to understand something, Carmen. My parents . . . they're very . . ." He sighed fitfully, trying to come up with a word that would adequately describe them. Finally, he decided on, " . . . Manipulative. That's what they are. Manipulative."

"What does it mean to be . . ." Carmen took her time over the word as she repeated, "manipulative?"

This time his sigh was one of exasperation. "It means they know exactly what to do to make me feel bad whenever they want to." He stood and paced to the other side of the room as he continued. "There's something you have to understand about me, Carmen. I'm not a very strong person."

She waved her hand through the air and laughed. "I know that."

He frowned at her. That wasn't the reply he had expected to hear. "You know that?" he repeated.

"Of course. Oh, you have much strength in your body," she allowed with a suggestive smile. "It is very exciting. But I know you are not so strong when it comes to other things."

"Like what?"

"Like me," she told him simply. "And like your parents."

He crossed the room again and rejoined her on the couch. "I've only stood up to them once in my entire life, and that was when I joined the Coast Guard. And it wasn't an easy thing to do. I sweated it for years before finally going through with it, and I've paid for it for years as a result."

"Why did you do it?"

The question stumped him. "Why? Because I felt so strongly about it," he told her. "Because I love the ocean. I love being out on the water. To coop myself up inside my dad's bank all day long would have killed me. When I joined the Coast Guard, it was because I felt more passionately about the ocean than I had ever felt about anything else in my life."

She squeezed his fingers tightly with her own. "So you must love something—feel passionately about it—before you will go against your parents wishes."

"Yes."

She released his fingers and cupped her hands together in her lap. "Then it is good that we do not see each other anymore. Because it is clear that you do not feel that way about me."

"I do care about you, Carmen," he said softly. "More than you probably know."

She didn't look up and her voice was quiet as she said, "But it is not enough."

When he didn't comment further, she asked, "Why did you come to the casino tonight? You said we needed to talk. That you had something to tell me."

He had told her that, he remembered. And at the time, there had been something he wanted to tell her. Now, however, he couldn't quite remember what that was. As he looked at her face, a face so beautiful it made his stomach clench in knots, nearly every thought in his head flew away like the wind. Only a flicker of something he couldn't identify remained behind, a vague, barely familiar notion of something he wasn't quite able to place his finger on.

"Nothing," he finally said. "It was nothing important. I guess I just wanted to make sure you were all right."

"I am fine, Baxter," she said. "Out of work temporarily, but that will not last long."

He nodded, then rose and headed toward the door. As an afterthought, he turned around and told her, "I've enrolled in some of the Spanish classes the base offers."

He could tell immediately that his revelation surprised her. "But why?" she asked. "You will only be in Puerto Rico for another month. Then they will send you someplace new. Someplace where you will probably not need to know Spanish."

He lifted his shoulders and dropped them again, then smiled. "Yeah, I know. But it just seemed like the thing to do for some reason."

He wanted to say more, was going to say more, but

the door to the manager's office opened then, and two men entered. One of them was one of the big tuxedos who'd peeled Mr. Dolan from his chest earlier. And the one with the medical kit was no doubt the doctor. After checking him over briefly and pronouncing him fit enough, the doctor cleaned a cut on his lip and a small abrasion on his head, taping a bandage over the latter. Carmen chatted with the bouncer in Spanish during that time, and Baxter was surprised to hear her laugh out loud at one point.

"What?" he asked. "What's so funny?"

"It is Mr. Dolan," Carmen told him. "Cosmo said that when he left the casino a little while ago, he was not alone."

"No?"

She shook her head. "He was headed back to his room with a woman who picked him up in the bar. To you that might not be so funny. But the woman in question was named Trixie."

Baxter smiled. "I know Trixie."

Cosmo smiled, too. "We should have known. Everyone around here knows Trixie."

Baxter couldn't imagine a sweeter revenge. "But not nearly as well as Mr. Dolan soon will."

"You better go," Carmen told him suddenly. "Ramon will not be happy if he sees you are still here. And I must clean out my locker, pick up my check, and go home. Good-bye, Baxter," she concluded softly. "Take care of yourself."

He didn't like the finality of her words, but didn't know what to say to contradict them. Moving to the door once again, he paused before exiting and turned to look at her one last time—at the black hair and ebony eyes, at the soft skin as dark and smooth as a pecan shell. Such a small detail, the color of their skin, he thought. So harmless, so superficial. Why should it bother his parents that Carmen's complexion differed from his own? Why should this one detail be so difficult to overcome?

Because maybe, he thought further, way down deep inside it wasn't his parents' approval he sought so desperately. Maybe, way down deep inside, what Baxter needed was his own.

It didn't seem right, saying goodbye to her that way. So instead he told her, "I'll see you around, Carmen."

He thought she shook her head almost imperceptibly at that, then assured himself he must be mistaken. Turning quickly, he exited the office and made his way back downstairs.

21

Dear Mom and Dad,

I had a dream the other night that I came back home to Cleveland, but that everything was different there once I arrived. It was scary, seeing how everything had changed, but at the same time, I felt kind of excited. Usually when I have dreams like that, I wake up feeling sad, but this time, for some reason, I didn't feel bad at all . . .

Rico's was virtually empty when Reuben stopped by to see Natalie the day after Nick walked out. A few guys from the base she knew only by their first names were shooting pool at one of the decrepit tables management provided, and a couple of locals sipped leisurely at their beers in a corner booth. Reuben seemed to fill the doorway when he entered, his presence seeming somehow ominous to Natalie.

She only glanced up at him once, then returned to filling out Rico's weekly bar order and tried to pretend her husband's ex-best friend was no one in particular.

"Are you ready to talk?" he asked as he sat down on the bar stool directly in front of her.

Natalie didn't look up. "I've already said everything I need to say."

"Well, I haven't."

"Oh, I think you've said more than enough."

"I haven't said nearly enough."

When she finally glanced up at him, she saw that he was tired and angry looking, and she frowned. Just who in the hell did he think he was feeling that way? she wondered. After what he'd generated yesterday, she figured she should have the monopoly on fatigue and resentment.

"Well, I don't want to hear anything more you might have to say," she told him. "In fact, I don't ever want to see you again."

"I don't believe you."

It was odd, she thought, how quickly and easily Reuben Channing had stopped being attractive to her. Somehow, after yesterday's explosion, she had too many other more important things to make her mind go spinning, and suddenly, there was simply no room in her head for Reuben. He looked no different than he ever had. His voice was the same, as was his posture, his attitude. Yet something had changed. Perhaps not with Reuben, but with her. She actually tried to conjure some of the fascination for him she had once had. But instead, worries about Nick were all that materialized.

"Say what you have to say," she said softly. "Then leave me alone."

He reached for her hand and wove her fingers with his. "Well, what I have to say is going to run a little bit counter to your instructions. Because alone is the last place I want to leave you."

She didn't remove her hand, but gazed at their entwined fingers and thought how strange her hand looked locked with his. "There's nothing there, Reuben," she told him. "I'm sorry if I misled you. I guess I misled myself, too. But when I think of you now, there's just . . . nothing. I have to focus on working things out with Nick. That's all that's important to me now."

"So you're going back to him."

"I don't know. I'm still not sure how things are between him and me. I'm still not sure what I want. But I do know one thing. You're not a part of my future."

"But—"

She shifted her gaze from their hands to his face, and whatever he saw in her eyes must have made him reconsider what he had intended to say. She wished she could tell him something reassuring, something that might make the entire situation come clear, but all she asked was, "Where do you want to be ten years from now?"

"I don't know," he said. "Do you?"

"I used to. I used to know exactly where I was going to be at any given time in my life."

"But you don't now."

She shook her head silently.

"Then how does that make us any different from each other?"

She didn't answer his question, instead posing one of her own. "Why did you try to make Nick believe there was something going on between us?"

"Because there is, that's why."

"No, there's not. Nothing substantial anyway. There never was, and there never will be."

"All that time we spent together didn't mean anything to you? All those times you kissed me, you were just killing some time?"

She drew in a shaky breath and released it slowly. She couldn't remember when she had ever found herself embroiled in such a nightmare. "Okay," she conceded reluctantly. "I admit we had some fun together."

"And the kisses?" he asked.

She paused only a moment before saying unwillingly, "They were okay, too, I guess."

"Just okay? Are you telling me I'm the only one who lost a lot of sleep those nights?"

"No," she said softly. "But I didn't stay awake in bed thinking about making love to you. I stayed awake wondering what kind of terrible person I was for betraying my husband. Betraying him with his best friend. And just because what we did was . . . enjoyable . . . didn't make it right. God, what we did was anything but right."

"There's nothing wrong with two people doing what comes naturally," Reuben told her.

"And there's nothing natural about lying to your husband. About hurting him so badly that he can't bear to speak to you, to look at you."

"Look, Natalie," he tried again.

"Reuben, I think you should just go. I don't want to see you anymore, and you will undoubtedly forget all about me in no time."

"We need to talk more about this."

"No, we don't."

"Yes, we do."

"It's Nick I need to talk to now, if I can get him to speak to me. Anything you have to say isn't important."

"It's very important."

Natalie studied him for a long time, noting the rugged features of his face that had become almost as familiar to her over the past several months as Nick's were. Since coming to Puerto Rico, she had probably spent more time with Reuben, seen more with Reuben, and shared more adventures with Reuben than she had with her own husband. Reuben had stirred something deep inside of her that she hadn't felt for a long, long time. Not since those early days with Nick had she experienced a more heated response to something as simple as a kiss.

But there was nothing much more to him. Reuben Channing was nothing less than fascinating, attractive, and stimulating. And, she thought for the first time since meeting him, he was nothing more. Why hadn't she seen all that before?

She freed her hand from his and folded it over her other one on top of the bar. "Go home, Reuben," she told him softly. "It's over."

"But—"

She surveyed him intently, unable to gauge what he was thinking or feeling, surprised to realize that she didn't really care. He wasn't important to her. Not the way Nick was.

For better or for worse, that's what she and Nick had promised each other. Well, she couldn't imagine things between them getting much worse than they were now. Still, she had made that vow, and so had Nick. And if there was one thing he had never done to her before, it was to go back on his word.

"Go home, Reuben," Natalie said again. "And thanks for everything. But I won't be needing a ride home from work anymore. I won't be needing anything from you."

Nick's new wedding ring arrived in the mail two weeks after he had left Natalie alone in their apartment. She opened the package from Carroll's Fine Jewelers of Cleveland almost fearfully, rubbing her thumb over the pearl-gray velvet box for several moments before opening it. Inside, she found an exact replica of the ring she had placed on her husband's finger nearly ten months ago. She hurried to the bedroom and removed her own ring from the jewelry box where it had lain untouched since May, then plucked his from its box to compare the two. Where her ring had dulled a bit and sustained an occasional tiny dent in the soft metal, Nick's new ring was shiny and flawless, as bright as a new beginning.

She had tried to see him that evening after she had spoken with Reuben for the last time. She had gone to the cutter where she found Baxter standing watch, and he'd told her Nick and Jack had gone into town and he wasn't sure when they'd be back. He'd grumbled further about how he'd finally freed himself of Jack's residency on the boat only to have Nick move in next, muttered something about the questionable mental health of his crew, and then wished Natalie the best of luck with her husband.

She had met with equally dismal success when she'd tried to telephone Nick, and he had managed to avoid her every further visit to the base. Then, of course, the cutter had gotten underway for a week, and she'd had no way to communicate with him, even if he'd wanted to talk to her. Which obviously he didn't, she had realized. And as a result, she had given up trying to see him, hoping instead that he might come around in search of her instead.

But he hadn't. The cutter had been back in San Juan for nearly a week now, and she'd heard not a word from him. There were times when she wondered if she would ever hear his voice or see his face again.

Natalie sat down on the bed and studied the rings some more. She should take Nick's to him, she thought. It was his, after all, and he had taken all of his other belongings from the apartment. Of course, she had no way of knowing if he even wanted his ring anymore. Indications would suggest not. But surely by now Nick had had plenty of time to think about everything—about them, about her, about the possibility of everything maybe working out. After all, she'd scarcely thought about anything else over the last two weeks.

Then again, she hadn't much come to any significant conclusions herself. Though that may have been because conclusions about two people were difficult to come by when one was so utterly alone.

She tucked Nick's ring back into its box and examined her own again. The metal had grown warm from her touch and seemed a bit shinier now due to her handling of it. Carefully, she slipped it over the fourth finger of her left hand and pushed hard to get it over her knuckle. It felt awkward there, the fingers on each side bumping it plainly when she pressed her fingers together. It looked nice, though, and it still fit pretty well. It might not be such a bad idea to leave it on. That way she'd always know where it was.

She really should take Nick's to him, she thought again, reaching for the gray velvet box once more as she rose from the bed. It belonged to him, and he had a right to do with it whatever he wanted. She only hoped what he wanted wouldn't be to chuck it over the side of the boat.

"You shouldn't have come," he told her when she stood facing him a short time later.

The cutter was unoccupied except for Nick, who was standing a twenty-four hour watch. Natalie had run into him on deck, but he had denied her permission to come aboard. She'd come aboard anyway, however, deciding quickly that because they were married they were essentially of equal rank, so she could disobey his order if she wanted to.

"I have something that belongs to you," she told him, extending the box that contained his ring.

Nick surveyed it suspiciously but didn't take it from her.

"It's your wedding ring. It came in the mail today. I thought you might want it."

"Why?"

She sighed fitfully. Clearly he had no intention of making this easy. "Because it's yours."

"What if I don't want it anymore?"

"I thought maybe you would."

"Why?" he asked again.

"Because nothing's really been settled between us."

He reached out his hand cautiously, plucking the box from her left hand as if it might explode if he weren't careful. Instead of opening it, however, he only continued to stare at Natalie's hand instead.

"You're wearing your ring again," he said.

"Yes."

"How come?"

She lifted her shoulders and dropped them again. "Didn't want to lose it, I guess."

He nodded slowly and stuffed the box containing his ring into his pocket. Natalie frowned, a cold spot at the pit of her stomach growing larger.

"Aren't you even going to open it?" she asked him. "Aren't you even going to make sure it's okay? That it fits?"

"It's not the same ring I had before, Nat," he said. "It's never going to feel the same as the original."

She tried to smile, but barely managed a grin. "Maybe it will feel even better than the first one."

"I doubt it. That one fit great."

Instead of reminding him that he was the one who'd lost that one to begin with, she simply suggested, "You could at least try this one on. See how it feels."

"Maybe later."

They were silent for a moment. There was so much Natalie wanted to say to Nick, so many things she still needed to explain. Unfortunately, she still wasn't quite sure how to mend the situation. For that she was going to need Nick's help. And clearly, he wasn't willing to participate just yet.

"Will you be coming home soon?" she asked. With a little smile, she added, "Amber and Geneva have been asking about you."

She thought she saw him smile back, but his expression changed so quickly that she couldn't be certain.

"Tell them I said hi," he replied.

"They were playing Roy Orbison the other night.

'Love Hurts.' I'm still trying to figure that one out. I'm not sure I want to know."

Nick actually chuckled at that. "My favorite of theirs is still 'Makin' Whoopee.' That's a pretty straight-forward one."

Natalie laughed, too, and met his gaze. "Nick, please come home."

His chest rose and fell as he inhaled an impatient breath. "I can't, Natalie. Not yet."

"Why not?"

He looked away, over her shoulder and out toward San Juan Harbor. "I'm just not ready yet. I'm still not sure how to deal with all this."

"I could help you. You could help me."

"It's not that easy. Everything with Reuben—"

"Reuben's gone," she interrupted him. "He's not coming back."

"I'm not so sure about that."

"I am."

He still didn't look at her, but he tucked his hand into his pocket, and she could see that he had closed his fingers over the box containing his ring. "I need more time," he said.

"How much more?"

"I don't know."

She tried to tell herself she could understand that, but realized that she understood nothing. "Okay," she told him. She took a step backward, toward the gang-plank. "I just wanted you to have your ring. And I wanted to tell you that Reuben won't be coming around anymore."

"How about you?" he asked.

"What about me?"

"Are you still . . . confused?"

"Yeah. Some. I guess. You?"

He nodded. "I'll see you, Nat."

She turned and carefully crossed over the gang-plank. When her feet were secure on the pier, she pivoted again to face her husband. "Nick?" she called back to him.

"Yeah?"

"I love you."

He looked at her, but didn't return the words. Instead, he only repeated, "I'll see you."

"Do you promise?" she asked.

He nodded again, but said nothing. He turned and headed toward the hatch, disappearing through it and pulling the metal door closed behind him with a clang.

And as hard as she tried to remind herself that Nick had never lied to her before, she couldn't shake the feeling that this time might be different. Things between them had changed, after all. And no matter what happened, the two of them could never go back to the way they were before.

Sadly, Natalie turned and made her way back to the apartment.

22

Dear Mom and Dad,

*I finally went into that bar that Nick always
told me to avoid because of the questionable
clientele. It's a really nice place, but not too many
women seem to go there. Except for a few with
moustaches. I think it might be a gay bar, but I'm
not sure . . .*

     Natalie, Sybil, and Carmen sat at one end
of the bar in The Palm Bar, Sybil's wide waistline
keeping her a bit further from the edge than the others. Natalie sat to her left, stirring her straw idly in the
few cubes of ice left over from her very tall planter's
punch, and Carmen sat on her right, staring blindly
into a wine glass stained at the bottom with a small
circle of red. All were dressed in their festive best.
And none was having a good time.

"You know, we should have done this a long time ago," Sybil said, trying to inject as much lightness and high spirits into her voice as she dared, all things considered. "We girls need a night out every now and then, and I've missed the female companionship."

When Natalie and Carmen continued to sit in silence, staring morosely out at the sparse population of the bar, she sighed. "Oh, hell, who am I kidding? I've missed any kind of companionship period."

"Did you ladies want another round?" the bartender asked when he reappeared. He was blond and shirtless and impossibly young, and he reminded Sybil of Sandy from the old *Flipper* series.

"Yeah, set 'em up again," she told him. "We're having too much fun to go home, aren't we, girls?"

Natalie and Carmen grunted their agreement. At least, Sybil thought it was agreement.

The bartender smiled. "Yeah, you can tell you three are in a gala mood tonight. The minute you walked in the door, I knew I was going to have to keep an eye on you. Party animals and troublemakers, the lot of you. Wild women. Oh, baby."

Sybil narrowed her eyes at him. "Oh, shut up."

He arched one eyebrow at her response, then went to fetch their drinks. When he returned, none of them had budged an inch, and Sybil could see that he was biting his tongue to keep himself from saying whatever was on his mind.

"What?" she said when he placed her ginger ale before her. "What is it you want to say? Come on, don't hold back. We can take it."

He eyed her thoughtfully for a moment before asking, "Are you sure you're in the right place? I mean, you do know what kind of a bar this is, right?"

Sybil looked around. "Gee, attractive, nicely dressed men, some of whom appear to be dancing together to an old Judy Garland number—and dancing better than your average man, I might add—no other women besides us, no one hitting on us despite our solitary status and the fact that we are relatively decent-looking women . . ." She placed a finger to her chin, feigning deep consideration. "Hmmm, let me think a minute. Could it be perhaps that we have stumbled into a . . . a gay bar?"

The bartender smiled. "Yeah, I'd say there's a real good chance of that."

"A bar where the only men present have absolutely no romantic interest in women, correct?"

"Correct."

"Then this is exactly where we want to be, right, ladies?"

Natalie and Carmen looked at her as if they hadn't been aware she was speaking until that moment.

"What?" Natalie said.

"I am sorry, Sybil, I was not listening," Carmen added.

"I was just telling Sandy here that we came to this bar because we knew there was no chance of any men bothering us, right?"

The other two nodded.

The bartender shook his head. "Man troubles, huh?"

"In every sense of the word," Sybil said.

"I have a man who does not want me to be his wife," Carmen told him.

"I have a man who's not sure he wants to be my husband," Natalie joined in.

"And I have a man who doesn't want to be a father to our baby," Sybil told him.

The bartender nodded sympathetically. "Sounds

rough all right. Well, if you've got man troubles, you're in the right place. Most of us here have them at one time or another." He started to turn away, then added, "Oh, and by the way, the name's not Sandy. It's Mike."

Sybil was decent enough to look sheepish. "Sorry."

He smiled. "No problem. Let me know if you need anything else."

"Thanks."

The three women sat in silence for a little while longer before Natalie broke it by saying, "This is getting us nowhere."

"You are right," Carmen said. "There is no point in sitting here feeling miserable."

"Right," Sybil agreed. "Especially when we could go anywhere and feel miserable."

"That's not what I meant," Natalie said. "We're doing nothing to solve our problems by drowning them in the beverage of our choice. There's got to be some way to fix all the stuff that's gone wrong. If we all put our heads together, we'll have to come up with a viable solution."

Sybil stared at her. She had thought that after nine months in San Juan, Natalie Brannon would have become a bit more worldly and considerably less naive. She would have guessed that any woman who had become embroiled in a love triangle—albeit a less than steamy one—would have learned a lot about herself and the opposite sex. She would have suspected that Natalie would understand by now how the world works, would see that nothing ever went the way it was supposed to, and that human beings had no control whatsoever over their destinies. Instead, Natalie Brannon still seemed to be—ugh—an optimist.

"Fix all the stuff that's gone wrong," Sybil repeated blandly. "Do you honestly think that's possible?"

Natalie nodded without hesitation. "Sure."

Sybil smiled indulgently and steepled her fingers together on the bar. "Let's review, shall we? My husband of nineteen years has left me because he doesn't want to face the responsibility of his child and is certain I betrayed him in every way by becoming pregnant without his permission. Carmen over there is in love with a man who can't make himself see past the color of her skin to love her back. You, my sweet, succumbed to the wiles of an older, more experienced man who happened to be your husband's best friend, and now have no idea what you want for your future.

"All in all," she concluded, "what we have here in a nutshell is a convoluted mixture of disloyalty, broken vows, narrow-mindedness, confusion, prejudice, infidelity, and jealousy. Pretty much a microcosm of the planet in general. And nothing any of us can do or say will change any of it."

"But—"

"Don't you see?" Sybil continued. "Things are out of our hands, kids. There's nothing more we can do."

"There's something I could do," Natalie said quietly. "I'm just not sure what it is."

"Baxter is taking Spanish lessons," Carmen volunteered suddenly.

Natalie and Sybil looked at her with wide eyes.

"Really?" Sybil asked. "Why? The change of command is only a month away and then he'll be long gone from Puerto Rico."

Carmen smiled. "He said that it seemed like the right thing to do."

Natalie and Sybil exchanged speculative looks before turning to Carmen again.

"So maybe all is not lost," Carmen went on. "Maybe there is still hope that all will turn out right for each of us."

Sybil shook her head. "I don't know. These guys have had a lot of stuff to digest over the last few months. Seems to me that if everything was going to work out, it would have been fixed by now."

"Not with me and Nick," Natalie protested. "Some things take time."

"You know, Natalie," Sybil said softly, covering the younger woman's hand with her own. "I like you a lot. You're a nice kid. But I think you really screwed up royally with this whole Reuben thing."

She hung her head and stared at the band circling her left ring finger, then rubbed absently at a wet spot on the bar. "I know."

"Then again, Nick did some pretty stupid things, too, before you came down here."

Her head came back up at that, and she studied Sybil closely. "What do you mean?"

Sybil sighed. "The next time you see him, ask him about a party at Booker's a couple of months before you moved down here. If he has trouble remembering, tell him to call me, and I'll be glad to refresh his memory."

"What happened?"

"Ask Nick," Sybil told her again. "Maybe it will help break the ice between you two and get you talking about all the stuff you need to talk about. Because trust me, the two of you have a lot of talking to do."

Natalie nodded but said nothing more.

"Do you have any information on Baxter?" Carmen asked.

The other woman chuckled, but shook her head. "Only that he really does seem to be a genuinely decent guy. You're right, Carmen, he may come around yet."

"But will it happen before he leaves Puerto Rico?" Carmen wondered aloud.

"That I don't know."

Silence consumed them again after that, and they sat in a companionable stupor. Sybil was torn between putting them out of their misery by calling an end to the evening or ordering another round to prolong it, when she looked up to see a familiar face entering the bar. He came in as if he knew the place intimately, and several of the other men raised their hands in greeting to him. Mike the bartender immediately reached for a bottle of very expensive single malt Scotch without even asking the newcomer what he would be drinking, as if he knew instinctively what the man would order. Sybil smiled as a number of questions she'd always had about Catch suddenly fell into place.

"Hi, Catch," she said when he took a seat at the opposite end of the bar.

He looked up quickly, clearly surprised to hear his name spoken by a female voice in the place. He smiled back at her when he recognized the trio of women and immediately moved down to join them.

"Hi, kids," he said as he settled on the bar stool beside Natalie. "Come here often?"

Sybil shook her head. "First time. And you can just imagine our surprise to discover what kind of place this is. Imagine our surprise to discover that they don't serve seafood here."

"Imagine."

Mike placed a drink on the bar before Catch, then

asked whether or not the ladies would care for another round. Before Sybil could reply, Catch insisted that the next round go on his tab, and Mike disappeared. He returned with three fresh drinks, placed them on the bar in front of the women, then turned to Catch again.

"Francisco was in here looking for you yesterday," he said.

Catch sipped his drink and showed no reaction. "Cisco knows where he can find me when he wants to."

"Just thought I'd mention it."

"Thanks."

"No problem."

Catch turned to Sybil. "How are you feeling?"

She spread her hands over her expansive belly and sighed. "Okay. Pretty good, actually. I'm starting to get antsy about the delivery, though. And I still have a month to go."

"It'll go by fast. Have you heard anything from Jack lately?"

She shook her head.

"You will. I know it."

"Got any premonitions for me?" Natalie asked.

Catch smiled at her. "I haven't seen you for a while, Natalie. How are you and Nick doing?"

"Not so good. We've been having some problems. He's staying on the cutter right now."

"I see. I'm sorry." He leaned further over the bar and looked at Carmen. "And Carmen? How's Baxter?"

"I do not know. We do not see each other anymore."

Catch nodded. "This is becoming an epidemic."

"Yeah, Eddie and Pete had a big fight last week, too," Mike threw in. "Who would have thought it from those two?"

"World's going to hell in a handbasket," Catch said.

"You can say that again," Sybil agreed. "Is anyone in the world truly happy, do you think?"

Catch shrugged. "Oh, I suppose somewhere, maybe high up in the Himalayas or something, there's probably some guy who's blissfully at peace with himself."

"But he's probably all alone, right?" Sybil asked.

Catch nodded. "Undoubtedly."

"That's what I figured."

"So you do not think it is possible for two people to find happiness together?" Carmen asked, clearly disturbed by the thought.

"I used to think it was possible," Sybil told her. "For a long time, I thought it was easy for two people to be perfectly happy together forever. I would have sworn that nothing could come between me and Jack. We survived a lot, especially in those early years, you know? I just thought after nineteen years, we could have worked through anything."

"It's not over yet, Sybil," Catch told her.

Not long ago, she would have believed that. Despite Jack's behavior, she would have thought the two of them still had a chance to work things out. But lately . . . lately she'd just become too tired to keep hoping. Jack had made his decision. And there was nothing in the world she could imagine that would make him change his mind.

"Yeah, I think it is, Catch," she said, biting her lower lip hard to keep from crumpling into tears. "I truly think it is."

23

Dear Mom and Dad,

I added it all up in my head, and between Nick's underways and watch standing, I've only seen him five days out of fifteen since we've been married. Strange, huh? You'd think our being separated so much would mean we make the most of the time we do spend together, but sometimes things get so tense between us, all I can do is wonder whether Nick likes it better being away. After all, the guys probably have lots of adventures when they're gone . . .

      Cruising the Dominican Republic was Nick's least favorite patrol. Not only was the local beer lousy, but the capital city of Santo Domingo was a town of stinking, open sewers, roach-infested, dirt-floored shanties, and skinny, pathetic-looking children. The smell of the place alone, something he usually noticed before the *Point Kendall* even made it all the way into port, was enough to make anyone who didn't have to be there turn around and head east for Puerto Rico. It was a journey the Dominicans seemed to undertake frequently enough. Fishing people out of the Mona Passage because they wanted to escape the destitution of their country for the indigence of another was a fairly regular occurrence for the crew of the cutter. The Dominican Republic was poverty at its most glaring, and there was nowhere on the island to escape it.

Except for the Club Med near Puerto Plata, of course, Nick recalled sardonically every time he approached Santo Domingo. There, all the wealthy tourists forked over thousands of dollars to sun and drink themselves into oblivion for a week. But their beer, imported from the finest countries in Europe, was way too expensive for a bunch of coasties. So now he and Jack and Baxter sat at one of the local establishments instead, trying their best to enjoy a free afternoon away from the cutter, each seeming less inclined to talk than they normally would be.

The late August temperature hovered at ninety degrees, and the humidity made the small, open bar feel even more close and uncomfortable than it already was. The tavern overlooked what the local tourist commission would probably call a canal, but the waterway was a thick, unnatural mixture of brown and green, and no doubt a carrier of raw sewage and any number of poisons. Across the way, four children splashed and frolicked in the water, hooting and laughing in the way children do when left unattended to play as they please.

Nick fought off an urge to shout out a warning to them. They probably played in these waters everyday. They were still too young to understand the dangers that faced them in their own hometown. Too young to realize the obstacles they would meet as they grew older. Too young to know that the atmosphere in which they were growing up would severely limit the kind of future they might enjoy. And too young to care about anything other than simply making the most of a sunny afternoon. It was strange, but in a way, Nick envied them, and he couldn't help but smile.

"Remember when you were that little?" he asked his companions as he pointed across the shallow canal toward the giggling children.

Baxter nodded. "Yeah, but we had a lot better places to play than the sewer."

"Oh, I don't know," Jack said. "I can remember a drainage ditch near my house being one of our favorite places to go after a good, hard rain."

"Yeah, but it probably wasn't a breeding ground for hepatitis and typhus, was it?" Baxter asked.

"No, but my point is that kids do dumb stuff that endangers them, no matter where they live. They don't think about what they're doing."

"But that's what makes them so much fun," Nick said. "I've got this nephew Dennis who's four, and—"

"Can the chatter," Jack interrupted him. "I hate cute kid stories."

"You hate kids period," Baxter said. "Even your own, evidently. When are you going to start realizing you're behaving like an asshole? I still don't see why you refuse to try and work things out with Sybil."

Jack tipped back his beer for a long swallow, grimacing at the bitter taste it left behind in his mouth.

His voice was noticeably tense when he replied, "I am not behaving like an asshole, and there's no reason to try and work things out with Sybil. She made her decision and I made mine. Whatever the two of us had once, it's gone now."

"So you're divorcing her?"

Jack's head snapped up at that. "What?"

"If there's no chance the two of you will be working things out, then divorce seems the likely conclusion, don't you think? Have you filed yet?"

"No, of course not—"

"Oh, so Sybil's going to do the filing. I guess that makes sense since she's the injured party. You did walk out on her after all."

"She is *not* the injured party, I am. She threw away everything we'd been planning for when she got herself knocked up."

Baxter emitted a rude laugh. "Oh, like she did it all by herself. Last I heard, it takes two people to make a baby."

"She's the woman," Jack pointed out unnecessarily. "And the woman's the one who has to carry the child. It's her responsibility to take precautions."

"And Sybil wasn't taking them?"

"She used a diaphragm," Jack said grudgingly.

"The only precaution that's one hundred percent effective in preventing kids is no sex," Baxter said. "What if you'd been using a condom when she got pregnant? Wouldn't that be your fault?"

"No."

"Why not?"

"Because . . . because . . ."

"It's a crap shoot, Jack," Baxter told him. "If you're going to have sex, whether you're married or not, whether you're using protection or not, you've got to be prepared for the possibility of children."

"And what if Carmen was the one who got pregnant?" Jack shot back. "What would you do? Marry her? From what I've seen of the two of you, that's not bloody likely."

"I don't know what I'd do," Baxter replied honestly. "But I sure as hell wouldn't turn my back on her if she were already my wife."

"Yeah, but you have no intention of making her that, do you? Even after stringing her along for almost two years. Hell, Skipper, I'm not the only one who behaves like an asshole sometimes, am I?"

Nick listened to the exchange in silence, hoping against hope that he had faded into the woodwork somewhere along the way. He'd never heard Jack speak to the skipper in a way that bordered on insubordination. He hadn't meant to get them started on this line of conversation. And now he scrambled for something that might possibly change the subject.

"Hey, how about them Indians, huh? Are they having a great season or what? Who would have thought they'd have a decent shot at the Series this year, huh? Man, I wish I could be back in Cleveland. Maybe I'll ask for a transfer back there next—I might even get it, who knows? I'm sure Nat would be glad to go home." He wondered at his last comment even as he was making it, curious about why Natalie would figure into his plans when things between them were in no way settled.

"Let's not argue about who's the bigger asshole here," Baxter went on, ignoring Nick's clumsy segue to fix Jack with a pointed gaze instead. "The point is Sybil *is* your wife. And when you married her, you agreed to stick with her no matter what. There are a lot worse things that can happen to two married people than having a baby. Call it crazy, but a lot of people think a baby is something to celebrate."

"A lot of people don't have their dreams crushed by a baby's arrival, either."

"No, but they have them crushed by other things. Loss of a job, infidelity, illness, death. A baby is nothing compared to stuff like that. Hell, Jack, nobody ever gets to have things exactly the way they want them. Nobody. What makes you so goddamned special that you alone should be the one who does? Quit being so selfish."

"I am *not* being selfish."

"Then what do you call it?"

Jack thought for a moment, knowing Skipper was wrong, but hard pressed to provide a reason why. Baxter simply didn't understand, he finally concluded. Despite his position and the responsibilities that went along with his job, he was really just a kid. And a privileged kid at that. He had no idea what real life was all about. Who the hell did he think he was calling Jack selfish?

He had opened his mouth to demand exactly that from his commanding officer when the shrill, piercing scream of a woman split the air outside the bar. All three men jerked their heads toward the origin of the sound and found themselves staring out over the water at the spot where the children had been playing only moments before.

There were two men there now pulling a body from the canal—the body of one of the children. Instinctively, Nick, Jack, and Baxter jumped up from their seats, toppling their chairs behind them. They

THE HONEYMOON   317 –

leapt over the wooden barrier that separated them from the canal, splashed through the water to the other side, and bent over the young boy. Baxter arrived first and identified himself as the CO of the cutter as he simultaneously pressed his fingers to the boy's throat, not sure anyone present would even understand him.

"No pulse," he told the others. "Somebody call an ambulance. We can do CPR until it gets here. Go on!" he shouted at the crowd that had gathered when no one made a move to leave.

"They probably don't speak English," Jack told him as he knelt over the boy, pressing his own finger to the child's throat.

"Well, hell, anybody can see what needs to be done here," Baxter said. "Ambulance," he repeated to the crowd of onlookers, forgetting in his panic all the meager Spanish he had learned so far. "Somebody call an ambulance."

Finally a man broke away and ran up the street. Nick could only hope he was going for help and prayed that it would come quickly. He watched as Jack cleared the boy's mouth and began mouth-to-mouth resuscitation. Baxter opened his palms over the boy's chest, pumping up and down in the technique all of them had learned but, surprisingly, seldom used. Slow and steady, up and down, the motion of Baxter's hands was mesmerizing. Together, he and Jack fell into a rhythm of CPR and mouth-to-mouth, a combination that he hoped could keep the child alive until help came.

A woman hovered near them, brushing fitfully at the child's shorts one minute and wringing her hands the next. The sounds she made at the sight of her child were something Nick was certain would take a long time to leave him. Nor would he likely forget the quiet. Despite the presence of dozens of people in the middle of town, there seemed to be no sound save the hiss of the wind around his ears. He brushed at the wet hair hanging in his eyes and was vaguely aware that his clothing reeked of the canal stench. But most of all, he was aware of the quiet.

"Someone's going to have to take over for me," Baxter said after some time. "Nick, you perform CPR and I'll do mouth-to-mouth for a while."

All three men traded positions in one fluid gesture, and then it was Nick whose hands pumped up and down on the boy's chest and Baxter who pressed his mouth to the child's. Jack sat back and watched the other two, breathing as evenly as he could to catch his breath.

"Where's the damned ambulance?" Nick grunted as he kneaded the boy's chest. "Didn't someone go for help?"

"Someone took off," Jack told him, "but I have no idea where he was going."

"An ambulance should have come by now. Where is it?"

No one seemed to have an answer. The crowd remained silent, Jack rose to pace restlessly, Baxter continued mouth-to-mouth, and Nick's fingers began to hurt.

"Your turn, Jack," he said some time later. "My hands are starting to cramp. I'll relieve Skipper."

Nick took Baxter's place as Baxter had taken Jack's a half hour before, breathing deeply in and out, offering his own breath to a still, silent mouth. The boy's skin was warm and dry now, but his eyes remained closed.

Nick guessed he was no more than twelve years old, if that. But dammit, he thought, as long as they had anything to say about it, the kid would see thirteen.

What seemed like hours could only be the passage of minutes, but his hands were still stiff and sore from CPR, and he started to feel a little dizzy. "Where's the ambulance?" he gasped between breaths without looking up from his task.

Baxter shaded his eyes with his hand and looked toward the nearest street, but there was no telltale whine of a siren, no flash of white or red. "I don't know," he said.

"How long has it been?" Jack asked.

Baxter glanced at his watch. "More than forty-five minutes."

"Somebody's going to have to take over for me here," Jack said. "I'm losing my rhythm."

Baxter moved in to relieve him, and Jack took Nick's place, beginning the cycle all over again. It was almost another hour before the howl of a siren finally greeted their ears.

"About time," Baxter said, shoving a hand through his sweat-soaked hair. "Jesus, it's about damned time."

"You got it okay, Jack?" Nick asked as he continued the steady in-and-out rhythm of air into the boy's lungs.

"I'm okay," Jack said without looking up. Then to the unconscious boy, he added, "And you'll be okay, too, now. Just hold on for a few more minutes."

Baxter met the ambulance as it slowed to a halt at the water's edge. When two men dressed in blue uniforms emerged from the cab, he demanded, "What the hell took you so long?"

The two men were expressionless when they looked at Baxter. Neither replied.

"What took so long?" Baxter repeated.

"*No comprendo,*" one of the men said before both opened the back of the ambulance and extracted a stretcher. "*Lo siento, no hablo inglés.*"

"Great," Baxter said, rolling his eyes.

Why had he waited so damned long to take Spanish? he asked himself. How they hell were they all supposed to communicate? He followed the two paramedics toward Jack and the boy, trying to explain in very limited Spanish and very elaborate—and no doubt ineffective—body language what had happened and what they had done before the paramedics arrived. One of the men ignored him completely, while the other continued to shake his head and mutter, "*No comprendo. Lo siento, no comprendo.*"

They unfolded the stretcher beside the boy, one of the men pushing Jack and Nick unceremoniously out of the way. When the paramedics reached down to pick up the boy, Jack stood over them and demanded to know what the hell they thought they were doing and how they were going to keep him alive without CPR.

"*No comprendo,*" the men said in unison, wheeling the stretcher slowly over the uneven ground.

Jack followed behind them, reaching for the boy to continue CPR, since these bozos evidently weren't going to, but the men held up their arms to keep him away. When they finally made it back to the ambulance, one of the men hoisted himself into the back while the other took his time in collapsing the stretcher. All the while, Jack stood by anxiously, knowing every second that passed was costing the boy plenty.

"Hurry up," he said. "You've got to—"

Finally, the stretcher fell flat, and Jack leapt forward to aid the other man in getting it into the back of the ambulance. Once there, the second man took a stethoscope and placed the flat part against the boy's chest. He listened thoughtfully for a moment, moved it to a different place, and listened some more. After a few more tries, he looked at his companion and said, "*Muerto.*"

The boy's mother, who had been standing beside Jack, wringing her hands and making that horrible, keening sound, fell to her knees. "*¿Muerto?*" she repeated. "*No. No está muerto, no.*" She covered her face with her hands and began to cry.

The paramedic removed his stethoscope, hung it back in its place, and reached for a paper sheet, which he unfolded and draped over the lifeless body on the stretcher.

Finally, Jack understood. "Dead?" he said. "You're telling me the boy is dead? After all that? After we kept him alive for more than an hour and a half, you just let him die?"

When he made a move toward the ambulance, the first paramedic held up an arm to restrain him. Jack shoved him aside and jumped into the back of the ambulance, pushed away the second paramedic, then tore the sheet off the stretcher.

"Jack—" Baxter said.

Ignoring him, Jack bent to listen to the boy's chest, frowned when he heard nothing, and started to pump his hands up and down again. He leaned over, too, and began mouth-to-mouth resuscitation again, alternating between the two.

"Come on, Nick, give me a hand," he instructed. "We can bring him around, I know we can."

Nick and Baxter exchanged a wary glance.

"Jack," Baxter said again, "it's not going to do any good. He's dead. The paramedic just said so."

"We can't just let him die. Not after all this."

"He's already dead," Baxter told him quietly. "There's nothing more we can do."

"The hell there isn't."

Baxter climbed up in the ambulance to stand behind him. "Jack—"

"I'm not going to stop."

"You can't keep it up forever."

"Maybe if we just keep it up for a little while longer."

Baxter sighed deeply. "We kept it up for an hour and a half, and it didn't bring him back. The boy's dead now. He's not going to come around." After a moment, when Jack continued with CPR, Baxter dropped a hand to his shoulder and added softly, "Let him go."

"No."

"Let him go."

"No."

"That's an order."

"No."

"There's nothing we can do to help him."

"I'm doing something right now."

"Let him go, Jack."

"No!"

Baxter turned to Nick, who stood at the foot of the ambulance staring with wide eyes. Jack's shoulders were hunched, the muscles in his back knotted, and he grunted painfully with every ineffective pump of his hands he offered. His hair hung over his eyes, dripping with sweat and the stinking water from the canal, but he seemed not to notice. Nick had never seen him so determined to do something, had never known him to so blatantly ignore an order from the skipper.

"Help me out here, Nick," Baxter said.

Nick scrambled into the ambulance and approached them slowly, mesmerized again by the motion of Jack's hands. They were red and stiff looking by now, and muscles twitched in his arms. "I . . . I don't know what to do," he said.

"You grab his left arm, I'll get his right," Baxter instructed.

"Don't do it," Jack warned them. "Don't even try."

"When I say three," Baxter said.

Nick's mouth went dry, but he met his commanding officer's gaze levelly and nodded.

"One . . ." Baxter began.

"Don't you dare," Jack told them. "I'm fine here."

"Two . . ."

"I'm warning you, Nick, don't do it."

"Three," Baxter concluded as both men reached down to tug Jack free.

"Noooooo!" Jack cried as they pulled him off the boy.

He kicked and flailed his arms fiercely, at one point breaking loose long enough to scramble back toward the body. Nick and Baxter grabbed him and jerked him back again, holding him tight despite his struggles. Once they had freed him from the body and pulled him out of the ambulance, the boy's mother climbed into the vehicle and threw herself over the lifeless form, wailing uncontrollably.

"Let me go!" Jack shouted, fighting harder to free himself.

"No!" Baxter shouted back.

"I can save him, I know it."

"We did what we could, Jack. There's nothing more we can do. He's dead."

"I can—"

"There's nothing more we can do," Baxter repeated firmly.

Jack stopped battling them then, and his body went limp. For a moment, Nick and Baxter continued to hold him, uncertain what he was trying to do. But when Jack began to cry, began to sob with a ferocity that rivaled the boy's mother's grievous sounds, Nick and Baxter let him go.

24

Dear Mom and Dad,

It's nice of you to be concerned about Amber
and Geneva, but I think they'll be just fine. I did
mention to Geneva your suggestion about checking into Mary Kay Cosmetics, Mom, and told
her about all the nice prizes that you won when
you were a rep. But they seem pretty content in
their line of work. She said to tell you thanks
anyway . . .

Natalie was lying on the sofa, thinking about Nick
when she first heard the sound. It came from outside
the front door, high-pitched and plaintive, and
seemed full of distress and confusion. She tilted her
head so that she would be able to hear it more clearly
when it happened again. There. Like an animal of
some kind. Like a . . . like a kitten?

She rose and padded to the front door, pressing her ear against it. The sound came again, over and over and over, and she smiled. Definitely a cat. A very young cat.

When she opened the door, she startled the creature, all eight inches of the pitiful little thing, and it hunched its back, fuzzed its tail, and hissed at her. Laughing, she scooped the miniature tabby up in one hand and nuzzled it.

"Oh, sweetie, I won't hurt you," she said softly. The kitten kneaded her chest with its tiny paws, and she pulled it away when its razor-sharp claws easily penetrated the fabric of her T-shirt. "Oh yeah. I forgot about how you little guys haven't had time to wear down the tips yet," she added, turning it upside down in her arms to rub its tummy. Or rather, *his* tummy, she noted when he was in his upside-down position.

He didn't appear to be underfed, and there was a piece of twine tied loosely around his neck, but no indication otherwise that he belonged to anyone. Wondering how the little guy could have made his way to the fifth floor on his own, Natalie scanned the foyer for some clue and saw a stack of cat food cans parked in front of Amber and Geneva's front door. There was an envelope, too—sealed against prying eyes, she noted when she picked it up to inspect it— but nothing else to offer her an answer.

The kitten weighed next to nothing in her hand, but his purr box hummed loudly enough to rival a Bengal tiger's. Natalie rapped twice on the door to the apartment across the hall, but received no answer. So, picking up one of the cans of food, she went back in to her own apartment with the little cat in tow, resigned to baby-sit until one of her neighbors came home.

He had eaten three-fourths of a can of cat food and consumed an entire saucer of half-and-half when she heard the sound of the elevator come to a stop outside. When the ensuing jingle of keys and rattle of grocery sacks halted abruptly, she figured whoever had come home had stumbled upon the cat food and note. Natalie pulled the front door open a second time to find a very startled Amber gazing back at her.

"Uh, I think someone left this for you," she said as she went out with the kitten in her hands. "I didn't see who. I heard him meowing out here and when you weren't home, decided to keep him company until you got here."

Amber smiled, shifting her grocery sack from her right arm to her left as she turned to insert her key into the front door. "I know who it's from," she said. She tossed her pale blond hair over one shoulder and pushed the door open. "Come on in," she added as she entered.

Natalie jumped at the invitation. She'd always wanted to see the inside of this apartment. Expecting to find whips and chains and any number of sexually suggestive toys lying around, she was somewhat disappointed to discover the apartment was very much like her own. Except that one of the walls was painted red. She found that kind of interesting. And the bedroom door was closed.

"So you know who this little *gato* is from?" she asked.

Amber placed her burden on the kitchen counter and came back to take the kitten from Natalie. "Actually, *gatito* is the Spanish word for kitten, and yes, I know who left it without even looking at the note. One of my clients. I mentioned to him last week how much I miss my cat back in Nebraska." Her smile became absolutely lascivious as she continued, "What I really said was—" She glanced over at Natalie quickly and seemed to think better of what she had intended to say. "Well, never mind," she concluded hastily. "It's not important."

She reached for the note and opened it, laughing low as she scanned the message inside. "He is such a poet sometimes. I never would have thought of rhyming haunt with—" She glanced up at Natalie once more. "Never mind," she said again as she folded the note closed.

"I fed him," Natalie told her, reaching out to scratch the kitten under the chin. "He's got a good appetite for such a little guy."

"All men have good appetites," Amber told her. "It's in their genes."

"Yeah, I guess that's true."

"Would you like a cup of tea?"

The invitation surprised Natalie. She nodded eagerly. "Sure. Tea sounds great."

"It seems strange to have you here." Amber went to the kitchen to fill the kettle with water and switched on the burner beneath it. "I mean, you've lived across the hall for how long now?"

Natalie mentally ticked off the total. "Almost ten months. Wow, has it really been that long? Sometimes I feel like we just moved in a few weeks ago."

"A lot has happened in ten months."

"I'll say."

"How's Nick?"

She hedged, uncertain how much to tell the other woman. "He's okay. I guess you know we've, uh, we've had something of a . . . a disagreement lately."

"About his friend, Reuben, you mean."

Natalie snapped her head up at that, fixing Amber with an intent stare. "How did you know?"

She smiled. "Because the front door of your apartment is as paper thin as ours is. It's hard to keep a secret in this building." The kettle whistled, and she lifted it from the burner to fill two expensive-looking china teacups. As she unwound two teabags and added them to the hot water, she continued, "Kind of a bummer, getting caught in the clinch like that, huh?"

Natalie felt her face turn flaming red. "Reuben caught me off guard."

Amber didn't look impressed. "Big deal."

Natalie glared at her. "It only happened a few times."

"And did he catch you off guard every time?"

She dropped her gaze back to the floor. "No," she replied reluctantly. "Not really."

It was none of Amber's business, Natalie told herself. This woman, of all people, was about as qualified to make judgments on another person's life as the devil himself was. Nevertheless, she found herself adding defensively, "I didn't know what to do to stop it."

"And now Nick knows about it."

"Yes."

"And you don't know how to explain things to him."

"No."

"Because you don't understand them yourself."

Natalie looked up again, surprised. "Yes."

Amber tugged the teabags out of the cups and brought them over to the coffee table. Automatically, Natalie followed her and sat down.

"You want milk and sugar?" Amber asked.

"Please."

When she returned from the kitchen, she was also carrying a plate filled with vanilla wafers and a jar of peanut butter.

"A wonderful taste combination," she assured Natalie. "Try it. You'll like it."

As she smeared a cookie with peanut butter, Natalie asked, "Is Amber your real name?"

She shook her head. "Anne. Anne is my real name. Geneva's real name is Jennifer. Boring, huh?"

"One of my sisters is named Jennifer."

"And she's probably like Suzy Homemaker or something, right?"

"Well, she is kind of dull sometimes," Natalie had to concede. "But I don't think that has anything to do with her name. It probably has more to do with the fact that she married a geek."

Amber nodded sagely. "Yeah, the wrong kind of man will bring you down so fast."

"I guess you'd know." The words were out of Natalie's mouth before she realized she had spoken them, and the cookie she was lifting to her mouth halted abruptly before she could complete the motion. "I am so sorry," she said quickly. "That was completely uncalled for."

Instead of being insulted, Amber only shrugged. "Geneva and I have never tried to hide what we do for a living."

Natalie had to admit she harbored a lurid curiosity about the whole thing. She wanted to ask Amber how she could do *that* with so many different men, wanted to know more about what precisely *that* involved. But she figured she'd probably learn more than she wanted to know, so she didn't pursue the line of questioning.

Instead, she asked, "So you know a lot about men, huh?"

Amber shrugged again. "Enough. More than most women, probably."

"Do you think—"

"Don't ask me for advice," Amber cut her off quickly. "That's not in my job description. If you've got a problem with two men, I don't want to know about it, okay?"

Natalie popped a vanilla wafer into her mouth and chewed to hide her disappointment. "Okay," she finally said.

The two women sat in silence for some moments, sipping tea and nibbling cookies like a couple of dowagers with no better way to pass the afternoon. Natalie was about to excuse herself and retreat to her own apartment when Amber settled her teacup back onto its saucer with a soft *clink* and fixed her with an intent gaze.

"Just be careful," she said. "And really think about what you're doing. It's so easy to lose sight of things sometimes, you know?"

Natalie nodded, a little confused by the words, but still grateful to hear them somehow.

"More tea?" Amber asked her.

"That would be great," Natalie said, surprised to discover she was enjoying her conversation with the other woman. "If you're sure you're not too busy?"

"Are you kidding?" Amber asked as she rose to return to the kitchen. "Daytime is my down time."

"I know you said not to ask you for advice," Natalie said as the other woman refilled their cups. "But could I ask you for a favor?"

"Sure."

"Could I maybe borrow that lion tamer outfit you told me about?"

Amber smiled. "Sure. You want the whip and chair, too?"

Natalie thought for a moment. "Why not?"

The other woman smiled. "It works best with 'Bungle in the Jungle.' Although Geneva has had a lot of success with 'Jungle Love,' too."

"I'll use them both," Natalie said.

"You, uh, you got something particular in mind for someone?"

She nodded. "Yeah. Nick and me. Maybe I'm just looking to bring a little romance back into our lives."

"If that doesn't do it, Natalie, nothing will."

25

Dear Mom and Dad,

The base is revving up for the change of command next week. They're bringing in some new guy to be the CO of the Point Kendall, and Baxter will be going somewhere else. Then a month after that, Nick will be transferred out, and shortly after that, Jack Ingram will be leaving the Guard for good. I can't believe it's been almost a year that we've been down here. It's going to be so weird when everyone goes their separate ways. It doesn't seem right somehow, to disband everybody like this. It's too bad things just can't go on the way they should. Some people just work so well together ...

Baxter stood at the Fuentes' front door with his fist lifted to knock, but hesitated. In his other hand he grasped a huge bouquet of lilies, holding them so tightly he knew they would wilt if he didn't surrender them soon.

He hadn't really thought this plan through very well. In fact, he hadn't much thought about it at all. The last thing he remembered was seeing the flowers in a florist's window near his apartment on his way home from work and thinking about how beautiful they were, and the next thing he knew, he was standing here, still in his work uniform, poised to knock. Without thinking further, he rapped quickly three times, wiping his palm on his pants before shifting the bouquet to perform the same service on his other hand. Footsteps greeted his summons on the other side of the door. He drew in a nervous breath and waited.

It was Rafaela Fuente who opened the door. He saw that she noted the flowers first, and she smiled broadly until she realized who was holding them. On recognizing Baxter, however, her smile fell, and she gazed at him through narrowed eyes.

"*Buenos días, Señora Fuente,*" he said in his best Spanish. He even remembered not to sound the *s* at the end of either word in the greeting, giving it the correct Puerto Rican pronunciation. "*¿Está Carmen en casa? Necesito hablar con ella, por favor. Es muy importante.*"

Her eyes widened in surprise at his use of Spanish, and he could see that she was more than a little confused by this new development. He just hoped like hell he'd said everything right. He'd be plenty embarrassed if, instead of requesting to speak to her daughter, he'd just asked to mow her lawn or something instead.

"Carmen no está," Rafaela told him as she began to push the front door toward him. *"Salió con otro. No volverá hasta muy tarde."*

Okay, he understood that, he thought as he performed a quick translation. Most of it, anyway. Her body language revealed what her spoken words hadn't. Carmen's mother was telling him that her daughter was out with another man, and Rafaela was trying to get rid of Baxter as quickly as she could. He supposed it was possible that Carmen was indeed not at home. But considering the fact that he could look past Rafaela and see a pair of her shoes on the floor beside the sofa, and her purse lying open on the sofa itself, he felt justified in remaining a little skeptical.

He placed his hand against the door that was fast closing against him to halt its motion and shouted "Carmen! *Soy yo,* Baxter. *Necesito hablar contigo,"* he added, fixing Rafaela intently with his gaze. *"Es muy importante."*

He heard commotion inside the apartment, then Orlando's face appeared above his mother's. Oh, great, Baxter thought. This was all he needed.

"The gringo speaks Spanish now," Orlando said in English. "So translate this."

What followed was a barrage of Spanish he couldn't begin to understand, but judging by the expression on the other man's face, he could pretty well figure out the gist of it. He was about to retaliate in the only language he had mastered completely, knowing Orlando's English was far better than his own Spanish, when the front door was pulled open wide and Carmen pushed her brother and mother to the side. She, too, began to speak rapidly in Spanish, and the three argued for some minutes before Rafaela and

Orlando grumbled and returned to the interior of the apartment.

Carmen looked upset and anxious when she turned to him again. "What are you doing here? Why have you come?"

He extended the flowers toward her, wincing at their battered state thanks to his attempts to break through the Rafaela/Orlando barrier. Nevertheless, Carmen smiled as she took them from him, fingering the delicate blooms carefully before lifting the arrangement to her nose to take in the sweet aroma.

"They are beautiful," she said quietly. "You have never brought me flowers before. Thank you."

"They're not as beautiful as you are," he told her. "And I should have brought you flowers a long time ago. I should have showered you with them every time I saw you. You deserve the best of everything, Carmen. I don't know why you ever settled for me."

She shrugged, but her smile remained unchanged. "You were very cute. And I liked the way your nose seemed to be sunburned all the time."

Her verb choice bothered him. "You, uh, you're speaking in the past tense there. Sorry, but we haven't gotten that far in my Spanish classes. If you want me to speak Spanish, we're just going to have to avoid the past and stay focused on the present."

"All right," she told him. "It is nice of you to come here to see me, but . . ." She glanced down at the flowers again as she continued, "Mami is not lying to you exactly. I have a date tonight. He will be arriving soon."

"Ah, see there? Now you've switched to the future tense," Baxter said, choosing to ignore the rest of her statement. "That's something I definitely need to work on."

She was smiling again when she met his gaze once more. "Perhaps it is something I could help you with."

He smiled back. "Perhaps it is."

They studied each other for a long time without speaking. Baxter noted with some annoyance that she had made herself look awfully nice for another man and glanced down at his soiled and not particularly fragrant uniform in comparison. He should have changed before he came over, he thought. But then, if he had, he might have missed her completely.

"I should go," he said. "And let you get on with your evening. I just wanted to tell you . . ." What? he asked himself. He had no idea why he had come over here.

"What did you wish to tell me?"

He sighed, opened his mouth to speak, then closed it again. And then he remembered something. Something that was indeed *muy importante*. "The change of command ceremony is this Saturday. I'll be leaving Puerto Rico shortly after that. They're sending me to Miami. I'll be the XO on a one-ten there. It's not exactly a promotion, but it'll look good on a resume. It will lead to better things in the future." He hesitated only a moment before adding, "I'm taking a couple of weeks off between assignments, so I don't have to report for duty until the first of next month. I thought I might spend the time in Puerto Rico. My rent's paid up through September anyway."

Carmen bit her lip thoughtfully, tightening her grip on the flowers she clasped to her breast. "Why are you telling me these things?"

"I, uh . . . I thought you might come to the change of command ceremony. I thought maybe we could have some lunch afterward or something. My parents are going to be there. But we don't have to invite them to come along. We could just say hello, exchange a few pleasantries. I just . . . I don't know. I thought you might want to come."

"I will come," she said quickly. "What time?"

The elevator doors opened at the other end of the hall and a tall, dark-haired, very handsome youth stepped off. Instinctively, Baxter knew it was Carmen's date, and he swore under his breath. The man looked understandably curious as he approached, but Carmen smiled and said something softly in Spanish that evidently placated him. With a nod to Baxter, he walked passed her and into the apartment, where he was met with enthusiastic greetings unlike any Baxter had ever received himself when visiting the Fuente home.

"What time?" Carmen asked again, her voice low.

"Eleven," he told her. "It's this Saturday at eleven. But if you want to come early, I won't mind."

She looked quickly over her shoulder and stepped outside the apartment, closing the front door behind her. Briefly, she pressed her mouth to his, then pulled away, rubbing his lips with her thumb to wipe away the lipstick left behind. It was something she had done frequently when the two of them had been together, and Baxter's heart picked up speed at sharing the gesture with her again. She turned toward the apartment to leave him, but he caught her free hand in his and lifted it to his lips for a quick kiss.

"Please come," he said as he released it.

She nodded. "I will."

He stood there for a long time after she had closed the door, listening to the laughter and chatter on the other side. At one time he had been convinced Carmen Fuente was better off with her family than she was with him. He had thought here was where she belonged. But things had changed a lot since his arrival in Puerto Rico. And soon he would be leaving the island behind. He had always associated Carmen with San Juan, had always thought she would be as much a memory of this place as would be Booker's parties, cobblestone streets, live salsa and cold beer under the palms. But somehow now, when he left Puerto Rico, he wanted to take more than a memory of Carmen with him. Unfortunately, he still wasn't quite sure how he was going to manage that.

26

Dear Mom and Dad,

You two weren't kidding when you said that the first year of marriage is the most difficult, most trying, most stressful year of a person's life. But it's also the most interesting. So many things have happened, and I've learned so much in San Juan. It just makes me curious about all the things that lie ahead . . .

Nick stood in his bedroom doorway and watched his wife sleep, remembering the last time he had seen her. She had asked him to come home. She had told him that she loved him. And he had simply left her like that, without saying a word or trying to understand.

Now she lay on her stomach with her fist doubled up by her face, her bare back tanned and dotted with a few mosquito bites. Her long hair fell over her jaw so that all he could see of her face was one slender cheekbone and one closed eye. In many ways, she appeared to be as lifeless as the little boy whose funeral he had attended with Jack and Skipper two days before.

But he could take comfort in knowing that when he touched Natalie, she would stir and awaken. Unlike the boy's mother, who had been crying the last time Nick had seen her, he himself still had the person he loved most in the world. He hadn't lost Natalie—not yet. And he wouldn't have to. Not unless he allowed Reuben Channing to come between them. Evidently, Natalie hadn't, because she was still sleeping in his bed and not someone else's. Noting the wink of silver and gold on the hand curled up on her pillow, he realized she was also still wearing her ring. The choice now, he supposed, was his.

"Natalie?" he called out softly.

She inhaled deeply, but didn't awaken.

"Nat?" he tried again. "I'm home."

The hand on her pillow lowered to the mattress, and she began to push herself up. Before she could move any further, Nick was in bed with her, turning her toward him and kissing her hello.

"Nick," she said softly when she was more awake. "You're home. You're really home. I was afraid you were never going to come back." She tilted her head back to kiss him again, but he pulled away. "Oh. Or maybe you're not home," she said when she noted his action. "What's wrong?"

He shook his head. "I just want to look at you. It's been a long time since I just sat here and looked at you. You're beautiful, you know that?"

She tugged self-consciously at her bangs. "Thanks. How was your underway?"

"Lousy."

"What happened?"

He skimmed the backs of his hand over her cheek and jaw, smiling that the two of them would exchange such ordinary, mundane conversation when they still had so many more important things to discuss. He leaned forward to kiss her lightly on the lips. "I don't want to talk about it, Nat. I want to talk about us."

She sat up straighter in bed, tucking the sheet around her as she went. "Okay."

"I'm sorry about the way I acted after I found you and Reuben together. I'm sorry I didn't stick around longer so we could talk about everything."

"Oh, Nick, you don't need to apologize for that. I'm the one who should apologize. I'm the one who—"

"Seems to me you already apologized a long time ago. I just wasn't in a frame of mind to forgive you then."

She searched his face, wanting desperately to believe that everything between them would indeed be all right. "I am so sorry, Nick. I never meant to hurt you. I never meant to mess things up between us. I just . . . lost sight of things for a little while. But I'm willing to do whatever it takes to set things right again. I've missed you. It's made me realize how very important you are to me. I love you. And I want us to work things out."

"Just tell me one thing and promise you'll tell me the truth."

"I promise."

"Do you . . . do you still think about Reuben? Or about any men? Tell me the truth, Natalie."

She smiled. "Yeah, I do."

"You do?"

She nodded. "I think about you. A lot."

He exhaled on a rush of air, and only then realized he had been holding his breath in anticipation of her answer. "But only me?" he asked.

"Only you."

He smiled back. "I believe you."

He caught her hand in his and pressed it to his lips, knowing there was something more he had to tell her, but fearful of destroying the tenuous peace the two of them had created. But he didn't want anything between them anymore. And he thought revealing what he had on his mind might help them both put things into perspective and relegate them to the past.

"I've been doing a lot of thinking over the past few weeks," he said. "About you and Reuben. You and me. And about something that happened before you came down here to live, before we got married."

Natalie curled her fingers more tightly around his. "Sybil told me I should ask you about a party at Booker's that happened before I came down here. Is this about that?"

"Yes."

"What happened?"

"I, uh . . . there was this girl named Charlotte there. She was visiting one of Booker's roommates—his sister, I think. Anyway, she and I got to talking, and one thing led to another, and—"

"Did you sleep with her, Nick? Tell me the truth." Natalie held her breath, praying with all her heart that he would answer the right way.

"God, no, I didn't sleep with her. I wouldn't do that to you. I *couldn't* do that to you."

She nodded slowly. "Yeah, I know. I couldn't do that to you, either."

"I'm sorry," he said.

"I'm sorry, too."

He kissed her briefly on the mouth, kicked off his topsiders, then climbed into bed beside her. But instead of pouncing on her and kissing her with the ferocity of a man who had been too long denied the passions of the woman he loved, he only lay beside her and pulled her close. When his hand splayed open over her heart, he sighed, feeling more content than he had in months.

"I love you," he told her.

"I love you, too." Snuggling closer, Natalie asked, "What happened to you on this last underway? You seem different somehow. I didn't think you were ever going to forgive me for what happened with Reuben."

For a long time he didn't answer her question, and Natalie had begun to think he had fallen asleep. She was about to close her eyes and join him in slumber when he moved a little closer and sighed.

"I saw someone lose somebody that was very important to them. Jack and Skipper and I, we kept this drowned kid alive for almost two hours, only to see him die because there was nothing more anyone could do."

"Oh, Nick." She rubbed her cheek against the silky black hair at the crown of his head. "I'm sorry."

He turned on the bed until he was facing her, then curled up in a ball against her, clutching her hard. "I don't want to lose you," he said. "I know we haven't even been married for a year, and that we've spent most of that time apart and that we still have some kinks to work out, but I can't imagine what I would do without you. I couldn't . . . I couldn't *manage*, Natalie. Do you know what I mean? I could never be happy again."

She nodded and held him close. "I know. I understand."

"A lot of people say the first year of marriage is the toughest."

"A lot of people are right."

"But we'll be through it in a couple of months."

"Yes, we will."

"The second year will be better."

She smiled. "I bet someday we think back on San Juan and remember it as the best time of our life."

Nick chuckled. "Well, I'm not so sure about *that* . . ."

Natalie squeezed him hard. "That's okay. I am."

She felt him move again, turning on his side to reach into his pants pocket for something. He withdrew the box containing his wedding band, opened it, plucked the ring from its resting place, and handed it to her.

"Once more with feeling?" he asked her.

Natalie smiled and took the ring from him, placing it over his finger. "For better or worse," she said as she slid the band of silver and gold over his knuckle.

"And it will only get better from here," he vowed further as he curled himself back up against her with a sigh.

She stretched out on the bed beside him, pulling him as near to her as she could, then closed her eyes. Neither had a thought for the physical act of making love. Love came in different forms, she supposed, just as romance did. It took a while to get this marriage stuff down pat. But after all was said and done, she and Nick were back on a pretty steady path. She only wished everyone could be as happy as she was.

27

Dear Mom and Dad,

Time's really moving fast now. Sybil's close to having her baby, Baxter's leaving the cutter, Nick's waiting to hear from his detailer to find out where he'll be going next. We're hoping—and we think it's going to happen—that we'll be coming back to Cleveland. It would be nice to be home with family again. I miss you guys a lot. I guess we don't realize how important people are to us until we're separated from them. You know, a lot of people I know could take a lesson from that . . .

The day designated for the change of command was a hot one, which was really no great surprise to Natalie, who fidgeted on her metal folding chair and fanned herself with her program. Carmen, who sat on her right, looked surprisingly cool in her red dress, but then she had grown up in this climate, so she was probably pretty used to it. Sybil, on the other hand, who sat on Natalie's left, looked hot and irritable and ready to explode—literally. The baby's due date was only three days away, but that probably wasn't the only reason Sybil looked so anxious. Jack was standing at the front of the room among the other members of the *Point Kendall* crew, and he was looking everywhere except at his wife.

Natalie had been surprised when Sybil had expressed an interest in coming to the ceremony today. Not only because of the situation with Jack, but also because she was obviously so uncomfortable in the late stages of her pregnancy. In fact, Sybil had told her some time ago that she had no desire to attend. But that morning she had shown up at the Brannons' apartment bright and early, and had asked them if they'd be interested in sharing a cab.

Natalie glanced down at her watch. They were already ten minutes late in getting this show on the road, and she wondered what the holdup was. She was leaning over to ask Sybil if she'd ever been to one of these things and what she could expect when Baxter and a man she had never seen before entered the room. Both wore what Nick had told her would be their "ice cream suits," high-collared, stark white uniforms decorated with an array of colorful ribbons and a few medals. They wore swords at their sides and white shoes on their feet, and all in all presented a very impressive front.

"Baxter looks handsome, no?" Carmen whispered as she leaned over toward Natalie. "I do not think I have ever seen him look so handsome."

Natalie had to agree that Baxter looked better than

she could ever recall seeing him. The other man with him was a Lieutenant J. G. Edward Pearson, who would take over the reins as CO of the *Point Kendall* once the ceremony was completed. It didn't seem right to Natalie, someone besides Baxter running the cutter. Ever since Nick had been assigned to San Juan, he and Jack and Baxter had been a team. Now that team was dissolving and would gradually be replaced by another. Eventually, no one assigned to the *Point Kendall* would be anyone she knew. It just seemed wrong somehow.

The ceremony itself wasn't particularly eventful and progressed rather quietly until the sword action that came in the second half. Natalie found herself making every effort to catch Nick's eye to see if she could make him laugh, but he was too fixed on the ceremony to fall prey to her. Her gaze roamed to Jack then, and she noticed that he was watching Sybil. When she turned to the woman beside her, it was to find Sybil watching intently the movements of the two commanding officers, completely oblivious to Jack's scrutiny. She was going to lean over and say something, but Baxter began to speak, so she refrained.

The ceremony ended with surprisingly little fanfare, and then everyone was free to get up and move around. Baxter was immediately overtaken by two people Natalie assumed must be his parents because they so thoroughly resembled him, and Nick came over to occupy the chair behind her. Jack, however, stayed where he was.

"So?" Nick asked as he cupped his hands over her shoulders. "What did you think?"

"It was nice," she told him honestly. "But kind of sad. It won't be the same without Baxter."

"Yeah, I know. Lieutenant Pearson is a nice guy, but you're right. Serving with Skipper was great."

"Will you call Lieutenant Pearson 'Skipper,' too?"

He shook his head. "He prefers to be called 'Mister Pearson,' so that's what we'll call him."

Natalie nodded her approval. "Good. Thinking of him as 'Skipper' would be like calling your mother-in-law 'Mom.' No offense, Nick," she added quickly.

He smiled. "None taken."

"What's his first name?"

"Ed."

"So I can call him Ed?"

"Yup. Just don't call him late for dinner. Come on, I'll introduce you."

"Uh, Nick," Sybil interceded, touching his wrist as he rose from his seat.

"Yeah?"

"Could you do me a favor?"

"Sure."

"Could you tell my husband—and please remind him that he is still my husband—that he's also about to become a father?"

Natalie, Nick, and Carmen all turned their attention to Sybil.

"Are you saying what I think you're saying?" Nick asked.

She nodded. "Yeah, the pains started about three o'clock this morning, but they didn't get too bad until a couple of hours ago. If the instructor in those childbirth classes was right, I'm probably going to need to get to the hospital pretty soon."

"Oh boy," Natalie said, dropping back into her chair. She took Sybil's hand and held it tightly in her own. "Are you okay? Do you need anything? What can we do?"

Sybil inhaled a deep breath and released it slowly. "You could tell Jack," she said. "I just think he ought to know."

"You're damned right he should," Nick said as he sprang up again.

He pushed through the throngs of people still swarming around Baxter and Lieutenant Pearson, ignoring a summons from the former as he made his way toward the last place he had seen Jack. He panicked when his XO wasn't where he had left him, searching the room frantically to locate him.

"What's wrong?" Baxter asked as he joined him. "What is it? You look like you've seen a ghost."

"Sybil Ingram is in labor," he said. "I'm trying to find Jack to let him know."

"He left for the reception a couple of minutes ago."

"Thanks. I'll go get him."

"I'll tell Natalie and Sybil where you went."

Nick ran across the base to the reception hall and found that quite a few people had already made their way over. Jack was talking to Baxter's parents near the punch bowl when he found him, and he sprinted over to interrupt the conversation.

"Sybil needs to get to the hospital," he said breathlessly.

Jack looked as panicked as Nick felt as he asked, "Why?"

"Because she's in labor. She's going to have the baby."

A long moment passed before Jack spoke again. When he did it was to remark in a deceptively bland voice, "So why are you telling me?"

"Why do you think I'm telling you?" Nick gaped at him for a moment before adding, "You are such a bastard, you know that? I can't believe how you're taking this." When Jack didn't comment, he went on relentlessly, "When I first found out what was going on with you and Sybil, I tried to understand why you were mad. Hell, I tried not to hold it against you when you moved out for a little while. A man needs space to think sometimes. But this has gone on long enough, Jack. Your wife is about to have a baby. You're going to be a father. It's about time you faced up to that fact and started acting like a man."

Jack set his punch cup down on the table with a heavy thump and turned on Nick. "You know, you're pushing it, talking to me that way. Not only do I outrank you, but I've got a hell of a lot more life experience than you have, you little—"

"Oh, big deal," Nick countered, all sense of propriety and military protocol forgotten now. His voice rose as he continued. "A lot more life experience has gotten you squat. Maybe I'm not as worldly as you are, but at least my wife and I are making an effort to work out our problems—and doing a pretty fair job of it, too. I'm not the one who's been grumbling about how unfairly I've been treated for the past six months. When Natalie and I had troubles, at least I did something to try and fix them." His voice became even louder as he added, "And when you get right down to it, Jack, catching your wife in the arms of another man is a hell of lot harder to deal with than finding out she loves you enough to have your damned baby!"

When he realized he had just shouted his last statement out loud and that everyone present in the room had heard, Nick ran both hands through his hair and shoved them into his pockets, then stared at Jack to keep himself from worrying about what everyone else was looking at. He took three deep breaths to calm himself before he spoke again.

"Sybil needs you now," he said more quietly. "And whether you know it or not, you need her more than you ever have before. Trust me on this, Jack. Maybe I haven't lived as long as you have, but this has been a hell of a year for me, too. If Natalie and I can work through our differences, you and Sybil can, too. Think about it."

Jack had stood silent throughout Nick's tirade, and remained so after he ended it. For a long time, neither man spoke, only glared at the other. Finally, Jack reached for his punch cup again and refilled it, lifting it to his lips for an idle sip.

"I'm not going to the hospital," he said when he had swallowed.

Nick shook his head at him. "Boy, you really are a class-A prick, aren't you? Then will you at least give me your car keys so Natalie and I can drive her there? I'm not sure there's time to call an ambulance."

Jack reached into his pocket and withdrew a ring of keys, which he tossed wordlessly to Nick.

"You know where she'll be," Nick said over his shoulder as he left. "Where your wife and your daughter both will be."

He didn't look back as he made his exit. Somehow, he was afraid of what he would see if he did.

Jack watched him go, forcing himself to remain steadfastly in place, trying to remember what he had been doing when Nick had interrupted his peace and quiet. Peace and quiet, hell, he thought even as the image formed. He hadn't had a speck of either since Sybil had laid that bombshell on him so many months ago.

A baby. God, it was really going to happen. He'd spent so much time denying it, had gone so long assuring himself that he wanted no part of it, that he hadn't once taken a moment to consider what it would be like when it happened. Now there was no escape. His wife was in labor. And once that baby was born, then according to the laws of nature, he would be a father. Within hours, it would all be over.

No, not over, he realized suddenly. Birth wasn't an end to something. It was a beginning. He remembered the drowned boy in Santo Domingo, recalled painfully the frail feel of the child's life slipping away beneath his fingertips. Death, that was the end of it. Not birth. Life was such a fragile thing, so easily lost, never to be regained. He didn't want to think about it.

"So, Jack, your wife is having a baby," Baxter's father said, intruding on his troubled thoughts.

He glanced up at the man, feeling for a moment as if he had forgotten where he was. "What? Oh, yeah. Yeah, she is."

"If you don't mind my saying so, you don't seem to be receiving the news with the usual fervor new fathers feel."

"It's, uh . . . Sybil and I have been having some problems. The news of a baby wasn't exactly good news."

Davis Torrance raised his hands in the gesture of surrender. "Believe me, I understand. And I can sympathize with your feelings completely. Children can be extremely troublesome things. And as hard as you work to make them happy, they can disappoint the hell out of you like that." He snapped his fingers together, then slapped Jack on the back hard enough to make his teeth rattle. "Don't let what that other fellow said bother you. You stand firm. Children aren't all they're cracked up to be, you mark my words."

Jack looked at him, horrified by the other man's

remarks. He knew a lot about Baxter's parents, had heard from his CO and seen for himself what kind of people they were. Jesus, was this what he was destined to become? A neglectful old man who couldn't be proud of his only child for his accomplishments simply because they weren't what he had planned for the child himself? In about twenty-five years, he'd be the same age as Davis Torrance. Would he be the same kind of man, then, too?

He tamped down the shiver that swam up his spine, and set his cup on the table again. He wasn't sure exactly what he was going to do and had no idea what caused him to react the way he did. He only knew suddenly that he needed to be with Sybil. Needed to know she would be all right, needed to make sure nothing happened to his daughter. Later, he'd have time to search through his feelings. Later, he'd figure out how to deal with everything else. If he hurried, he thought, he might be able to catch up with Nick. And if he was too late . . .

Well, he just wouldn't think about that right now.

28

Dear Mom and Dad,

Went to the much ballyhooed change of command ceremony today. It was pretty nice and everything, but the real excitement came afterward. You just never know what to expect at these military functions . . .

Carmen stood on one side of the reception hall, telling herself she was not hiding behind a group of happily chattering women, and watching Baxter as he spoke to his parents. She wondered why he had invited her to the change of command if he did not wish to talk to her. He had smiled at her during the ceremony—twice—and had lifted a hand in greeting to her after it was over when he had been surrounded by well-wishers. Then there had been some commotion when Nick and Natalie had taken Sybil to the hospital, and after that, Baxter had disappeared.

Of course, she could just go up to him and speak to him herself, she thought. But something—most likely the presence of his parents—prevented her from doing so. She remembered the way he had looked standing at her apartment door holding the flowers only a few days before. He had wanted to tell her something more that day. She had known he had. But between her mother and Orlando, and then having Nestor showing up when he did, she supposed the atmosphere had not lent itself to conversation.

And now Baxter stood with his mother and father, scanning the room. Immediately, Carmen knew he was searching for her. Recalling her last encounter with his parents, she swallowed hard. She did not like Davis and Elaine Torrance. She was still amazed that two such people had raised a son like Baxter.

He caught her eye then and quickly excused himself from his mother and father, hurrying across the room to where she stood.

"Where have you been?" he asked her, taking her hands in his. He kissed her briefly on the cheek. "I've been looking all over for you."

She closed her eyes as he brushed his lips over her skin, realizing how much she had missed even this small physical contact with him. "I have been right here all the time," she told him.

For a moment he only stared at her, a scant smile curling just the corners of his lips. Then quietly, he told her, "I've missed you."

Warm fingers squeezed her heart at the loneliness that laced his words. "I have missed you, too."

He looked down at his feet as he said, "Look, I know things didn't work out too well the last time you met my mother and father, but I'd appreciate it if you'd come over and say hello to them today."

She gazed past him at his parents, who were look-ing back at her and clearly concerned about their son's safety. She shook her head. "I do not think so."

"Why not?"

"Your parents do not like me," she said. "And I do not like your parents. They are not nice to me."

He frowned, but she could tell the expression was not meant for her. "I know, but . . ."

"I do not wish to put myself through something like that again. And I do not know why I should have to when you will be leaving Puerto Rico in two weeks anyway."

He opened his mouth to respond, but no words emerged. Carmen watched as he closed then opened it again, then closed it once more. He dragged his fin-gers through his hair, turned to glance over his shoul-der at his parents, then fixed her with an intent gaze.

"You remember a while back when I told you I'd enrolled in Spanish classes and you asked me why?"

"Yes."

"Well, at the time, I couldn't really give you a very good answer. Because at the time, I don't think I even knew the answer. But I've been thinking about it . . . about us . . . a lot lately, Carmen. And I . . ." He drew in a ragged breath and released it slowly. He bent for-ward until his face was only inches away from her own and said softly, "I love you."

Her breath, shallow to begin with, lurched to a halt in her throat. "You have never told me that," she whispered.

"I know, and I'm sorry. I think I've always loved you. I've just never let myself think too much about it. But now that I have been, I figure that's got to be the only explanation for why I can't get you out of my head. Why I can't stay away from you. Why I want nothing more than to be with you, under whatever circumstances are available."

"You have shown your love for me in strange ways," she said, not sure why she was trying to explain away his words of love when she had waited so long to hear them. "You have argued with me many times, over very silly things."

"I know that. And I'm sorry. All I can figure is that the arguing we've always done—that I've done— maybe that's just been my way of trying to keep you at a distance, because I was afraid of what would happen if I fell in love with you. But, hell, even that didn't work, because I always came after you. I always wanted—needed—you back."

"It is true that you do not seem to be able to leave me alone," she said with a smile. "You have always been that way."

He chuckled. "Yeah, well, you're irresistible. What can I say?"

"Tell me again that you love me."

"I love you. And I don't want to lose you. Ever. I know I've got a lot of nerve asking you this, after everything that's happened, but . . . I want you to come with me when I go to Miami. I . . . I want you to be my wife."

It was the question she had dreamed about, the question she had been waiting nearly two years for him to ask. What he wanted her to do was what she had been aching to do virtually since the day she had met him. Why then could she not shout out her agreement and hurl herself into his arms?

"I do not know," she said, surprised at how calmly she was able to speak.

Baxter's expression would have been the same if she

had just thrown her cup of punch into his face. "You don't know? But I thought . . . that is, you always said—"

"Many things have changed in the past months," she told him. "I have seen how much your parents will not like us being together. My family does not like us being together, either. Mami and Orlando may change their minds once we tell them we are to be married, but I do not think they will ever be happy about it. And your parents—"

"Hey, my parents can shove it."

"Baxter, that is not—"

"I mean it, Carmen. I've spent the last six years trying to get them to forgive me for doing something that's made me incredibly happy. Does that make sense to you? And I could live the rest of my life trying to please them, but they never will forgive me for not following in my father's footsteps, so what's the point? I don't care what they think anymore. I'm tired of doing everything I can to win them back, only to have them ignore me at every turn. You're right. They aren't very nice people. And I'm not going to worry about them anymore."

"What do you think they will do if we marry?"

"Oh, they'll probably never speak to me again. They'll probably disown me and cut me out of their will and instruct every single one of my relatives to never mention my name in their presence again."

She looked at him sadly. "Having their families so unhappy is not a good way for two people to begin a life together."

"But that's the point, Carmen, don't you see? It will be our life *together*. You and me. That's all we need."

She searched his face for more reassurance, wishing with all her heart that everything between them and their families would work out. But she knew there was little chance of that ever happening completely. Baxter's parents would never accept her as one of their own. And even if her own family could condone her marriage, they would never have the love for her husband that she would like them to have.

"It will not be easy, what you want us to do," she said. "There will be difficult times in the future."

"Yeah, well, nothing between us has ever been easy."

She smiled sadly. "You are right. So tell me," she added. "Yes?"

"What does learning Spanish have to do with this? You never explained."

He smiled, lifting one shoulder in a shrug. "Well, I just figured our kids are going to be fluent in Spanish, thanks to their mother, and I don't want them swearing at me behind my back without knowing what they're saying and being able to defend myself."

She laughed. "They will never use language like that around their father. Our children will be good children." She squeezed the hand she still held in hers. "And we will always be proud of them, no matter what they decide to do when they are grown."

"So you'll do it?" he asked. "You'll marry me?"

She placed her palm flat against his jaw and locked her gaze with his. "As long as you will promise me that you will always love me, and will always put me before anything else in your life. If you can promise me that then I will marry you."

He circled his arms around her waist and pulled her close, mindless of anyone who might be watching them. "Not a problem," he assured her. "Not a problem at all."

29

Dear Mom and Dad,

Funny what it takes sometimes to get people together. Talk about your extreme scenarios. Remember when Becky was in labor, and Daddy just paced and paced until he wore a hole in the carpet at the hospital? But worrying didn't make it happen any faster, did it? And everything worked out just fine. Just goes to show you have to go with the flow. Oh, and Nick and I have the most wonderful news . . .

P.S. But no, it's not that I'm pregnant. Hold your horses, will ya . . . ?

The hospital maternity ward was nearly empty at close to nine P.M. Evidently it was a slow day for having babies. Natalie flipped idly through a six-month-old issue of *Good Housekeeping* while Nick leaned against the wall beside her and stared out into space. The silence surrounding them was maddening at times, broken only by the whisper of rubber-soled shoes on carpeting and the occasional summons of a doctor's page from the speakers overhead.

"How long is this going to take?" Nick asked, rubbing his hands over his face.

Natalie didn't look up, focusing her attentions instead on tearing out a recipe for chocolate fondue. She didn't think anyone would mind. The magazine had been sitting here for six months after all. "When Becky had her first, she was in labor for thirty-two hours."

He dropped his chin toward his chest and stared at her in disbelief. "Are you kidding?" he asked. "She was in labor for a day and a half?"

She nodded. "Almost. Of course, with Jennifer, little Michelle came in about two hours. I guess you just never can tell."

He looked at his watch. "We've been here for almost eight hours. You'd think we'd have heard something by now."

"The baby will come when she's ready."

"Yeah, well I'm going to have to go get something to eat if she doesn't show up soon."

They looked up suddenly at the arrival of Baxter and Carmen, who bustled into the waiting room then all smiles and rosy cheeks.

"What's the word?" Baxter asked.

Nick shook his head. "Nothing. We haven't heard anything since we sat down in here."

"How is Sybil doing?" Carmen asked, taking a seat on the other side of Natalie.

She shrugged. "As well as can be expected, I guess, all things considered. This can't be easy for her. Even in the best of circumstances, childbirth must be a pretty trying experience."

Carmen nodded. "I wish there was something we could do."

"Everything will be okay. It's just going to take some time."

"So how was the reception?" Nick asked. "We didn't even get to have any cake and punch."

Baxter and Carmen exchanged a wary look and laughed a little nervously.

"You missed the fireworks, too," Baxter said. "And boy, were they bright. Seemed to go on forever."

"Fireworks?" Nick asked. "No one said there was going to be fireworks."

"They came as a surprise to most of the people there, I think. Carmen and I were expecting them, though. They started right about the time we told my folks the news."

"What news?" Natalie asked.

Carmen lifted her left hand for the other woman's inspection, showing off a modest-sized sparkling diamond that winked beneath the fluorescent lights overhead. "We just bought it," she said. "We are engaged to be married."

Natalie squealed with delight and jumped up from her chair, embracing the other woman fiercely. "Congratulations!" she cried. With another squeeze, she released her friend and went to hug Baxter, as well, who was releasing Nick's hand from its congratulatory shake. "It's about time you two came to your senses," she told him as she let him go. "When's the big day?"

"Soon. I am going to Miami with Baxter in two weeks, and we wish to be married before we leave."

"That's wonderful," Natalie said, nodding in approval. "I'm really happy for you both."

"Thanks," Baxter said, smiling at his fiancée. "Oh, and that reminds me. Your orders came through today, Nick. In all the confusion, I forgot to tell you." He pulled an envelope from his pocket and handed it to the other man. "I think you'll be pleased."

Natalie clapped her hands together. "We're going back to Cleveland, aren't we?" she asked. "We're going home."

Nick scanned the contents of the envelope, lifted his eyebrows in an expression she wasn't sure she liked, then shook his head and said, "Well, not exactly, Nat."

Her face fell. "We're not going home?"

He shook his head again.

"Then where are we going?"

He looked at Baxter, then back at his wife. "Well, actually, we, uh . . . we're going to Hawaii."

Her eyes widened in surprise. "Hawaii?"

He nodded. "I put it down as one of my choices on a lark. I didn't think for a second that I'd get it. I thought for sure they'd send me back to Cleveland. But instead . . . " He sighed. "I'm supposed to report in Hilo on October fifteenth."

She opened her mouth to utter an objection, but closed it just as quickly. "October fifteenth," she repeated. "That's our first anniversary."

"Right."

"And we're going to Hawaii."

"Yup. So what do you say? You want to give this honeymoon business a second shot?"

She smiled, liking the way he'd put it. "Yeah, you know, it might not be such a bad thing at that."

"And we will be going to Florida for our honeymoon," Carmen said. "I have always wanted to see Disney World. Baxter says he will take me."

Another arrival in the waiting room caused them all to look up again. Jack Ingram stood beside a nurse, cradling a tiny bundle of flannel in his arms.

"It's a girl," he said. He wore hospital scrubs and looked tired and stunned, but he was smiling as if he'd just witnessed the most amazing discovery known to mankind. "I, uh, I guess you all already knew that—I mean, I already knew it, too—but, um, she still came as kind of surprise to me."

Natalie smiled. Jack had shown up at the hospital in a taxi only a few minutes after she and Nick had arrived with Sybil. At first Sybil had told him to turn around and go home, that he was too damned late and that she didn't want or need him there with her when she delivered. As an orderly had helped her into a wheelchair, Jack had told her that was just too damned bad, because he wasn't about to leave and miss the birth of their child. They had still been arguing when they'd disappeared down a corridor behind a nurse and doctor. Their voices had carried for a long time after that. Natalie could just picture what the delivery must have been like.

"She's beautiful, Jack," Nick said as the group of four huddled around the newborn.

"I think she looks like a raisin," Jack said. "But she's got a good set of pipes. Squawked like a seagull the minute she got out."

"That's a good sign," Baxter told him.

Jack nodded.

"How's Sybil doing?" Natalie asked.

"She's exhausted. You can't imagine what she went through in there. It was . . . it was . . . it was . . ." He sighed, a broken, wistful sound, and pushed a fist against his eye. "She did great, though. She just needs to rest now."

"So you have a daughter," Carmen said, touching her finger to the baby's cheek.

Jack cuddled the infant tighter. "She's going to take sailing lessons as soon as she learns to walk. And she's going to learn how to tend bar. That'll come in handy on a boat. And it's going to work out really well, because she'll be able to get into all those small, tough-to-reach areas on *Errukine* that need maintenance, but are so difficult for me to get to."

"Sounds like you're going to turn her into a real salt," Baxter said with a chuckle.

"The saltiest baby in the seven seas," Jack agreed. "Look, I need to get back to Sybil, and the nurses have to do some stuff to my daughter."

"Have you picked out a name for her?"

"Sybil wants to name her after her grandmother. Sophia. So that's what we're going to go with. Sophie for short."

"Sophie Ingram," Natalie said. She crooked her fingers beneath the minuscule hand that had freed itself from the confines of the blanket. The tiny fingers curled over her own and she smiled. "Happy birthday, Sophie. And welcome to the world."

More than an hour passed before Sybil woke up again. Jack sat beside her bed, his hand tucked beneath hers, and recalled again the awesome event he had witnessed that afternoon.

He had just planned to come to the hospital to make sure Sybil would be okay. He hadn't intended to be with her through the delivery. But without thinking about it, and before he'd realized what was happening, he'd been donning scrubs and was standing beside her in the delivery room, holding her up when she needed to push, and wiping her forehead when she needed to rest. He hadn't given any thought at all to everything that had happened over the last six months. Because, suddenly, none of that mattered.

Sybil stirred, moving a little restlessly on the bed, then winced in pain. Jack's fingers flexed, weaving themselves with hers, and he stood over her.

"Do you want anything?" he asked. "I can call the nurse."

"Sophie?" she asked as her eyes fluttered open. "How's Sophie?"

"She's in the nursery. They had to take some blood and do some tests. But they do it for all the babies," he hastened to add when he saw the concern in her eyes. "She's fine. She's perfect, Sybil. I've never seen anything like her before."

She smiled. "She is pretty amazing, isn't she?"

He nodded. "Incredible."

The fingers he had twined with his tightened, pulling him closer. When he bent over the bed, she lifted her other hand to his face and threaded her fingers through his hair.

"It's been so long since I touched you," she said. A single tear escaped from her eye, sliding down to disappear in her hair. "Just touched you. You've put me through hell for months, Jack. I should hate you for the way you've treated me. But instead, all I want is for you to climb into this bed with me and hold me, and promise me you'll never let me go."

He complied with her wish immediately, dropping the metal rail closest to him, nudging her carefully to the other side, and stretching out alongside her. For a long time, neither spoke, but simply lay in each other's arms remembering what it was like to be close. Jack lay with one arm beneath her neck, tangling his fingers in her hair, splaying his other hand open over her still swollen belly, wondering what it would have been like to feel his child moving while she was still in the womb. He wondered about a lot of things he had missed over the last several months.

"Jack?"

Her voice, sounding so quiet and thin in the otherwise silent room, startled him, because he had thought she was asleep. "Yes?"

"What are you going to do now?"

It was a question he had asked himself earlier that day, and one for which he had yet to form an adequate answer. After a moment's thought, he said, "I don't know."

"You could come back to *Errukine* if you want."

He sighed. "Are you sure you want me back?"

When he felt her turn to look at him, he turned his head, too, meeting her gaze levelly.

"Yes, I am," she said. "We have a lot to talk about. The best way to do that would be for you to come home. Where you belong. For good."

"I'd like that," he told her. "I just didn't think you'd want—"

"I do want." She smiled at him. "I want so bad."

His gaze traveled toward the ceiling, and he sighed

from somewhere deep in his soul. "There's so much," he said. "Just so much inside me right now. I've never felt this way before."

"I know. It's like that with me, too. It isn't good for us to be apart. It isn't natural, you know? The two of us, we're like two halves of a whole. Or two-thirds, now, I guess is a more appropriate description. Sophie makes up the rest."

"I wish—" He broke off without completing the thought. There were so many things he wished. And it was too late for all of them. Looking over at Sybil, he saw her looking back at him the way she had nineteen years ago, the day they had married, when their lives had held nothing but promise. He smiled. Maybe it wasn't as late as he thought.

"I took the servicewide exam this month," he told her. "I thought maybe if I could make chief before I retired in January, it would bring my pension up a little."

Her expression didn't change as she said, "That's good."

"Of course, now it could mean something else. Something more."

"Like what?"

He shrugged. "My time in San Juan will be up come January. If I make chief, it would open up more possibilities for me when I transfer out. I could be the officer in charge someplace. Maybe put in to take over the reins of a tug or something."

Sybil hesitated only a moment before asking, "Would the hours be better than they are on the *Point Kendall*?"

"I'd be home most of the time, have more regular hours. I'd have to be out a few days from time to time, but there wouldn't be any of this week-in, week-out crap."

"So . . . so you'd have some time to spend with your wife and daughter?"

"Yeah. A lot more time than I have been lately, that's for sure."

She snuggled up as close to him as she could, tucking her head beneath his chin and draping her arm over his middle. "Jack?" she said softly.

"Hmm?"

"We'll get around the world someday. I promise you that."

He pulled her closer still and planted a kiss on the crown of her head. "Believe it or not, Syb, that doesn't seem nearly as important to me now as it once did."

"But we will do it."

"I know we will."

"And in the meantime, we'll have a different kind of adventure."

He smiled as he bent his head toward hers again, and this time when he kissed her, he pressed his mouth over hers and tried to tell her everything he'd wanted so desperately to tell her for months. That he was sorry. That he loved her. That the arrival of a child meant more to him than he could ever have known. But most of all, what he tried to tell her as he held her close was that, as long as he had anything to say about it, they would never, ever, be separated from each other again.

Epilogue

Dear Mom and Dad,

By the time you get this letter, Nick and I will probably be home visiting before we go on to Hawaii. It's going to be strange leaving Puerto Rico behind. I've been thinking, though. You know how you've been saying Pensacola doesn't really seem to be the place for you to retire? Well, I know this great little apartment building in Condado Beach, and I also know for a fact that one of the units will be vacant soon (if you don't mind the cucarachas*) . . .*

The sun shone brightly the day of Baxter and Carmen's wedding, the way it always seemed to do in Puerto Rico. Jack stood up as best man, while Natalie served as matron of honor. Nick and Sybil and baby Sophie sat on the groom's side in the little church in Old San Juan, while the bride's side was considerably more populous with every member of the Fuente family.

After a quick reception at El Patio de Sam, the party broke up, with the six friends and a baby returning to the Ingrams' boat for cocktails and final farewells. Night had fallen by then, and the full moon shone over the marina like a bright promise.

"To newlyweds," Sybil said, lifting her wine glass high.

"To newlyweds," the others joined in.

"To babies," Natalie toasted afterward.

"To babies," the other agreed.

"To new beginnings all around," Nick said with a smile.

"To new beginnings all around."

"You know, we keep toasting like this," Jack said, "and none of us is going to be able to see straight."

"To not seeing straight," Baxter said, lifting his glass again. The others followed suit.

"Hey, I have a question," Nick said, putting an end to the toasting momentarily. "Who was that woman Booker brought to the change of command? Last I heard he was at forty-eight, just two states shy of completing his goal."

"Yeah," Jack said with a nod. "He needed Arizona and Wyoming. He'd even gotten the District of Columbia, for good measure."

"Well, don't count your winnings yet, guys," Baxter told them. "Because the woman he was with at the ceremony was one Uta Nordstrom. From Oslo, Norway."

"Norway?" Nick asked. "What the hell good is that going to do him?"

"None," Baxter said with a laugh. "And it's tearing him up inside, believe you me. He is completely smitten with this woman, to the point of actually being faithful to her. But he got so close to reaching his goal, that he's strung tight as a spring."

"Gee, what a dilemma," Natalie said dryly.

"Oh, yes," Carmen agreed. "I feel so sorry for him."

"Knowing Booker, though, he'll figure a way out of this somehow," Sybil said with a shake of her head.

"Not this time," Baxter told her. "I think he's in it deep."

"Oh, Jack, by the way," Sybil asked as she stood up to go below for another bottle of wine. "Do you know where Catch was headed when he pulled out yesterday morning?"

Jack shook his head. "No. As usual, he didn't say. Why?"

"There were a couple of guys nosing around the marina who were asking about him yesterday afternoon. They said they'd be back. Jack . . . they were DEA."

That brought all heads up.

"Drug Enforcement Agency?" Jack asked.

"Uh-huh. You don't think Catch . . . ?"

He thought for a moment, then shook his head slowly. "Nah. Couldn't be."

Sybil nodded. "That's what I thought, too, but . . ."

He shook his head again. "Couldn't be," he repeated. "Maybe they were just friends of his. He has a lot of friends, you know."

"I suppose . . ."

"Oh, Nat, I forgot to tell you," Nick said as he turned to his wife. "After you left for the wedding this afternoon, the phone guy came and installed our phone."

She nearly dropped her drink overboard. "You're kidding."

He shook his head. "Nope. We've got a number and everything."

"Did you tell them they're going to have to come back and get it in two weeks when we leave again?"

He shook his head. "I figure I'll let the landlord handle it. He never did fix our intercom after all."

"You know," she said with a sigh, "I'm really going to miss this place when we go."

"Me, too," Nick said.

"It's been special for all of us," Baxter added. "In one way or another."

The others nodded their agreement. "And it's been a great place for a honeymoon," Natalie added with a smile.

"One more toast," Nick said, standing to lift his glass high.

The others groaned.

"No, come on. One more. You'll like it."

The others lifted their glasses halfheartedly.

"To honeymoons," he said.

Everyone present stood as well, lifting their glasses into the night. "To honeymoons," they chorused.

"Long may they reign," Nick added.

And as the moon began its slow arc across the sky, the three couples looked forward to the many honeymoons ahead.

Winner Take All by Terri Herrington

Logan Brisco is the smoothest, slickest, handsomest man ever to grace the small town of Serenity, Texas. Carny Sullivan is the only one who sees the con man behind that winning smile, and she vows to save the town from his clutches. But saving herself from the man who steals her heart is going to be the greatest challenge of all.

The Honeymoon by Elizabeth Bevarly

Newlyweds Nick and Natalie Brannon are wildly in love, starry-eyed about the future...and in for a rude awakening. Suddenly relocated from their midwestern hometown to San Juan, Puerto Rico, where Nick is posted with the U.S. Coast Guard, Natalie hopes for the best. But can true love survive the trials and tribulations of a not-so-perfect paradise?

Ride the Night Wind by Jo Ann Ferguson

As the only surviving member of a powerful family, Lady Audra fought to hold on to her vast manor lands against ruthless warlords. But from the moonlit moment when she encountered the mysterious masked outlaw known as Lynx, she was plunged into an even more desperate battle for the fate of her heart.

To Dream Again by Laura Lee Guhrke

Beautiful widow Mara Elliot had little time for shining promises or impractical dreams. But when dashing inventor Nathaniel Chase became her unwanted business partner, Mara found his optimism and reckless determination igniting a passion in her that suddenly put everything she treasured at risk.

Reckless Angel by Susan Kay Law

Angelina Winchester's dream led her to a new city, a new life, and a reckless bargain with Jeremiah Johnston, owner of the most notorious saloon in San Francisco. Falling in love was never part of their deal. But soon they would discover that the last thing they ever wanted was exactly what they needed most.

A Slender Thread by Lee Scofield

Once the center of Philadelphia's worst scandal, Jennifer Hastings was determined to rebuild her life as a schoolteacher in Kansas. She was touched when handsome and aloof Gil Prescott entrusted her with the care of his newborn son while he went to fight in the Civil War. When Gil's return unleashed a passion they had ignored for too long, they thought they had found happiness—until a man from Jennifer's past threatened to destroy it.